CAN'T WE ALL JUST GET ALONG?

When any Yavi project posed a greater threat to Earth, GIs on both sides died restoring the balance in chilly, undeclared brushfire wars. Trueborns called the arrangement Cold War II. The only things a GI hates more than getting killed in an undeclared war are the people who are trying to kill him. Trueborn soldiers hated Yavi soldiers, and the Yavi returned the favor.

The Yavi stood, hefted his glass mug like a Trueborn baseball, and spilled his beer.

As the two soldiers glared at each other, I smiled at the Yavi. "Let me refill that for you. On the house."

The Yavi ignored me and wound up to peg a fastball at the Trueborn gunny.

The gunny snatched a bar stool and turned it legs-up, like a bat. The legs trembled in his bony hands. "I remember my pugil-stick drill. You remember yours, 'salesman'?"

Brawls we … as hard on furniture. M… 't defusing the crisis. I … the safety.

A salesma… ut a soldier would. Both …

I shifted … back and forth from one torso to the other. "Free City of Shipyard Municipal Ordinance 6.21 authorizes the use of deadly force by a licensed establishment owner in defense of property. I own this place. That's my beer stein and my bar stool. So can't we all just get along?"

BAEN BOOKS
by ROBERT BUETTNER

Overkill
Undercurrents
Balance Point (forthcoming)

UNDERCURRENTS

ROBERT BUETTNER

UNDERCURRENTS

This is a work of fiction. All the characters and events portrayed in this book are fictional, and any resemblance to real people or incidents is purely coincidental.

A Baen Books Original

Baen Publishing Enterprises
P.O. Box 1403
Riverdale, NY 10471
www.baen.com

ISBN: 978-1-4516-3828-8

Cover art by Kurt Miller

First Baen Paperback printing September 2012

Distributed by Simon & Schuster
1230 Avenue of the Americas
New York, NY 10020

Library of Congress Cataloging-in-Publication Data 2011014194

10 9 8 7 6 5 4 3 2 1

For Bill, Rick, and Debi

If a ship's master misreads the current,
they take away his ship.
If a spy misreads the undercurrents,
they take away his head.

—Attributed to Admiral Wilhelm Canaris,
Commandant of German Intelligence,
at Flossenburg Concentration Camp,
Bavaria, Earth; April, 1945, as he awaited
execution on suspicion of plotting
to kill Adolf Hitler.

One

"What do you make of it, Sarge?"

The sergeant watched the Tressen sentry tug his face scarf back up as wind-driven snow needled the boy's cheeks. North of Tressel's Arctic Circle, winter days were short, and this one was already dying. In the fading light, the sentry hiked up his greatcoat and bent forward so he could peer down at the object that his kneeling platoon sergeant was studying.

The object protruded from a drift at the end of the snow furrow the sentry's boot had plowed when he had tripped over the thing. It resembled an overturned white kitchen pot. A knee-high white wire stuck up from the bowl, thrashing in the mounting gale like a fern stalk.

The sergeant cocked his helmeted head as he knelt, as careful not to touch it as a hot stove.

The kid rolled his eyes. "Sarge, if it didn't blow up when I *tripped* over it—"

The sergeant cut the kid off with an upraised palm. "The fish-eaters love second-touch booby traps."

The kid smiled. "Come on, Sarge. There's no rebels up here."

The kid was almost certainly right. There had been few rebels *anywhere* since before the sergeant himself had been a green, stupid boot. But the object was too civilized for this wilderness, too sleek for this time. The sergeant stood back, hands on hips. "Well, I think it's got something to do with wireless."

It had been pure stupidity turned to luck that the kid had chosen to piss fifty yards in front of his fighting hole instead of in the designated latrine trench behind the perimeter. One of the boy's buddies in the positions to his left or right might have shot him for an intruder. In fact, they should have. Their failure to do so would make for a lively instructional conversation later. Albeit a one-sided one.

The sergeant looked up at the flakes suddenly swirling around the two of them. Blizzard coming, and a long night as well. He sneezed into his mitten, wiped snot on his greatcoat, then dug inside his pocket for his signal whistle.

"Maybe our *guests*"—the sergeant spat the word—"will know what this thing is."

The soldiers of the Yavi intelligence unit that the sergeant's platoon had been ordered to escort weren't of this world, but they were as human as the sergeant was. Yavi and Tressens were fruit of the same tree, abducted from the Motherworld thirty thousand years ago, or so the historians claimed. But Yavet had civilized faster than Tressel. Yavet's technology was, they said, a century ahead of Tressel's. Yavet had even leapfrogged Earth, the Motherworld herself, by twenty years, they said.

Whatever they said, the sergeant thought that if the rest of the Yavi resembled these intelligence poofs, the Yavi were twenty years more arrogant than the Trueborns, too. And it was hard to be more arrogant than a Trueborn Earthman.

The sergeant untangled the signal whistle's lanyard, fumbling with mittened hands. Then he raised the whistle toward his lips.

Since the private had led the sergeant out here to the object, the kid had been shifting from one foot to another with ever-increasing frequency. At that moment he stepped forward, pointing with one hand. "Okay if I go over there and take a leak now, Sarge?"

The private's single step yielded three results, each bad.

The first result was bad for the private. His step moved his helmeted head into the path of a rifle round then inbound toward his sergeant, which round was meant to prevent the sergeant from blowing his signal whistle.

The round perforated the private's steel helmet like a finger through tissue, then split his head like a scarf-wrapped melon.

The impact of bullet against helmet, then bone, deflected and split the round so that its fragments sang harmlessly past the sergeant's ear. The explosion of the boy's head shocked the sergeant into frozen paralysis for two heartbeats.

The next result occurred two seconds later and was bad for the sergeant. A bolt-action Tressen service rifle with iron sights can accurately engage a stationary target from three hundred yards at a rate of one round every two seconds, if operated by an exceptional marksman. With the private's head removed from the line of fire, the follow-on round struck the sergeant an inch below his left eye.

The sergeant's head snapped back. Then his brain and skull atomized. His helmet fell on the snow, rocking like an inverted tortoise shell, while blood and brain-tissue mist condensed in the cold, then rained down around it.

The third result of the private's step was bad for the marksman. Distance and swirling wind had carried the rifle shots' reports away from the Tressen defensive perimeter. Blowing snow already dusted both bodies and would soon bury them. Therefore, the marksman's efficient violence would have gone undetected, as planned, until the gathering storm passed. But during the two seconds after the private intercepted the first shot, and before the follow-on shot struck, the wind shifted as the sergeant's last breath escaped through his signal whistle.

A gust carried the whistle shriek back, inside the defensive perimeter, then up and over the topographic crest of the ridge along which the perimeter stretched, and finally down into the shallow valley beyond.

In the valley, already shadowed by the Arctic night, driven snow fogged the glow of floodlights atop plasteel scaffolding. The floods lit a freshly blasted pit as wide and deep as an amphitheater, and in the pit's center bustled a dozen Yavi and two dozen Tressens. The Yavi, warm and faceless in visored body armor that glinted under the lights, directed the Tressens, who shivered beneath steel helmets and within bulky greatcoats.

The whistle's alarm caused both Yavi and Tressens to look up simultaneously.

Fluttering invisible above the pit, a hummingbird-sized

surveillance 'bot recorded the image of the work party's reaction, then transmitted the image as a signal too faint to be detected even by Yavi listening equipment. The 'bot's signal barely carried as far as the relay pod that the poor, headless sentry had tripped over. The pod, in turn, recrypted the image into an equally faint signal that reached out barely three hundred yards. There the image displayed on the visor screen of a white-armored figure. The armored marksman crabbed backward, then lay belly down in the snow, now hidden from view on the reverse slope of the next ridgeline.

"Dammit!" The marksman pounded the snow, frustrated first by the necessity of shooting two grunts who presented no physical threat, and second by the fact that their deaths hadn't salvaged the mission. The marksman's junior teammate had already perished four days earlier in a crevasse fall, taking the team's uplink transmitter down with him.

The marksman bit down on an inner helmet switch that signaled the relay transmitter and the imaging 'bot to incinerate themselves. Then the marksman considered a range of lousy options.

The rifle was Tressen manufactured, obsolete even locally. Its extra bulk during evasive action outweighed any future utility it might have in a shoot-out, if this fiasco deteriorated further. If found, the weapon would be assumed stolen, which it was, then abandoned by an Iridian rebel, which it was not. The marksman's armor, if found, would not, however, be assumed to be of Tressen manufacture. The suit looked like it came from another planet. Because it had.

The marksman chinned the helmet's visor display to meteorologics. The squall would strengthen for the next twenty-six hours. Windblown snow should cover tracks and discourage pursuit. The marksman's armor was less advanced than Yavi armor, but it could sustain its wearer under blizzard conditions for days. If the Yavi and the Tressens could be evaded in the meantime.

The marksman left the rifle behind, then ran into a thickening curtain of blowing snow, away from the patrols that were sure to follow.

Two

"Stop here and let me out!" Major Ruberd Polian shouted over the blizzard at the skimmer's driver, as the skimmer slid up alongside the two snow-dusted bodies.

"Yes, Sir!" The driver reversed thrust, Polian lurched forward until his armor's helmet banged the skimmer's windscreen, and the skimmer following behind them slewed and nearly rear-ended them.

The driver's eyes widened. "Dammit!"

He wasn't reacting to what he had just done to his commanding officer, Polian realized, but to the two headless bodies alongside which the driver had stopped the skimmer.

The kid turned his head away and gagged. "Sorry, sir."

On Yavet, Polian's father had been a cop. One evening Polian had pulled up crime-scene images from the old man's personal 'puter while it lay on the hall table. Polian had gagged at the sight of mutilated corpses, and those were just holos. When his father caught him, he had slapped Polian. "There's nothing wrong with what I do!"

Polian touched the kid's arm. "Don't worry. If a soldier ever gets used to it, it's time to quit."

The kid nodded, wiped his eyes.

Polian turned to the two cub lieutenants in the skimmer's rear seat. The one on the left, fat-cheeked and soft, looked half sick from the bumpy skimmer ride. "Sandr, you dismount here, with me." The kid on the right was lean and hard. "Frei, you take command of both skimmers."

Lieutenant Frei smiled, but craned his neck at the storm that swirled around them. "Sir?"

"Lay out a patrol grid." Polian waved a hand at the snow curtain and at the bodies. "Comb this area until you find the people who did this." Polian pointed at the lean lieutenant. "Full armor. Full sensors. Weapons locked and loaded. Shoot anything that moves. I don't want anybody else ending up like these two because somebody got careless."

Polian and the soft lieutenant jumped the three feet over the skimmer's side and sank knee deep in snow.

Polian brushed snow off his thigh plates, muttering into his open mike. Polian hated losing soldiers, even Tressens. So he had just ordered Frei to shoot first. But as an intelligence officer, Polian knew that he should have ordered Frei to risk more lives, if necessary, to capture an interrogable prisoner.

This was an obvious Iridian rebel hit-and-run. Obvious to some, anyway.

Alongside Polian, the skimmer, freed of the weight of two passengers, bobbed up like a dinghy at sea. He frowned behind his visor as something tugged at his mind, and he muttered, "Undercurrents . . ."

Sandr, alongside him, asked, "Sir?"

Polian waved a gauntleted hand. "Nothing."

On Polian's twelfth birthday, like every legally born Yavi, he had received a pass for a day outside. It was the day when every father spoke to every son about what it meant to be a man. Polian's father had taken him uplevels, to Skyceiling, where they rented an open skimmer, filter masks, and waders. They had driven to the sea, dismounted, and stood on the beach, staring out through the haze at the gray, opaque waves.

Then Polian's father had dragged him by the hand out into the sea. When the water reached as high as Polian's waist, Polian's father released his son's hand.

Polian turned to his father, eyes wide. And then something beneath the surface tugged at Polian. Gently at first, then stronger. A crosscurrent of water, beneath the still surface, swept Polian's feet off the shifting seabed and dragged him out toward the emptiness.

He screamed, clawed for his father's arm.

The older man allowed him to drift for a moment, then caught his son's hand, pulled him upright, and stared down into his eyes. "Undercurrent. You see one thing on the surface. But underneath, things are moving in a different direction. And the difference can kill you. Ruberd, if you're gonna be a cop, you have to be tougher. And you have to learn that a good cop never forgets to read the undercurrents."

The experience had been intended to teach Polian what it would take to follow in his father's footsteps. Instead, it had turned Polian bookish, the bright kid in class rather than the bold one. And a bright kid who became an analytical-intelligence officer, not a cop. But Polian never forgot to read the undercurrents.

Aboard the skimmer, Lieutenant Frei touched his helmet faceplate with a salute to Polian. The driver twisted the wheel, swung the vehicle away from the excavation site, and both skimmers vanished into the swirling snow within twenty yards.

Polian turned, then looked down at the corpses.

Alongside Polian, Lieutenant Sandr threw back his visor, bent at the waist, and vomited into the snow.

Polian sighed, but didn't afford Lieutenant Sandr the sympathy he'd shown the skimmer driver.

It was, Polian knew, because Sandr was too much like Polian himself. Sandr was uplevels raised, a bright, bookish boy. A degreed xenogeologist. University boys skated basic and went straight to intel officer's training. Sandr had never learned what the downlevels kids did, either from life or from the tongue and baton of a basic instructor. Neither, Polian knew, had he.

So Polian had assigned the patrol to Frei, born to be a line officer, a leader of men.

On the other hand, officers like Polian and Sandr, who would be a staff officer, an advisor to commanders, as Polian was, had their place. A xenogeologist ought to be good at puzzles. And Polian had a puzzle on his hands.

Polian knelt alongside the nearest body, a raw private by his sleeve flashes, and rubbed at a black smudge on the side of the body's greatcoat. He rubbed the black stuff between his gauntlet fingers. Soot.

Inside his temperature-controlled armor, Polian felt cold congeal in his stomach. Undercurrents tugged harder at his mind. “Sandr, wipe the drool off and give me a hand here.”

It took both of them to roll the headless body, already frozen stiff as a log, over onto its back.

Within the snow hollow vacated by the torso was a deeper pit in the snow, displacing the volume of a flower pot. The smaller pit had icy, blackened sides.

Polian stood back, hands on hips, then pointed at the pit. “What do you make of that, Sandr?”

“Sir?” The boy genius cocked his helmeted head. “Uh, well . . . these two made a fire to keep warm. Somebody spotted it and shot them. This fellow fell on top of the fire as he died, and smothered it. Bandits would have ransacked the bodies for valuables, so it must have been rebels.”

Polian sighed, pointed at the other body. “That sergeant had twenty years in, by his sleeve hash marks. An experienced soldier wanders fifty yards in front of his lines to build a fire?”

“Oh.”

“And where would he get firewood?”

The xenogeologist turned and looked into the storm as though trees might have sprouted on the barren, snowy plain while they spoke. The kid shrugged. “I guess the rebels just stumbled across these two, killed them, then tried to burn the bodies, to cover up.”

Polian sighed again. Xenogeology must not be that tough. “I agree with you that these two weren’t shot by bandits. We’re a hundred miles above this planet’s Arctic Circle. The nearest settlement is at Northern Terminus, where we jumped off, one hundred six miles west. Any bandit who tried to make a living at this spot would starve waiting for victims."

Sandr spread upturned palms. "That leaves the rebels. As I said. Sir."

Polian pressed his lips together. Then he said, "Iridian rebels haven't done more than blow up the occasional railroad track in years. See any tracks?"

"I understand, sir. That doesn't mean they couldn't have followed us up here."

"How? By dogsled?" The largest land animals evolved to date on Tressel were bow-legged amphibians that couldn't survive an autumn frost, much less a blizzard. The only vehicles on Tressel capable of crossing the frozen wasteland between the northern terminus of the Arctic Railroad and this excavation site were Polian's skimmers. The skimmers had been downsmuggled a component at a time.

"Well, these two didn't shoot each other!" The lieutenant gulped. "Sir."

Polian nodded. "On that, we agree again. Sandr, you graduated Intelligence Officer School, yes?"

The kid straightened. "Perfect scores on every exam, sir."

Polian rolled his eyes behind his visor. He made a mental note to tell Intel School's faculty where they could put their exam program.

"Do you recall any remote covert sensor, in even a half-modern intelligence inventory, that isn't equipped with a pyrotechnic self-destruct?"

The kid furrowed his pale brow behind his visor. "No. But the soot couldn't be from a self-destruct.

Technologically this planet's a hundred-plus years behind us, almost that far behind even *Earth*. The Tressen military has no modern covert sensors. And so the rebels *certainly* don't have them."

Polian stared at the kid as wind rattled snow against their helmets.

Finally, the boy genius said, "Oh."

Two hours later, a detail made up of Tressen soldiers had tagged and bagged their mates' frozen remains, improvising from sample sacks intended for storage and transport of this mission's objective.

Polian's earpiece crackled; then Lieutenant Frei said, "Sir, we got ten yards' visibility out here. So far we've cleared about four square miles."

Polian ground his teeth. Too slow. If these guys could evade as well as they could shoot, they would lose themselves in the storm. "Visibility stinks here, too. What do your thermals show?"

"Actually, sir, that's why I'm reporting. The sensors weren't showing much in this crud. Then Mazzen said, well, these are *prospecting* skimmers, so why don't we switch over to their magnetometers. We did, and five minutes later we found a steel rifle! Obsolete local military. Bet we find the serial number matches one the rebels stole from some armory, and the ballistics match with the bullets that—uh."

Polian exhaled. Of course the gun would be a locally manufactured piece. And of course it would turn out to be the "murder weapon." But this was a covert operation that could change human history, not a homicide investigation. Nonetheless, initiative should be encouraged. Mazzen was a sharp kid, NCO material. Polian said, "Tell Mazzen good thinking, for me. And that he's breveted to corporal."

Polian could *hear* Frei smile. "Outstanding, sir! He'll appreciate that, Major! The rebels must be carrying rifles, shovels, helmets—hell, pots and pans—all kinds of metal. We'll get 'em now."

Inside his helmet, Polian shook his head. "Okay. But stay sharp. Eternad armor barely shows on normal sensors. A magnetometer's blind to it."

"Eternads, sir?" Polian could hear the smirk in Frei's voice, too. Frei said, "Only Trueborns use Eternads. And they don't carry bolt-action rifles."

Three

The marksman burrowed into the snow, panting. It was full dark now. But colder, which meant that a heat source stood out more against its surroundings.

Eternad armor vented body and mechanical heat in irregular patterns. That theoretically camouflaged the wearer's passive infrared signature. But Eternads blew less deceptively than Yavi armor did. And Yavi passive sensors were sensitive enough to detect even Yavi armor. Being twenty years behind the bad guys was a bitch.

The marksman shut down all the suit's external sensors and the heater, cutting what the suit blew, then waited for the exhaust-temp and heart-rate displays to drop back into the green. The rest was welcome.

Minutes passed while the wind howled. The overall situation was more frustrating now. The signals spooks had got it right. The Yavi *had* inserted a unit here on Tressel, clandestinely and illegally. That had been expected, because clandestine and illegal was how the baby-killers always worked. Of course, it had been just as illegal to insert the marksman's team in response.

Well, hardly "just as." The Tressens, who were even bigger villains than the Yavi, knew the Yavi were here. In fact the Tressens had welcomed these Yavi, according to the images. The Tressens were providing security and labor to help the baby-killers get whatever it was they wanted up here in the frozen north.

And whatever the two most isolated and autocratic rogue worlds in the Human Union wanted was certainly bad for Earth. And probably worse for the rest of the Union.

But the chance to record proof of the plot had now gone up in smoke, literally. Earth couldn't afford to confront its two most bellicose neighbors with a conspiracy that the Motherworld could neither prove nor understand.

The Motherworld also couldn't afford to have a covert spook of its own captured here on Tressel. Trueborns were the Good Guys, the ones who played by the rules. The marksman's presence here violated about a dozen rules derived from the Sovereignty Clause of the Human Union Charter.

The heat-signature readings and heart rate on the marksman's visor display dropped back into the green. *Time to run like you stole something, again.*

The marksman sucked on the helmet's water nipple, chinned the suit's sensors back on, then stood in the storm and waited for them to activate.

A shadow barreled out of the blowing snow just as the marksman's helmet sensors flashed red and howled.

The Yavi skimmer's front debris guard slammed the marksman's chest plate. A four-ton object moving at twenty miles per hour met a stationary object that weighed, all-up gear plus living tissue, one hundred eighty-one pounds. The result was predictable.

The marksman thought, somersaulting through blowing snow, that physics were a bitch.

Then there was pain, and, finally, darkness.

Four

Polian stood over the dented, twisted armor suit that lay in the snow, glinting in the foggy cone projected by the skimmer's headlights. Polian shook his head. "How long ago did you hit him?"

"An hour, sir. Give or take." The skimmer's driver knelt alongside his machine, wedged a boot against the bent debris guard. He grasped the plasteel tubing in two gauntleted hands, grunted, and pulled the guard back to a semblance of functionality.

Polian cut his helmet mike so he could swear, because Frei stood beside him.

Magnetometer! If they had been running normal thermal sensors, they might have detected this spy and taken him alive instead of pulverizing him. Now all Polian had was a third corpse. A corpse wearing Eternad armor, certainly. But the Trueborns would claim, successfully, that didn't prove anything except poor inventory control. They would deplore the black market in restricted technology and ask the Yavi to help them tighten their security. It was so predictable, so phony.

Polian bent down and peered at the dented armor's opaque faceplate, upturned toward the storm. One fact was undeniable. This one had been a covert-ops specialist, alright, and a good one. Crack shot with a gunpowder antique. Smart enough to discard the rifle, both to mislead and to lighten his load. He had probably shut down his own sensors to reduce his heat signature, and it had worked. Just dumb bad luck for him that the skimmer, blind to his presence, had whacked him.

Local technology had yet produced no vehicle that could keep up with a skimmer over snow, and as Polian knew from recent experience, smuggling anything as big as a skimmer down from orbit was nearly impossible.

That meant that this guy had route-marched at least a hundred and six frigid, snowy miles to catch up with them. But not just this guy.

Polian turned to Frei. "Get back on your grid. Pick up the search where you left off. And keep the thermal on this time!"

The younger man eyed the storm swirling around them. "Sir? There's no other tracks. And we respooled the sensor recordings while we were waiting for you. There was just the one set of vitals."

"Trueborn special-operations teams work as matched pairs. There's another snake in this snow someplace."

Frei saluted, then turned to the skimmer crew.

Partner or not, wearing Eternad armor or not, this guy had been a hard case to have followed them up here. From the tracks in the snow, after the skimmer bounced him, he had still crawled fifty yards from where he had landed before he collapsed.

Polian whispered to the motionless faceplate, "Oh, you lucky sonuvabitch. If we had taken you alive we might have turned you over to the local spooks. You self-righteous pricks call *Yavi* intel inhumane? Nobody can make a subject suffer like the ferrents can."

Polian stood, stretched, and started to turn away.

Then the corpse groaned and twitched one arm.

Polian's jaw dropped. Then he smiled.

Ten minutes later, two Tressen privates had gotten the Trueborn spy, armor and all, lashed to a skimmer's rear rack. None too gently, and the spy moaned.

After waving the two Tressens out of earshot, Polian leaned down until his helmet was a handspan away from the spy's opaque faceplate, and popped his own faceplate open. Then Polian reached down and worked the exterior faceplate latch on the spy's helmet. He wanted to see the fear in the murdering bastard's face, eye to eye, when he told the spy what the ferrents would do to make him talk.

Polian popped the spy's faceplate open and stared down.

Polian's eyes widened. "What the hell?"

Five

As I stood behind the bar at Jazen's, I polished its nickel surface with a towel in one hand. I like the place neat, because I'm Jazen. I also like the place peaceful, because I'm too familiar with other times than peace. Therefore, I snaked my free hand beneath the bar until my fingers brushed the stock of the sawed off shotgun. The gun lay alongside the little paper garnish umbrellas. Like every bar in Shipyard, Jazen's needed the former more than the latter.

I had just three customers, normal because the next cruiser wasn't due in to the Port of Mousetrap until the next morning. What wasn't normal was that each of the three smelled like a different kind of trouble.

The first customer sat at the bar, a graying Trueborn gunnery sergeant, retired. I knew that from the ID he had shown. Not that I'm nosy. Shipyard's no place for the nosy. But active duty and vets with ID got two for one at Jazen's ever since I took it over. And always would. The gunny had availed himself of my generosity and belted enough doubles to put an ex-GI like me under the table. I hated to concede any field to the jarheads, but in that activity they practiced harder than we did.

He shot me a drowsy glance, then lifted his empty glass with a hand that wobbled. Raw field regrows usually wobbled, and vet bennies didn't cover fine-motor neural rehab.

I smiled. "Take a coffee break, Gunny? On me." A passed-out drunk was bad for business, which didn't bother me. But the old soldier had given his arm, and a lifetime, to his service. Refusing him anything that I had *did* bother me.

He nodded, lurched to his feet, saluted, and turned for the door. That caused his gaze to cross the second of my three customers. The second was a Yavi, in civvies but with head shaved high and tight, who sat alone at a table staring into a beer.

The gunny muttered, "Don't care to drink with baby-killers anyway."

The Yavi's forearms, which were tattooed, and as muscular as the gunny's had been once, tightened. The Yavi's business chip, which entered him in a drawing for a free full-body massage next door that nobody ever won, claimed he was a manufacturers' rep. I grew up on Yavet, one of the few Illegal babies that the customer and his ilk hadn't managed to kill. Therefore, I recognized him for Yavi military in civilian drag.

Obviously, the gunny had recognized him, too. Which was going to be a problem.

Yavet and Earth were the Human Union's only nuclear powers, and they were within twenty years of one another in technologic development. Yavet lagged Earth in just one discipline, but it was a honker. Only Earth had starships.

The Trueborns let anybody and anything ride their ships, because they believed everybody should be free. Of course, "free to ride" didn't mean "ride for free." Open access made Earth rich. And the access wasn't entirely open. The Trueborns refused to carry military. Except their own, and the Legion, which was an Earth-based independent contractor. Both of whom were, of course, even-handed peacekeepers.

This infuriated Yavet, which was overpopulated, over-polluted, and proud to be both. Yavet needed *lebensraum* worse than a teenaged boy needed a free full body massage.

But without starships, Yavet could no more expand than a sixteen-year-old without a car could get laid.

So the Yavi did what they could get away with to grow their influence. They smuggled military to the outworlds aboard Trueborn starships. The Trueborns let them get away with it as long as the influence growth was minute. When any Yavi project posed a greater threat to Earth, GIs on both sides died restoring the balance in chilly, undeclared brushfire wars. There had been so many such brush fires that the Trueborns called the arrangement Cold War II. The only things a GI hates more than getting killed in an undeclared war are the people who are trying to kill him. Trueborn soldiers hated Yavi soldiers, and the Yavi returned the favor.

The Yavi stood, hefted his glass mug like a Trueborn baseball, and spilled his beer.

As the two soldiers glared at each other, I smiled at the Yavi. "Let me refill that for you. On the house."

The Yavi ignored me and wound up to peg a fastball at the gunny.

The gunny snatched a bar stool and turned it legs-up, like a bat. The legs trembled in his bony hands. "I remember my pugil-stick drill. You remember yours, 'salesman'?"

Brawls weren't so much bad for business as hard on furniture. My friendly offers of freebies weren't defusing the crisis. I drew the shotgun and clicked off the safety.

A salesman wouldn't recognize the click, but a soldier would. Both men froze.

I shifted the saloon gun's stubby barrels back and forth from one torso to the other. "Free City of Shipyard Municipal Ordinance 6.21 authorizes the use of deadly force by a licensed establishment owner in defense of property. I own this place. That's my beer stein and my bar stool. So can't we all just get along?"

Neither man budged, while their breath rasps echoed off the bar's hewn nickel-iron walls. The gunny gave away too much in age and bulk to the Yavi to win the fight. However, if he managed to break a chair over a Yavi, he'd brag at the Shipyard VIW Post for years. But if the Yavi blew his cover, his superiors would cashier him, or worse. And he knew it.

The Yavi slammed his mug back down on his table. "Fuck it." Then he spun on his heel, walked out the open door into the passage, turned right, and was gone.

"Gutless weasel." The gunny snorted. He replaced the barstool on the floor with quivering hands, nodded to me, and stalked out, too.

The Gunny turned left, and I exhaled audibly.

My third—and now only—customer had sat silently at a corner table during the flap.

He watched the door until the sound of both mens' footfalls faded. Then, while I slid the shotgun back underneath the bar, he stood and carried his glass back to me.

I had noted when he came in that he was as militarily erect as the other two and carried himself with that sense of entitlement that outworlders immediately recognize in any Trueborn. When he had come in, he had said he was a cruiser tourist. However, the only cruiser due for the month was still inbound, so that was a lie. But the Free City of Shipyard ran on cash in the fist, not on truth. Therefore I had shut up and poured.

The liar laid a bill on my bar. "For the whisky."

I pointed at the bill. "You got imported. There won't be change back from that."

He raised his eyebrows. "Imported?"

I nodded, swept up the bill. "Authentic Tennessee sour mash." I figured one obvious lie deserved another.

I eyed his glass. Still full. Which either meant he knew Shipyard bootleg will make you blind, or he was on duty. Probably both.

He said, "I hear Jazen Parker inherited this place. You him?"

I shrugged. "You can hear anything in Shipyard." But he had heard right about how I got the bar. The mother of an only child I had served with in the Legion left Fatso's to me when I was, uh, between jobs, two years before. She left it to me partly because she couldn't leave it to her son. I had been with him when he died in action.

Partly because she felt guilty about having fingered me for a bounty hunter who almost killed me, too.

The liar looked around the empty cavern. "Business good?"

"Profitable enough when there are cruisers in the port." I leaned forward, palms on my bar. "And there aren't any in the port. So who the hell are you, really?"

He shrugged. "Let's say I'm a messenger. Somebody would like to see you, Lieutenant Parker."

A spook. I shook my head. "Just Parker. I resigned my commission two years ago, when my hitch ended."

I began my military career, if you call mercenary work military, with a two-year Legion hitch. Legion enlistment got me off Yavet ahead of the bounty hunters, but my Legion time ended, shall we say, poorly. My second hitch was in the Trueborn military-intelligence service. That got me commissioned as an officer and a gentleman, but ended even worse. Twice bitten, thrice shy.

He shrugged again. "It was a gesture of respect. I saw your file. It says a lot good about you."

I shrugged back. "You saw I've got a shotgun under this bar, too. My file says I'm not afraid to use it. As a gesture of respect, I won't. If you drink up and leave."

He raised his hands, palms out, and smiled. "Just doing my job, sir. The Old Man's here. Came all the way out just to see you."

I raised my eyebrows. It was one of those lies so obvious that I knew it was true. Everybody within the hollowed-out moonlet that was the interstellar crossroad called Mousetrap knew the next cruiser wasn't due in until tomorrow.

However, less than everybody knew that a VIP and his personal security detail could launch from an inbound cruiser in a fast-mover and beat the cruiser in by a full day. Cruisers drift in through the North Lock, then down Broadway, the fifteen-mile-long axial tunnel that cores Mousetrap like an apple, to the berths at the South End. But fastys could enter Mousetrap very privately. The moonlet's skin was peppered with abandoned interceptor sally ports that still worked fine if you knew the codes. Which was exactly the way Lieutenant General Howard Hibble, aka King of the Spooks, aka the Old Man, would make an entrance.

The security-detail spook shrugged again. "He just wants to visit."

"I'll be here 'til closing."

"You know he can't come up to Shipyard."

I knew nothing of the sort, but I was curious. And my calendar wasn't exactly full. "Where, then?"

"At the Pseudocephalopod War Museum, First Battle of Mousetrap exhibit. In an hour."

Forty-one minutes later I stepped off the Southbound tuber at Museum Station and blinked at the contrast. I always did when I traveled from Shipyard to the South End.

Mousetrap was originally mankind's interstellar Gibraltar, our bulwark against the Pseudocephalopod Hegemony. Since we won the war, the South End had remained the crossroads of the Human Union, the gateway to the temporal-fabric insertion points that led, directly or indirectly, to the five hundred twelve planets that comprised the Human Union. As such, the South End was insufferably bright and clean and quiet.

After the war, the North End, where the great ships that won the war for us had been built and berthed, had been abandoned by the Human Union. Eventually Mousetrap's unemployed shipwrights had squatted there, then declared themselves an independent and, uh, socially liberated community. Today the Free City of Shipyard, where nothing was free but everything was available if one paid cash, was the graffiti-tagged nest of addicts, villains, and libertines that I called home.

The Museum and War Memorials saw little traffic when the Port was between cruisers, but today Museum Station was so deserted that I heard my shoes squeak on the floor tile as I walked.

I looked down the platform. The crawl above the museum entrance read "Closed this afternoon. Private event."

I smiled. Somehow, I had the feeling that, despite the sign, when I got close enough that my ID, but nobody else's, tickled the sensors, the doors would slide open anyway.

Ten minutes' walk down the dim museum corridor I came to the First Battle of Mousetrap Gallery and saw Howard Hibble for the first time in two years. He sat with his back to me, staring through the glass wall at the static displays beyond. He teetered on a hovering scooter, his bony hands grasping the tiller. Not because he was obese. Howard was as gaunt as ever. But because he was old.

"How's the saloon business?" He spoke without turning. I suppose he saw my reflection in the glass, the way I saw his. He wore civvies as wrinkled as his skin, and they bagged on his skinny frame as badly as his uniforms always did. Old-fashioned glasses covered his eyes, the kind that hooked over his ears and rested across his nose.

"Better than the spook business, if you've got time to waste on me." I pointed through the glass at the display of twodee photographs from the start of the war, when the Slugs blitzed Earth seventy years before, and at his picture in an intelligence captain's uniform in particular. "You haven't changed much."

He shrugged. "Trueborn medicine and near-light-travel time dilation."

I snorted. "I mean the spook theatrics." I threw my arms wide and spun in a circle. "*Here* you meet me?"

"It seemed appropriate, considering. Besides, your parents—"

I stopped spinning and pointed at him. "Exactly! The only reason I signed on with you was because you said you'd tell me the truth about my parents."

He raised a bony palm off the scooter's tiller and shook his head. "No. I told you I knew your parents during the war and that your separation from them at birth wasn't the abandonment it's seemed to you over the years. That was the truth."

I cocked my head. "Oh. And I suppose you're here now to tell me the rest of the truth, finally?"

Behind his glasses, Howard Hibble rolled sleepy eyes. "It was classified then, it's classified now."

I returned his eye roll. "Come on, Howard! What could be classified about a war that we won thirty years ago? Against an enemy that doesn't exist anymore?" I pointed at a different holo display. "Jason Wander, GI hero of the Battle of Ganymede." And another. "General Jason

Wander, goat of the First Battle of Mousetrap, hero of the Second Battle of Mousetrap."

"It doesn't say he was the goat."

"No." I waved my hand down the corridor. "But of all the heroes, he's the only one without a picture here. Or anywhere. I've looked all over the Net. And after Second Mousetrap—poof—he just disappears from the history chips. And so does Admiral Mimi Ozawa."

"I told you he and your mother were alive and working for me, at least part-time. I can tell you that's still true."

"Where? Doing what? Why the whitewash of what they did in the war? And why did they leave me on Yavet with the midwife who delivered me?"

"I can't answer your questions directly. Jazen, you know I trust you. But, operationally, you have no need to know the answers."

"Then I have no need to continue this conversation." I turned away.

Howard said, "But I can offer you a job where you would need to know."

I stopped. Only someone who has no past understands why it's important. "Desk job?"

"Case officer. I'll be honest. It's extremely dangerous. The incumbent senior on the team that your team would replace was, in my opinion, our best. The team went silent a month ago."

Incumbent case officers? Why not just call spies spies? Because Howard Hibble was hooked on euphemistic understatement. That also meant that when he called the job "extremely dangerous," the job was a death sentence.

I snorted. "Went silent? You mean went dead, Howard."

"I mean went silent. We've lost contact with teams in the field before but recovered them eventually."

"I was barely past rookie when I left. You must have two hundred case officers more experienced than me. Why replace the best with me?"

"You have unique qualifications."

"Such as?"

"You'll find out as you go. If you go."

I wanted to know why my parents abandoned me. I wanted to know how my parents had screwed up the end of the war. Screwed it up so badly that they both got expunged from history. But I rolled my eyes up to the dark museum ceiling. "No. In fact, hell no. Howard, this rabbit-in-the-hat crap is why I quit in the first place."

The King of the Spooks shook his head, then dropped his voice. "We both know that's not why you quit."

I bit my lip, looked away from the displays, into the dark, and swallowed while my eyes burned. "You're right." I blinked, drew a breath. "But I'm past that. Now I've got a saloon to run." I turned and walked away.

Howard let me stalk to the end of the corridor. Then his whisper echoed to me. "Jazen, don't you want to know who the missing incumbent senior is?"

Six

Dawn on the streets of Tressia was calm and greased with the oil smoke from a half-million chimneys. Polian walked, hands in civilian coat pockets, eyes cast down at the cobbles, and frowned. Not at the feel of the coat. Tressen textiles had a hand-woven texture that he enjoyed. But the day ahead was the first of the thirty-one since he had returned from the Arctic that worried him.

He passed through a manned security checkpoint, a vestige of the day when rebel sabotage was a real threat and not just an excuse for the Interior Police to search the citizenry.

Then Polian was within the Government Quarter of Tressen's capital. Polian frowned again because the sterile, boxy Tressen government buildings were set back thirty yards on both sides of a boulevard that was fifteen yards wide itself. Worse, the capital city of Tressen, in fact the entire nation, was open to the sky. Polian had grown up like every legal Yavi, beneath the levels' comforting ceilings.

He swore as he walked. Trueborn psychologists called

the Yavi discomfort with open spaces agoraphobic. Yavi psychologists called it normal. Leave it to the Trueborns to define any behavior except theirs as aberrant. The polite term for Trueborn self-absorption was "Terracentrism." Polian preferred to call it arrogance.

He rounded the last corner and let his eyes rest on the clinic. Its architecture was pleasantly different from the sterile Tressen boxes that it predated. Neo-Iridian, it was all white marble with arched doors and windows, crenulated parapets, for this world a regular castle. But in front of the castle squatted a long-hooded Tressen automobile, so black and anonymous that it could only be Interior Police. It was parked at the curb in front of the clinic's arched entrance. Behind the car squatted a swollen-tired Tressen ambulance, rear doors swung open, exposing an empty interior waiting to be filled. Because half the clinic had been cleared, and now housed only one patient, that meant Polian's worry about day thirty-one was justified.

Polian ran the remaining distance and reached the clinic's front doors just as a patient-loaded gurney's end bumped them open in front of him. Polian planted a hand on the rolling bed's foot rail and stopped it.

He shouted, "What do you think you're doing?"

The two trench-coated men pushing the gurney looked up at Polian. The one on the left peered from beneath the brim of his slouch hat with eyes as black and cold as marbles. "Custody transfer, Mr. Polian. The IP has humored you for a month."

The man, an Interior Police chief inspector by his lapel badge, shifted his weight and shoved the gurney toward the waiting ambulance. Polian planted his feet, shoved back until the gurney quivered, and stared at the cop. Every member of the Interior Police that Polian had encountered had the same attitude and dead eyes.

The locals called the IP "ferrents," after an indigenous species of anvil-headed, rat-sized amphibians. Partly because the IP wore ferrent-colored brown leather trench coats and slouch hats. Mostly because ferrents—the four footed kind—had a singularly disgusting habit of nosing around in other creatures' dung.

Polian looked down at the bandaged, unconscious figure strapped to the gurney. "Thirty days was a reevaluation date, not a turnover deadline." He peered over the ferrent's shoulder at the lab-coated physician who stood behind them in the corridor. "Doctor, what'll happen if she's moved?"

The physician glanced sideways at the ferrent, around spectacles fashioned from bent wire. "As I explained to the chief inspector, each surgery has improved her chance of regaining consciousness. I think that in a few more days—"

The ferrent rolled his eyes. "*More* days? She was unconscious when she got here. After a month of your coddling, she's the same. Our methods have gotten the attention of subjects less lively than she is."

Ferrent "methods" would only kill her. That she die, and painfully, suited Polian fine. But not until she talked.

The doctor and this idiot ferrent knew only that the woman on the gurney was a high-value detainee and that Polian was a civilian with an odd accent and too much stroke. And that was all they needed to know.

So Polian simply sighed and exercised his stroke. He stared at the ferrent. "Would you care to see my papers?"

The man scowled and stared at Polian's chest.

In a leather wallet in his breast pocket, Polian carried a simple letter on the personal letterhead of, and signed and sealed by, the chairman of the Republican Socialist Party and chancellor-for-life of the Tressen Republic. It advised the reader to render all assistance to the bearer that he might request. It encouraged the reader to contact the Chancellery directly if further clarification was required.

So far, further clarification had never, ever been required by anyone who saw the letter.

Undoubtedly, the ferrent's predecessor had told this new ferrent about the fiat letter, if the doctor hadn't. Polian cursed himself silently for keeping a predictable schedule. The ferrents had expected to steal the woman before he arrived, then fumble and shuffle about her whereabouts while they worked her over. They had nearly succeeded. The Trueborns had a saying that possession was nine points of the law. Evidently the Tressens did, too.

The doctor laid a hand on the ferrent's coat sleeve and shook his head. The gesture measured the power of a simple Chancellery fiat letter. Just as no sane civilian Yavi back home laid hands on a government representative, no sane Tressen laid hands on a ferrent, unless the consequences of holding back were worse.

The ferrent glanced down at the hand quivering on his sleeve, then up at Polian. After two breaths, the ferrent nodded to his trench-coated companion, and the two relaxed their grips on the gurney rails. The senior ferrent narrowed his eyes at Polian and pointed. "I don't know who you are, but I know you'll regret this. This woman is trouble."

Polian warmed to his role and mocked a pout. "Ah, women! How many years have the Interior Police been chasing Celline? Or does she chase you?" To the remaining Iridians, and the Tressens who covertly sympathized with them, Celline was hope. To the ferrents, her rebellion was an infuriating symbol of their impotence. To Polian, she was irrelevant. But she was a momentarily amusing pin with which to prick this ferrent's ass.

The ferrent's pointing finger shook. "We don't chase myths. The last Iridian royal was hanged years ago."

Polian smiled again. "Then why is her wanted poster still hanging in the employee lounge? Just an oversight, I'm sure. A rebellion could never survive for thirty years. Not against you ferrents."

The doctor coughed a laugh into his hand. He had probably never heard anyone call a chief inspector of the Interior Police "ferrent" to his face.

The ferrent folded his pointed finger into a fist, shook it, then waved his subordinate to follow him as he stalked out the doors.

Twenty minutes later, in the windowless hospital room to which the anonymous patient had been returned, Polian stood alongside the unconscious woman while she breathed.

He stared down at her. With the bruising faded from her cheeks, she was a beautiful woman, but somehow not a regal one.

Polian stroked his chin and thought out loud. "Well,

whoever you are, you're no more an Iridian than I'm a Tressen. You're a Trueborn from your toes to your eyeballs. You've got an athlete's body. Or a soldier's." He ran a finger along the intravenous feeding tube taped to the woman's emaciated arm. "Well, you did have a month ago."

Her wounds had been so massive that her stable survival was, considering the primitive state of Tressen medical practice, miraculous. Back home, Yavi medical technology could have healed her to interrogatable condition long ago. And Yavi interrogation methods would then have wrung her dry within days. For now, all Polian could do was wonder. "How much do you know? How much does your partner know? How much of what you know have you passed on to your masters?"

Wonder, and wait on the next damn Trueborn cruiser to bring the next Yavi "humanitarian" delegation to Tressen.

He sighed at the serene, silent spy. "Well, once we succeed here, nothing the Trueborns know will help them."

Seven

"Those are the roughest holy men I've ever seen." The blue-eyed, pale kid seated across from me stared past me at the far side of the main dining salon of the Human Union Bastogne-class cruiser *Emerald River*. The twenty Yavi who were seated there wore cleric shawls and bowed their shaved heads in post-meal prayer. But they were the fittest priests *anybody* had ever seen.

Three days after my conversation with Howard Hibble, *Emerald River* had slid her ancient, mile-long bulk out Mousetrap's South Lock. Bound, as scheduled, for Tressel, she carried me, along with an insertion-support team and the rookie case officer with whom Howard had paired me. This lunch was my first meeting with my new junior.

I glanced over my shoulder. "They aren't preachers, Weddle, if I know my Yavi. And I do. I grew up on Yavet."

My new partner wrinkled his forehead. "You? You look as Trueborn as I do."

Actually, nobody looked as white-bread Trueborn as

Weddle. Fortunately, the look blended with the Tressens with whom we would be mingling.

"Long, boring story. Weddle, there are two kinds of Yavi. The first kind are the general population. Short, docile, beat down by generations of overcrowding." I jerked my thumb at the Yavi lunch group. "The second kind of Yavi are those jokers. Military, and cops who act like military. The second kind make sure the first kind *stay* docile. They make decent soldiers, and excellent bullies."

The bulk of *Emerald River's* cargo consisted of farm implements, electronics, and the latest consumer goods from the Motherworld. Those items would be off-loaded at intermediate planetary waypoints. Once the cruiser reached her turnaround point, which for an embargoed world like Tressel was a geosynchronous parking orbit, she would off-load in orbit her remaining cargo. That consisted of a minimal volume of unembargoed humanitarian items, mostly medical supplies and the freely distributed Trueborn holy books called Gideon Bibles.

Emerald River would also off-load a personnel pod carrying the twenty liars who sat on the other side of the dining salon.

The cargo, human and otherwise, would be shuttled down aboard old-fashioned chemical-fueled space planes operated by neutrals under contract with the Union.

Once on Tressel, the twenty liars would not distribute holy books. They would do what Yavi covert military parties did on every outworld. Build Yavi influence, at the expense of Earth's influence, by espionage and violence.

Not that Weddle and I were much better. We were supposed to be tourists. He wore a flower-print shirt and kept poking his own cheek with the umbrella garnish that stuck up out of his drink.

Neither we nor the Yavi were fooling the other. The charade had teetered at an uneasy balance point for decades.

Neither the Trueborns nor the Yavi wanted Cold War II to explode into Interstellar War II. The Yavi had the Human Union's largest population and correspondingly largest gross planetary product. The Trueborns had the smug prestige of being the cradle of mankind. More importantly, the Trueborns controlled the starships that connected the worlds of the Union.

Like any other belligerent couple, each of the two cultures thought it held the moral high ground.

Earth had waged and won the war that eradicated the Pseudocephalopod Hegemony and saved the human race. In the process, Earth had lost sixty million people and had stolen starship technology from the Slugs fair and square.

For its part, Yavet had produced mankind's most numerically prolific and technically advanced society, albeit one that executed unpermitted babies at birth, raped the environment, and generally made Earth's last-century Nazis look soft.

The Trueborns refused to share C-drive with Neo-Nazis. The Yavi refused to be judged by holier-than-thou hypocrites. The only thing stupider or worse than the rivalry would have been all-out war. Avoiding which was, therefore, the overriding goal and sworn duty for which every spook case officer would joyfully sacrifice his or her life. And/or the life of his or her partner. It said so right in the oath.

I forked up my last bite of blueberry pie, then glanced at my 'puter. My new junior looked across at me like a puppy.

I suppose I looked at Kit that way when I was the green junior case officer and she was my senior. Weddle and I would henceforth be, as Kit and I had been, as every case officer team was, closer than siblings. Well, not exactly. If Kit had been my sister, our off-duty, uh, interaction would have gotten us arrested some places in the Union. But Weddle and I would train together, eat together, study together, and depend on one another for our very lives.

I slapped my palms on the tablecloth, like the impatient older brother I was about to become. "Weddle, time to save the universe. Or die trying."

Part one of universe-saving for a case officer team is insertion prep. Prep was normally conducted on dirt, and took months. Weddle and I were being prepped for this insertion on the fly, in weeks.

Mostly, that didn't bother me. A kid who grows up denied the right to go to school, which was how I had grown up on Yavet, grows up thirsty for knowledge.

During my two years on Earth I had read everything I could lay hands on. Mostly, a soldier can lay his hands on military history, but I had sponged up other things, too. A playwright named Shakespeare came highly recommended. They said he wrote in the language that became Standard, but at first I barely recognized it. I even read a Gideon Bible once.

I always enjoyed the classroom segments of an insertion prep. Say that for Howard. He had been a professor before the Slug War. So spook branch always force-fed a case officer the natural history of the planet for which he or she was bound, its human history, and a dumbed-down helping of any science the case required.

We got our physical exams updated and a comprehensive prick-and-swallow to immunize us against local diseases.

The physical training and hand-to-hand combat segments of insertion prep were usually just to maintain established fitness and skills. But in my case they were a sweaty and necessary evil. Two years of saloon keeping, in the spun-up rotational gravity of a hollow meteor with a mass less than Manhattan Island's, had been no health-club membership. Weddle kicked my butt daily in all phases.

Running we did by laps around one of the outer decks, like hamsters in a cosmic wheel.

Case officers ran wearing full rucksacks, to simulate field conditions. The only thing more precious to a case officer in the field than his or her partner and weapon was the equipment in his ruck. However, on the last lap packs were dropped for a final sprint.

It was called the burn lap, but not just for what it did to your lungs and thighs. A case officer's pack was only dropped if the bad guys in hot pursuit got danger-close. And only after yanking a timer cord that caused the pack, and its classified contents, to burn like Krakatoa. And, with luck, take down some bad guys.

Kit and I had always run the burn lap competitively. If I won, we showered *ensemble*. Sometimes even if I lost. Though then I had to listen to her crow about how second place was just first loser. That was one of her favorite gungho–isms.

But the part of prep I really cared about was the

mission-specific case briefing. The CB began after *Emerald River* made her last jump through the temporal fabric, which left us a week of near-light travel away from Tressel parking orbit.

The first thing that made this particular case briefing abnormal, considering Howard's security fetish, was that the CB was conducted in the echoing emptiness of *Emerald River*'s Bay Twenty-four.

Cruisers were originally built as warships. But there were no other ships left in the universe to make war on. Lacking need to project military power, the Trueborns used their cruisers to project mercantile and cultural power across five hundred and twelve planets. All concerned got richer and smarter. However, the Trueborns got richest and smartest.

Emerald River's belt line was ringed with thirty-six launch and recovery bays that had once housed interceptors and attack transports. In civilian service, most of the bays were empty. But the bays, and the C-drive engineering spaces in the booms behind them, were still sealed off from forward-area passengers, especially curious Yavi "civilians," by a locked and loaded marine platoon.

The second thing that made this case briefing abnormal was that the King of the Spooks himself had made the trip with us and was briefing us personally.

Howard Hibble's voice echoed in the hangar-sized, pie-slice–shaped bay, and nobody could hear it except me, Weddle, and the three cleared members of the insertion team.

We sat, hands folded, around a table set up on the deck plates while Howard slid back and forth on his scooter the way a lecturer paced a stage. The only other things in the bay were three sealed plasteel cargo containers. Those were packed with mission-specific equipment. The stuff the spooks thought I needed to know about would be explained to me.

Howard said, "Six months ago we developed intelligence that Yavet and Tressel intended to form a clandestine alliance."

I raised my eyebrows, but I didn't ask how we came to know that. Spooks are closemouthed, even among themselves, about "sources and methods." "Sources and methods" meant how and/or from whom raw information was obtained. "Developed intelligence" was what spooks made of all the information they assembled. It might mean that we had it all on holo. Or it might mean that Howard had a wild-ass hunch.

I furrowed my brow. "Tressen's a fourth-rate civilization stuck at the end of a jump line. What could be in *that* for the Yavi?"

Howard pursed his lips. "Well, I have a hunch about that."

I knew asking what Howard's hunch was would be as futile as asking about sources and methods. Howard's hunches had proven world-savingly right often during the last half century. That's why the tight-ass Trueborn military let him run his branch like a libertarian bus wreck.

Howard made a thin fist. "But we need proof. That's why we inserted Colonel Born's team."

My heart skipped when he mentioned Kit's name. Howard normally ignored rank and called people by their first names, just one of the anarchic quirks that drove the regular army bughouse. Calling Kit by her rank was, I think, his attempt to depersonalize the situation and keep me focused and quiet. It didn't work.

I interrupted him. "What happened to her, Howard?"

"We don't know, Jazen."

"What feedback have you gotten from the local contacts?"

Howard shook his head. "None. The team went in barefoot. We haven't had reliable human assets on Tressel for years. Kit freelances and improvises better than anybody I've ever seen. Well, almost anybody."

"Then you want us to follow her?" The only reason I was once again sitting in a starship, surrounded by spooks thinking up ways to endanger me, was Kit.

Howard shook his head. "We don't know what's happened to her, but any step we followed when we inserted her team could have been the step that got them in trouble. So we're changing everything up for you two. Except that once your feet are wet, you'll be unsupervised, like she was." He blinked. "Is."

My breath caught and my heart thumped. She was alive down there somewhere. I had to believe that.

So I nodded at Howard. "Understood."

Weddle just sat, arms folded and eyes locked on Howard like a good junior. At my first briefing, as a good junior, I had done the same thing. Actually, my eyes had been locked more on my senior than on my briefer.

Really, what I meant by "understood" was that whatever spy foolishness Howard wanted me to pursue, my personal first priority was Kit. The sheer hostility of the planet and society we were going to operate in would isolate me. I would be free to pursue my priority first and Howard's spy foolishness second. I wasn't sticking my neck out for some secret handshake. I was sticking my neck out for Kit. So my spy oath was a lie. But lying was what spies did.

"How soon does our Scorpion drop?" I wrinkled my forehead and looked around the empty bay as I said it. It should have occurred to me sooner that the insertion vehicle wasn't in the bay with us.

Normally, a case-officer team entered an area of operations like any other cruiser passengers, except with phony ID. But in closed and hostile environments like Tressel, insertion was done by ferrying the team down to a planet's surface at a remote location, unannounced and undetected, in a Scorpion T. Spook Scorpion transport variants were as fast and shifty as Scorpion fighters, but with a radar cross section smaller than the bluebird of happiness and a heat signature fainter than that of day-old pizza.

From orbital strap-in to disembarkation on the ground normally took ten minutes. Things might get hairy later, but insertion by Scorpion had the drama of a limo ride from the airport.

Howard frowned and shook his head. "We inserted Kit's team by Scorpion. So that's the first thing we're changing for you." He waved at the peephole in the personnel hatch that led into the bay from the passageway. The hatch undogged from the other side, and two more spooks, each wearing coveralls and paratroop jump boots, came in, walked to us, and saluted Howard.

Howard returned the salute with a limp hand.

The redheaded para turned to me and smiled. “Good thing you’re not afraid of heights, Lieutenant.”

I wrinkled my forehead. “Huh?

Eight

Twenty minutes later, Howard and the other briefing spooks adjourned for coffee and probably a game of chess.

Weddle and I stood in the empty, echoing bay with our respective trainers, arms outstretched like scarecrows.

The redhead, who turned out to be an Airborne School jumpmaster, knelt alongside me. He was fitting an Eternad armor suit he had unpacked from one of the plasteel crates. As he worked he tapped suit features and lectured. "Thigh scabbard. One each twenty-four-inch synthetic koto-steel bush knife—"

I sighed and tapped my opposite thigh pocket. "One each search-and-rescue pyrotechnic canister."

He stood, slipped the helmet down over my head like a coronation. "I gather you've worn Eternads before, Lieutenant?"

I nodded.

"When last, sir? The latest evolution's had a couple tweaks."

Successive evolutions of the Eternad fighting suit had

been saving Trueborn GI lives, including mine, since clear back at the start of the Slug War.

"Couple years." I sniffed the prior occupant's sweat in the helmet pads. "I think somebody's been wearing this suit ever since."

He smiled. "We're fitting each of you to a suit that's broken in. Seventy percent of new suits experience out-of-the-box glitches. Can't tolerate that when we're already pushing the equipment's limit."

I frowned out through my open faceplate. Pushing my equipment's limit? Eternads store a GI's body-movement energy, then use it to run their computers and sensors, and to heat and warm the GI. They synthesize or purify air, and water if necessary. They keep out any water that *isn't* necessary, such as the kind one might fall into. They also keep out vacuum, bullets, shrapnel, chemical and biological agents, and the occasional mosquito. But they're light enough and supple enough to let the GI double-time a marathon. Eternad armor's limit is hard to push.

He snapped my visor shut to pressure test the seals, so I was talking to myself when I asked, "What the hell does that mean?"

Ten minutes later, my suit was fitted and cooling me. Meanwhile, the spook had unpacked another plasteel. The jigsaw he had laid out on the floor was sleek and radar-absorbent black. He held a cylindrical section alongside my suit's thigh, cocked his head, then replaced it with a different one.

I popped my visor as he said, "The fairing pieces look different outside the wind tunnel."

"Wind tunnel?"

He stared into my helmet. "General Hibble didn't tell you?"

I sighed. "Why don't you?"

He glanced at the closed hatch, then back at me, and lowered his voice. "Sir, Weddle's a master parachutist. But they did say you're Airborne qualified?"

I nodded. "Made it through jump school."

He smiled and raised a fist. "Air-*borne*!"

I bumped his fist with mine while avoiding a visible eye roll. "All the way." I left the military for many good and sufficient reasons. Somewhere on my reason list was gung-ho phobia.

The jumpmaster ratcheted the suit's right forearm until it matched the length of my own. "Basically, sir, this jump will be just like a static-line school jump. Only from a little higher altitude."

My heart skipped. "Jump?" I had graduated jump school because my military operational specialty required it, but it scared me green. Now it was clear that Weddle and I weren't going to step out onto Tressel's surface from a Scorpion, like exiting a taxi. We were going to parachute to the surface.

I frowned. "A little higher" meant something different to someone wearing paratroop jump boots than to sane people. "Not a HALO jump?"

Super spooks like Kit Born, and special-operations troops since long before the Slug War, often jumped High Altitude-Low Opening. HALO jumpers exited an aircraft in the frozen stratosphere, breathing bottled oxygen and bundled against the cold, then fell arms and legs splayed and belly-down for most of ten miles before they opened their chutes. While falling they attained a terminal velocity of one hundred twenty miles per hour. Very stealthy. Very scary.

He raised his palm and shook his head. "HALO? Oh, no, sir!"

I exhaled. "Good."

"A Scorpion that low might be detected."

This time, I rolled my eyes visibly. "Detected? The Tressens only invented aerial searchlights six years ago. They couldn't detect a Scorpion if one fell on them."

He shrugged. "General Hibble's afraid the Yavi might have smuggled in modern air-defense detection systems, and crews to operate them, to help the Tressens."

There was no paranoid like an Intel paranoid. But I sighed. After all, something had tripped Kit up. If I hoped to get her out, Weddle and I had to avoid whatever it was.

The jumpmaster pointed at the bay outer doors, which, because of rotational gravity, we were actually standing on. "It's really pretty simple. A cruiser moves by gravity manipulation. It doesn't really orbit, just mimics orbit to match speed and trajectory with conventional shuttles that actually do need to maintain orbital velocities to stay aloft. So the ship will simply drop down and circle the planet twenty-five miles lower, for a brief interval."

"You're afraid the Tressens will notice a four-place stealth aircraft. So you're going to use a mile-long spaceship instead?"

"We've already told the Tressens that the *Emerald River* will be varying her altitude this trip. As a humanitarian favor. The diplomats won't let us drop off satellites around Tressel. So we're doing atmospheric research, to increase the accuracy of Tressel weather forecasting. Perfectly logical."

Spook logic was not Aristotelian logic. One minute paranoia drove them. The next they were overconfident enough to hide in plain sight behind some obvious lie.

The jumpmaster said, "While the ship's at the lower altitude, we'll open the bay doors. Low-thrust boosters attached to your suits will kick-start you two out into space. Then you'll just fall through the atmosphere until your altimeter reading opens your chute."

"Uh-uh." I shook my head. Bad logic was arguable. Bad physics wasn't. "That won't work. We'll burn up like old space capsules."

He shook his head back at me. "Nope. The old space capsules actually *were* in orbit. They used atmospheric friction to decelerate them from orbital velocity so they could fall back to the surface. Friction absorbs speed energy by turning it into heat energy. Like car brakes. But this ship will be moving geosynchronously. Moving at the same speed as the atmosphere. For you two it'll be like jumping out of a stationary balloon's gondola. Just from higher up."

I glanced over at Weddle, the master parachutist who was barely old enough to shave. He and the other jumpmaster were chatting it up, smiling.

I cocked my head. I had bet my life on Eternads before. If white-bread Weddle could do this, I could. But the jumpmaster had mentioned pushing the suit's limits. "Can the suits stay pressure tight at a hundred twenty miles an hour?"

The jumpmaster frowned. "One twenty? Sir, that's

where things get a little complicated. Terminal velocity is the speed at which a free-falling object's atmospheric drag equals gravitational acceleration. For a parachutist jumping from ten miles up, terminal velocity *is* about a hundred twenty miles per hour You'll be falling through near vacuum at first. So atmospheric drag won't retard your acceleration much for the first hundred miles or so."

My eyes popped wider. "I fall a hundred miles?"

He wrinkled his nose. "Give or take."

"How fast?"

He turned his palms up. "Well, the density of Tressen's upper atmosphere's different from Earth's, fortunately."

"How fast?"

He shifted his weight. "We've calculated that you shouldn't break the sound barrier."

I smiled. "No, really."

"Really. Actually, if you did go supersonic, that could be a problem. The fins we're adding to the suit's thigh plates will keep you falling headfirst—"

"Headfirst? Nice touch. Thanks. But no." Spook jump school had included one sky dive–style belly-flop familiarization jump. "I'll just belly flop. That'll slow me down."

He paused and stared at me. "—Headfirst. In practical vacuum you can't stop spinning if you start. If you belly flop, then start to spin, you'd spin flat, like you were an old holodisc on a turntable. When you reached one hundred forty-five rpm, centrifugal force would pancake your brain flat against the top of your skull."

"Oh."

"That would snap your brain off of your brain stem."

I swallowed. "Which would kill me."

He shook his head. "Actually, no."

"Great news."

"You'd already be dead. Increased pressure in your cranial blood vessels would have ruptured them before that."

I nodded. "Okay, then. Headfirst."

He paused again, hands on hips, and sighed. "Sir, this will go smoother if you just trust us. We've thought this through."

I nodded. "Sorry. It's just that I'm the one doing the falling."

He grinned at me and pumped his fist. "And what a ride, huh? Air-*borne*, sir!"

I sighed. "Yeah. All the way."

He wrinkled his forehead. "As I was saying, the problem if you go supersonic in the headfirst attitude is that your head becomes supersonic first. A moment before your torso does."

"So?"

"So the buffeting instability of an object's transonic passage can cause the object to disarticulate along planes of weakness."

I stared at him.

He said, "Uh, back in the day, experimental aircraft used to break up. After all, we still call it the sound barrier. The human body, even in armor, is weaker than an old jet fuselage."

I frowned. "I'd break when I hit the barrier?"

He nodded. "Ever shoot a chicken into a boulder?"

No, but it sounded like some of Howard's twisted minions had.

He thrust up his index finger. "But we're attaching speed-sensitive dive brakes to the suit. They'll slow you automatically. Heck, you won't exceed six hundred miles per hour. Probably."

"Probably?" My voice rose. "*Probably?*"

He turned his palms up and cocked his head. "Given budget and time, we'd have tested this technique better, Lieutenant. But this case requirement just came up. We needed technology that was already on the shelf, and—"

I sighed. Everybody who works for Howard sighs a lot. "And cheap?" Spook budgets had been unlimited during the Slug War, when human existence hung in the balance. Mankind had mortgaged its future to build Mousetrap and the cruiser fleet. But now we were still paying off the debt decades later.

He flicked his eyes down at the deck plates, then looked up. "This concept was developed clear back in the space-capsule days, so the old astronauts could escape from a malfunctioning reaction-propelled spacecraft. After we got C-drive, spacecraft didn't really need the technology."

I raised my eyebrows. "But back in the space-capsule days it *did* work?"

"The odds of a successful outcome are five in ten."

"This saved five astronauts? I never heard of even one."

"Our simulated odds. Nobody's ever actually done this and lived. General Hibble prefers to say that nobody's actually done this and died."

"Yet." I stared up at the bay roof plates. I scuffed my boot toe across the deck.

Then I sighed, unclamped my helmet, and tugged it

off. I stripped off the rest of the suit, dropped it to the deck plates, and stood there barefoot in my skivs.

"I know, sir. I jump out of perfectly good airplanes every week back home, for fun and for jump-pay qualification. Weddle's a better jumper than I am. But if I were in your boots, sir? Honestly?" He shook his head.

I sat down at the table and crossed my arms. "I want to see Howard. Now."

Nine

Ten minutes after I had mutinied, the vast bay had been cleared except for Howard and me. Riding his little scooter, he circled my chair. "I warned you that this would be dangerous, Jazen."

I swiveled my head and stared at him as he orbited me. "No, Howard. Dangerous is shooting and drowning and fighting six-legged telepathic monsters. This is a science project. And I'm the hamster."

"Jazen, the rest of the Union thinks Earth succeeds because we're rich or lucky. And we're both. But the truth is that we succeed because we take risks. When the need is great enough, we dive in at the deep end, then scramble to learn to swim. I can't tell you how many times I saw your father improvise like that."

My father? Where did that come from? I shook my head. "Don't try to play that card with me! You say you can't tell me about him. But you trot him out as soon as you need to manipulate me."

He didn't answer, just drifted his scooter to a girder

supporting the bay wall. He dug a penknife from a pocket, scraped a paint chip off the girder onto the blade, then rotated it in front of his eyes like a jeweler appraising a wedding ring. "Look at these layers. You know, I'll bet the *Emerald River*'s been repainted and updated a dozen times since the war. You knew your mother commanded her once, didn't you?"

He paused to let me sniff the bait.

I sighed. Then, manipulation or not, I swallowed it whole. "What was she like back then?"

He smiled and stared into the space between us. "Admiral Ozawa was as fine a ship handler as the war produced. Mimi could fly anything, though. Not just cruisers. She started out as a fighter jock. And the handsomest woman who ever wore a flight suit. At least, your father seemed to think so every moment they were together."

He slid the scooter alongside me, then leaned close. "Not that they were together much. Or that there weren't painful adjustments to make each time they got back together. That's the nature of relationships in the military, Jazen. The separations and the stresses grow people apart. But they can grow back together, too, if they try. Your parents did."

Back together. I believed him because I wanted to.

"Got one of your hunches about whether Kit's still alive, Howard?"

"If they had captured or killed her, they'd be parading their Trueborn spy to embarrass us by now. Or at least they'd be looking to exchange her for one of their captured coverts. If the team's on the run down there, Tressel's no picnic, but she's survived worse."

"Howard, if it were my mother down there, what would my father do?"

"Saving Kit's secondary to your mission, Jazen."

"Yeah. Howard, what would he do?"

"Everything."

I nodded. Then I stood, lifted the suit off the deck plates, and stuck a foot into the leggings.

I believed Howard about Kit's chances because I wanted to, just like I wanted to believe about the chances for Kit and me. But Howard's reasoning about the probability that she was still alive made sense on an objective level, too.

Howard waved at the personnel hatch, and Weddle and the rest of the briefers reentered.

Howard squinted at his 'puter. "Study hard, you two. You drop in sixteen hours."

Ten

Fifteen hours and fifty-nine minutes later I hung head down in my Eternads, festooned with fins and dive brakes that were supposed to keep me from disintegrating at six hundred miles per hour. I hung in a drop cradle that the spooks had bolted above the centerline of the launch bay's doors. Twenty feet away, in an identical cradle, Weddle hung. Between us in a third cradle hung a man-sized, finned object that looked like a day-glo orange, old-fashioned gravity bomb.

The bay had already been evacuated, first of spooks then of air, so the only sounds I could hear were on the hardwired intercom that was plugged into my suit's thigh connector, and any sound that was conducted through the solid cradle connected to my suit.

I must have looked as vicious as a bat big enough to bite rhinos, but I felt like vomit waiting to happen. Eighteen inches below my helmet's crest, on the opposite side of the bay-door plates, things began going bump, even louder than the blood pounding in my ears.

I chinned my intercom mike. "What's that noise?"

Howard's voice crackled in my ears. "Don't worry. It's abnormal, but it's according to plan. The ship's dropped twenty-five miles. That puts it into atmosphere just dense enough that frost condenses on the shaded portion of the outer hull. When the ship's rotation brings the frost into the sun and heats it, chunks break off."

"Why the hell would you plan that?"

"The main reason the ship's altitude has to be lower is so your free-fall velocity doesn't reach the sound barrier. The condensation chunking's a phenomenon that we hadn't anticipated until last week. But we realized that the chunks will be a bonus. They're about the same size as you two, and of the equipment drone. When you drop, any radar analyst should dismiss you as just chunks of ice."

Eye roll. "Radar analysts? Howard, I'll blow every radar analyst on Tressel."

"Better safe than sorry."

"What if either of us collides with an ice chunk?"

There was the deer-in-the-headlights pause of a spook who just thought of something too late. Then Howard said, "Well, the suits are very tough."

He didn't add "probably," which I was tired of hearing anyway.

A third, distant voice crackled. "Bay doors will open on my mark."

I drew a breath and closed my eyes.

Howard said, "Be careful down there, Jazen."

"Mark."

The bay doors rumbled, I opened my eyes, and the last remaining air blew hull-plate dust out into blackness. The intercom's crackle cut off knife-sharp as the cradle clamps released me and the hardwire jack unplugged.

Bang. Hissss.

The rocket booster that pushed me toward the planet below really *was* gentle. At least gentler than a jump-master's boot on a reluctant student jumper's ass.

A jolt smacked me through the armor's backplate as the spent booster separated itself from me. I felt myself fall in silence while I stared down at white, swirled clouds. They looked to have been painted above blue ocean that stretched to a curved horizon in every direction.

As the jump-master and I had practiced while I hung in the cradle, I kept my body rigid, hands tight to my sides, ankles together.

Twenty yards to my right I could just make out Weddle falling in formation like a wingman. I wasn't about to crane my neck to look at him, much less wave.

I shot down toward Tressel like a plasteel arrow. The only sound audible in the suit was my rapid breathing. I spoke out loud inside my helmet. "Not so bad."

Then I noticed another object tumbling along at the edge of my vision, between Weddle and me. White and ragged.

Blam.

Something struck my left boot. One of Howard's bonus ice chunks. Probably.

"Goddam your science projects, Howard!" My view changed to blackness, then back to the planet, alternating. The collision with the ice chunk had set me somersaulting, head over feet, at a slow and constant rate.

As I rotated, I saw a half-dozen ice chunks flying in formation. Above, alongside, and now below me.

"Oh, crap!" I wasn't flat-spinning toward cerebral hemorrhage, but there was nothing, not even air, to grab hold of as I fell. I couldn't stop my tumbling. Within minutes the atmosphere would thicken. My speed would increase, maybe not beyond the sound barrier, but even at a modest four hundred miles per hour the wind would tear an extended limb off my body the way a Visigoth tore a leg off a roast goose.

Howard had the uplink to *Emerald River* blocked, so I couldn't ask for advice. I couldn't spot Weddle, but he was a master parachutist. So I chinned the emergency suit-to-suit. "Weddle? I got hit. I'm tumbling. What do I do?"

Nothing.

"Weddle? Goddammit, chin on your suit-to-suit!"

Another object tumbled into view, smaller and darker than the flying icebergs.

It was an Eternad helmet, dented. Probably by the impact of a falling ice chunk.

"Oh, fuck."

The helmet disappeared from view as I spun. "Weddle?" They say there are no stupid questions, but that one was close.

I made another revolution and glimpsed the helmet again. Something red and white flapped out of the helmet's neck ring.

Weddle's spinal cord, or what was left of it.

I squeezed my eyes shut and gagged.

When I opened them, Weddle's head was gone. Mercifully for both of us, I suppose. I couldn't spot the rest of him, which, along with the ice storm, seemed to have fallen away from me, below.

A small favor. With each revolution I glimpsed the black space above me. *Emerald River* soon shrank to rice-grain size as the gulf between us widened.

But as *Emerald River* shrank, another speck, gray against the blackness of space, grew. Something was gaining on me.

Again, I said, "Oh, crap."

Eleven

One minute later I was twenty miles closer to Tressel and to impersonating Humpty Dumpty. My visor display pegged my speed at four hundred miles per hour. The sky was more deep purple than black, and the speck chasing me had swollen to the size and color of an orange.

The speck wasn't Weddle's decapitated corpse. It was the equipment drone that had hung in the cradle between him and me, and dropped seconds after us.

The ED was an unpowered, streamlined pod packed with the team's weapons and equipment. It was equipped with a parachute system in its tail similar to the ones that were supposed to waft us down in one piece.

It's hard to land parachuted objects, human or inanimate, close together even when they're dropped from an airplane. Dropped from a hundred miles up in space, keeping Weddle, the ED, and me usefully close together at landing was like dropping three olives into the same martini glass from a skyscraper's observation deck. But that was just the kind of challenge that Howard's geeks relished. So they had repurposed another obsolete, cheap, on-the-shelf technology, then let my life depend on it.

The ED was a dumb-bomb casing sans explosives, but the spooks had fitted it with a smart-munition kit.

Smart-munition kits had revolutionized Trueborn warfare during what they called Cold War I. A dumb bomb's nose was fitted with an eye that detected a specific frequency of laser light. When the eye saw the light, it signaled fins fitted on the bomb's ass end. The fins ruddered the bomb so the eye kept pointing at the light source.

That light source, back during the Cold War, was a laser beam reflecting off a target. The beam was shot at and kept on the target by an aircraft or even by a GI on the ground aiming a glorified flashlight. Smart bombs were so accurate that they could literally fly down a chimney, if the target was properly laser-illuminated. Smart-munition kits worked. Even better, they worked cheap. There were moments when the hype about Trueborn cleverness seemed justified.

Since I was the target that the ED needed to steer toward, and I was falling headfirst, the spooks had installed a laser beacon on my boot sole. Weddle's suit had a secondary beacon, but the thought was that a master parachutist could steer toward me and the drone easier than I could steer toward either of them.

The spooks had also put a laser range finder on the ED that measured the distance to my beacon, then deployed or feathered the ED's dive brakes if it began catching up too close to me.

The ED would follow me down until both my chutes

and its chutes popped. We would then be so close to the surface that my equipment would land within shouting distance, but not on top of me. The briefing spooks hand-waved a bit about the not-on-top-of-me part, but otherwise the concept seemed sound.

During the early free-fall moments the ED's eye was locked on to my boot-sole laser beacon. Therefore the ED had, as a matter of physics, slid into the same imaginary elevator shaft I was falling down, plummeting directly behind me. Good thing, because the ED's fins had no air to rudder against anyway at super-atmospheric altitude.

Then I had started tumbling through the barely thickening atmosphere. As far as the ED's eye could see, my sole beacon had disappeared. When we were both falling streamlined, our speeds would have matched. Now I was spinning like a lazy snowball, so I was accelerating slower than the drone was. But the drone didn't slow itself down to avoid me because it couldn't see me. It just barreled down toward me like a runaway bus with a sleeping driver.

The gap between me and the drone shrank so that I could make out the four-inch–diameter ceramic nose cone. Through it the laser sensors peered but saw nothing.

My heart pounded. Collision with an ice chunk had killed my junior case officer less than a minute into the mission. Another collision had set me tumbling, which was probably going to kill me. Now I was about to get rear-ended by a runaway bus, which would make things worse. Or would it?

At my current speed, even the whisper-thin Tressen

atmosphere screamed by my helmet and warmed my suit's outer skin. Twitching an arm was like lifting weights, but I just managed, and my attitude in the slipstream twitched, too. Not much. But maybe enough.

My twitch shifted my trajectory so that the ED didn't hit me, but drew alongside me like a bus passing in the fast lane. The shock waves spreading off the drone's nose, like swells off a boat prow, interfered with the waves I was throwing, and buffeted me.

I gasped as my head-over-heels tumble corkscrewed into a yawing, off-axis spin.

The mental picture of Weddle's bloody cervical vertebrae forced itself into my consciousness. My head pounded and my stomach rebelled.

"Gaakk!" I spewed bile and Meals Utility Desiccated onto my inner visor. The ventilator shrieked as it sucked puke, but for critical seconds I was blind.

The drone wasn't moving much faster than I was. My only chance was to grasp one of the ED's tail fins as it passed me, then hang on so that I stopped spinning and resumed a headfirst dive, following behind the drone like a hitched trailer.

But even with the rigid support of the Eternads, reaching out into the slipstream at almost five hundred miles per hour could tear my arm from its socket.

I panted inside my armor. If I reached, I might die in moments. But if I missed this bus, if the drone passed by and left me tumbling, I would just keep tumbling. Even if the slipstream didn't "disarticulate" me, the chute, which was designed to deploy freely, would foul. Tangled lines and canopy would simply form a pretty carbon-fiber-reinforced streamer behind me. I would slam onto Tressel and explode in a shower of bone, tissue, and puked-out desiccated turkey.

I gritted my teeth, made a gauntleted fist, and inched it toward the drone.

The new irregularity to my profile made me yaw worse.

Pop.

I yelped inside my helmet as the slipstream dislocated my wrist. My reach had been too aggressive. The Eternads' rigidity kept things attached, as far as I could tell, but the pain was knife-edge.

Now my chances depended on just one hand. I waited until my tumble corkscrewed me around, so that the good hand was alongside the drone's fins.

The drone's rear fins were passing my head now. Three heartbeats from now my last chance would be gone.

The sky had bloomed indigo, and the slipstream of the still-thin atmosphere boomed as the shock waves bounced me against the drone.

I grabbed for a tail fin and caught something.

I tried to tighten my fingers around it and realized I had hold of the left access-panel release.

The panel peeled back like banana skin. Then the slipstream ripped it loose. Items of spy crap spewed into the troposphere, then tumbled alongside me like a highly classified meteor shower. A four-inch gap opened between the drone's fin and my fingers.

"Arrr!" I forced my hand back and death-gripped the fin.

This time, I held on. The speed differential between my slower fall and the drone's fall yanked me into the wind shadow behind the ED.

Pop.

I yelped. I had separated my shoulder once before, falling off a hovertank fender onto a boulder. I got chewed out by a sergeant for clumsiness and had to route-march behind the tank for six miles so I would learn to be more careful next time. This time the separation felt more severe, but so were the consequences if I let go.

The drone, now with me flapping behind and screaming inside my armor, flashed into high clouds. Ice crystallized on the outside of my vomit-smeared visor.

"Dammit." Blind again. I chinned the visor's defroster. By the time my view cleared, the drone and I had popped out of the clouds into an overcast day.

Below me was supposed to be the Eastern Sea of Tressel, off the coast of the part of Tressen that had once been the Unified Duchies of Iridia. A boatload of Iridian partisans, of questionable friendliness, was supposed to fish me, Weddle, and the drone out of the sea after I landed.

The sea was blue. What I saw below, through a film of Turkey With Giblet Gravy Paste, was only half twinkling blue. That was the sea, muted sunlight reflecting off waves. Half my field of vision was scum green laced with barf brown. The drone's trajectory was dropping it and me too far toward shore.

I clung to the drone's fin. The thicker atmosphere down here was slowing the drone and me. The plan had been that in the thicker air I would "steer" myself toward the target landing zone in the sea, while the drone followed. Unfortunately, I had wound up behind the drone, so instead the drone and I remained a trailer following a runaway bus, bound wherever wind and gravity took us.

The landing, it became clearer with each yard of free fall, was not going to be in the twinkling blue sea, where a boatload of friendlies would rush to collect me. The drone and I were plummeting inland. I had to correct course.

Crack.

The altimeters on the drone and on my chute pack popped the small drogue chutes off my back and out the drone's tapered tail.

"Crap!" I let go of the drone's fin like it had caught fire and spun myself away. Either the drone's drogue chute or the main chute that the drogue was tugging out would foul my own chute. If that happened, being off target or losing my equipment wouldn't matter. The drone and I would hit like dropped rocks.

Whomp.

I screamed as the shock of my main chute's deployment jerked my wrecked shoulder.

Happily, my chute's opening separated me clean from the ED, which dangled beneath its own intact chute a hundred feet below and four hundred feet to my left.

A mere thousand feet below, too close for meaningful course alteration, Mother Tressel rushed up to greet me.

Unhappily, her kiss was going to be sloppy.

Twelve

I grimaced as I yanked the toggles that controlled my chute canopy, struggling to sideslip so that I would land in the sea's open water. But a thousand feet disappear fast, and the wrist at the end of my dislocated shoulder refused to cooperate, so one toggle worked and the other didn't, and I just corkscrewed down into the inland swamps.

My boots crackled sideways through leathery foliage sixty feet above mud. Then the first substantial branch caught beneath my shoulder and spun me. Pain seared my shoulder as the impact popped the joint back into place.

Then my canopy hung up in the treetops. I swayed as I dangled. Water the color and consistency of old gravy lapped at my boot toes. I twisted as I dangled. I was down in one piece, but where? Dragonflies as big as vultures zigged through mist patches adrift above the water.

Based on my briefing, I had landed in the Tressen Barrens, one hundred thousand square miles of brackish coastal swamp that would, in a couple of hundred million years, provide this planet with more coal than Trueborns had hubris.

The "trees" were cycads, meaning their trunks had the proportions and texture of pinecones, with palm-frond branches feather-dustering from their tops. The biggest land animals in the Barrens were dog-sized, bow-legged, flat-bodied amphibians that sunned themselves on the trunks of fallen cycads that were as mottled brown as they were. My visor display measured ambient temperature at ninety-nine degrees Fahrenheit with ninety-four percent humidity.

Inside my suit I thanked Mr. Eternad, if such a person existed, for climate control, like a million other GIs had over the last century.

Unfortunately, no smiling friendlies waited to greet me. Fortunately, the drone lay just a hundred feet away, orange fuselage crumpled but otherwise whole, on a mudflat.

Whatever equipment had spilled out during free fall was lost to me forever, scattered and splattered over square miles of this swamp. But the drone contained, if it was still inside, a heliograph signal mirror with sight and tripod mount. I could use it to signal the friendlies of my whereabouts. If I could change my whereabouts to the seashore. If the friendlies were close enough and vigilant enough to spot a signal. And if they were really friendly.

There was also a meds kit that would allow me to make a field reduction of my dislocated wrist. The kit also contained happy pills more serious than the ones in my helmet dispenser. The happys would allow me to keep going, since I couldn't wait for the wrist and shoulder to improve.

First I had to escape my chute harness. I tried to punch

the chest release plate, but with the bad wrist all I did was demonstrate how loud a human scream sounds inside an Eternad helmet.

The branches of the cycad from which I dangled drooped beneath my weight as I struggled. I now splashed knee-deep in the swamp.

My good hand was free enough to tug my bush knife from its thigh scabbard so I could cut away the shroud lines. After thirty seconds of sawing, I plopped into waist-deep water.

The plop stung enough that I popped a couple of helmet happys, pending a dose of the hard stuff from the meds kit.

I slogged toward the drone, shoulder and wrist throbbing, knee-deep in opaque water, across a slick mud bottom. Ten minutes later I reached the drone. By the time I crawled up onto the mudflat, I was wheezing like a plasteel lungfish and my sweat had maxed my ventilators.

A flat-headed amphibian the size of an alley cat had beaten me to the drone, attracted, I suppose, by the friction warmth generated by the drone's passage through the lower atmosphere. The flat-head squatted in the recess that housed the drone's remaining access-panel release. She—enough females have ignored me that I just know—squatted there, oblivious to my approach.

I didn't know what to expect from her. The Tressen Barrens faunal brief mostly lost my attention because Barrens operations were labeled "I.S.," for "Improbable Scenario." Or, as case officers restated the acronym, "Ignorable (I'll just say here) Stuff."

The amphibian turned one glassy frog eye to me,

decided I was no threat, and looked away.

I stepped forward, shooing her off the drone. Finally she plopped onto the mud and waddled off. Then I dug gauntleted fingers into the hinge-release recess and tugged the pin. I touched something squishy, jerked my hand from the release recess, and glanced down. Before the amphibian had left, she had deposited a load of (I'll just say here) stuff.

While I swore and wiped my fingers on ground moss, the drone banana-peeled itself open, and I catalogued what equipment I had lost.

My heart sank. Where the uplink case had nestled there was now a bare socket and two torn tie-down straps. The uplink encrypted messages, searched the sky for, and then locked on to, receivers aboard any cruiser within a hundred thousand miles. Then the uplink squirted the messages to the receivers in a beam no wider, or more detectable, than an invisible pencil one hundred thousand miles long. Because this fiasco was so secret, we were only supposed to use the uplink in life-threatening emergencies, or to summon the pickup Scorpion.

Without the uplink, I was now invisible to the spooks up above.

Well, fortunately that wasn't entirely true. Both Weddle's armor and mine had a transponder built in to the left shoulder that squirted a simple, brief "here I am" to the sky every sixty seconds, once it was activated. It was activated either by the wearer, voluntarily, or involuntarily by the suit, if the suit detected a really miserable set of wearer vitals.

Weddel's vitals, obviously, were as bad as could be. If

his transponder had survived the fall, which was possible but doubtful, the spooks up above us thought we were someplace where I wasn't.

I side-tapped my temple pad to turn my transponder on. The little green light didn't flash. I tried again. Nothing.

"Crap." My heart rate rose, a vital which the suit was perfectly happy to display for me.

I reached up with my good hand and gently touched the suit's shoulder plate. The good thing about Eternad armor is that it gives itself up to absorb a severe impact so the wearer's body doesn't absorb it. My shoulder plate had done its job somewhere during my fall, and therefore my arm remained attached. But the shoulder plate was caved in by a dent the size of a tennis ball. Somewhere in there were the mashed remains of my transponder.

There was a worst-case search-and-rescue backup plan for barefoot case officers. Like most Hibble plans it was well-intentioned, obsolete, and cheap.

It consisted of laying out fabric panels in a prearranged pattern on open ground. Those panels would, theoretically, be spotted by a lookdown resource; then somebody would come and give the officer a lift home. "Lookdown resource" normally meant a satellite, of which we had none orbiting Tressel, thanks to the diplomats. That meant that Spook Central would have to import, then deploy, a recon Scorpion to do the looking down, which could take weeks. Meanwhile the barefoot officer had to stay put around the panels. I couldn't stay put even for hours.

I sat back on my armored butt, rested my good hand on the ground, and said aloud to the swamp, "Crap."

I had wanted to be independent, not orphaned. Before I even started, I had lost my partner, my overhead support, and, for a while at least, the use of my left arm.

I sat in the alien mud and felt sorry for myself for sixty seconds. Then I stood up and reassessed, one hand on my hip while I favored the sore-wristed hand. I needed my local help now more than ever.

That meant I had to make it to the coast with the heliograph.

Even healthy, I couldn't carry much more than half the load. That was part of Weddle's job. So, what to take along?

A GI's first priority is to keep his weapon with him. His second is to get it back if he loses it. His third, failing one and two, is to steal someone else's. But the deadliest thing I could aim and fire one-handed, until I got into the meds pack, was a sidearm. A rifle was less valuable at the moment than the daylight I would waste prepping it.

I glanced around the swamp. No need for a gun to counter an immediate enemy threat. There wasn't a Tressen within miles.

But did I need a gun to counter natural threats?

I wiped my fingers clean with a cycad frond while I considered. Basic planetology rubs off on a GI after a few tours, as inevitably as frog shit. These amphibians and cycads looked and behaved like amphibians and cycads that had already evolved, then gone extinct, on planets like Earth and Yavet. "Like environments evolve like faunas." Tressel was a warm, wet, slow-evolving rock. Earth was a warm, wet, fast-evolving rock. Thus, Tressel had giant frogs. Earth used to have giant frogs.

The geneticists doubted that interplanetarily disparate species, however overtly similar, would voluntarily interbreed. Having seen my first Tressen lady frog, I doubted it, too. But then I'm not a gentleman frog.

I peered across the swamp. Somewhere out in the mist croaked a male who thought that frog was hot merchandise. But somebody else out there thought she was lunch.

I wrinkled my forehead. My meager memory of the brief was that the Barrens's top land predators weren't much bigger or meaner than the misshapen frog that I had just shooed off the drone.

I rubbed my good hand on my armored thigh. Supposedly, they actually tested an Eternad boot once by leaving it in a tiger cage. After a week the tigers had lost three teeth chewing on the boot, which was unscratched. I reached the conclusion that no gun was required here in the Barrens, at least on land.

The shallow swamp water held shellfish that looked, as I remembered, like lobsters or scorpions. I had lost even minimal interest in the segment about them when I learned that they didn't even have tail stingers. I didn't recall how big they were, but they sounded less threatening than the frogs.

I would have to lead the partisans back here to recover the rest of my gear, anyway. I ignored the weapons pod, bent on one knee and raced the sinking sun until I had set my dislocated wrist, loaded a watertight backpack with the heliograph, and dropped a couple serious happys.

By the time I straightened up and stretched, my visor display predicted three hours more of signal-sufficient daylight. Overland I would have to hack through vegetation with the suit's bush knife, unable to trade hands and distribute the workload. Worse, I would likely have to detour around the densest thickets. I squinted up at the gray sky and shook my head. Overland I'd never make the coast before dark.

I turned toward the sludge-brown bayou I had landed in, while my shoulder socket throbbed against my armor's underlayer. The bayou curved, but wound directly toward the ocean. Fallen fronds on the water's surface drifted seaward as fast as a man could walk.

I nodded to myself. Improvisation separates good case officers from dead ones.

Eternads weren't diving suits, but they were watertight enough for waterborne assault, even for underwater demolition missions in a pinch. In my suit I could float on the outrunning tide like a human beach ball. I would reach the ocean in a half hour. During which I could rest my arm and conserve my energy. If time in the field teaches a GI anything, it is never walk if you can hitch a ride.

I punched up the suit's overboard mode, then gritted my teeth. The micropump between my shoulder blades pounded my damaged joints as its vibration inflated the suit's flotation bladders. Then I waded out knee-deep, lay back, arms and legs splayed, and drifted, belly to the sky. As I pinwheeled slowly downstream atop the warm water, dragonflies whirred across my field of vision against a lattice of cycad branches and gray sky. The surface current rafted me toward the coast. I smiled at my ingenuity and enjoyed the ride.

As the good ship *Jazen* drifted, so did my mind. The happys I had dropped spread a warm buzz throughout my body. Yo ho ho, a pirate's life for me.

Two minutes and two hundred yards later, I turned my head to watch a pickle-sized pink worm wriggle toward me across the surface. It was probably toxic, the pink color a defense mechanism advertising "Don't eat me!"

I wrinkled my forehead as I yawned. There had been something in the brief about the pink worms, but what? The nagging thought caused me roll onto my belly, then stand in water that proved to be waist deep. The little worm danced across the surface. I fingered the bush knife in my leg scabbard with my good hand.

The worm had something to do with the big lobsters. They—

Whoom.

Brown water turned white as it foamed up around the worm, then geysered up. Something grabbed me around the waist and squeezed.

Thirteen

Lobster, my ass. Muddy water flooded over my faceplate and closed out the daylight as a monster dragged me under and toward the channel's center.

Desperation concentrates the mind, and now the brief about the scorpions flooded back over my drugged brain.

Barrens scorpions weren't, biologically speaking, scorpions. But they weren't restaurant lobsters, either. They were Tressel's version of pterygotid eurypterids, giant nightmares that had evolved, then died off, on Earth and Yavet during those planets' respective Paleozoic eras. Pterygotid eurypterids filled the brackish-water estuary-predator niche until they went extinct. Then crocodiles moved in and replaced them.

The scorpions hunted by lying in opaque water that hid their ton-plus bulk, navigating with dinner-plate–sized compound eyes. They lured prey with wormlike stalks that periscoped above their manhole-cover–sized flat heads. Apparently some animals were dumb enough to buy the worm trick. I now knew of at least one.

The scorpion clamped me with its two pincers. One vised my left thigh, the other my waist. The scorpion dragged me backward toward the channel's deep center, thrashing a horizontal fluke flexed by tail muscles four yards long and a yard wide.

The scorpion's mouth, on the underside of its flat head, was too small and mandibular to bite chunks off prey. So the scorpion battle plan was to crush and drown prey, then store the carcass under a rock for leisurely nibbling, after rot softened the meal.

The beast shifted its pincers to better grip this hard-shelled, unfamiliar fish.

I broke free and slogged, gasping, into the shallows. There I drew my puny bush knife while I screamed at the idiot who decided not to bring a gun.

The bug shot after me into the shallows, then rose up on eight legs. Water streamed off its armored back and off its two snapping pincers, upraised like a boxer's gloves. It punched one pincer at me, and I slashed with my knife. The blade exploded water but slid off the bug like a toothpick off a lobster claw.

Meanwhile the scorpion's other claw thrust beneath the water, clamped my ankle, and dragged me down again.

I hacked every appendage I could reach with the bush knife, but this time I couldn't break the monster's grip. The good news was that the Eternad's strain gauges stayed in the green. This monster wasn't strong enough to crush up-to-date plasteel.

The bad news was that, according to the suit's sensors, the water in the deep center of the channel was saltier, and therefore heavier. It lay beneath the layer of fresh water that was flowing seaward. The salty undercurrent was drifting the bug and me inland. That was fine with the bug, who preferred brackish water to the saltier open sea, and disastrous for me.

One reason that the scorpion liked inland waters was that Tressel's Paleozoic ocean was chock-full of fish big enough and mean enough to eat it.

I wasn't strong enough to break free of this beast, but, with the help of the suit's buoyancy, I could force the pair of us to the surface. I blew the floatation to max, and the two of us popped up like a buoy.

The surface current was still running out to sea. After only moments on the surface and above the undercurrent, the scorpion and I reversed direction and floated seaward as we struggled, whether the beast liked it or not.

For the next ten minutes we drifted down the cycad-roofed bayou like it was fight night in the tunnel of love, pummeling one another without result.

Then the leafy cycad roof vanished. The estuary spilled its fresh water out into the sea, where it would blend with the salty ocean.

Heh, heh. As soon as the scorpion sensed the change of salinity, it would drop me like a hot amphibian and swim back to the shelter of its swamp.

I looked skyward. Still daylight. Once freed, I would swim ashore and set up the heliograph tripod.

I punched the air with my injured fist, grimaced, but hooted at the scorpion anyway. "End of the line, dumb ass!"

Ten minutes later, the dumb ass and I continued to

drift out to sea locked together, only one of us really fighting anymore. He may have been uncomfortable in salt water. He may have feared open-water predators bigger than himself. But he was *too* dumb to let go of a meal once he had clamped onto it. No wonder his kind were headed for extinction.

I pushed myself up against the bug's claws and stretched my neck. The waves were only a couple of feet high, but that was enough to obscure my vision. I couldn't see any friendlies. If they had hung around the landing zone, if they had ever been at the landing zone, they probably couldn't see me.

If night fell and the friendlies gave me up for dead, I might as well be. The distance between me and my objectives would be as unbridgeable as the light-years I was from home. I might as well have hit the mud at terminal velocity, or become bug food back in the swamp.

I was down to one option. I hated to use up my one and only signal pyrotechnic. If a bomb explodes in the ocean and no one hears it, does it make a sound?

I eyed the sinking glow of the sun beyond the overcast. Time was running out.

Digging into my suit's thigh pocket, I tugged out the pyro signal canister and hefted it. It felt heavier than the Mark II I was used to. I read the stenciled instructions.

MARK IV ENHANCED SEARCH AND
RESCUE PYROTECHNIC DEVICE

PULL PIN AND THROW

Well, that part remained idiot-proof. There was more.

CAUTION: DO NOT DEPLOY
WITHIN THIRTY YARDS OF PERSONNEL
OR CONCUSSION-SENSITIVE EQUIPMENT

Seriously? It was a glorified firecracker, for God's sake. I reduced the gain on my helmet audio and pulled the pin. Then I chucked the canister into the water, where it splashed down four yards away.

Foom!

Even muted, the sound knifed my ears. Blue sea spouted against the gray sky, and threw me and the bug twenty feet.

We splashed back into the water, sank, then surfaced in a froth. I said, "Wow."

A pall of purple marker smoke blotted out the daylight as it drifted across me.

Not us. Me.

The bug was gone. Maybe dead. Maybe scared. I didn't care which.

I was free at last. I floated on my back and paddled my unencumbered feet. "Woo hoo!"

The purple smoke dissipated.

I stopped woo-hooing and listened to the waves as they metronomed against my helmet. There was no other sound, such as a friendly voice.

I trod water and thrust my uninjured arm above the wave crests so I could periscope the vicinity with my finger cam. I didn't see land. The estuary outflow had carried us farther than I had realized.

I was free. But I was alone. And it was getting dark. I said to nobody, "Oboy."

At least it couldn't get worse.

My foot felt cold. And wet. The pyro's concussion had ruptured a suit seal. I was sinking slowly, but I was sinking.

Blup.

I turned my head as a dead fish bobbed to the surface alongside me. They *had* been serious about the thirty-yard safe radius.

Blup. Blup. Blup.

Two minutes later I stopped counting the concussed, belly-up Paleozoic fish that surrounded me.

I periscoped another brief snapshot. Silver in the distance, a fin that appeared to be attached to something bigger than the scorpion cut the water. It was inbound toward me and my fish fry.

The brief about open-water fauna I *had* paid attention to. Tressen sea rhizodonts reached lengths of up to twenty-five feet, had four hundred needle teeth per jaw, foul dispositions, and insatiable appetites. They ate pterygotid eurypterids, if any ventured beyond the swamps, for breakfast.

I trod water and reached for my bush knife as the cold of inflowing water in my suit reached my knee.

I had been wrong. It could get worse.

Fourteen

Ten minutes after I spotted the first fin, the first rhiz brushed against my thigh plate as it swooshed past in the twilight, mouth agape to scoop dead fish into a lower jaw studded with more four-inch teeth than I could count. For the moment, I suppose I smelled and felt as appetizing as driftwood. But if these monsters decided I was food, I wasn't sure whether the suit would keep them out indefinitely. And I didn't know how deep these fish might dive or how deep the suit would stay pressure-tight if one dove and took me with it.

Bump.

A big one thumped my back, and I sucked a breath and clenched my teeth. The happys I had taken, back in the relative safety of the lair of the giant scorpions, were wearing off. My shoulder throbbed, and my cold, wet leg was growing numb.

It was nearly full dark now. There were no friendlies.

Beneath the surface, something clamped against my boot.

I kicked.

It held fast.

Fifteen

I thrashed in the dark sea, paddling but going nowhere against the thing that held me.

My eyes swelled and burned. I had reenlisted. I had traveled halfway across the known universe. I had jumped out of a perfectly good spaceship, fallen a hundred screaming miles, and fought a swamp monster for her. It was bad enough that I would never see her again. The worst was that she would never even know I had tried. I punched a wave and struggled harder. "Goddammit!"

"Stop kicking, you stupid bugger!"

I rolled onto my back. A dark silhouette loomed against the purple twilight sky.

I floated alongside an open boat under sail. The boat carried two human beings who were tugging at a grapple that was hooked around my boot.

Splash.

The smaller of the two humans let go of me, poked a pitchfork-sized trident into the waves, and discouraged a rhiz.

Then I relaxed, let them reel me in, and extended my good arm. The larger man hooked a hand under my backpack and tugged me as I kicked my boots; then I tumbled over the gunwale into the boat.

I rocked in the slop that sloshed the boat's bottom while I stared up at the two silhouettes and coughed. A rhiz, silver and thrashing and as long as I was tall, thrashed in the boat's belly, clamped ineffectually to my armored calf. The smaller man pounded the fish with a club until it let go, then watched as it thrashed slower and slower, until it lay motionless and gasping.

The boat was thirty feet long, with square cloth sails. Just an open wooden tub with a tiller aft and benches and lockers along its sides. Iridian lober boats, and lobers, who fished for trilobites and lobe-finned fish, hadn't changed much in a thousand years.

The smaller figure turned to the one who had pulled me in. "You think this is one of them?"

The voice squeaked. A girl, not a man.

"Who else would he be?" Deeper voice.

"There were supposed to be two."

"All these rhiz? The other one's bait by now."

I raised my eyebrows and didn't bother to switch on my translator. Apparently one thing *had* changed in a thousand years. I resented the tidal wave of Earth culture that swamped the rest of the Human Union as much as anyone raised on an outworld did. But Terracentrism had its virtues. At this moment the Trueborn mission schools, and cowboy holos and comic chips that had made Standard *the* language, even in literal backwaters like this one, sounded pretty good.

Rhizodonts twice the size of the one for which I had been bait thumped the open boat's hull planks. The man who had pulled me aboard was lean, with a gray beard and Iridian-green eyes, and wore a lober fisherman's leather armor. I cleared my throat. "Thanks."

The bearded man snorted. "None returned. Your bomb's attracted half the rhiz in this bay."

"It attracted you, too. I had to do something."

"We were where we were told to be! You weren't."

"I'm sorry. You turned out to be too small a target from a hundred miles up."

The man snorted again. "Iridia's always too small for the Trueborns."

I sighed inside my helmet. Decades earlier, Earth tilted against Iridia and toward Tressen to end a bloody, stalemated war between them. The Tilt ended the war, alright. But the Tressens turned their victory into a campaign to eradicate Iridia from the face of this planet.

Earth didn't like genocide any better than the next smug, patronizing superpower. But Earth had its hands full saving the human race from the Slugs. So Earth imposed isolating sanctions on Tressen, then washed its collective hands of the Iridians. No wonder Kit had to go in here friendless. And no wonder these two weren't overjoyed to see me.

But they were the closest things to allies I had.

I sat up in the boat and popped my visor. "I'm Jazen. You?"

The man just stared at me.

I eye-rolled. It was possible to overdo operational security. "Look, I need to call you something."

The gray-bearded man shrugged. “I’m Pyt. The girl is Alia.”

I squinted at the smaller Iridian. Her strawberry-blonde hair was pulled back, and her shirt hung on an eleven-year-old’s board-flat frame, but girl she was.

I nodded. “We need to retrieve my baggage, Pyt.”

“Why?”

Because without it I’m just an ignorant stranger. With it I’m an ignorant stranger armed to the teeth. “Because that’s where the diamonds are.”

Pyt fended off a rhiz with his trident, then jerked his head shoreward. “We need to get away from this bait shop anyway. How far?”

I shrugged and punched up the Equipment Drone’s locator, then pointed over the gunwale. “Thousand yards inland. That heading.”

Two dark hours and two scorpion encounters later, the little boat creaked and rolled as it sailed away from the Barrens with my stuff aboard. We were bound south, toward the rock-bound Iridian coast.

The moon had risen, and reflected off the waves like a rolling carpet of silver coins.

Pyt sat in the boat’s stern, the tiller pressed between his arm and torso, while he shucked a raw trilobite with a lober’s hooknife. The girl slept, wrapped in blankets, in the prow.

Pyt nodded at the sea and smiled at me. “Beautiful, no?”

I hung my helmetless head over the gunwale and dry heaved for the second time. I gasped and spat at the waves. “I hate water.” The rhizodont alongside me banged its tail against my belly. “Can we throw that thing out? ’Cause I’m not eating it.”

Pyt shook his head. “Never waste something you can cut into bait.”

“And I thought you were keeping me around just for the diamonds.”

That finally coaxed a smile from Pyt. He said, “You Trueborns don’t sail, then?”

I wiped drool off my chin, dug out a motion-sickness cap from the meds kit, and gulped it dry.

My shoulder throbbed. While I was in the meds kit, I punched in the details of my brachial injuries, selected the two caps the screen prescribed, and swallowed them. The sedative in the first one would knock me out. The second contained nano machines, activated by stomach acid, that would swim through my bloodstream and repair my arm damage.

Pyt watched in silence as I played doctor.

Finally, I answered him. “Some Trueborns sail.”

Kit had a rich kid’s shelf full of yachting trophies, not to mention a boathouse full of day sailers, at her parents’ beach place in the Caribbean. One weekend on leave down there she had tried to teach me the difference between a jib and a bowline. But we were alone together, and we ended up, uh, distracted. Well, I was distracted and she had let me be.

I gulped a breath and said to Pyt, “But I’m Trueborn by blood only. My parents were born on Earth. I was born and raised downlevels on Yavet. Like living in the bottom of a layer cake. I never saw an ocean until I joined the Legion.”

He frowned. "The Legion? I agreed to guide a Trueborn military officer. Not a hired murderer."

"The Legion was a long time ago. I am a Trueborn military officer. I'm also a saloon owner on holiday."

He rolled his eyes.

"Look, I didn't abandon Iridia. The diplomat assholes who did that retired before I was born." But I was sent here by the diplomat assholes who replaced them. "My partner's already dead."

Pyt stiffened, started to say something. Then he turned his face away and stared at the shore.

I, in turn, stared out across the empty sea. My partner? Somewhere out there the white-bread junior case officer who I had barely met was already two separate chunks of rhizodont bait. I didn't know whether Weddle sailed, like Kit did. I didn't know his parents any better than I didn't know my own. When I tried to picture his face, all I could see was the bloody stump of his spinal cord flapping out of his helmet as it tumbled through the sky. I dry-heaved over the side again.

I wiped my eyes. My two allies seemed in no hurry to get to know me any more than I had been in a hurry to get to know Weddle. So I studied them. Both wore brown leather-plated armor. The case brief said the Iridian lober culture was a littoral-zone subsistence economy.

Family units hand-fished for needle-toothed, lobe-finned fish and trilobites. Trilobites were millipede shellfish, some with back spines that would make a porcupine jealous.

Pyt looked to be fifty, broad-faced and lean, with hair that had once been brown. The girl, Alia, couldn't have been older than eleven. Unlike Pyt, she had delicate features and strawberry-blonde hair. But she cocked her head just in the way that the man did. A daughter who favored her mother?

Pyt had lost the little and ring fingers of his right hand at the first joint of each. Digital amputation was one of a lober's many occupational hazards. The rule of thumb, so to speak, was one finger joint lost for each five years fishing. The girl still had all ten fingers.

I saw a watertight locker in the stern that was the right shape to house long guns, but the Iridians weren't hunters by nature. They weren't killers, either. Like most partisans, Pyt and Alia hardly looked the part. But they had fished me out of a mess. I had to trust them if I was going to accomplish anything.

I also had to heal. My shoulder muscles spasmed as the drugs began working.

I rolled onto my side, helmet faceplate open, in case I heaved again. Then I counted back from a hundred, waiting for the cap to settle my stomach, the sed to knock me out, and the nanos to sail my bloodstream like microscopic hospital ships.

The boat rocked, the crew snored, and I hadn't slept since before the pre-drop briefing.

The last number I remembered was eighty-six.

Kit's finger traced my lips as she smiled down at me, smelling of lemons. I smiled back as I took her finger between my lips.

Then the smell changed as she leaned down and whispered. "Are you a knight?"

I woke with sun in my eyes and the girl staring down at me through my open faceplate.

Sixteen

"What?" I groaned and slid my eyes until I saw Pyt dozing in the stern alongside the tied-down tiller.

Alia touched the finger that had rested on my lips to my Eternad armor's breastplate. "Are you a knight?"

I squinted at her and tried not to move my shoulder. "How would you know what a knight is?" The largest land animal on Tressel wasn't big enough to carry Lancelot's chain-mail undershirt. Steel-armored knights belonged to the history of planets that had evolved horses.

The girl pointed at the sleeping man. "Pyt gives me books. So, are you?"

"I dunno. What do you think a knight is?"

"A hero. Protects the weak. Fights for the right."

I shook my head. "I protect me. I fight for a paycheck."

She frowned. "Well, I hope you turn out to be *some* kind of hero."

I stared, straight-faced. "Why?"

"Pyt says if all you have to offer is the diamonds, you'll be thrown to the rhiz."

I cocked my head. "I dunno. They're pretty nice diamonds."

Her eyes lit. "Can I see them?"

I nodded and pointed at a yellow, locking hard-shell case among the equipment boxes. "In there."

Alia retrieved the case, pushed her thumbs against the latches, then frowned. "How do I open it?"

"You don't." I sighed. "The case will blow up if it's opened without my thumb on the left latch."

Alia scowled and drew her hooknife. "Then I might cut off your thumb. I'm ruthless."

I coughed to cover a smile. Not the least tragedy of civil war is that it really did create ruthless eleven-year-olds. I'd seen too many of them. But if Alia had been one of them, she could have cut my throat with that hooknife while I slept.

I said, "Don't bother. Unless my thumb's attached to me and I'm alive, the case won't open." Which was true. "But I'll let you take a look at the diamonds. Heck, I'll let you weigh them. Twelve hundred carats of perfect blue-white Weichselan diamonds, cut to a fenceable average weight between one half and three carats each."

Diamonds were perfect universal value totems for espionage bribes and barter. They were desired, portable, unattributable, durable, and scarce. And Howard's spooks had long ago figured out how to make diamonds into checks that only their case officers could cash.

Alia narrowed her eyes. "You will?"

Pyt woke, then stood behind us, yawning, while he laid a hand on the girl's shoulder. "He will because the Trueborns have coated them."

Alia wrinkled her forehead at me while she jerked her thumb toward Pyt. "What's he mean?"

I said, "He means that in four days the diamonds will turn to powder. Unless I deactivate the coating. The idea is to encourage you to keep your promise and discourage you from cutting me into bait with your hooknife."

It's a basic tenet of spookology that effective lies are grounded in truth. The diamonds were coated, alright. But unlike thumbprint-recognition locks, which were real technology, the magic coating was gray household glaze. I could no more turn diamonds into powder than I could turn carriages into pumpkins. But case officers had told the coating lie for so long, and so well, in so many places, that most outworld partisans we worked with had heard it and believed it.

At least so far.

Alia returned the case to the spot where she got it, then stepped over the still-twitching rhizodont and relieved Pyt on the tiller.

Pyt watched her go, then said to me, "It's ironic. The Trueborns do these things because *they* don't trust *Iridians*."

I shook my head. "That's got nothing to do with it. When you're as far from home as I am, you don't trust anybody."

Pyt stepped over my outstretched legs, went forward, and did sailor things with ropes.

I sighed. Maybe the myth of Trueborn magic was all that was keeping me alive.

I sat up in the rocking boat and my shoulder throbbed less due to real Trueborn magic. I wrapped both arms around my knees and also blessed the thousands of little nano 'bots who had exhausted themselves overnight. Their tiny mechanical corpses were now drifting through my veins. They would make their way to my large intestine, then to an uncelebrated burial at sea, in the usual way.

Later my hosts sat down in the stern and breakfasted on raw trilobite. I wasn't invited, but wasn't disappointed. I dug a Meal Utility Desiccated out of one plasteel, then sat with my shoulders against the deck planks while the MUD's paste heated. Meanwhile, the boat scudded south in silence, driven by what sailors like Kit called a fair wind.

An hour later I had moved up into the bow and sat next to Pyt as he stood scanning the horizon to our front with brass binoculars. I pointed at my jumbled gear. "I could use a hand to break out some of this."

"You want your weapons."

"Among other things."

Pyt jerked a thumb at the diamond case. "You already have your insurance against Iridian treachery."

"I'd like to have some insurance against Tressens."

"The nearest Tressens are a hundred miles north, aboard a cutter based at Vilus. The old tub never ventures more than thirty miles from its mooring."

The swamp shoreline had given way to pink rock cliffs striped with emerald moss.

When the fisherman lowered his glasses, I pointed at the landscape and asked, "It is beautiful. Is that Iridia?"

He shook his head. "The Tressens say Iridia doesn't exist anymore."

"Are they right?"

He shrugged. "You can judge for yourself. After we take you where you're paying us to take you."

"And when will that be?"

"It's a straight run down the coast. If the weather remains fair, two days."

"And then?"

"And then you'll pay us and we'll leave you alone." Pyt walked back to the stern and traded places with Alia, who was handling the tiller.

I sighed.

Two days. Howard Hibble liked to quote a long-dead Trueborn general named Patton, who had said that a commander shouldn't give soldiers orders, he should give soldiers objectives, then be astonished at their ingenuity in achieving them.

My objective according to Howard was to find out what the Tressens and the Yavi were up to, and report back. My objective according to me was to find Kit. It seemed to me that the two objectives were compatible, but mine came first. Now that I was free of Howard, I had two days to devise my plan to find her. It wouldn't be easy.

She had left no trail as far as the spooks knew. Her team's uplink and transponders were as silent as mine. I knew the landing-zone coordinates where Kit had disembarked. I knew her mission, which was the same as mine. I knew what equipment she carried. Most importantly, I knew her and how she thought, maybe as well as any living human being did.

Still, I was searching for what the Trueborns called a needle in a haystack. Worse, the haystack was an entire planet. Worst of all, the needle was trying not to be found, and Kit Born excelled at that. I held my arm, which throbbed worse now that I was moving around, and probably hurt more because I didn't know what to do next.

Alia came forward, carrying the binoculars, and settled across from me in the bow, replacing Pyt as lookout. But Alia stared at me, wide-eyed. "Did you really fly through the sky?"

I winced at a shoulder twinge. "Trueborns can't fly. I fell."

Alia pointed across the boat toward my helmet, which sat upside down beside me. "What do all those things in there do?"

"Nothing you need to know. Look, I need to think—"

She reached for my helmet. I snatched it away and jerked my thumb at Pyt. "Didn't your father teach you to leave other people's stuff alone?"

"Pyt's not my father. I mean, he is, but not my real one."

"Oh. What happened?"

She looked down at the binoculars and fiddled with the focus ferrule. "Pyt won't tell me. At least not all of it. That's the worst part."

I swallowed and nodded. "Yeah. It is."

I poked two fingers inside the helmet and switched on the visor displays. Then I slipped the helmet over the girl's head, and she grinned out at me through the faceplate while the displays cycled before her eyes like multicolored butterflies.

"Stop playing! You're on watch!" Pyt shouted, frowning, while he worked the tiller.

Alia began tugging the helmet off.

I patted it back onto her head. "Push your chin against the soft knob on the left. The second one."

She pushed, then gasped as the green reticle frame of the mag optics framed her eyes. "Binoculars!"

I grinned in at her. "Better. And they work in the dark."

Alia turned her face forward and scanned the horizon. "I just saw a fish jump! I could've counted his scales!"

"If you select loop memory, you can go back to the image and you can count them. It records what you—"

"Smoke!" Alia pointed at the horizon. I looked where she pointed, but saw nothing.

Pyt called Alia back to take the tiller, then ran forward, snatched the binoculars from her, and trained them in the direction where the girl continued to stare. "Where away?"

The girl pointed. "Four points starboard."

Pyt peered through the binoculars, shaking his head. "There's nothing—" Then he gripped the binoculars tighter. "Gods!"

Alia looked up at Pyt. "Is it a cutter?"

I looked where he pointed. Now a tiny black smudge shimmered on the blue horizon.

"What else makes that much smoke?" Pyt lowered his glasses and chewed his lip. "How the hell would they know we're here?" He cut his eyes away from his binoculars and stared at me. "More to the point, why would they care?"

I motioned to Alia, now back at the tiller, to take off my helmet. As she tugged, Pyt cupped a hand and shouted back, "Make for the Inside Passage!"

Alia held out the helmet to me. I reached for it just as the girl responded to Pyt's course-change order.

Before I touched my helmet, the boat heeled over, turning shoreward, and my helmet rolled, then bounced across the curved deck like a bowling ball.

I scuttled on hands and knees through the bilge sloshing in the boat's belly. For what seemed like minutes, I pursued my helmet. Each time I caught up to it, Pyt ordered evasive action, the boat changed direction, and my helmet and I tumbled in opposite directions like spilled marbles in a bowl.

Pyt snapped, "They're unlimbering the four-inch!"

Our boat heeled over again, and for the second time I cursed myself for failing to break weapons out of the sub pod. A TAR's stock against my sore shoulder would have felt good just now, even if sinking a tub full of Tressen bullies would cause an interplanetary incident.

"Muzzle flash!" Pyt shoved Alia flat.

Moments later I heard the overhead rush of an artillery round, then the following report of its firing.

Whoomp!

A high-explosive round detonated in water nearby. The boat rocked and threw me onto my back.

Pyt sniffed. "One hundred yards long if it was one!"

I didn't sniff with him. Tressens were capable gunners, given the equipment they had. The next round would be fired from even shorter range, as the distance diminished between the warship and our tiny fishing boat.

I gave up on my helmet chase and poked my bare head above the gunwale.

The cutter was close enough to see with my naked eyes,

now. Two hundred feet of gray, angular, riveted iron, she trailed black smoke from her stacks and pushed white water off her bow, what Kit had called a bone in her teeth.

My tank commander's eyes made the range just over a mile, closing fast.

The four-inch gun on the cutter's foredeck flashed again. I counted heartbeats.

Whoomp!

White water geysered again, this time a hundred yards short of us.

The Tressen swabbies had bracketed us with just two rounds.

I craned my neck and looked out across the bow. A narrow opening in the hundred-foot-tall pink cliffs lay dead ahead of us. How far? Three hundred yards? Too far?

The muzzle flashed again. Alia heeled us so violently that lines groaned and snapped.

Whoom!

The round's concussion lifted our bow and tumbled me backward, away from the gunwale. Spray rained down into the boat and trickled off my face to puddle in my armor's neck seal.

A Tressen four-inch naval gun delivered a thirty-one-pound high-explosive projectile. I had seen old 105 mm howitzer projectiles that weighed half that much level small houses. One round on target would vaporize this boat and everybody in it.

The girl's maneuver had fooled the Tressen gunners, who had led us just too far. They were too good to be fooled twice.

Pyt picked his way over nets, rope, and the twitching fish to the stern and pushed Alia away from the tiller and forward, toward me. "Over the side with the both of you! You can swim to shore. Once they get the boat, they won't bother to come after you."

Alia clung to the mast. "I won't leave you, Pyt!"

If I left the boat and my equipment without at least one local partisan to guide and vouch for me, I would once again be an ignorant stranger with no hope of finding Kit, much less busting the Yavis' plot. I flicked my eyes from Alia to Pyt. "I'm staying."

Our boat bobbed in the waves. While the three of us stared at one another, stalemated.

Great. In crises, one course of action that usually fails is doing nothing.

I stood and visored a hand above my eyes. I held my breath and watched for the next, and final, muzzle flash.

Seventeen

"Hold your fire!"

The Tressen cutter captain's jaw dropped. He lowered his field glasses and turned, chest out, to the tall man in civilian clothes who stood beside him on the cutter's bridge. "What, sir?"

Polian lowered his own glasses, which had been focused on the tiny sailboat in the distance. But he kept his eyes on it. "Hold your fire, Captain!"

The captain frowned but barked over his shoulder, "Hold fire!"

"Hold fire, aye!"

The captain's command was relayed as the gun crew ahead of and beneath the bridge slammed a shell into the four-inch deck gun's breech, locked it in place, then scurried aside and stood at attention on the plank deck.

The captain's eyes bugged beneath gray brows at Polian. "Sir, it is bad enough that I have, at your insistence, wasted fuel oil and ammunition pursuing some lober boat. I have found it for you. Now you intend to let it get away?"

Polian kept his eyes on the tiny boat as it inchwormed from wave crest to trough, toward the cliffs. "I do not."

"Then may I ask—?"

"No."

Eighteen

I finally captured my helmet, tugged it on, sealed the neck ring watertight, and ducked below the gunwale.

When the cutter's deck gun fired for effect, my armor would probably protect me from shell splinters and the secondary shrapnel which the boat would become. It was probable, but less so, that the Eternads would save me from concussion pulverization. I'd had tanks shot out from under me, even dinosaurs. But never a boat.

I knelt in bilge, listening to it slop and to my heart thump. I looked left and saw Pyt huddled, his body shielding Alia, who squirmed to peek over the gunwale.

If it hadn't been for me, the two of them wouldn't be facing this. I scuttled to them and spread my armored arms across the two of them. As if it could help.

Finally I realized that I should have been hearing the shriek of an incoming round or the blast of the round's detonation. But all I heard was water swish and raspy breathing.

How long since the last round? A decent naval deck-gun

crew, even while adjusting fire between shots, should put a round downrange every ten seconds.

It had easily been over a minute since the last shot.

I chinned up my helmet optics and focused on the cutter's deck gun. The stripe-shirted crew stood lined up at attention, as they had when I looked last. They should have been spinning elevation and deflection handwheels, ramming a shell home, something.

I turned to Pyt, who still kept a hand on the tiller as we ran for the cliffs. "Why are they waiting?"

He turned back to me, eyes wide, and shrugged.

I turned and looked across the waves at the shadowed shelter of the rift in the cliffs.

I shook my head and said to nobody, "Too far."

Nineteen

Polian gripped the cutter bridge's steel rail ahead of him. He was a ground trooper. It had never occurred to him that large ships could move so violently that handrails were needed. But that hadn't stopped him from commandeering her.

When Polian had read the Tressen report that the regularly scheduled Trueborn cruiser would dip lower to conduct "atmospheric tests," the paper had seemed to stick to his fingers. The Trueborns were providing too much information. An undercurrent tugged at his instincts.

Until the delegation currently circling the planet above him in that cruiser arrived on the surface of Tressel, Major Ruberd Polian was Yavet's ranking representative on Tressel. As such he was free to chase every undercurrent that tugged at his instincts.

The bookish boy finally had an opportunity to be the bold one, and Polian had seized it.

But why would the Trueborns even bother with such a

ruse? The Tressens barely believed that giant ships, invisible beyond the atmosphere, really circled their planet, anyway. They would never have noticed.

Polian had plotted the track of the orbiting cruiser on a Tressen globe in a wooden stand, using a length of twine. How convenient that the Trueborns had chosen to sample the atmosphere one hundred miles above a desolate part of the Iridian coast, far from prying eyes.

It was probably an inconsequential coincidence. After all, unlike Yavet, most of sparsely populated Tressel was far from prying eyes. But good intelligence officers didn't believe in coincidence.

Polian was convinced that the remaining Trueborn spy of the pair was at large, and a threat to expose the Yavi presence, if not the mission itself, here on Tressel. The "atmospheric sampling" was too coincidental. Were the Trueborns somehow picking up the at-large team member? If not, was he—or she—uplinking critical information about the hidden developments in the Arctic? Polian had weighed the risks, and he had acted.

Even so, when this old steamer's lookouts had spotted the dumpy fishing boat, Polian had doubted his action. To be sure, the boat was Iridian. Its crew were presumably Iridians.

Iridians were, by statutory definition, enemies of the Tressen state, which justified blowing them to hell. But the cutter captain was right. Using a warship to blow up lober fishermen was like steamrolling flies.

Then, at that moment, a figure stood up, unsteady, in the boat. It could have been a fisherman in lober's armor. The telltale blue-black color could have been a trick of light. Or it could have been a Trueborn case officer wearing a suit of Eternad armor, faceplate open.

If the figure was a simple fisherman, Polian should let the Tressens blow the boat to hell. But if there was the smallest chance that it was a Trueborn spy? The woman's missing partner?

Polian pointed at the opening in the cliffs toward which the fishing boat ran. "Can you follow them in there?"

The captain shook his head. "We'd rip out our bottom a thousand yards offshore."

"Then can you put a marine detachment over the side in one of your launches?"

The captain shook his head again. "With the head start that boat has? Behind those cliffs there's an uncharted network of long shore passages. They twist and braid like yarn. They're barely wide enough and deep enough to pass a launch, and there are falls and rapids around every bend. The Iridians have been fishing and smuggling the Inside Passage for six hundred years. We'd never find them."

Polian nodded. "Then we can't give that boat a head start." He turned his head to the fresh-faced Yavi in civilian clothes who stood behind him and the cutter captain. "Lieutenant Sandr, have the Tressens put the skimmer over the side."

"Combat, sir? The skimmers aren't even supposed to be on this planet."

Polian turned and faced the kid. "That Trueborn spy that Frei ran over wasn't supposed to be here either, Sandr! Take the squad. The skimmer should be able to chase down that little tub out there before it disappears.

If it does make it beyond the cliffs, it should be easy enough to track. The boat and crew you can feed to the fish if you like. But bring me back the one wearing black armor. Alive enough to question! Or I'll feed you and your squad to the fish. Clear?"

"Yes, sir!" Sandr swallowed, saluted, faced about, and double-timed off the bridge.

A Tressen junior naval officer stood at the opposite side of the bridge, staring back over his shoulder at the cutter's captain. "Sir? They're getting away! We have them bracketed. One round . . ."

The captain shook his head as he stared at the Chancellery envelope that protruded from Polian's breast pocket. The captain squeezed his binoculars. "Ensign, have this gentleman's contraption swung over the stern."

Twenty

Alia grinned while she pounded one fist on our gunwale. She shook her other fist at the cutter. "You can't catch us now!" She kept her feet even as our boat leapt, then crashed down in the chop along the cliff base.

I lacked the girl's sea legs, so I death-gripped the bucking gunwale with both hands.

Trueborns have a saying—it only took me a couple years on my parents' world to learn that Trueborns have a saying for everything—about the folly of counting unborn poultry. But I grinned, too.

I nodded down my optics and zoomed on the cutter's gun crew. They hadn't budged. In another minute our progress would interpose the cliffs between us and the cutter. At the big ship's stern, something moved.

I pointed and called over surf crash to Pyt, "What are they doing?"

He squinted at the big ship. "The cutter would ground in the shallows. So they're putting in a shallow draft launch to chase us." He leaned into the tiller while Alia tugged on lines for reasons I didn't understand. Their combined action slipped us past surf that boiled around a garage-sized boulder.

Then Pyt shook his head. "I don't understand why they're bothering. A motor launch is barely faster than we are. And once we make the Inside Passage, they'll never find us."

I watched as the Tressens swung the craft that would hunt us out on davits over the ship's side and lowered it on ropes and pulleys toward the waves.

I rolled my eyes. "Crap."

Pyt raised his glasses, focused; then his brow wrinkled. "The fools are putting their launch in upside down!"

I cocked my head. A twelve-place skimmer's inverted-bathtub hull *would* look like an overturned open boat if you had never seen an air-cushion vehicle. I sighed again. "It's not a boat. It's a light-duty utility vehicle. It blows air out from beneath that skirt around its belly and floats above the water. Or the land."

Pyt snorted. "They have no such—."

Alia said, "It's true! It looks just like the pictures!"

Pyt turned to me, green eyes ablaze, and pointed at the skimmer. "You haven't punished Iridia enough? You've given more machines to the Tressens? To hunt down the last of us?"

"We didn't do that. That's a Yavi machine."

"Yavi?" Pyt frowned.

I said, "Another planet. If you think the Trueborns punished you, wait 'til you meet some Yavis."

In the distance, the skimmer floated in the water, awaiting a helmsman. A dozen riflemen scrambled over a cargo net draped over the cutter's side and dropped into the open skimmer's troop space as it bobbed.

Nine of the squad wore Yavi body armor and carried assault rifles with barrels so slender that they had to be Yavi needle guns. One man, thinner than the others, wore Tressen naval coveralls and carried a gunpowder sidearm. The last two Yavi carried crew-served needle machine guns. The gunners levered the needlers into the skimmer's midships gun mounts and fitted their drum magazines with a weary competence that couldn't have been Tressen. I whistled. "And you're about to meet some."

The skimmer driver fired up his vehicle, and that familiar sucking whine snarled across the water. A fog of atomized seawater obscured the skimmer's skirt, and the vehicle rose two feet above the waves.

Pyt's eyes widened, and he glanced back and forth between the passage entrance, now thirty yards ahead of us, and the wobbling skimmer. "How fast is that thing?"

The skimmer's driver got his vehicle trimmed. Its nose dipped, and it shot toward us, accelerating toward sixty miles per hour.

Pyt swore.

Alia slapped her forehead. "Ooh!"

Then our creaking boat passed into shadow, behind the cliff's shoulder. For a moment, we could neither see nor hear the dozen heavily armed troops bearing down on us. There was only the creak of our own hull as we sailed on at one sixth the speed of our pursuers.

Pyt unlatched the locker in the stern, withdrew two single-shot rifles and cartridge bandoliers, and handed one to Alia.

Then both of them turned and stared at me.

Pyt pointed a three-fingered hand in my direction. "You brought these devils upon us. You get rid of them!"

Twenty-one

"Rover, we've lost sight of the boat from out here. Do you have visual on it yet?" Polian's heart pounded as he awaited the skimmer's reply, and he squeezed his handtalk so hard that it squirted from his fingers. It clattered across the bridge's deck plates, and Polian kicked at it before he snatched it up.

The Tressen captain stroked his moustache to conceal a smile. "I sympathize with your frustration. But we did everything precisely as you asked. We could have blown those fish-eaters out of the water. We've done it before. Your mission, your command, sir. But if they escape . . ."

Polian faced away from the Tressen captain, stared out at the sky, and swallowed hard. Aboard the Trueborn cruiser circling invisibly above, hiding under a priest's prayer shawl, rode this mission's real commander.

Polian was the acting senior command authority for Yavet's entire presence on Tressel, but only until General Ulys Gill hit dirt. Gill was replacing Polian's unexpectedly and ironically dead boss, a this-century warrior slain by last-century Tressen influenza. With no suitable replacement on hand, command had plucked Gill off the almost-retired shelf and packed him off to Tressel with the next available detachment. Polian hardly welcomed the change. By reputation, the old moustaches had scant patience with staff officers, especially those who acted like line officers then got it wrong.

"Base, this is Rover." Sandr's voice shrieked as he shouted to be heard above the skimmer's roar. Polian had almost forgotten that he had a question pending to his subordinate.

Sandr said, "No, we've lost sight of them. Once we clear the point, we should reacquire visual."

Pop-pop-pop. Pop-pop-pop. The sound of needle-gun bursts drifted to Polian as the squad pressured up its mounted crew-served weapons.

"Rover, this is Base. Does that sailor with you know where he's going?"

"Generally. But he says nobody knows the channels and rapids ahead like the fish-eaters."

Polian blew out a breath. Why did everything on this simple planet have to be not simple? "You have the sensors calibrated, then?"

"Much as we can in a new environment, sir. But it should be simple enough to follow the boat's telltales."

Pop-pop-pop. One more pressuring burst.

Sandr said, "And when we catch it, sir, we'll razor every living thing in it."

"No! Rover, I want that boat interdicted. But I also want someone alive enough to tell me where it was headed and why."

Twenty-two

Pyt steered our boat into a passage darkened by hundred-foot-high rock walls that narrowed upward to a slit. The channel was too open to be a cave, too narrow to be a fjord, too broad to be a crevasse.

Boom.

A swell tossed the boat against the cliff and knocked me off balance. I tripped over coiled rope, fell headlong against a bait barrel, and landed on the still-twitching rhizodont. It managed a slow snap at me, and I kicked its head. I grabbed at Alia's arm to stand and knocked her down, too.

She pulled herself upright, gasping.

Alia furled the sails as the swells swept the boat down the passage, thumping against rock hard enough to crack our hull's planking. She unlashed a wooden pole, three times her height, from the mast, then stood in the bow, using the pole to fend the boat off the cliffs.

I called back to Pyt, "What do you want me to do?"

He waved a hand, palm down. "Sit down! Shut up! We've done this a thousand times."

Ten minutes later the passage widened and the swells spilled out into the unconfined area and dissipated. Our boat slowed with the current, and I looked back up the passage, half expecting to see the skimmer bearing down.

Alia aimed her fending pole into the water, then walked from bow to stern pushing the pole against the bottom, speeding the boat through the widened grotto.

Fifty yards ahead, the grotto channel split into three more passages. Pyt steered us into the leftmost channel.

I turned back to him. "What if they follow one of the other channels?"

He smiled. "That's the beauty of the Inside Passage. The falls at the end of either of those channels will crush a Tressen launch like an egg."

The Inside Passage referred to what the xenogeologists called an inundated tectonic compression zone. That was an expensive description of the place where a continent and a seabed pressed against one another, butting heads until one yielded to the other. However, in this case, both landmasses had pushed back, stubborn and unyielding.

Like, shall we say, a Trueborn senior case officer with an idealistic board up her adorable ass, and a reasonable but pragmatic, some would say nihilistically cynical, junior case officer.

Like Kit and me, the landmasses had finally buckled and shattered, one worse than the other. The resultant jumble of cliffs, drowned canyons, channels, rapids, and falls created a sheltered inland waterway that stretched along the shore of half a continent. The Inland Passage had connected and defined the Iridian nation for centuries.

Pyt knew his world. But he didn't know any others.

I walked back and stood alongside him to answer his question. "Remember, that thing can do things a Tressen launch can't."

"I saw that thing. It's too large, too heavy. If they choose the wrong passage, it won't survive either of those falls. So two chances in three we're done with them."

I shook my head. "They won't choose wrong. The skimmer's got sensors that detect heat and motion residues. Even micro rippling left behind in water. It's a mechanical bloodhound."

Pyt crossed his arms and just stared at me. Bloodhounds wouldn't evolve on Tressel for eons. He frowned, then nodded. "I understand. You're saying they can track us. What do you suggest?"

I sucked in a breath. A case officer who was building local relationships was taught that the first request for advice or aid was a golden opportunity. If the case officer offered good ideas or useful materiel, a bond formed. If he blundered, the opportunity transmuted from gold to lead, and the locals wrote him off as worthless.

Worse, this problem wasn't, for example, a child's toothache that I could cure from the meds kit. If I couldn't think of something, we would find ourselves in a twelve-on-three firefight with a dozen trained killers.

I rummaged through the jumbled gear in the tiny boat, searching more for an idea than an object, while Alia stared at me. I tried to look like I had a clue.

Twenty-three

"Talk to me, Sandr." Polian paced the cutter's foredeck as it rocked at anchor. The ship lay fifteen hundred yards offshore from the mouth of the passage in the cliffs, behind which the sun was now sinking.

"Sir, we've reached a decision point here."

"You finally have them in sight?"

"Uh . . ."

Polian rolled his eyes. "A skimmer can't catch a wooden sailboat?"

"Major, these channels, they're a maze. And the boat's been running with a strong current. The current doesn't benefit us, because we're above it. That's not a problem by itself, but our beam is broader than theirs, and the passage actually narrows upward in places, bottlenecks in others. So we're reduced to a pace not much faster than double time."

Polian squeezed his eyes shut. "But you haven't lost them?"

"No, sir. But we've just entered a grotto. It has three

other exits. This coastline is a regular maze once you get behind the cliffs."

"So you take the passage that the sensors show that they took."

"Sir, the sensor calibration's still pretty coarse. We've got residual moving-target indicators and heat and organic traces extending down two divergent passages. Obviously, one indication's false. We're sorting relative strength and quality, but . . ."

Polian squeezed his handtalk. He had assigned Sandr, the fledgling staff officer, to chase the boat in order to build the boy's decision-making skills. So far it wasn't working. "While you're sorting, they're opening the gap, son! Ninety percent of command is being right in time. Worst case, you backtrack. Choose a passage, Lieutenant."

Silence.

Polian's handtalk crackled. "Yes, sir. Here we go."

Polian smiled. Lessons learned in the classroom were forgotten in the field. Lessons learned in the field, however, became reflexes. The next time crisis forced Sandr, the bright but timid kid, to decide, he wouldn't hesitate—he would leap.

But personnel development was ancillary to Polian's primary objective. He had overreached by exposing his covert force to chase a counterespionage hunch. If he caught a spy, he was a genius. But unless Sandr caught that boat, Polian could only look like an idiot who had chased a tub full of fishermen.

Polian turned away from the sunset and flipped up the collar of his Tressen jacket against the rising wind. Then he looked back up at the bridge. The ship's captain looked down, his features obscured beneath his cap-bill shadow. But Polian swore that the bastard was laughing at him.

Twenty-four

We had been drifting down our passageway for twenty minutes, bumping against the rock walls. When we slowed, Alia poled.

I kept staring back over the stern, snoopers on in late afternoon dimness, audio gain maxed. I expected to hear the snarl or see the snout of the skimmer every moment, but behind us there was nothing. Finally, I unwrapped a protein bar and chewed it while I bent and broke out weapons. Then something occurred to me.

All three of the channels among which we had chosen ran roughly parallel. Two of the channels led to waterfalls. I ran my fingers along our boat's rickety wooden top rail. Then I pointed at our route, wrapper in hand, and asked Pyt. "What's at the end of this?"

He turned his eyes up toward the dimming sky sliver that glowed between the canyon walls. "Just a splash of white water. This is the easiest passage."

"Good. I hate amusement rides as much as I hate water."

An hour later, Alia shipped her pole because the current now carried us faster than she could pole. The narrow channel became a gorge barely wider than our hull. Distant thunder rumbled.

I turned to Alia, cupped a hand, and shouted. "Rapids?"

She shook her head and shouted back, grinning. "Better! Dead Man's Falls!"

As the boat accelerated on the current, the distant thunder became a steady roar.

I shot Pyt a bug-eyed glance. "A splash of white water?" The thunder, confined and booming off the gorge walls, now shook the boat so hard that the rope lines quivered. I pointed forward and screamed at him, "A *splash*?"

Pyt shrugged, then tossed me a rope coil. "Would it have helped you to know?"

"You goddam liar!"

"I didn't lie. It is the easiest passage. Watch how I tie myself in, then you do the same."

Twenty-five

Alone at a polished wood table in the cutter's officer's mess, Polian sat hunched over a mug of tepid local tea and ground his teeth. He tugged back the sleeve of his Tressen jacket and eyed his 'puter.

If he were back home, with a lousy brigade recon platoon, he could have simply put up a drone and tracked this boat forever. Polian sighed. It was a rule of covert operations that the equipment they let you bring was always one item short of the equipment you needed.

So, with a permanent change in the human balance of power at stake, here he sat. Reduced to awaiting progress reports about a rowboat race, relayed in the clear on glorified portable telephones with awful reception. He should have taken command of the skimmer himself. But this expedition into which he had thrown his troops was already Polian's first real foray from staff officer to commander. The experience would grow Polian as a commander, just as it would grow Sandr, and Polian had seen too many grandstanding commanders who led from the front unnecessarily.

A Tressen seaman rapped on the mess hatchway's steel surround as he turtled his head in through the opening. "Sir? Your man on deck says a call is coming in on your wireless."

The sailor jumped aside, wide-eyed, as Polian sprinted past him to the passage ladder.

Polian took the ladder two steps at a time, barked a shin as he emerged from below decks into twilight, and limped, swearing under his breath, to Frei, the budding line lieutenant, whom Polian had assigned to monitor the handtalk.

Polian snatched the handtalk from Frei, and a voice, not Sandr's, crackled in Polian's ear. "—at first light. Or we can give it up."

Polian panted. "Rover, this is Base. What's your situation?"

"Base, we've taken a casualty."

Polian closed his eyes and gripped the handtalk. Polian recognized the voice now. Mazzen, the brevet corporal. That meant the casualty—

"Sir, the lieutenant's dead."

Polian stepped back, off balance, though the ship wasn't rolling. His shoulders slumped. He should have gone himself. "How?"

"The passage we took. It wasn't the one the Iridian boat took, sir."

Polian wrinkled his forehead in the fading light. "Then how—?"

"They spoofed us, sir. Tied some big, half-live fish to a barrel and let the current carry it. The sensors aren't close-calibrated, so we got mass and residual motion and organic indicators from it. Took a while to catch up with it and recognize the decoy."

"But Sandr?"

"Sir, the decoy suckered us into a gorge that led to a waterfall. Dropped straight down two hundred feet to solid rock. The passage was too narrow for us to turn the skink around. We barely stopped in time. Then we had to reverse out with everybody fending off the walls with their weapon stocks. We lost a man overboard." There was a pause. "Me. I was a goner. Except Lieutenant Sandr dove in after me and got a line on me. But nobody had a line on him."

Another pause.

"He didn't hesitate a heartbeat, sir. If he had, I wouldn't be here."

Polian leaned against the deck gun and wiped his eyes. "I understand." Polian stared across the calm sea at the last red glow of daylight above the cliffs. Somewhere beyond those cliffs was Mazzen and the skimmer, the Iridian boat, and what remained of Sandr. Sandr, who had died because he, Polian, who had no experience of command at all, had some addled aversion to leading from the front. And he, Polian, had filled the kid with stupid notions of responsibility and decisiveness, as if he himself understood them.

"Sir, he hit the rocks headfirst. Armor or not . . . We haven't been able to reduce the remains, sir. Honestly, we'd probably lose somebody else trying. I'm sorry, sir. I know you and the elltee . . ."

Polian straightened and drew a breath. "So, where are you now?"

"Back in the intersection. Now we're calibrated. And we've got reliable residuals to track. With snoopers we can make better time than the rebels can. The Tressen guide says we can still overtake them within an hour, now that we're both navigating in darkness."

Polian rubbed his forehead with numb fingers. "Yes. Of course."

Alongside Polian, Lieutenant Frei cleared his throat. "Sir? I overheard. If Mazzen waits, there's time for the Tressens to ferry me out to the skink in their launch. I could take Sandr's place and direct the pursuit."

Polian blinked as he felt swelling around his eyes. Then he clapped the boy on the shoulder. "I appreciate that, Frei." Polian shook his head. "But it's my place to go."

Frei opened his mouth, then closed it.

Polian thumbed the handtalk. "Mazzen? Hold your position."

"Hold? Sir, I—yes, sir."

"I'm on my way to join you."

"Oh. But if I may, sir? A question?"

"Shoot."

"How did fishermen a hundred years behind the times learn to spoof a sensor array?"

Polian felt blood rise in his cheeks. The guilt for Sandr's death didn't rest entirely on Polian. "They didn't, Mazzen. But once I get out there, we will find the bastard who did this. And he'll pay for it."

Twenty-six

I clung to the ropes around my waist that lashed me to the quaking boat and stared at the girl. Alia sat across from me, roped the same way and staring back. We teetered on the lip of the first, twenty-foot stair-step drop of Dead Man's Falls. The roar of the falls drowned the hull's creaks. And probably the grinding of my teeth.

The girl sat serene, staring ahead as the bow dipped. As Pyt had told me, they had done this before. The distances between Yavet and Tressel, and the differences between life on each of them, could scarcely have been greater. Yet the girl and I were alike. For practical purposes she was growing up orphaned by parents she never knew, as I had. Like every Iridian, and every child born Illegal on Yavet, she was subject to summary execution for the crime of living.

The boat passed its tipping point, and I must have yipped. She looked at me with the Iridian green eyes that marked her and shrugged. "Don't worry. The next steps aren't any worse."

Boom.

The keel struck a boulder, and the boat rolled right.

Boom. Back left.

Spray drenched my armor. Inside it, my underlayer was already sweat soaked.

Pyt, back on the tiller, straightened us, and we careened between glistening black boulders and over the second twenty-foot step.

All three of the channels among which we had chosen plunged down the same two-hundred-foot-high escarpment. Name notwithstanding, Dead Man's Falls made the plunge in survivable twenty-foot drops. The other channels' falls, Pyt had told me, dropped sheer.

My improvised sensor decoy must have worked, or the skimmer would have caught us well before we reached these falls. So were the Yavi all dead? And if they were, had I killed them?

I swallowed. As an officer in Earth's army, I had taken an oath to defend my parents' homeworld against enemies and oppressors, and Yavet was certainly both. I had spent my growing years on Yavet hiding from a government that wanted Illegals like me dead. But still I had been raised a Yavi.

When you're young, committing to anything is hard. But, as the girl and I knew, being alone was harder.

The channel beyond the falls was narrow, flat, and slow. Daylight was now gone from the canyon floor.

I panted.

I turned to Pyt. "Can we stop here?"

He nodded, glancing back over his shoulder at the now-distant falls. Then he grounded the boat, its prow grinding up onto a half-moon–shaped beach pocketed in a bend and walled by cliffs. While Alia made the boat fast, Pyt grabbed my elbow and took me aside. "What are you thinking, Jazen?"

I pointed back along the channel in the direction of Dead Man's Falls. "The Yavi must have bought our spoof, or they'd have been on us an hour ago. If they went over your falls, fine. But if they didn't, they'll backtrack. Then come after us down this channel."

He nodded. "We have to assume the worst, then plan to deal with it. I agree."

I nodded back as I rummaged through my gear. "If they make it over the falls, running won't save us. The skimmer's faster than we are, and they won't fall for a decoy again."

He crossed his arms. "Then we fight."

I shook my head. "Force against force? A dozen Yavi commandos would annihilate the three of us in a fair fight."

Pyt narrowed his eyes. "You're suggesting we run away?"

I shook my head again. "I'm suggesting we make it an unfair fight." I knelt and popped seals on a plasteel. "We call the equipment I have in this container force multipliers. If the skimmer makes it over the falls, the Yavi will be channeled down that gorge for a hundred yards. And they'll be as shell-shocked as I was for a couple minutes."

Pyt smiled. "We lay an ambush?"

I shook my head one more time. "I lay an ambush. You two continue downstream."

Pyt frowned. "You? That's—"

"See this?" I held up a curved slab of olive plastic, as rectangular and thick as a Gideon Bible.

Pyt ran a finger across words molded into the slab's convex plastic face like a book title, in Standard. He read aloud, "This Side Toward Enemy." Then he sniffed. "We already have mines. We use Tressen artillery shells when we can steal them, and nails in gunpowder when we can't."

I sighed. Trueborns, for all their self-proclaimed goodness, had invented more ways to slaughter people on the cheap than any three outworld societies combined. Pyt probably didn't realize that improvised explosive devices, the poor man's force multiplier, had been invented on Earth a century before.

Even the IED's regular-forces cousin, the command-detonated directional antipersonnel mine, hadn't evolved much. Why mess with a bad thing?

I rotated the mine as I pointed out its features to Pyt. "This beats a bucket of nails. Convex slab of plastic explosive, here. Harmless as cookie dough without a detonating cap. Seven hundred rifle balls stuck into the explosive's front. The cookie's sealed in weatherproof plastic. Blasting cap in the back, here. Detonation wires out the back, here. There's even a peep sight, here on top. Emplace, back off, send a spark to the cap, and . . . boom!"

Pyt jerked his hand back off the mine's face.

I set the mine down and unboxed another. "Any man-sized target within a sixty-degree arc fifty yards downrange will take a bullet."

While he hefted the mine, I laid out a half-dozen more. "I'll set these along the gorge, just beneath the waterline, angled up, and detonate them when the skimmer's inside the kill box. Skimmer armor's like kitchen foil. One mine should disable everyone in the skimmer, armored or not, but a little overkill won't hurt. Two mines I'll hardwire back to me, to be detonated on command by me, from cover, fifty yards downstream. I'll set four more to detonate automatically, as fail-safes. Two on photoelectric trips, two on temperature sensors."

I peeled Cosplas off a heavy machine gun, stripped and reassembled it. "When the first mine blows, I'll fire straight down the gorge. Enfilade fire. Like knocking down dominoes." I palmed back the gun's charging handle, released it, then tapped the handle to seat it. "Yavi body armor may protect them from some of the mine shrapnel, but it won't stop a heavy machine-gun round."

"We know ambush technique. You could use some help."

I swept a hand above the equipment containers. "Sure. If I had a day to teach you new techniques to ambush armored troops in a skink. These will be Yavi, equipped like nothing you've ever seen."

I twisted a buzz bug to activate it, then said, "Pick a number between one and five."

Pyt wrinkled his forehead. "Three."

"Now pick another."

"One. Why?"

I coded the bug, then handed it to him. "Keep this in your pocket. It's a wireless receiver. If the Yavi don't show up, or the ambush succeeds, I'll transmit a burst signal from my helmet comm. The receiver's silent, but if you're within twenty miles of me, my signal will make it vibrate.

If you receive three vibes, one minute apart each, wait for me at the next fork. If you receive nothing, keep running. If you receive any other pattern, keep running. Any other pattern could be a spoof transmitted by the Yavi. Clear?"

"Clear." Pyt nodded slowly. "But I would have expected a Trueborn to make those he had paid for take the risk. Not himself."

I watched the girl, who had rolled up her pant legs and was wading in the stream, chasing shellfish, then cocked my head inside my helmet. "Me, too."

Twenty minutes later, I was alone in the gorge. I had set passive listeners to warn me if the skimmer closed in while I was prepping the ambush. Then I had waded back upstream and emplaced mines to envelop the ambush kill zone.

By the time I had run det wires, set aiming and ranging marks for the gun, and scooped out a firing position on the little beach, I was wheezing. The warning sensors remained quiet. I lay on my back alongside the gun on its bipod, popped my visor, and stared up at the night-sky sliver that showed between the gorge walls. As I watched, a streak flashed across the sky, as fleeting as the meteor "shooting stars" that lit Earth's night skies.

I smiled. I had seen enough old-style orbitals cross above enough battlefields to recognize the difference between spacecraft and meteors. The streak was a downshuttle. Soon that shuttle's human cargo would be standing in immigration and baggage-claim lines, bitching about the discomfort and inconvenience of shuttling in this day and age. I smiled. I would gladly have traded my planetfall experience for theirs.

In the cool darkness, listening to the distant falls purr, I yawned. If this plan did come to a firefight, I needed to be fresh. I maxed my sensor alarms and checked the gun and the mine det clackers one more time. Then I popped two dozers from my helmet dispenser. The nice thing about dozers was that when you woke, you woke one hundred percent alert. I chased them with fortified water from my helmet nipple.

While I waited for the dozers to kick in, I visualized myself lying on a starlit beach less hostile than this one, with Kit alongside me. Pyt was right. Why was I lone-wolfing this ambush when the book dictated that I enlist expendable locals to do it? I was in this to save the damsel and run, not to stick my neck out for some child I hardly knew. Wasn't I?

Before I could answer my own question, I slept.

Twenty-seven

The skimmer crept down the pitch-dark gorge, floating a foot above the current roaring beneath it. Polian fended the skimmer off the rock wall, green in the amplified light of his snoopers, with a gauntlet.

"All stop!" The Tressen seaman seated alongside Polian touched the skimmer driver's arm, and the skimmer stopped and hovered. The seaman turned to Polian. "This one's more rapids than a sheer fall, Cap'n." He cupped a hand around his ear. "The pitch of the sound tells you."

Polian ground his teeth. The pitch hadn't told this man enough last time. And so a promising officer, who was a good kid, was dead. But this Tressen was the best guide Polian had.

"Sir, I got organics a thousand yards dead ahead! We're catching them!" the specialist monitoring the sensors whispered into his helmet mike.

Polian frowned. "Movers or stationary?"

"Uh. Actually, they *are* stationary, sir."

Mazzen, the brevet corporal, frowned, too. "Maybe they wrecked on the falls."

Polian shook his head. "They know this place. They didn't wreck themselves."

"But if they think we wrecked, they may have put in for the night."

Polian stared around them at the narrow gorge. It would become even narrower, and more demanding of their attention, when they reached the falls or rapids or whatever rumbled up ahead. He shook his head again. "He's too smart to assume that. They've set an ambush at the base of the falls."

Polian turned to Mazzen and pointed at the gorge walls. "Can you get six men up to the top of this canyon?" Polian pointed at the sensor image and the map onscreen. "Move down past the falls on foot? Flank them?"

Mazzen's boots clanged as he popped his climbing crampons. "Hour up the wall, sir. Another hour hump downstream. Thirty minutes to down rappel." He smiled. "Actually, we wouldn't need to down rappel. We could take 'em under fire from above. Hell, chuck grenades down on them." Then Mazzen frowned. "But I suppose you want them alive, sir?"

"I do. As soon as you're in position above and behind them, we'll bring the skimmer forward and distract them."

Ten minutes later, Mazzen's team clung to the gorge wall thirty feet above the skimmer, already looking as small as a half-dozen green monkeys climbing a green curtain.

Polian tapped the specialist's shoulder and took the sensor-display tablet from the man. The target indicator hadn't moved. It was, of course, possible that they really had misjudged the success of their little decoy game and stopped to rest. That would make capture even easier.

Polian opened his visor and let the night air and the roar of the undercurrent wash over him. Actually, it didn't matter what their mind-set was, or whether they were asleep or awake. He whispered to the shapeless blob on the tablet screen, "You're mine now."

Twenty-eight

I woke, belly down in my slit trench, because a hand grabbed my shoulder as my sensors screeched.

I spun onto my back, drew my bush knife, and pressed it to my attacker's throat.

"Jazen! It's me!" The girl's eyes bulged.

I recoiled, whispering, "Alia? What the hell?"

Pyt, speaking from over my shoulder, said, "Iridians don't cut and run. Alia had to remind me of that."

I thrust my knife back into its scabbard then pounded the boulder. "Crap!"

Alia's face fell.

My army, a half-handed, middle-aged stepfather and a prepubescent girl, stood there jut-jawed. They clutched their hunting rifles like they thought they were three hundred Trueborn Spartans at Thermopylae. Pyt, I guessed, also came back to see whether Trueborns were, to use an expression that made no sense on a world without mammals, all hat and no cattle.

I cupped Alia's chin in one gauntleted hand, until her

eyes met mine. "You're very brave to come back. But I didn't send you downstream to protect you from a fight. I'm wearing armor that will barely show on Yavi sensors. The two of you will glow in the dark like vending-machine rubbers."

Alia wrinkled her forehead. "Like what?"

I raised my eyebrows at Pyt and shrugged while I answered Alia. "Never mind. Look, if the Yavi know we're here, this won't be an ambush. It'll be a clusterfuck."

Alia wrinkled her forehead again.

I pointed at an upturned rock ledge. Needle guns were designed to kill selectively in civilian crowds, not penetrate cover. "Both of you get behind that. Maybe they won't—"

Wheet. Wheet. Wheet.

The remote sensors I had set downstream klaxoned in my helmet. At the same instant, a new sound mingled with the falls' distant rumble. The skimmer's whine.

I ran, crouching, back to where the pair huddled behind the slab and pointed at the sky. "Keep your eyes on the gorge rim. If they know we're here, they may try to flank us. Shoot anything that moves." If a Yavi did poke a helmeted head over the rim above us, the Iridian rifles wouldn't dent his helmet. But the shots might slow him down, and they would warn me that he was there.

Whirrr.

I maxed my snoops and focused on the lip of the first cascade, six hundred yards away. The skimmer's snout peeked out above the precipice, then withdrew.

Bam. Bam. Bam.

Two hunting rifles rattled behind me.

"Jazen! They're up above! All around us."

The skimmer peeked out again, this time slewed broadside.

Prraaap.

The skimmer's side-mounted needle gun hosed the rock ledge with a burst that sang away in a shower of orange ricochet sparks and spent rounds.

Thump.

An object, dropped from above, half buried itself in the sand ten yards from me. Illumination canister. Its fuse fizzed; then the charge burst in a white, arcing flash.

My snoops compensated. The Yavis' snoops would, too. Neither I nor they needed illumination. The canister had been dropped to momentarily blind my two would-be helpers.

Meanwhile, the skimmer refused to enter my kill zone.

Alia called, "Jazen! We can't see!"

I fired twenty machine-gun rounds at the spot where the skimmer had been seconds before. As much from frustration as from murderous intent or tactical cleverness. The burst's tracers zigzagged in green streak ricochets, then disappeared harmlessly up the gorge.

The skimmer showed its snout again. I aimed, fired. And the gun jammed after a single round.

Something wriggled against the gorge wall, above and to my flank, like a spilled basket of cobras.

I groaned. Rappel ropes.

My side was outnumbered, outgunned, blind, surrounded, and had ceded the high ground to the enemy. I had been wrong. This ambush would have to get lots better to rise to the level of a clusterfuck.

I swung the gun around to pick off as many of the Yavi as I could as soon as they began bouncing down the rock walls toward us. I tried to clear the jam, failed, and tried again.

Finally, I drew my sidearm in one hand and my bush knife in the other and faced the still-unused rappel ropes. "Well, a few of you baby-killers are going down with me!"

It was the kind of guts-and-duty drivel that Kit had always spouted when her back was to the wall. Now, finally, she had me doing it, too. Unfortunately, she would never know about it. No one would.

Twenty-nine

"Base, this is Flanker. We're in position above the objective. We will down rappel on your command."

Polian, seated in the skimmer, enveloped in nitrogen fog from the needlers' bursts, chinned his helmet comm and replied to Mazzen. "Any effective resistance? Because you'll be sitting ducks while—"

The sensor specialist seated behind Polian tugged his arm and thrust the handtalk at him. "Sir, it's Lieutenant Frei. From the cutter."

Polian sighed. If he had had another suit hotted up, Frei would be wearing it. Then he and Frei could be conversing on any one of a half-dozen nets that the suits supported. Instead Polian wormed the handtalk in through his open visor until it rested alongside his ear.

Frei's voice buzzed at him. "—immediately."

"We're in a firefight, Sandr. Later."

"He said to tell you it's a direct order."

Polian stiffened. "What? Who?"

"General Gill, sir. He hit dirt two hours ago."

"He's not due for two days!"

"Yes, sir. He traded downshuttle slots with one of his aides."

Polian blew out a breath.

Frei said, "He's—frankly, sir, he sounded pissed you didn't meet the downshuttle, even before I told him we were out here. And when he heard we've gone operational, and about Lieutenant Sandr . . ."

Polian squeezed the handtalk. Gill didn't understand.

"Sir, he's ordered us to cease operations instantly and return to Tressia with all deliberate speed."

"Okay. We should wrap up out here within two hours. We'll be back aboard the cutter with prisoners before dawn."

"Uh. I kind of told him that, sir. He asked me whether I had a hearing problem, because if I did a court-martial would fix it."

Gill was focused on the mission, which was appropriate. And a new commander usually made an example early to establish authority. But Gill needed to know the gravity of the threat that had drawn Polian out here. "Frei, patch me through to the general."

"Just lost the link, Major."

Only fool officers jumped into a situation about which they knew nothing and undercut the commander on the ground. Polian had no reason to think that Gill was a fool. And even if he were, Polian's oath contained no escape clause for orders issued by fools. In the darkness, Polian turned his head and swore. Then he said, "Understood. Out."

Polian considered explaining to Mazzen, but Mazzen

had taken the same oath. Polian dialed up CallAll, then sounded recall.

Mazzen's voice broke in over the electronic bugle. "Sir? Did you hit recall by mistake?"

"No mistake. Get back here at the double crack."

"But—yes, sir."

Polian slumped back against his seat's safety harness. While he waited for the squad to reassemble at the skimmer, he stared at the tablet's screen. Three distinct images glowed there now. The two boat rebels. And a tiny flicker, scarcely bigger than a small rodent. To Polian's trained eye, the flicker was the telltale of a third adversary, wearing a suit of Trueborn Eternad armor. If the Iridians hadn't been there, shining like beacons, the skimmer would have blundered into the trap. Polian held the tablet in one hand while he made a fist of the other and pounded his thigh plate.

The sensor specialist said, "Sucks, doesn't it, Major? I mean, we *had* the bastards! And now it's over."

Polian stared at the tiny flicker that he held responsible for Sandr's death and imprinted on his brain the distant face of the spy he had glimpsed through binoculars from the cutter's deck. Then Polian shook his head. "It isn't over."

Thirty

I aimed my rifle at the cliff tops, waiting for the first Yavi head, hand, or foot to poke over the edge, and listened to my heart pound.

Nothing.

I glanced back toward the falls. No skimmer. In fact, no sound of a skimmer.

Pyt low-crawled out from behind the rock slab to me, then whispered, "What are they waiting for?"

I shook my head and whispered back, "Dunno."

I checked the downstream sensors. The skimmer was gone, or at least had retired out of sensor range. I scanned the cliff top again. My helmet indicators all lay flat in the green.

Twenty minutes passed. Then I stood up and showed myself. Nobody shot me, or painted me with fire-control sensors, or did anything at all.

I wrinkled my forehead inside my helmet. "They're gone."

We waited another hour. Then we crept to the boat,

loaded the gear, and pushed off silently downstream, with my armored ass steering while the two Iridians lay sheltered in the boat's belly.

After the current had carried us six miles without incident, Pyt crawled back to me, smiling. "We made it!"

I nodded. We had, though it made no sense.

The gorge widened, and the expanding sliver of sky began to glow with false dawn.

Alia also crawled to us in the boat's stern. Her eyes were alight, her cheeks aglow.

A Trueborn warlord named Churchill wrote, while a young soldier, that there is no feeling so exhilarating as to be shot at without result. I suspect he wrote that before he saw his first friend take a bullet.

I turned to Pyt. "So, when do I see Celline?"

Alia wrinkled her glowing forehead and opened her mouth, but Pyt silenced her with a hand on the girl's forearm.

Pyt slipped alongside me and replaced me on the tiller. "Dusk tomorrow, if the weather holds."

Alia frowned. Then Pyt tapped the girl's shoulder and led her forward to rig lines.

Thirty-one

The unmarked Tressen staff car's brake squeal woke Polian; then its deceleration pitched him upright in the auto's front seat. The car stopped and idled at the striped sentry box set beside the gate in a wire fence line.

While the car's driver presented his pass to the Tressen gate sentry, Polian stretched and rubbed the stubble of two days' travel on his face. Polian was supposed to be a missionary, not a soldier, so the look was consistent. But Gill probably wouldn't see it that way. Polian was prepared to be relieved because he had compromised this mission's security. He was more than prepared to be busted—maybe even court-martialed—because his blundering had gotten a good young officer killed.

The sentry glanced through the window at Polian without studying him, then stepped back and raised the gate.

The car rolled forward into the military compound on the capital's outskirts, passed barracks and administration buildings, then swung onto a dirt track that led to a windowless warehouse and stopped.

Polian stepped from the car, cleared another sentry, then stepped through a man-sized door, set in a vehicle-sized rolling door, and into the building's incandescent-lit interior.

Gill stood, back to Polian, wearing a black civilian suit, a cleric's shawl draped round his neck, hands clasped at the small of his back. He was tiny for a Yavi military man, as short and slight as a girl, with cropped white hair rather than the current shave job. He stared down a row of thirty parked skimmers, all painted in gray and white arctic camouflage.

Polian tucked his civilian cap beneath his arm, shot the cuffs of the shirt beneath his Tressen jacket. Then he straightened and cleared his throat. "Sir, Major Polian reports."

Gill stepped to the nearest skimmer and laid a hand on its empty gun mount. "At ease, Major. A handful of patrol vehicles. Not much equipment for a two-leaf general, do you think, Polian?"

"Sir? It's not my place to think—"

"Major, it is always an officer's place to think." Gill pivoted and faced Polian. Dark eyes alight beneath thick brows, he slapped his palm against the skimmer's flank plates. "When I arrived, you had decided to go off and run an operation. Even though you're a staff officer by training and experience."

Damn right I had, and I'd do it again. But it went wrong and compromised this operation and got a good man killed. Polian swallowed, hard. "Yes, sir. Operations aren't my business. I screwed up."

Gill waved a thin hand as he shook his head. "Son,

operations have been my business all my military life. And I can tell you there is no way up which I have not screwed. That's the beast's nature. I didn't stand you down because you chased your instincts. I certainly didn't stand you down because things got difficult. I stood you down because you weren't there to meet me."

Polian felt blood color his cheeks. *For a moment I thought you were reasonable. But, you pompous old son of a bitch, you're going to discipline me because I didn't greet you with roses and a kiss on your balls!* "It was inconsiderate of me, sir."

Gill raised his palm again and shook his head, smiling. "Major, you aren't hearing me. I don't care a rat fart whether my staff sucks up to me. I do care if I can't get their advice when I'm fresh on dirt. Do you know who *did* meet me, in your absence?"

"Uh, no, sir."

"The commandant of the Interior Police."

Polian closed his eyes, then opened them.

"Evidently his organization's been trying to get custody of some female prisoner. He insisted I turn her over to them immediately."

Polian's heart sank, and he blurted, "General, the ferrents are goons. They'll kill that prisoner without learning a thing!"

Gill snorted. "Major, do you really think I'd undercut an officer of mine? On a matter I know dick about? I told him I'd sleep on it."

"Oh. Thank you, sir."

"Don't thank me, Major. Just don't leave me uninformed again. Polian, an intelligence staff officer's job is to suspect everything and to predict the future. A commander's job is to listen to his staff, then *make* the future. Son, from now on I'll do the operational commanding, and you suspect and predict. Fair enough?"

"Yes, sir." Polian slumped, relieved.

Gill nodded. "Alright, then. Major, speaking as my staff intelligence officer, what's the single most important thing I need to do right now?"

Polian drew back. "Oh. Uh. Well, I'd continue to keep the woman prisoner away from the ferrents. Their techniques could spoil her value."

"What value does she have?"

"I think she's a Trueborn spy."

Gill raised his eyebrows. "A Trueborn? Here? You think the Trueborns would risk meddling in Tressel politics again? The Tilt was decades ago, and half the outworlds still hate 'em for it."

"Sir, what we're attempting here can reverse the balance of the Cold War. If Earth even suspects that, they couldn't risk *not* meddling."

"The Interior Police say the woman's just a suicidal Iridian rebel who shot two careless infantrymen. They also say that you commandeered a Tressen warship on a hunch, to chase some Iridian fishermen."

Polian stiffened and nodded. "Sir, the woman was wearing Eternad armor."

"So are half the crooks and insurgents in the Union. The black market's lousy with it."

Polian shook his head. "She was too competent to have been a local. And the fishermen spoofed our sensors. Iridians shouldn't have been that sophisticated."

Gill narrowed his eyes. "As I heard it, they dumped a half-dead fish in the water and we chased it. How sophisticated is that?"

Polian swallowed. "Also, I saw . . . I think I saw another person in the fishing boat. Also wearing Eternads. Trueborn case officers operate in pairs. And we intercepted the boat near the track of the Trueborn cruiser's orbital dip, which is where the fishing boat would have been if it was rendezvousing with a Trueborn fast mover."

Gill raised his palm. "Or if it was fishing. The woman was captured fifteen hundred miles away from whoever you saw."

Polian shook his head again. "Sir, one way to resolve this is to get her to talk. One of our interrogation specialists is part of the team that downshipped with you. I've seen the ferrents in action. If they work her over first, there won't be a mind left to interrogate."

Gill crossed his arms, then extended a bony hand and rubbed his chin. "Major, the Trueborns say 'finders, keepers.' What if I tell that Tressen cop that we found her, so we're keeping her?"

Polian grinned. "Thank you, sir." Then he frowned. "But the ferrents won't like it."

"Son, if I had spent my career doing what idiots liked, I'd be behind a desk wearing another leaf."

"If you say so, sir."

The general turned back and stared at the skimmers. "How about you show me what I'm in command of? Besides these tubs."

"I thought you might want a tour, sir. I took the liberty of arranging one. How soon do you want to leave?"

Gill rubbed his parchment cheeks with both hands and yawned. "I'm an old man, and I have been in travel status too long. By the look of you, you're a young man but you have, too. Let's both get some sleep. We'll leave in the morning."

Thirty-two

The sun had already set when Alia and I jumped over the side into knee-deep water, while Pyt manned the boat's tiller. We tied lines to two charred posts that had once been a dock.

Since we had left the ambush of an ambush that never happened, we had dodged through a maze of rock-walled canyons without incident. I had assumed that our course had carried us farther inland. In fact, we had run parallel to the coast, and this place was an inlet, so close to the sea that I could hear ocean waves break in the distance.

Alia and I unloaded my gear and piled it fifty yards from the shoreline. I shucked my Eternads in favor of local clothing that I borrowed from Pyt. My outfit comprised baggy cloth trousers and a buttoned shirt, a pocketed vest, and hide boots that would have been comfortable if they had fit.

Trueborns were by definition alien and by reputation assholes already. Case officers tried to minimize those disadvantages in first meet-ups by going as native as the situation allowed.

I also unloaded the diamonds, a day pack filled with basics, and a sidearm. Then I left Alia to camo the cache with moss while I went and sat with Pyt.

I wanted to know where we were, and why. But it had been a long and exhausting time since I fell out of the sky. Pyt and I sat silent and cross-legged, ate, and rested while Tressel's only moon rose and began its brief dash across the night sky. I watched Alia as she scurried back and forth, collecting moss, arranging, than rearranging it. "She's a good kid."

Pyt sipped tea. "The best."

"She's almost been killed three times since I met her. Why would you involve an eleven-year-old girl in something like this?"

"It takes two to sail the boat, especially if one has just half a hand. Iridia has too few grown sons left. Besides, she insisted."

I snorted. "She's a child. You could have said no."

Pyt set his mug down in the moss and shook his head. "Jazen, if an Iridian owes a blood favor, the obligation passes to the legacy. Alia's family saved my life."

"Oh." I cocked my head. "Alia said you wouldn't tell her what happened to her parents. It sounds like something heroic happened. Why should that be a secret?"

Pyt stared at the ground while he answered me. "The situation is very complex."

I nodded. "Right." It was a crappy, evasive answer. No crappier or more evasive than what Howard Hibble wouldn't tell me about *my* parents. And I didn't have time to deal with complex collateral crap here and now.

One hundred yards from the two of us, atop a rise that

must have had a terrific view, angular piles of stone shone black, lit in animate shadows by the racing moon.

I pointed at the stone piles. "That was a building once. What is this place?"

Pyt said, "The last place on Tressel where the Tressens would look for us."

"That's a good place to be. But why?"

He turned a full circle, pointing into the darkness. "They think this place frightens and shames Iridians."

I wrinkled my forehead and shrugged. "It's quiet. It's pretty."

"It was meant to teach us a lesson. Jazen, this was—is—Cella."

I nodded and whistled. Cella had been the home of the grand dukes of Northern Iridia. The castle had served as the seat of Iridian government for six centuries. It had symbolized everything that Iridians loved about their land and their way of life. Its image was even on Iridian money.

We sat in an elongate, weathered depression perhaps eight feet wide and two feet deep. The depression stretched away into the darkness in both directions. It was overgrown with the local moss that passed for grass. I scuffed the moss with my boot toe and turned up a corroded cartridge case. "This was one of the siege trenches?"

Pyt nodded. "The rains collapsed them years ago."

After the Tressens, with Trueborn help, won the last war between the Tressens and the Iridians, the Tressens had occupied Iridia. They also denied Iridians the right to own property, the right to procreate more Iridians, and the right to vote. Voting's no big deal in a dictatorship, but the other stuff rankled the Iridians.

The Tressens knew that the difference between a rankled mob and an effective rebellion is leadership. Therefore, they hanged the sitting grand duke of Iridia, ending a benign patriarchy that had been stable for six centuries. The Tressens also took over Cella. This was supposed to decapitate any potential rebellion. But the Iridians stole their duke's body back. The Tressens responded to this act of defiance by rounding up and exterminating all the Iridians they could lay hands on. What followed, as the Trueborns say, was history.

The history chips mark the beginning of the organized Iridian Rebellion as the day that Iridian rebels stormed and retook Cella. Celline, the last duke's maiden daughter, led them. Celline thus became the first duchess of Iridia in six hundred years who did more than christen ships and throw alms to the poor from a balcony, while her duke ran the country.

Pyt stood, and I followed him up the rise to the castle's ruins. He knelt in front of the first half-buried granite block we came to, laid his forehead against the stone, closed his eyes, and sobbed.

I bowed my head, too, but watched him from the corner of one eye.

Celline's rebellion had begun well, with the symbolic reoccupation of Cella. However, the Tressens had a knack for nipping stuff in the bud. They marched an expeditionary force of two full divisions to Cella, surrounded it, and laid siege. Cella's defenders, ill equipped and outnumbered four hundred against twenty thousand, vowed to die rather than surrender.

The Tressens were happy to oblige them. But the

Iridians defended the castle with skill and courage for fifty-one days. Three thousand Tressen troops died retaking Cella, which reduced their happiness. Therefore, the Tressens publicly mutilated the Iridian defenders' bodies. Then they hung them from Cella's spires and blew the place to rubble. Then they burned the rubble.

Afterward, the Tressen troops took turns urinating on the smoldering ashes. Apparently, in Iridian religion, that prevents dead souls from entering the afterlife. Nice touch.

After a minute, Pyt stood, stared at the ground, and wiped his eyes. "This is consecrated ground to an Iridian. Do you know what was done here?"

"I do. They were very brave." Actually, they were more than brave. Martyrs usually get nothing for their sacrifice but remembered. But the stand made by Cella's defenders diverted and tied up the Tressen expeditionary force for almost two months. That allowed Celline, who, to the Tressen's dismay, turned out to have left Cella, to organize a proper rebellion. It persisted for decades, an everlasting carbuncle on the Tressen body politic.

The rebellion's persistence, I supposed, was why Howard had used whatever feeble contacts Earth still had on Tressel to entice some Iridian rebels to pluck me from the sea and bring me to Celline. In the absence of a proper indigenous intelligence apparatus on Tressel, I was supposed to persuade Celline to help us crack the Yavi-Tressen plot, and, if feasible, determine the fate of my predecessor case officer.

Thus the diamonds. Frankly, my spook and Legion experience had taught me that idealistic insurgents wouldn't trust a meddling superpower just for money. If all you brought rebels was diamonds, they would likely take them, then run. Or take them, then kill you. Too many case officers had learned that lesson the hard way.

But Howard Hibble was supposed to be the premier genius of espionage poker in human history, and I was just a GI schooled by hard knocks. So if Howard thought Celline's cooperation could be bought for diamonds alone, I had to play the card that Howard had dealt me.

However, I couldn't even try to bribe Celline until I found her.

I looked around at the so-called rendezvous. The night was still, except for insect thrum and distant wave rumble. If the most important Iridian alive was nearby, where were the sentries? I had been lied to enough in my life to know that Pyt had lied to me about what happened to Alia's parents. I began to wonder again about Pyt and Alia's bona fides. Whatever local asset of Howard's had contacted them had probably been naive. Certainly, the asset had been untrained. Had we been spoofed by imposters? Were these two just swindlers out to score a handful of diamonds?

I eyed my 'puter. "Pyt, you're supposed to be helping me. How long do I have to wait?"

He snorted. "The Trueborns were supposed to help Iridia. We're still waiting."

My doubts resurged. Even if Pyt and Alia were rebels rather than petty crooks, Howard Hibble had pinned Earth's hopes on my gaining the trust of a people whom Earth had sold out. Twice.

Not that Howard had a better option. Earth's intel

apparatus on most outworlds was awful. On Tressel, it was nonexistent.

Earth's outworld intelligence gap had arisen logically enough. On Earth, modern nations spied on one another by electronic eavesdropping, by database hacking, and by delegating hands-on rough stuff to remote 'bots. Live spying was a lost art.

But outworld cultures like Tressel's barely had telephone wires to tap. They certainly had no 'puters to hack. If you wanted their secrets, somebody had to break into a file cabinet and take them. It was easier to train a human case officer to pick a lock than it was to program 'bots for the operational nuances of five hundred different worlds. And cheaper. Which, in the post-war fever to cut defense budgets, counted for more.

So, on the outworlds, the Trueborns had relearned to spy the old fashioned way. Routine on-planet gathering was handled by spooks who posed as embassy officials, and as business travelers. These imposters recruited and handled sources among the locals.

Rough or sneaky stuff was left to a new generation of human blunt instruments, case officers like Kit Born and even me. We got briefed, imported into a situation, then we worked with intel and logistic support from each planet's permanent embassy spooks. We did whatever we were ordered to do, then we got out. Some places the system worked.

But on Tressel, Earth had shut down its embassy and cut trade ties years before. This was supposed to harshly punish the Tressen butchery. To me, helping the butchered by abandoning them to the butchers seemed idiotic. Maybe that's why I was a blunt instrument, not a diplomat.

The diplomatic quarantine of Tressel, breached only by a trickle of "humanitarian" contacts, left the planet cut off, blind and deaf about the rest of the universe. But the quarantine reciprocally left the Union's sole superpower blind and deaf about Tressel. And so I was left to depend on one-handed Pyt and eleven-year-old Alia.

"Your stuff's all ashore, Jazen." Alia walked up the rise to us, boots dripping.

I turned to Pyt. "Now what?"

"Now we take you to Celline. In return for which you give us clean diamonds."

Pyt led Alia and me past the ruins, away from the water, and down into a rocky valley. The moon set, and in the suddenly black night Pyt and Alia lit torches to light the way. Without snoops, I needed the light as much as they did.

We descended the valley for five miles, by my pace count, until Pyt halted us at a rock overhang. The gap beneath the overhang was filled by overgrown cut stone. A rusted iron gate blocked the wall's only opening.

Pyt handed his torch to Alia, who held it while Pyt manipulated the gate latch.

When Pyt tugged the gate open, the metal screech echoed in the darkness.

I had to crouch as I followed Pyt down the passage that led away from the gate. The flickering torchlight lit walls scarred by tools. The passage was more mine shaft than cave. A hundred yards in, the passage widened and its ceiling rose, so high that the torchlight didn't illuminate it.

Cool air that fluttered the torch flames told me there was another way out.

Dim shapes hunched in the darkness, stretching away in a double row. Pyt walked to the first one and held his torch above it. The thing was a waist-high granite box ten feet long, with a carved lid.

Pyt said. "This is the crypt of the dukes of Iridia. We came in through the original entrance. You are looking at the sarcophagus of the first duke."

"The history books don't mention this place."

Pyt shook his head. "Iridia's been at war with Tressen off and on for six centuries. Family crypts are private places."

"Ah." I nodded. If I were a God-fearing Iridian with hopes for the afterlife, I wouldn't want Tressens peeing on my grave, either.

Alia and Pyt led on up the center aisle, torches held high, with me trailing behind in the dark. We walked between two rows of sarcophagi, the fifty-six dukes of Iridia on our left and their duchesses on our right. Our breathing and footfalls echoed off the chamber walls.

The stonework became more ornate and skillful the farther we went, as the dukes got richer, the coffin makers more skilled, and their tools and materials more sophisticated. At about three hundred years before the present, the sarcophagus lids began to bear carved, reclining likenesses of their occupants.

The more I thought about it, the more secure this meeting place seemed. Obviously, the Tressens didn't know it was here, or it would have been razed years ago. There were apparently at least two ways out, and the narrow, echoing entry passages prevented approaches by bad guys in numbers, or without warning. So Celline and her infrastructure might be competent, after all.

My step picked up. It was easier to persuade competents than fools. If I could persuade her, I might find Kit after all. I might even accomplish my mission for Howard.

Things were looking up.

When we reached the casket of Duke fifty-six, the one whose hanging precipitated the rebellion, I realized that I had been counting the ducal caskets to my left as we walked.

I also realized that the row of duchess caskets to my right didn't end.

Hair stood on my neck as Pyt passed his torch above the fifty-seventh casket in the duchess's row.

The sarcophagus's lid was set with the alabaster death mask of a young woman, hands folded across her chest. Where the prior duchesses held dainty carved stone bouquets, or jeweled scepters, the young woman clasped the hilt of a simple broadsword.

My jaw hung open as I squinted from the sarcophagus lid to Pyt and back. "What the hell? Are you telling me—"

"Our arrangement was to take you to see Celline. Here she is. We've performed fully."

I stood in the darkness, sputtering. "I—she's dead? Celline's a fucking mythic figurehead?"

"Hardly a myth."

"When did she die?"

Pyt paused, glanced sideways. "Years ago. The rebellion would have died with her if the word had gotten out."

I stepped back deeper into the shadows and leaned against Duke fifty-six's casket. Pyt was right. Morale-wise, one living legend is worth a thousand pep talks. But if there was no Celline to direct a rebellion, there was no Celline for me to persuade. And without her live leadership, reports of the health of the Iridian rebellion were probably overstated anyway. All I had seen of that rebellion was these two.

I stared at Pyt and Alia. "Then are you just a couple of diamond thieves, after all?"

Alia stepped toward me, chest out. "We're patriots, not thieves."

I pointed from Pyt to Alia. "Assuming I believe that, do you two have a network? Eyes and ears to help me locate another Trueborn agent on Tressel?"

They stood mute. Of course they didn't.

I sighed, then held out the diamond case to Alia. "Here. Not that you've earned 'em. But before you die, you might as well meet one guy who keeps his promises."

Alia narrowed her eyes. "What about the coating, Jazen?"

I shook my head. "The coating's phony. Just like your warrior queen. The diamonds are fine."

Alia's lower lip stuck out. "You lied to us. Heroes don't lie."

"*You* lied to *me*! Everybody lies, Alia. Welcome to life."

Pyt said, "I'm sorry, Jazen."

"Sorry?" I threw my hands up in the darkness. "What do I do now? I need intelligence, not transgenerational con men." I sat cross-legged on the floor in the dark and rubbed my forehead. I could leave these two and find a safe open spot to lay out my phone-home panels. With luck I'd be on my way off this clown show of a rock within a couple of months.

Alia opened her mouth, but Pyt shushed her.

Or I could retrace my steps, then stumble around this planet on my own looking for Kit until my accent and my incompetence got me killed.

I stood and shifted the sidearm at my waist. "See you two around."

"No, Jazen!" Alia stepped toward me as I turned, and the light of her torch fell across my face for the first time.

From the darkness, a woman's voice gasped.

I froze there in the torchlight.

After four heartbeats the voice said, "Who *are* you?"

Thirty-three

Just before midnight on the day after Polian had met General Gill, the two of them dismounted from the Tressen military two-car train that had brought them north on steel rails from the capital. Ice Line Station, on Tressen's flat, frigid northern prairie, marked the end of that line. The place was just a huddle of huts, windows dark in the night, that existed only because at this place one railroad ended and another began.

Along with a half-dozen Yavi commandos, Polian and Gill stepped off onto a wind-scoured iron transfer platform that bridged the space between the train that had carried them north and the train aboard which they would continue their journey.

Oil lamps suspended beneath the platform canopy swayed in the wind, and the lamps threw elongate shadows into the dark beyond the platform.

All the men lumbered, bundled in civilian Tressen winter wear. Their armor and two skimmers were loaded, beneath tarps, on the flatcar behind the train's passenger coach.

Polian walked along the platform, pointing with a blunt mitten at the spiked wheels of the new train's engine while he leaned toward the general to be heard above the wind. He lectured the general, who walked a pace back, hands clasped behind his back. Beyond the ice train's black bulk, the frozen river, the riverbank, and the sky merged into a monochrome ebony wall.

Polian said to Gill, "North of here—the Ice Line—the Tressens don't lay rails. The rivers are frozen as hard as iron three-fourths of the year, and the mines are inoperable during melt season, anyway. So these locomotives tow sledges on tracks cut in the ice."

Gill turned back to the first train as the Tressen platform crew and the commandos rolled the covered skimmers' cargo pallets across the platform and onto the transfer train's waiting flat sledge.

Gill shook his head. "Mag levs on wheels. Straight off a history chip."

Polian continued, "Our new train will head north at first light and take us a hundred miles farther. The last hundred miles can only be covered by skimmer."

Chains rattled in the darkness as the commandos locked the skimmers down on their new flatcar.

Gill squinted into the featureless blackness that surrounded them. "So we travel in daylight. Any sights to see along the way?"

Polian stared into the night. "Yes. Unfortunately."

Thirty-four

My heart skipped at the sound of the woman's voice. Pyt and Alia had led me into a trap. I reached down and unsnapped my sidearm holster's flap.

Before my pistol cleared its holster, the crackle of released rifle safeties echoed off the dark Iridian crypt's walls. A half-dozen men seemed to materialize from the darkness and formed a semicircle around me, rifles aimed at my head. One stepped forward and pressed a knife long enough to be a sword against my throat while he twisted the sidearm out of my holster.

My pistol clattered on the crypt's rock floor.

Only then did a silhouette glide out of the shadows toward me. The woman was as tall as I was, slim and athletic. She wore a simple battle-dress uniform, trousers bloused over boots, and a single ammunition bandolier crossed her chest. Her hair was blonde and pulled back, and I guessed she was in her forties. Her eyes were even more bright emerald than Pyt's or Alia's, and she carried herself with that confidence common to Trueborns but uncommon in outworlders. When she turned her head, her silhouette against the torchlight matched the profile of the young woman whose stone image adorned the sarcophagus. I smiled in spite of my predicament. Reports of the death of the fifty-seventh duchess were exaggerated.

Pyt stepped toward her and dropped his head. "Ma'am."

She flicked a hand, motioning him closer. He whispered in her ear.

She stared at me with those big eyes, her chin elevated. In fatigues and over forty, she was a knockout. She must have been a goddess at her coming-out party.

She said, "Lieutenant Jazen Parker. Pyt says that you're odd for a Trueborn."

I stood motionless, then swallowed, and the blade's steel pressed against my Adam's apple. Head back, I croaked, "I wouldn't believe much Pyt says. He also told me you were dead. Ma'am."

She smiled. "It can be a convenient fiction."

"Yep. You could've had the diamonds for nothing and been rid of me."

She glanced at the rifles pointed at me. "We still can."

I shifted my weight, and the blade at my throat scraped unshaved whiskers. "We need help. It's in your interest to help us."

She smiled. "Forgive my skepticism. Iridians have met few Trueborns they could trust."

"Me, too."

She raised her eyebrows and half smiled. "That sounds familiar."

I wrinkled my forehead. "I—why?"

She waved away the man who held a knife to my throat.

He frowned, then withdrew his blade and stepped back with a nod. "Yes, ma'am."

Celline leaned toward me and squinted.

I rubbed my throat. "What *is* it?"

She stepped back and glanced over at the man who had held the knife to my throat. "Can we make it across the Corridor at the appropriate time, Captain?"

"Of course, ma'am. We always have."

"I mean if we take Lieutenant Parker here with us. He's favoring a shoulder, and limping."

The captain eyed me. "That would be a question for our guest, ma'am."

She looked me up and down. "I would bet he has a foot soldier's genes."

It was an odd way to phrase a vote of confidence.

I pointed at the captain. He was as gray as Pyt and probably older. "I can keep up with *him*, if that's what you mean."

The captain frowned. "We'd best move out, then, ma'am."

She stared at me again and sighed. "This isn't the time or the place to get to know you, Lieutenant Jazen Parker."

After a hundred yards by my pace count, down a tunnel that led away from the crypt, we emerged into the now-moonless darkness of a cool Iridian night.

Within the first hundred yards I regretted my representation of fitness. My shoulder remained worse than expected, the Iridian boots were hell, and Celline's troops double-timed when the terrain and light allowed. Sandwiched front and back by two troops with sidearms, I struggled.

I didn't know where we were going, or why. I didn't know who my captors were, though I had a pretty good idea.

But at least my potential ally was alive, and so was I. Unless the pace killed me. Or my potential ally did.

Thirty-five

Polian turned his back to the wind that had screeched unchecked across a hundred miles of drifted snow, all the way from Tressel's North Pole. He flapped his arms against his Tressen overcoat. However comfortable Tressen clothing otherwise was, it was impossible to keep warm up here in the stuff. Sheep, and wool, still lay eons in Tressel's future.

He stepped into the wind shadow thrown by the ice train's now-still locomotive. The train had reached its northern limit as surely as his overcoat had. It was impossible to travel any farther in any conveyance the Tressens had yet invented.

He watched his men—now they were Gill's men, from a chain-of-command standpoint—unload and prep the skimmers. Meanwhile, the Tressens bustled around the train that had brought them all this far.

Polian and Gill stepped inside a frigid shed and began changing into heated armor for the trip. The skimmers' thin, retractable canopies were designed to keep sun and rain out, not heat in.

Gill's limbs quivered like parchment-swathed branches beneath his underlayer as he tugged on his armor. He gazed out the shed window. Beyond the complex of drifted-over sheds that formed the Northern Terminus of the ice-train railroad, the train that had brought them blasted its whistle and began to move south with a fresh crew.

Gill pointed at the train as it rolled away. "That train's going back empty. You said the iron mines are south of here. So why does this place exist?"

Polian's teeth chattered as he pointed past the sheds at the never-melted snow. "No function, today. Years ago, this is where the Tressens brought the Iridian troublemakers." There was, Polian remembered, a Tressen saying that the only Iridian who didn't make trouble was a dead one. "After the war, Iridians were forced from their lands and told they were being relocated north to settle the northern wilderness. That was a raw deal. But about what the Iridians expected from the Tressens. They boarded the trains grudgingly, but they boarded. Of course, they would have balked at the truth."

"What was the truth?"

"The Tressens hauled the Iridians up here by the trainload, like cattle. Then they dumped them into fenced-off compounds in the snow without food, water, or shelter. The Iridians died of exposure, dehydration, starvation. There was a macabre efficiency to it. All it took was enough personnel at this end to assure the trains could be turned around, and to keep the Iridians inside the fences until nature killed them."

Gill stared into the darkness, and Polian wondered what he was thinking.

Polian said, "The Tressens didn't even need to bury the bodies. They just let the wind cover them with snow. If our train had stopped during the last sixty miles, you couldn't have walked a hundred feet from the tracks without tripping over a corpse."

"This is the graveyard of a nation?" It was cold, but Gill shivered visibly.

Polian nodded. "When the bodies filled up one compound, the Tressens just extended the ice road a bit farther north and fenced off a new compound. Nobody at the south end had any idea what was going on because this place is so inaccessible."

Gill sighed. "Did you ever wonder whether we're so different, Major?"

Polian stared at his new boss. If you have more people than resources, why waste the latter growing the former to adulthood? An overquota Yavi terminated at birth wasted no resources and created minimal societal entanglements. That wasn't cruel. It was basic civics to every Yavi. Especially to Yavi like Polian, whose father, the vice cop, terminated Illegals daily. When you thought about it, Iridians were just Illegals who had already consumed more than their share.

Polian and Gill buckled into their skimmer seats, and the skimmer's relief driver pulled the compartment door shut behind them. The hovercraft's starter whined, then it rose and wobbled in the wind.

Polian wrinkled his brow as he stared out at glistening white snow and steel-blue sky. It almost seemed like Gill questioned the basic morality of the society he had defended for all his life.

Well, if Gill did question Yavi society, that was more than the Trueborns did with Trueborn society. Their blindness to their own idiocy took away an impartial observer's breath. An "inalienable right" to life was not only absurd, it begat chaos. Idiots begat more idiots. Trueborns thought they dominated the Union because they were just, but the truth was that they were just lucky.

The driver backed the skimmer off the platform, spun it around, and idled two feet above the crusted snow. The escort skimmer, bearing the protective troops, fell in behind them, then the little convoy shot north across the barren whiteness.

Polian gazed out through the skimmer's side curtain as the featureless snow whisked past. The nations of Earth still fought among themselves. The Trueborns allowed idiots to beget idiots; then the productive parts of Trueborn society supported them. Worse, because they were lucky enough to control interstellar travel, the Trueborns exported their idiots and their idiocy.

Polian sat back, let the skimmer's vibration lull him, and smiled. Well, the Trueborns' luck was about to change.

Thirty-six

The Iridian rebel column of which I had become an unwelcome part marched like foot cavalry until the first pale light of Tressel's sun diluted the darkness. As it became brighter, I could see that they were aging foot cavalry, but spry for geezers.

We halted suddenly, by which time my borrowed boots had raised, then broken, blisters on both my feet. I estimated by pace count that we had moved inland fourteen miles.

Alia, who had been tasked to lead three soldiers back to retrieve, then carry, my gear, came and knelt alongside me while I sat on a rock and tugged off one of my Iridian boots.

The brushy knoll atop which we had halted offered some cover. I looked out across the dimly visible broad valley that stretched away to our north and south and swung my hand. "Is this the Bloody Corridor?"

Alia cocked her head. "How do you know about the Corridor?"

"I did my homework. That's what you should be doing. Not playing soldier."

"I'm not playing!" She turned away and crossed her arms.

According to the case brief, the naked, jumbled rock terrain that comprised the Iridian coastaI zone was a fifteen-mile-wide maze of flooded channels and jumbled ridges and canyons. It stretched north all the way to the Barrens, and the swamp's natural barrier defined part of the Iridian-Tressen boundary. The inland portion of northern Iridia was a plateau carpeted with impenetrable tree-fern forests.

A single, mile-wide rift valley, the Iridian Corridor, bisected Iridia at the transition between the coastal zone and the Iridian Central Plateau.

After the war, when the Tressens needed a railroad to bring oppressors in to Iridia and take spoils out, they chose the easiest route, which was down the Corridor's flat, unforested center.

Emerging industrial cultures live and die by their railroads. The Trueborns fought incessant internecine wars that they misnamed "civil." Jefferson Davis, a warlord during one of them, had observed that an invading army dangles within an invaded country like a spider, suspended from the slender thread of the supply line that connects it to its home. In Davis's America, and in post-war Iridia, steel rails, not silk, formed that fragile thread.

The Iridian rebels hid in the forests of the Iridian Plateau, from which they raided the Tressen railroad, cut the spider's thread, then disappeared. In response, the Tressens built a string of fortified strongpoints up and down the railroad. At first, the fortified line was there to protect the railroad, and to split Iridia in two, with the interior cut off from the sea. Later, the strongpoints served as bait. The Tressens tried to draw the dwindling rebel army into set-piece battles, by which the Tressens could bleed it. The conventional wisdom was that every yard of what came to be called the Bloody Corridor was a death trap. That was probably hyperbole, but I wasn't looking forward to crossing a mile of open ground to prove it.

Nonetheless, ten minutes later I had my boots back on, and our platoon-sized unit dispersed in a line along the brushy ridge, crouched, and waited.

As the dawn trickled light across the Corridor, I saw the railroad, no more than a fragile black ribbon, a half mile to our front, laid across a mossy plain. A half mile beyond the rails the ground sloped upward to the Plateau's still-dark and welcome forest.

The Corridor was heavily fortified at points where rebel attacks had succeeded in the past, and at bottlenecks where repairs to destroyed track would be difficult. This place was neither, just a slightly narrow section of the valley. Today, Celline wanted safe passage, not a fight.

I fidgeted and whispered to Alia, "Okay. I know that you're not playing. We're going to cross a mile of open ground in a line, to minimize our exposure time. But every minute we wait, it gets lighter. Why?"

"Celline knows what she's doing." Alia cupped a hand behind her ear. "Listen."

Whooo.

The distant steam whistle echoed, faint and on our right.

Six minutes later, a five-car Tressen armored train chugged past us, headlight burning a yellow hole in the dark, trailing an inky snake of black smoke spewed by the moss-refined oil that powered Tressen civilization. Behind the locomotive and tank tender rumbled an iron-riveted, enclosed troop car. An armored, manned guard turret whiskered with machine guns grew from the car's roof like an angular wart. Behind the troop cars trundled two empty flatcars, their decks ajangle with tie-down chains.

Likely, on some days, the flatcars carried armored cars that could be ramped off to chase down items of interest—such as us—that the train's lookouts spotted on its morning run to clear the corridor for the day's traffic.

My heart pounded. Even without mech support, the troops on that train, and their heavier weapons, would cut Celline's merry band into fish bait if they spotted us.

Alia pointed to our left, in the direction the train was bound. "The train stops every morning three miles south, at the strongpoint beyond that rise. The train brings hot breakfast and mail. Any patrol that might have spotted us will have turned for home as soon as they heard the whistle. That's why we cross here."

The strength of regular armies was disciplined adherence to established procedure. The weakness of regular armies was that irregular armies turned that strength against them.

The train vanished over the rise, and the rebels, Alia, and I were off at a dead run, downslope in the half light, each soldier maintaining separation and depth with the soldiers on his flanks. Occasionally, a section leader would slow or speed up an element with a hand signal.

Trueborn infantry still were instructed in troop movement without intra-unit radios, but I doubted that the average contemporary grunt could get out of his own way without a noncom in his ear.

Every trooper hit the gravel roadbed within a five-second interval, and the formation slowed for a heartbeat while we trued the line.

As we paused on the elevated roadbed, I wrinkled my nose and asked Alia, "What stinks?"

She pointed between the cross ties, at a litter of rotted fish flesh and bone. "The trains that go north carry fish to make fertilizer for Tressen. The railroad always smells like this."

We crossed the tracks and ran, maybe faster to escape the smell, and were in among the fern trees on the opposite slope ten minutes later, without incident.

Two miles into the woods we stopped again. My feet screamed, my lungs burned, and I bent, hands on knees, gasping, while the unit set a defensive perimeter.

In contemporary warfare, regular infantry, with their sensory advantage, own the night and laager up by day. On most outworlds the situation was reversed. Darkness was the irregulars' friend, not the regulars'. We would laager here for the day.

Fine by me.

Celline's troops dug fighting holes, then settled down in them to eat and sleep in shifts. Our defensive position had been well chosen, in a thicket so dense that a dragonfly, much less a Tressen, couldn't have walked within fifty yards without being heard. I dug a hole anyway.

Nobody offered to share trilobite jerky, which didn't

hurt my feelings. I hotted up a Meal Utility Desiccated, salved my blisters, shot up my shoulder, and slept for three hours.

"A word, Lieutenant Parker?"

I woke to see Celline bent, hands on knees, over me.

I sat up, rubbed my face. "Sure. Yes, ma'am."

We walked to a trickling stream that lay within the defensive perimeter but out of earshot of the others.

The duchess sat on a flat rock and motioned me to sit on one across from her.

The afternoon was warm, and dragonflies hummed at a distance, just loud enough to be heard above the gurgle of water over the stones.

She rested her elbow on a raised knee and cupped her chin in her hand. "What am I going to do with you?"

I had expected some diplomatic foreplay. On Earth I saw a holomentary about the queen of England meeting commoners. Mostly she asked them where they were from. I cleared my throat. "Grant me a favor, I hope. Ma'am."

"The favors Iridia has done for the Trueborns in the past were repaid with treachery."

I squirmed on my rock. She had the diamonds, which would buy a lot of boots and ammunition, but the deal had been that they earned me an audience, not a favor. A case officer's first rule vis-à-vis local allies was that a deal was a deal. The second rule was to find something you and your host could agree on.

"I understand, ma'am. Where I grew up nobody trusted the Trueborns, either."

"Oh. Tell me about where you grew up."

I sat back. Suddenly our negotiation had regressed into

small talk. Maybe the custom in Iridia was that the monarch small-talked later, rather than sooner.

What to say about my heritage? There are two kinds of Yavi Illegals. Those who lie about it and dead ones. But one reason I had quit the spook business was because I was tired of lying. I leaned forward, hands on knees. "I was born on Yavet."

She cocked her head, frowned. "You look—I find that hard to believe, Lieutenant."

"I look Trueborn because my parents were Trueborns."

She sat back and smiled. "I find that easy to believe." She nodded.

I said, "But we were separated when I was born. I've never met them."

Her eyes softened. "That must have devastated your father."

My *father*? I snorted. "It was no picnic for *me*. The midwife who delivered me raised me, hid me downlevels because I was an Illegal. I finally joined the Legion to dodge the vice cops. After the Legion, I fell into a hitch as a Trueborn case officer. Turned out that the King of the Spooks had served with my father."

The duchess's jaw dropped. Then she nodded. "Ah. Yes. The King of the Spooks. It all makes sense now. Hibble is so—the Trueborns have a word—Byzantine."

It was my turn to drop my jaw. "You know Howard?"

"For too long. Though indirectly. Jazen, are you aware that an Iridian who owes a blood favor to a father owes it to the son as well?"

I nodded. Like Pyt owed Alia. "Yes, ma'am, I heard that." I wrinkled my brow. "Are you saying . . . ?"

"I owe Jason Wander my life, and more."

I sat there, still and silent while the dragonflies droned.

The "unique qualifications" for which Howard Hibble had re-recruited me were my genes. I was the only available Trueborn who still had a friend on Tressel. And an influential friend, at that.

I shook my head and muttered, "Howard, you devious rat bastard."

Celline threw back her head and laughed. "You sound just like your father. He said worse about Hibble. Often. You don't only *look* like Jason, you know."

"Honestly, ma'am, I barely knew *that*." I stared into the shadows. Rat bastard though he was, Howard had made good on his word back in Mousetrap. The answers I had needed all my life were here, at least some of them.

Celline leaned forward. "But you didn't come so far to listen to an old woman reminisce. How can I—how can we—help you?"

"I . . ." Actually, I ached to listen to her memories of my father. But she was right. Kit could die while Celline told me stories. Or the Yavi could take over the universe. I set my astonishment aside. "I need to find two more Trueborns. Case officers like me. We lost contact with them six weeks ago."

She nodded. "Where are they?"

I squirmed. "Honestly, I have no idea."

She raised her eyebrows. "This is a big world, Jazen. And my people are small within it."

I nodded. It was futile.

But she said, "Where do we begin?"

I rubbed my forehead. A good spook who didn't want

to be found wouldn't be found, and Kit Born was the best. But, like one of those invisible subatomic particles, a spook could sometimes be identified by the disturbance caused in the surrounding area. "See whether the Tressens have been looking for somebody, somebody unusual. Or if some other people, unusual people, have been looking."

She smiled. "The Tressens are always looking for somebody. But I take your point. We are few, but a few sets of eyes and ears still watch out on our behalf. How soon do you need to find your colleagues?"

I scratched my head. I had witnessed, in fact been the target of, a mechanized attack by Yavi military, operating openly off a Tressen warship. The Cold War between the Trueborns and the Yavi had stayed cold for decades because both sides honored delicate etiquette rules. The Yavi had just broken the rules worse than a food fight in church.

The Yavi wouldn't risk turning the Cold War into a hot war unless they were close to something huge. Especially a hot war that, without starships, Yavet could neither wage nor win.

I frowned at my new old friend and answered her pending question. "Ma'am, we need to find them yesterday."

Thirty-seven

Polian watched the Tressen sun creep along the arctic horizon, low and cold even at mid-morning, its glare veiled behind the snow fog boiling from the skimmer's skirt. As he watched, the skimmer crossed the red line of outermost sensor pickets, got pinged by the sentry equipment on the defensive perimeter, and sent back the day's response authentication.

If the planners had allowed him to equip the Tressens with proper equipment to begin with, the woman never would have gotten close enough to be a problem, either for Yavet or for him.

The long-coated sentries who flagged the skimmer down, ancient rifles at the ready, were still Tressen. Polian didn't trust the locals, but Yavi on dirt here remained too scarce to do without.

Four minutes later, the skimmer cleared inner-perimeter security, then greased to a stop alongside the main excavation. The driver turned to Polian; he nodded, and the skimmer sank onto the snow and shut down.

Almost before the engine vibration died, Gill was out and legging it through the snow, down into the pit, where the six Yavi combat engineers working the site were drawn up in a tiny rank at attention.

Polian caught up to Gill, then fell in behind him as the old soldier inspected the troops.

Gill stepped from one to the other and looked them up and down. Gill, visor up and breath fog curling in the Arctic cold, paused in front of one man, spoke, received a nod back and a laugh, then clapped the kid on an armored shoulder.

After Polian dismissed his men to return to their work, he turned to Gill. "What would the general like to know about our operation?"

Gill smiled at him. "Start with everything. Let the old man stop you if he's already heard it."

Polian stepped to soil mounded in the bucket of a hydraulic excavator, dug out a glassy, spherical stone the size of a bird's egg, and held it up between his thumb and forefinger. It glowed red with inner fire despite the waning daylight. "Cavorite. It took the Slugs three million years to discover and tame it. It took the Trueborns one war to steal and misname it."

Gill raised bushy eyebrows as he extended his palm. "What's wrong with the name?"

Polian dropped the stone into the general's glove, and the older man held it up to the sky as he turned it in his fingers.

Polian smiled. "It's named for a fictitious Earth metal that was supposed to block gravity."

Gill said, "But on Tressel this metal's for real?"

Polian shook his head. "No, sir. That is, cavorite's not metal, and it's not from Tressel, at least not originally. That stone's a meteorite that fell here as part of a shower forty thousand years ago."

"Fell from where?"

"That stone is the product of a collision between this universe and another universe that abuts this one. The core mote in that stone isn't metal. It isn't even matter. It doesn't block gravity. It *eats* it."

Gill stared at the stone. "And the mote generates the force that moves starships?"

"No, sir. Gravity is the force. One of the basic forces of this universe. Cavorite is antithetic to gravity." Polian took the stone back and turned it. "Right now, this stone, and all the matter in this universe, stays where it is because the gravitational forces generated by the mass of this universe act uniformly on it from all sides." Polian tipped his hand, and the unsupported stone fell to the snow. "If I take away the gravity pulling on one side of this stone, like I just took away my hand, the gravity of the rest of the universe pulls the stone the other way. Cavorite doesn't so much block gravity as it eats gravity."

Gill toed the stone in the snow. "Doesn't seem to be hungry just now."

Polian smiled as he stooped and retrieved the stone. "Modulating the removal and replacement of the shielding. Harnessing the power. That's the real secret of C-drive. It's the part that took the Slugs so long, sir."

"And only took the Trueborns the time required to steal it from the little maggots."

Polian nodded. "And the Trueborns inherited the only

source of propulsion-grade cavorite in the universe, to boot."

Polian swung his hand at the surrounding landscape. "But Bren's not the only source any more! These meteorites are sprinkled across an impact zone a hundred miles long. Clear back across the trace of the ice-train railroad we came north on. But the quality back there's unsuited for propulsion."

Gill narrowed his eyes. "How did we find this?"

"We didn't. Two years ago the Tressens approached one of our missionary teams with a sample that had been gathering dust in a mineral-specimen storeroom. The Tressens had literally stumbled across it when they built the ice-rail line."

"I'm surprised they knew what they had."

"Actually, they didn't. At the time the stuff was discovered, the Trueborns still had a diplomatic presence on Tressel. All the Tressens knew was that the Trueborns were inordinately nosy about this stuff."

Gill toed a stone in the snow again. "I take it there's more where this came from?"

Polian led them up out of the pit, scuffed the snow with his boot for thirty seconds, then bent and plucked up another stone slightly smaller than the first. "The bolides are very low density, and they struck the surface at a low angle. Some buried themselves, but sixty percent of them skidded, bounced, or barely dug in. They're literally scattered across the surface beneath the snow, even forty thousand years after they fell. When we arrived, we expected it would take months to evaluate the deposit. Then years more to mount a clandestine mining operation."

Gill rubbed his chin. "Major, what would the Trueborns do if they knew about this?"

"If I had their monopoly and found out that it was at risk, I'd go to war to preserve it."

Gill nodded. "I agree. And if you're right about this woman and the fellow in that boat, the Trueborns may be on the brink of finding out."

Polian dug another glowing stone from the snow, tossed it in his palm, then dropped it again. As he gazed back to the south, he sighed. Somewhere down there, he was convinced, a Trueborn who had slipped through his fingers like a cavorite stone was doing whatever he could to find out exactly.

Thirty-eight

Two days after my conversation with Celline, her group and I had settled in at one of a network of rebel camps that were hidden in the Central Plateau's forests. Celline shifted constantly among the camps, both to show the flag for her troops' morale and to minimize the possibility of her capture.

The camp nestled at the base of an overgrown escarpment peppered with shallow caves. The units in camp spent most of their time training, which didn't surprise me. What did surprise me was that there seemed to be half as many units as there were available billets, and most of the soldiers were so old that they didn't really seem to need training. One troop wasn't only younger, she got different training. Pyt tutored Alia daily in everything from algebra to written and spoken Iridian, which the Tressens had outlawed. He also taught her pugil-stick drill.

A modern army takes real-time communication and surveillance for granted. On Tressel information was exchanged slower, especially among the rebels. Celline had circulated urgent inquiries across the Iridians' human intelligence network, such as it was, looking for clues for me.

While I waited for intel returns, I hung out with the only other person on post who had free time and a juvenile streak. One afternoon, with Pyt's blessing, I chased Alia up a scree slope at the cliff base. I had told him I would give her some escape and evasion training. We were playing hide-and-seek, which, when I thought about it, was pretty much the same thing.

I scrambled to the junction where the scree met the cliff, panting, and realized that Alia had vanished.

Then I saw that beyond the scree the cliff tucked back into a cave's mouth fifty yards wide, a hundred yards deep, and twelve feet tall. More like the underlip of a ledge than a cave. I bent, hands on knees, and squinted into the dimness. I didn't see Alia, but I did see a jumble of unnatural shapes.

I shuffled into the darkness toward the closest object. It seemed to be an up-angled log, but the cavern smelled of old canvas, rusted metal, and oil. I reached out to the shape and touched not wood but steel, a horizontal, tapered tube as big around as my bicep.

I pulled out my pocket flash, which was cheating for hide-and-seek, but spies cheat all the time.

The thing I had touched was an old-fashioned, wood-spoke-wheeled, breech-loaded artillery rifle. I shone the flash around the cave and saw a jumble of military hardware. Water-cooled machine guns on tripods, their blunt muzzles angled toward the cavern's ceiling. More artillery pieces, hand-cranked wired field telephone kits. The back wall was piled to the ceiling with wooden packing crates, to the extent that I could see the back wall. The part I couldn't see was obscured by parked vehicles of various sizes, from two-wheeled gun caissons to rusting, boxy trucks.

Calling that scrap heap an armory was a stretch, but museum almost fit. Especially for a former tanker like me.

Alongside the trucks were parked four tanks. "Tanks" was as big a stretch as "armory." They closely resembled the first tracked armored vehicles, which on Earth were rolled out well over a century earlier, to break the stalemate in a trench war similar to the meat grinder that had ended with the rape of Iridia by Tressen.

The tanks' tracks stretched around rhombohedral flanks plated with riveted steel armor from which bulged sponsons set with side-firing cannon. I had seen holos, mostly remastered sepia-toned twodee motion pictures, but for a tanker to see one of these in the steel was like a paleontologist staring at a live dinosaur. I walked to the closest old crawler and rapped on its plating.

"Who's there?" Alia's giggle echoed from inside the dinosaur's belly.

"A tank driver."

The tank's main hatch, which was just a steel door set in the beast's flat flank, squealed, and Alia poked her head out. "You drove one of these?"

I walked to the machine's rear, and clambered up the forward-sloping rear tread like it was a shallow ladder. "I was a hovertanker. Hovertanks don't have tracks. They ride on an air cushion, like the skimmer that chased us. I've driven crawlers. But never any this old. Does the army ever use these?"

"They're museum pieces. Slow. Hard to maintain. Fuel is scarce. They're as useless as the rest of these supplies, because we've learned to avoid set-piece battles, anyway." It wasn't Alia who answered me, but Celline.

She stood silhouetted, hands on hips, against the bright light oval formed by the cave mouth.

I visored my hand above my eyes and blinked. "Alia was learning to hide."

Celline crouched so that she could peer at Alia over the tank's hull, then spoke not so much to me as to the girl. "I wish she were as good at Iridian grammar as she is at hiding." Celline stood and looked at me. "Jazen, I came looking for you because we've heard something back."

I leapt off the crawler's back and landed, crouching, on the cave's dirt floor. "Where is she? They."

Celline walked to the tank and laid one hand on the right six-pounder's barrel while she held her other hand out, palm down. "It's just raw information, Jazen. Nothing definite."

I raised my eyebrows. "Well? Ma'am."

She said, "A physician—a Tressen who was once married to an Iridian—on the staff of a clinic in Tressel occasionally assists us. He was treating a comatose woman who, he was told, had been struck by a lorry. He doubted that."

"Why?"

"An accident victim usually doesn't have an armed ferrent posted at the door to her room."

My heart skipped. "What do you mean, 'was' treating? Is she . . . ?"

"Alive, as far as the physician knows. He's no longer attending her. There was some sort of argument between the Interior Police and an anonymous man over her treatment. The man seemed influential."

"Why?"

"Only someone influential would dare argue with a ferrent, Jazen. Shortly after the argument, our friend the doctor was relieved from the case. The patient was moved to a more secure location within the clinic. And she was placed under heavier guard, by people who didn't look like ferrents."

I frowned. "Could this prisoner be just a routine criminal?"

"Perhaps. But the ferrents don't deal with routine crimes. And it's the only lead we have for you, so far."

"Then I need to talk to this physician."

Celline shook her head. "Just tell us what information you need. We'll send someone. You can't go. Not with your accent."

"What's my accent have to do with it?"

"You would certainly have to speak to someone."

"Why?"

"The clinic's not just in Tressen. It's in Tressia, the capital. In fact, it's in the Government Quarter, six blocks from ferrent headquarters. Interior Police on every other street corner check the identity papers of everyone who enters the Government Quarter."

"Then I'll go with whomever you were going to send, and they can do the talking. Ma'am, I don't just need to talk to the physician. If this is the person I'm looking for, I need to see this place if I'm going to make a plan that gets me in and gets me out of it."

Celline shook her head again. "If you go with one of our men, you would just endanger him more. We've heard that the Tressens are double-checking pairs of adults traveling together. A new protocol."

I puffed out a breath. "We can thank the Tressens' new buddies for that profile. The Yavi must have told them that Trueborn case officers come in sets of two."

Alia said, "They never check Pyt and me at all."

Eyes wide, I looked down at the girl, who had crawled out from beneath the ancient tank to stand beside us. "You've been to Tressia?"

Celline nodded. "Pyt's been traveling there for us for years. The Tressens tolerate a black market in medical supplies, which we need."

Well, that explained how "we" knew the doctor.

Celline laid her hand on Alia's head and smiled down at her. "Alia's presence can be disarming."

Using a child as a disguise seemed callous. But a child who grew up with a target on her back, the way I had grown up with a target on mine, accepted callous as normal. Undesirable, but normal.

I narrowed my eyes at Celline. "Tressia's nearly four hundred miles from here. If I hike fifty miles a day, it would still take a week. I don't have that long."

Alia shook her head. "Walk? We don't walk. We can get there and back in two days—"

"We?" I pointed from Alia to my chest and back. "We? This wouldn't be a shopping trip with old Pyt.

This will be dangerous. No!" I crossed my arms. Then I paused and cocked my head at Celline. "Did she say two days?"

Thirty-nine

Polian wrapped his hands around his warm tea mug as he stared from the clinic's empty visitor's lounge down the building's white-walled entry corridor. Three days had passed since he had briefed Gill in the snow-covered arctic pit, and during the entire return trip Polian had rarely even been chilly in his armor. But psychologically he craved the tea mug's warmth. The human mind convinced itself of things that weren't true. This morning, Polian was counting on that weakness.

The door guard unlocked, then opened, one of the translucent entry doors that spanned the corridor's far end. The door's hinge creak echoed through air that smelled of disinfectant as daylight flashed in.

A man dressed in Tressen civvies, tall even for Yavi military, stepped through sideways. The tall man wrestled a metal case with both hands, then set it down in the corridor and flexed his fingers while the guard closed and relocked the door. The man was slender, hawk-faced, and the echoes of his panting breath displaced the sound of the door lock clicking.

After a full minute, the man picked up the case again, walked down the corridor, and set the case down in front of Polian. "I lugged my equipment nine blocks from that damn boarding house. If you had put me up in a hotel commensurate with my rank I could have gotten a cab."

Polian sighed. A Medical Corps major had no rank as far as real officers were concerned. Polian shook his head at the interrogation specialist. "Every hotel desk clerk and cabbie in this city reports to the Interior Police. I don't want the ferrents to know you're here."

The interrogator pulled out a chair and reached for the teapot on the table.

A physician, in fact the one who had laughed at the ferrent when Polian had his run-in, passed them on his way toward the clinic's occupied rooms. He glanced up from a clipboard at them, then looked away.

Polian stood and grasped the tea pot and two mugs. "We'll take it with us. The ferrents will get wind of what we're doing here too soon as it is."

Polian led the interrogator down the hallway perpendicular to the entry hall, past rooms that had been emptied at his order, until they arrived at a closed, steel-riveted door, in front of which a Yavi sat at a desk. The man sprang up from his chair, which, like the desk, Polian had insisted be placed in the corridor. The man's civilian jacket gapped and revealed the pistol he wore in a shoulder holster beneath his jacket.

The guard nodded at Polian, turned, and unlocked the heavy door.

Beyond the open door, the woman lay in the bed in the

center of the windowless hospital room, eyes closed, breathing regular.

The interrogator set his case on the room's floor alongside a plain table and chairs. He glanced around the room, nodded, then circled the woman like a wolf.

Polian poured tea into two mugs, set the pot on the table, and handed one of the mugs to the interrogator. "We took her into custody forty-six days ago."

The interrogator sipped the bitter local tea, puckered his lips, then nodded. "And somehow these witch doctors have managed to keep her alive and repair her since then. I read her file. Grade-four concussion. Skull fracture. Thoracic trauma. Compound fracture of the right radius and ulna. All complicated by hypothermia, after her suit quit. I suspect her survival's more a function of her toughness than their brilliance."

"Is she tough enough to bring up?"

The interrogator shrugged as he bent, opened his field case, and began removing equipment. "I'll run some tests here and let you know."

"How long?"

The interrogator shrugged again. "Come back in a couple days."

It was, Polian thought, lack of urgency that separated soldiers from professionals who wore the uniform while they plied a civilian trade. Polian dragged out a chair, sat, and poured himself fresh tea. "I'll wait."

Forty

A day after Celline told me about the Tressens' suspicious prisoner, I crouched in the deepening darkness of Tressel moonset, alongside Pyt and Alia, barely breathing. We hid in the underbrush at the forested edge of the Iridian Corridor. Six hundred yards to our front, a dozen Tressen infantry, rifles held across their bodies at port arms, walked in two lines, one on each side of the Corridor's parallel rail lines, one for southbound trains, one for northbound.

Pyt leaned toward me and whispered, "They make one pass down this section every night. Then they tuck in to the strongpoint beyond the rise until dawn. They rarely send out patrols after moonset, because it's too easy for us to ambush them."

I glanced at Alia. She, like me, wore the rough vest and trousers of a fisherman ashore. I said to Pyt, "I still don't like using the girl."

"You need someone with you who can do the talking. Any adult would trigger suspicion. Jazen, we all owe a debt to something greater than ourselves. Fate chooses some of us to repay that debt earlier than others."

I rolled my eyes. "I've already had one partner who thought she was born to save the universe. I hope you didn't choose me another one."

"Only Celline chooses for Alia."

I supposed that, technically, Celline chose for all Iridians. But it seemed a stupid way to put it.

The moon disappeared below the horizon, and the night blackened.

Alia pointed at the tracks. "Patrol's gone."

Alia and I gathered our battered fisherman's rucksacks, Pyt grabbed up two shovels, and the three of us sprinted out of the treeline and ran, crouched, to the tracks.

We picked a spot five yards to the side of the northbound track. While Alia kept watch in the direction of the strongpoint, Pyt and I carved two shallow trenches in the roadbed gravel. I grimaced as every spade stroke rasped metal against rock and echoed through the night. I also held my breath as we raked up rotting fish bits that had fallen off into the roadbed.

Finally, Alia and I lay down, face up, in the trenches, rucksacks at our sides. Pyt raked rock and soil back over us in a thin layer. He left openings for our eyes, protected by goggles, and mouths, which we covered with scarves. Then he redistributed the rest of the spoil. By morning, the dirt would dry to the same tone as the undisturbed roadbed, and we would be invisible. At least, that was what they told me, and the rebels had hopped freights here before without incident.

Pyt knelt beside us. "Are you both alright?"

Alia said, “I hate this part.”

I started to speak, got a mouthful of sand that leaked past my scarf, spat it out. “Who wouldn’t love being buried alive in fish guts?”

Pyt, outside my narrow range of vision, patted the soil piled on my belly. “Godspeed, both of you.”

I heard his footsteps fade. Then there was no sound but the breeze humming across the unobstructed ground.

“Jazen?”

“I didn’t go anywhere. God, the smell is awful.”

“You’ll get used to it. But not the cold. And having to pee.”

“What’s the best thing to do now?”

“Sleep. The sun will wake us before the patrol train arrives.”

Forty-one

"Major?"

Polian awoke on the cot that the staff had wheeled into the woman's room when the interrogator laid a hand on his shoulder.

Polian sat up, rubbed his face, then smoothed two days of wrinkles from his Tressen civvies. He glanced toward the room's closed door. Last night's evening dishes still teetered, unremoved, on a stand by the door. He stared at the interrogator, who needed a shave, rubbed the stubble on his own chin, then glanced at his 'puter. "It's three a.m.!"

"Best time to bring a subject up. Circadian rhythm's at low ebb. Her resistance is at its daily low point."

Polian sat up straight. "Now? She's healthy enough?"

"Most of the impact trauma has either healed or been repaired. Her immune system's functioning normally. Brain activity's as vigorous as a comatose patient's can be."

Polian swung his legs over the cot's side and pulled on his shoes. He stretched, then yawned. "So?"

"So I've looked at everything I can. I think I can bring

her up. Very slowly. Very short duration, but I think she'll respond. And survive it without regressing."

The woman's bed was now surrounded by equipment, from which insulated wire leads slithered across the sheets and attached to her forehead and chest.

Polian stepped alongside the bed and peered down into the woman's slack face. He was a field officer, accustomed to more basic methods. He had read plenty of enhanced-interrogation transcripts, but he'd never actually seen how they were developed.

The hawk-faced interrogator held an injection gun in a surgical gloved hand. "Well? It's your call."

"We could lose her?"

"Doubt it. But anything's possible. How bad do you want to know what she knows?"

Polian nodded. "We need to know what the Trueborns know, and we need to know it last week. Do it."

The interrogator lifted the woman's arm out from under her bedsheet and laid it flat. He squeezed her limp arm until he found a vein, then pressed the gun's mushroom-shaped tip against the spot.

Zee.

The interrogator removed the gun's flat muzzle from the woman's forearm, stood back, and squinted at the digits on the screen nearest to the woman's blonde head. They had been frozen on zero since the interrogator hooked the screen to his subject. Now they flickered and increased with each second that passed as the drugs stimulated her system.

Polian asked, "How long until we know if she's going to respond?"

The interrogator tapped a finger on the tiny intravenous spigot that connected the woman to whatever they chose to fill her with, then waved his arm at the displays that surrounded the woman. "I could quote you numbers that you could watch for on the screens. Heart rate. Respiration. Brain function. But generally the subject comes up when they come up. I can tell you what to expect when she does. She'll be articulate and lucid, and apparently aware of her surroundings. But she'll answer any question put to her as readily as if you asked her the time. No resistance whatsoever."

"Any chance she'll spoof us?"

The interrogator shook his head. "On the old cocktails, maybe that happened one time in two hundred. The juice I've shot her up with's the best we got. Spoof us on this stuff? Maybe one chance in three hundred thousand. As to how long she can stay up—"

"Haaahhhh!"

Polian's own heart skipped as the woman sucked in a massive breath. The sheet rose as she arched her back, and her arms, one still immobilized in a flexicast, flailed.

Her eyes flew wide open.

Polian touched the interrogator's arm. "Should I get somebody else to—?"

She tried to sit up, but the interrogator laid a hand on her shoulder. "You don't want to sit up."

"I don't want to sit up." It was a croak. She pointed at her throat. "I'm thirsty."

The interrogator moistened the woman's dry lips with gloved fingertips, then let her sip water from a squeeze bag. "How do you feel?"

"Like I got hit by a train."

Which she had, approximately.

"My arm hurts. My head hurts. My boobs hurt. I have to pee."

"You have a catheter. Just relax."

Polian shook his head as he watched, entranced. Most of the interrogator's craft had actually been developed for civil work with Yavet's citizens. Polian knew from his father, though, that most day-to-day Yavi police work, like most military interrogation, relied on simpler physical "persuasion" and mental coercion. Somehow Polian had expected this format to be more foggy and adversarial. But it was like a doctor-patient consultation, or a civil deposition.

"What's your name?"

The woman stared at the ceiling. "Catherine Trentin Born."

"They call you the whole thing?"

"They call me Kit."

"Kit, do you have a job?"

"I'm a colonel in the United States Army, seconded to the Peacekeeping Forces of the Human Union."

"That sounds interesting. Kit, are you a particular kind of colonel?"

"You bet your ass. Senior special-operations case officer."

Polian's jaw dropped, and he turned to the holocams and eyed their red lights to be sure this was being recorded.

He stepped alongside the interrogator and whispered, "I knew it!"

"You don't have to whisper. Once she's engaged, she's

only stimulated by questions directed to her. The rest is background noise. Ask her something yourself."

Polian stepped alongside the hospital bed and cleared his throat. "Kit, why did you come to Tressel?"

"To find out what the Yavi are up to."

"Kit, why did you think they were up to something?"

She lay there, but shrugged. "That's what the baby-killers *do*."

Polian ignored the slur. "Kit, did you have specific information, though?"

"Abnormal amount of covert military traffic directed to Tressel."

"Kit, how many case officers are here with you?"

"None."

"Kit, you're a senior case officer. Don't case officers work in pairs, a senior and a junior?"

"None alive. The junior I inserted with died in the Arctic."

Polian stared down at her and tugged his lip. He was already convinced that she wasn't holding back or lying. But he also knew the puzzle pieces he held, and they didn't fit. She couldn't be the only Trueborn spy alive on Tressel. "Kit, there wasn't anyone else?"

She blinked. "There was. Before."

Ping. Her heart-rate monitor warning light flashed red.

Ping. A light on the brain-scan screen winked red.

The interrogator laid a hand on Polian's forearm. "I have to put her back down."

Polian shrugged the hand away. "Not now! Just a few more—"

Tears welled in the woman's eyes as she lay there. She clenched her fists.

"Now! This line of inquiry's too stressful for her."

Polian set his jaw. "Stressful? All I asked her was—"

"Major, overstress triggers a biochemical reaction to the cocktail. If we go on, I may have to reset the mix. That can take days. Or—I've lost subjects altogether. Keep this up and I won't be responsible if she winds up vegetative."

Polian paused. Then he stepped back and slapped his palm against the table so hard that the interrogator's instruments jingled.

The interrogator stepped alongside the woman—the spy, Polian corrected himself—and injected her.

Thirty seconds later, her fists unclenched and her tears stopped. She lay back, closed her eyes, and slipped into a deep-breathing sleep.

Polian watched the interrogator reset the alarms of the monitors wired to the woman, then asked him, "How long?"

"Until what? She'll be eating solids by noon, walking tomorrow. The day after that, she'll have given us ninety percent of what she knows."

"Why won't she give the last ten percent?"

"Oh, she *would*. But her body wouldn't tolerate the cocktail. She'd die before she talked. The last ten percent we get the old-fashioned way."

"I'm going to bring Gill down here to see her."

The interrogator raised one finger. "If you do, don't mention the last ten percent."

Polian's forehead creased. "Why not?"

"I've worked with him before. Old-school rules of war.

Bond of shared soldierly duty. That stuff." The interrogator stepped to the table, lifted the lid on the empty teapot, peered in, and frowned.

"You disagree?"

The interrogator set the teapot on the table, then shook his head. "Why split hairs about torturing an assassin whom you'd shoot on sight if you encountered her in the field? I'm a perfectionist, not a moralist. I just figure if you pour out a jug and leave ten percent inside, your job's only half done. When I'm done, the subject's empty."

"Empty? Does that mean dead?"

The interrogator shrugged. "Only if I do it right."

Forty-two

Whooo—whooo.

The distant train whistle woke me as I lay under the cobbled blanket that Pyt had piled on me the night before. Cold, numb, and with a full bladder, all I could see was clouds overhead. All I could hear was the wind, and all I could smell was rotten fish. "Alia?"

"Good. You're awake."

My nose itched. The sole of my left foot itched. My back, between my shoulder blades, itched. "Does the patrol train ever stop here?"

"They might have today if you didn't wake up. You snore loud."

"Mean girls don't grow breasts, you know."

"Very funny. Obviously mean boys still grow whiskers. Because you have too many."

I stared at the overcast sky through dusty goggles and sighed. Now my stubble itched, too. "Any more fashion tips?"

"Those stripes on your arm look stupid. You should wash them off."

I smiled under my bandana. My Legion graves-registration bar code.

"Can't. They're burned in clear down to the bone."

"Eeew! Why?"

"Identification. In my old job, the bones might be all that was left."

"Who would take a job like that?"

"I took the job to get away from the place where I grew up. The people in charge there killed children like me just for being born."

"Oh." Silence. Then she said, "Just like here. Except I can't get away."

It was my turn to be silent. I lay there and counted my unscratchable itches.

Ten minutes later the ground all around me shook as the northbound Tressen patrol train rumbled closer.

I held my breath. Pyt had camouflaged us in darkness. If he had left a foot, a sleeve exposed? If the rocks atop my chest had been shifted overnight by my heavy breathing? All it would take to get us captured or killed was one bored GI glancing down at the roadbed.

Ruummbblle.

I squeezed my eyes shut.

The whistle sounded again, its pitch different. The interval as wheels clacked across rail joints increased. The train was slowing!

My heart skipped; then I remembered. The reason we were dug in here was because the railroad at this point sloped upward to the north. The grade increase minimally slowed the short, relatively light patrol train.

But once the patrol train had cleared the Corridor, the

fully loaded northbound freights that would follow would be slowed to the pace of a brisk walk.

An hour later the day's first freight shook the roadbed, each set of wheels clanking over the uneven joint between rails that was closest to us. As Pyt had instructed me, I counted, two clicks per axle, two axles per car. A normal freight was manned only at the engine and caboose, with a hundred unwatched boxcars in between.

When I heard car number thirty pass, I pushed my way up from my shallow grave. Right arm. Left arm. I arched my back; rocks clattered as they tumbled off my belly. Sputtering dirt and wiping it from my mouth, I got to my hands and knees and looked forward and aft. I half expected to see riflemen dashing along the roadbed toward us. As the sear of returning circulation burned my thighs and arms, I saw nothing but open ground and a swaying, rumbling, and endless wall of boxcars.

"Jazen!"

Alia sat, half out of her hole, legs still covered, and tugged at her rucksack.

I kicked away rocks, dragged the dusty bag free, and she stood, brushing herself and panting.

Then I kicked dirt and rocks back into the holes to obscure the evidence of our visit. Pyt said a half-ass job would do. Rainy season was beginning, and the rain would tidy up.

The unconscious clock in my head had counted the passage of twenty more cars.

"Come on!" I grasped her hand and my own bag, and we sprinted until we matched speed with a boxcar's door, open like the others to ventilate the stacks of slatted fish crates inside.

I chucked my bag onto the car's floor as I ran, snatched Alia's bag and tossed it in, too. Then, as she grasped the boxcar's doorframe, I boosted her in, then heaved myself up behind her.

The two of us sprawled, puffing, on the dirty straw that covered the parts of the boxcar's floor not occupied by crates.

After three minutes, I sat up, my rucksack pillowing my back as I leaned against stacked, gray crates. She sat up across from me, grinning as we savored the simple joy of hopping a slow freight.

"Hungry?" Alia tugged a silvery carcass out between a fish crate's slats and chucked it at me.

I blocked the fish with a forearm. "Remember what I said about mean girls."

"Is she mean?"

"Who?"

"The woman we're trying to find."

"Only to mean people."

"Then she's a warrior princess. Like Celline."

"She's—yeah, sort of." I squirmed at this line of inquiry.

"Is she beautiful?"

I felt myself flush. "That's not important."

"Princesses are always beautiful. Celline is."

I turned and stared out the door at the passing landscape. "Yes, she is." Time to change the subject. "What do we do at the border?"

"She'll kiss you if you save her, you know. A princess always kisses the hero."

The train rocked us as I shook my head. "She's not that kind of princess. Care for a fish?" I pegged one at Alia.

She covered her head with both hands and squealed.

Then she frowned. "The border isn't guarded anymore, since Iridia became part of Tressen. Pyt cried about that the first time we went across. And nobody goes near a stinky fish train in the rail yards. It doesn't get scary until we get to the ferrents in town."

We rode in silence for ten minutes, until Alia looked up at me and cocked her head. "Then what kind of princess is she?"

Forty-three

Polian stood in rolled-up shirtsleeves, arms crossed, in the clinic's muggy observation closet. Alongside him stood the interrogator and General Gill. The three men stared through the one-way glass at the woman in the brightly lit psychological-interview room beyond.

The woman—the assassin, Polian corrected himself—paced the interview room's floor, still unsteady and pale, but ambulatory. She wore a borrowed nurse's smock and trousers, and a modern plastine cast still protected her mended right arm from wrist to elbow.

As they watched, she lowered herself facedown on the floor, gritted her teeth, and tried to lever her body up with her arms in a Trueborn calisthenic. Her right arm gave way and she fell, panting. Moments later she tried again.

Alongside Polian, General Gill ran a manual pencil down the Tressen paper pad upon which Polian had written his summary of her last session.

The interrogator said, "We don't have the equipment to copy the holo for you, but the gist—"

Gill kept reading. "Amazing. Not just her physical recovery. Apart from these officers of ours who she accounted for personally . . ."

Polian glanced up as the woman, her recently fractured arm trembling, completed a sixth push-up. He grimaced. Two of the officers she had "accounted for" had been friends of his. And he held her responsible for Sandr.

The interrogator pointed at a paragraph further down the page. "It's not just the assassinations. General, she's confessed to outworld tampering in places where we barely knew there was anything to tamper with. The propaganda value of that holo—"

Gill laid his jacketed arm on the interrogator's. "This isn't about propaganda. It's about maintaining this operation's security. If we do that, Yavet won't need propaganda. You're sure she hasn't uplinked anything about the cavorite mining?"

The interrogator shrugged. "That's what she said. We can spool the holo for you. But if there's another team operating on Tressel, she's in the dark about it."

Gill stepped to the window and laid his palm on the glass, as though trying to touch the woman. "How has she been treated?"

The interrogator glanced at Polian and raised his eyebrows. "The drugs are painless. Now that she's off them, she's feisty. She has no conscious recollection that she coughed up the dirt that's summarized on that notepad. Far as she knows, she's still a good soldier."

Gill raised his own eyebrows as he turned to leave the observation closet. "And what's wrong with that?" He turned to Polian. "Major? I'd like to have a word with her."

By the time the guard opened the door to the interview room, the woman was seated at the table in the room's center.

She looked up, recognition in her eyes as she saw Polian and the interrogator.

She pointed at Gill, gray, slight, and a head shorter than Polian, then said to Polian, "If he's the bad cop, this is gonna take a really long time."

Gill crossed his arms. "I take it then that you haven't been mistreated?"

"And I take it you're the boss of these two."

Gill shrugged.

The woman said, "I call getting run down by an illegal military vehicle mistreatment."

Gill stiffened. "If we're going to discuss illegal activity on an outworld, let's begin with the two Tressen infantrymen you killed."

She paused at the mention of the dead soldiers, then shook her head. "No idea what you're talking about. I got caught in a snowstorm while I was out jogging."

In his mind, Polian saw his murdered friends, and Sandr, and even the two decapitated Tressen GIs he didn't even know. He stepped around the table and cuffed the smart-mouthed woman with the back of his hand.

The blow knocked her backward and toppled her chair.

Gill grabbed Polian's arm. "Major Polian!"

The woman rolled to her knees, then stood. Her blue eyes burned at Polian while she laid a hand on her cheek. Then she smiled, and blood trickled from the corner of her mouth. "Seriously? You *really* need a better bad cop." She stepped toward Polian and drew back her fist.

Gill pushed Polian back and stepped between him and the woman. "Sit down, Colonel Born!"

The woman's eyes widened at the mention of her name and rank. She paused, then picked up her chair and sat.

Gill said, "Colonel, I have an opinion about whether your conduct has been professional. The truth about it, and its consequences for you, will be decided in good time. However, not solely by me, certainly not by this gentleman. In the interim you will be treated as a soldier."

The woman raised her eyebrows, then snorted. "That's enlightened, coming from a baby-killer."

Gill ignored her and turned to Polian. "Major, apologize to the prisoner."

Polian felt his eyes bulge. "Sir? She's a terrorist, not—"

"She's a prisoner of war! And if you wish to remain an officer under my command, you will treat her as such." Gill stared up at him, jaw thrust out, hands on hips.

Polian ground his teeth, then stared at the woman. "I'm sorry I struck you."

She smirked. "Struck you, *ma'am*? If I'm a colonel and you're a major . . ."

Polian squeezed his eyes shut. "Ma'am."

Thirty minutes later, after Gill had left the clinic, Polian and the interrogator stood together again in the observation closet. The woman lay face to the wall on a cot in the interview room's far corner, apparently sleeping.

The interrogator said, "I warned you about him."

Polian asked, "How do we get the last ten percent out of her?"

"Gill said—"

"Gill said a tribunal would judge her. A tribunal acts on

facts. Intelligence gathers facts. I'm the only intelligence officer within a hundred billion cubic light-years. How long to complete her interrogation by conventional methods?"

The interrogator pointed at Polian's chest. "This is strictly on you."

"How long?"

The interrogator stroked his chin. "Anything that results in blood loss, you're looking at another day from now to set it up clean. Electricity?" He shrugged as he peered up at the primitive incandescent bulb that hung above the woman. As he watched, it flickered, and she glanced up at it.

The interrogator said, "The current's unreliable here. I'd need to adapt my gear, probably the clinic's, too." He rubbed his chin again. "Might have an early glitch or two. I'm a neurologist, not an electrician. Figure a couple hours longer. But shock done right leaves no permanent visible deformity. You might want to think about that if you don't plan to tell Gill."

The faces of old friends, and of Sandr, whose blood was on this woman's hands, swam in Polian's memory. "No marks? How painful is it?"

"Electricity? With careful modulation you can drive a subject insane without killing her. And eventually, of course, you *can* kill her with it."

Polian stared at the assassin one more time, then removed his Tressen jacket from the hook alongside the door. As he turned the doorknob, he squinted back at the interrogator. "Electricity, then. Tomorrow night."

Forty-four

The freight rolled through the outskirts of Tressia at dawn, past houses, factories, and the rest of a city drab in stone and brick.

Then we passed a tarmac strip that stretched parallel to the tracks for, I estimated, just over two miles. In the distance, at the runway's end, stood a complex of buildings that didn't belong to this world. Alia pointed at the complex. "That's where the shuttles land and take off. Pyt says it was built there so all the new goods could be put right on the trains."

I snorted. I knew the place, though I hadn't seen it before. Spaceport Tressel. Spaceport was a stretch. Mousetrap, now that was a spaceport. Of course, the Tressens barely had aeroplanes, so it must've seemed magical to them.

Spaceport Tressel was a presently deserted nonworking model of superpower noncooperation.

The Cold War began warm and fuzzy, with Trueborns and Yavi competing for hearts and minds on developing outworlds by bribes consisting of obsolete leftovers. The Trueborns gifted the Tressens with finicky, last-generation chemical-fueled shuttles remaindered by the Trueborn manufacturer. The Yavi one-upped the Trueborns with a glittering, stadium-sized prefab-dome hangar-terminal complex. But the finicky shuttles' guts hated Tressel's climate. The giant dome that sparkled so impressively beneath the summer sun leaked like a geodesic sieve during the rainy, influenza-scourged Tressen winter.

Then came the war, the Tilt, and the embargo. Today the shuttles hung parked in orbit, operated by a subsidized, arm's-length contractor. The space planes landed on the overgrown flats of Spaceport Tressel only when a cruiser visited, and left before the crew caught the flu.

Conventional wisdom held that the Yavi won. At least they netted a glitter-domed symbol of Tressen-Yavi cooperation out of the deal.

I stared at the deserted strip, but it offered no clues. Kit's team hadn't arrived there. Their insertion point had been an isolated, empty clearing thirty miles from this city. But the Yavi, whom I was convinced that Kit and her junior had somehow encountered, did arrive and depart Tressel here.

Our freight slowed to walking pace after we passed the shuttle strip and ten minutes later rolled to a stop in Tressia's central rail yard, just one of string upon parallel string of anonymous, identical boxcars and flatcars.

We slipped down into the chill morning and dodged through the yard, crabbing under row after row of carriages. The few yard workers we saw didn't merely ignore us; they distanced themselves from us.

Alia said, "Dressed like this we look like Tressen settlers. They hop freights down in the southern settlements all the time. Especially this time of year."

"This time of year," late fall on into rainy winter, was the annoying time that modern societies called flu season. Pre-vaccine societies called it influenza season, but for them it wasn't annoying: it was a time of angst and death. Without vaccines, the flu laid the strong low and killed the weak. Desperate settlers from the south brought their sick children north for "modern" medical care that was little more than hand-holding.

It took Alia and me, rucksacks in hand, an hour to walk to the office of the Iridian-sympathizing physician who had tipped Celline's network about his mysterious female former patient.

His office was in the city's Old Quarter, a warren of narrow, cobbled streets and stone buildings. The tight-packed buildings stood no higher than three stories, except for church steeples, not for aesthetics or to honor the almighty but because that was as tall as the architects of the time had been able to stack stone.

The gray and black was relieved only by red ribbons that hung from half the doorways. The ribbons flapped in the breeze generated by chugging autos and rattling lorries as they passed. Pedestrians, heads down and hands in pockets, filled streets that a Trueborn would call over-crowded and a downlevels Yavi would call sparsely populated.

No pedestrian bothered us, and those who approached us from downwind gave us a wide berth. What fear of influenza didn't do, fish stink did.

The row house that served as the physician's office was easy to find. Flapping red ribbons hung not just beside the building's door but from both stoop rails. The ribbons warned passersby that the influenza was inside. Generally, those homes were cleared and shunned. A doctor's office didn't have that luxury. Tressens had reached that unfortunate stage of medical acumen where they understood that close contact spread disease but couldn't do much about the disease once it had spread.

The office vestibule was so crowded that we had to step over the outstretched legs of waiting patients to reach the reception nurse. After one sniff, she hustled us through a second waiting room, crowded with sad-eyed adults and weeping children, into an examining room.

We exchanged our travel outfits for laundered clothes that had been packed in oilskin bags. Then we sat on straight chairs and waited, hands clasped between our knees.

The doctor swept in, gray and weary, wearing a starched white long coat and spectacles rimmed with copper wire that hooked behind his ears. He smiled when he saw Alia and chucked her under the chin. "You've grown! How are you feeling?"

"Fine."

"That's because you were inoculated."

He turned his head toward me and frowned. "Where is the other gentleman?"

"He didn't come this time. I'm—"

The physician raised his palm. "What I don't know the ferrents can never beat out of me." He paused and fingered a stethoscope that hung around his neck. "I'm afraid you've come at a bad time. There's no vaccine. At any price."

I wrinkled my forehead. "Influenza vaccine's not embargoed. The Trueborns send Tressel tons of it. Free."

"Oh, they do. But it's all diverted to Party members' families. They resell any leftovers they don't ruin. But they won't trickle into the black market for a couple of months yet. That's when the other fellow usually visits."

Alia said, "He's not here about the medicine."

The physician kept his eyes on me. "Well, he should be!" He pointed at the closed examining-room door. "Did you look at those people waiting to see me? This pandemic will kill one of every five out there. More, among the children!" He held up a quivering finger. "And not one has to die! Not one! All I have to give them is sympathy, hygiene advice, and a red ribbon for their door. Your people should do something about it!"

I raised my eyebrows and laid my palm on my chest. "*My* people?"

He eyed me, head to toe. "You look Trueborn. You sound Trueborn."

I shook my head. The Trueborns weren't my people. The Yavi weren't my people. I was a waif abandoned by the former, a criminal guilty of being born among the latter. I didn't have a people. I had a job.

I pointed at the closed door, and my finger shook as hard as the physician's had. "The people out there won't die because of me! They won't die because of the Trueborns, either! Blame the Republican Socialist Party!"

The physician paused, steadied himself with a hand against the door jamb, then rubbed his forehead. "I'm sorry. You're right. That's why I help the cause." He looked up. "If you're not here for vaccine, then you're here about the woman."

I nodded and leaned forward. "How is she?"

"Someone saw her walking at the clinic yesterday. Which is miraculous, considering her initial condition."

My heart leapt. "What does this woman look like?"

"Well, like the very devil when they brought her in." He turned his eyes to the ceiling and tapped a finger on a tooth. "I saw her prone, of course. Measured out, I should say, perhaps half a head shorter than yourself. Lovely fair skin, the few bits that weren't bruised. Blonde hair, cropped like a boy's. Superb muscle tone. Eyes an extraordinary shade of blue, to the extent I saw them with the lids pulled back."

The Trueborns called the shade Caribbean blue, and Kit's eyes were better than extraordinary.

I scooted farther forward on my chair. "Scars?"

He lifted his trouser leg and drew a finger diagonally across his left ankle. "Prominent one, just here. A knife, probably." He pointed a finger at his chest. "Depression the diameter of a one-crown coin, just here, below the clavicle. Old gunshot entry wound if I'm any judge."

I sank back on the chair and closed my eyes. "Yes!" Kit was alive. And walking!

He said, "You know her, then?"

"Where is this clinic?"

"It's Republican Socialist Memorial."

I stared at him.

He said, "Formerly Daughters of Iridia Medical Center? The Alabaster Castle!"

I turned up my palms. "Which is where?"

He eyed my fisherman's outfit. "Ah, yes. You're not from here."

I pressed my palms together. "Please, Doctor. This is really important."

He turned to Alia and raised his eyebrows.

She nodded.

Alia and I left the physician after I pumped him for another half hour. We came away with a plan, and with time to kill before we implemented it.

We scouted eat-in bakeries in the Old Quarter until we found one that baked and served brot.

Brot was a bland Iridian flatbread. Brot was served toasted, then spread with trilobite roe. The roe actually tasted like, because it was, a sort of poor man's caviar. But there was no brot-of-the-month club, because trilobite roe looked exactly like human snot. It took us an hour to find a place that still catered to the Iridian taste for brot.

The bakery was set two steps down below street level, with narrow windows, and was a block outside the Government Quarter. We sat at a toy of a table in the corner, out of the baker's earshot. We ate our brot, with tea that smelled like wet cat fur, and watched people's legs and feet go by. Too often, we also saw hearse wheels roll past.

Alia poked a brot crust into roe puddled on her plate. "*Is* it your fault?"

"The doctor didn't say anything was my fault! It's not my job to fix the world."

"I see. It's only your job to rescue her tonight."

I shook my head. "No. Tonight's a reconnaissance. Plan first. Rescue sometime later."

"Then why do you have guns and all that other stuff in your rucksack?"

I raised my eyebrows. "Nosy girls don't grow breasts, either."

She wrinkled her nose at me and glared. Then she said, "You were asleep. I was bored. Well, why do you?"

"No plan survives contact with the enemy. So plan for every contingency. She taught me that when we were together."

"Together. Like kissing and stuff?"

Especially and stuff. I looked down into my tea and swirled it. "Together. Like senior and junior case officer. Partners."

My eleven-year-old inquisitor raised her chin and narrowed her eyes. "Uh-*huh*."

I turned to the bakery owner behind the counter and waved for the check.

At dusk, we lined up at a sand-bagged sidewalk checkpoint, behind a dozen homeward-bound day workers waiting to pass through Tressia's cordoned-off Government Quarter.

My heart thumped as I toed my heavy rucksack forward each time the line advanced. For all the burying alive and hopping of freights, this was the biggest gamble so far in our journey. I could have made it safer by caching my weapons and gear and going unarmed through the checkpoint. But I had left my firepower behind once before on this planet and almost got pinched in half by a giant crab.

Alia and I reached the head of the line.

A uniformed ferrent wearing an ankle-length coat, armed with a slung rifle, waved us forward. "Papers?"

I feigned a cough so deep that my shoulders shook, covering my mouth with my hand. Then I held our forgeries out to him.

His eyes widened as he saw my fingers and the papers, dripping with green trilobite roe. He waved them back at me unexamined. "You have business in the Government Quarter?"

I coughed until my shoulders shook while I nodded.

Alia looked up at him as she wiped roe from her nose with the back of her bare hand. "My father's sick."

The ferrent frowned as she flicked green slime off her hand onto the sidewalk. "So are you, missy."

"The doctor told us to go to the clinic."

The ferrent shook his head. "The doctor's an idiot, then. They don't take walk-ins."

The line behind us swelled.

Alia snapped off a sneeze that sprayed saliva in the ferrent's general direction.

He cringed. Then he waved us past the checkpoint. "Try if you want. Just get away from me."

Alia raised her rucksack and held it in front of the ferrent's face. "Aren't you supposed to look in our bags?"

My heart skipped. The machine pistols and surveillance gear in the bag dangling from my shoulder suddenly weighed a ton.

The ferrent glanced at the bag she held in front of his nose and shook his head. "Move along!"

I shook like an out-of-tune Tressen lorry as we walked

away from the checkpoint. After fifty yards, we turned a corner, and I grabbed her by the shoulders and squinted down at her. "Look in our bags? What the hell were you thinking?"

"Pyt says attack can be the best defense." She rolled her eyes at me. "Before I showed him my bag, I rubbed a goober as big as your nose on my bag handle."

She squirmed, and I realized my fingers were digging into her shoulders.

I relaxed my grip and drew a breath. "Oh."

She grinned. "Did you see his face when I sneezed on him?"

"You know, you were fine back there. In fact, really good."

"Of course. Celline says girls lie better."

We resumed walking down the dark street in the moonlight.

Alia hiked her rucksack up across her shoulder as we walked. "I could be your new partner."

I smiled. "Maybe."

"But no kissing."

I smiled again. "Too many whiskers?"

Alia shook her head. "You're already taken."

We ducked down an alley and waited. The streetlights in the Government Quarter were shut off after moonset.

Republican Socialist civil servants were no more inclined to work late than any other kind, so the lights in the Government Quarter were mostly superfluous in the evenings. And the Tressens' electrical grid was so feeble that after moonset they redirected most of the juice to still-inhabited parts of town, where it was needed. After moonset, the Government Quarter turned as dark as a cave, so I put on snoops and led Alia by the hand the rest of the way to the clinic.

The clinic's grounds were easy to find. They were the only island of light in the deserted Government Quarter.

But they weren't deserted.

I muttered, "What the hell?"

Forty-five

Polian dabbed softly with a towel at the spot where the woman's fist had struck his jaw, and winced. He watched his two corporals wrestle her into the metal skeleton chair. The interrogator had ordered the chair bolted to the floor in the center of the clinic's psychological-interview room. Insulated cables clamped to the chair snaked six feet across the floor and connected to a satchel-sized console laid out on a simple table. The console, in turn, was connected to the wall outlet by a thicker cable.

A third soldier sat dazed on the floor, his back against one table leg. He grimaced, slid his trouser leg up to expose the kneecap she had kicked, then gently prodded the dislocated bone.

The interrogator peered at Polian's jaw and whistled. "That's gonna leave a mark. I told you we should have drugged her lunch."

Polian shook his head. "No. I want her to feel every jolt."

The two corporals tied her onto the chair's legs and arms, securing her at the ankles and knees, then wrists and elbows, with thick tape over her smock and trousers. Finally, they taped thin copper wires, that were wrapped at one end around parts of the chair frame, to her palms and the soles of her feet.

Only then did the interrogator step forward and stand in front of her with his arms crossed. "Colonel, please don't think I will enjoy this night. But I find that these interviews are easier for everyone if the interviewee chooses to cooperate. I also find that some interviewees make that choice if I explain the process."

The woman stared at him, cocking an ear toward him as she whispered, "What?"

The interrogator bent closer and stared into her eyes. "Electricity will be applied through the electrodes affixed to your palms and to the soles of your feet. Later the electrodes will be relocated to your genitalia. Initially, while I'm checking the modifications I've made to the equipment, the damage will only hurt your vanity. Static buildup that will cause your hair to stand out. As I increase the voltage, the pain will—"

She snapped her head forward, and her skull struck the interrogator's nose so hard that Polian heard a crack like a snapped chicken bone.

The interrogator staggered back, hand up to stanch the blood gushing down across his lips and chin.

She stared at him, eyes narrowed. "How 'bout that? Already you're not enjoying this night."

Polian stepped alongside the interrogator. He passed the man the hand towel with which he had been dabbing his jaw. Then he peered, wide-eyed, at the man's swelling nose, and whistled. "That's gonna leave a mark!"

The interrogator glared at Polian across the wadded towel as he pressed it to his nose and a bright red stain blossomed across the fabric.

Polian raised his eyebrows. "Mind if I chat with her while you fix that?"

He removed his Tressen jacket, folded it, then laid it on the table. Then he stood, hands on knees, at a safe distance from the woman and smiled at her. "Me? I'm not like the gentleman you just sucker punched. I *am* the bad cop. Very bad. I don't want to make this interview pleasant. I want to hurt you. Like you've hurt so many fine soldiers."

She shook her head. "Baby-killers aren't fine soldiers. The only thing I've ever hurt is your rotten system."

It was, Polian thought, a genuinely felt, if futile, posture. Zealots actually took pride in enduring pain for a cause. He needed to change her attitude.

The interrogator stepped forward, his nose now bandaged. Arms outstretched, he rammed the bloody towel that he had used to contain his nosebleed into her mouth until she gagged. "These walls are thick. But not thick enough to muffle the screaming you're going to do. I'm not going to play good cop anymore, Colonel. We'll move quickly through the preparatory stages and get right to the really horrifying stuff."

" 'Ite me, ah'hole."

Polian walked to the table and flicked on the hologen that lay alongside the electrical console. He let the recording of her first session run until the moment when she said, "You bet your ass. Senior special-operations case officer." Then he paused the recording so that her image hung in the air in front of her, her lips parted as she prepared to reveal a lifetime of secrets that would humiliate her nation.

She stared, and her eyes widened.

Polian smiled at her and pointed at the image. "You have no memory of this at all, do you? You've hurt my cause over the years, Colonel. I'll concede you that. But this confession holo will hurt your cause worse. Far worse. Your epitaph won't be heroine. It will be traitor."

For the first time, confusion then fear sparked in the woman's eyes.

Polian smiled more broadly. It was one thing to endure pain for a cause. Quite another to suffer it for betraying one. Stripped of pride in her own heroism, she would crumble quickly. She would talk, then she would plead, weeping, for them to let her shame die with her. Then she would die.

He turned to the interrogator and nodded. "Let's get started."

Forty-six

I tugged Alia behind a building across the street from the clinic where Kit was being held. Then I adjusted my snoops for the available light and peered around the building's corner.

Alia whispered, "What do you see?"

I saw a white building gingerbreaded with arched windows and parapets. "He wasn't kidding. It is a castle."

"Of course. Where else would they hold a princess?"

I adjusted the snoops' magnification. "One Interior Police staff car and two covered lorries. They're just sitting in front of the clinic at the curb. They're seventy-five yards away from us. Twenty yards in front of the building."

"More guards? Then they know we're here!"

I shook my head, and the image blurred for an instant. "The doctor said the guards he's seen since the argument have all been Yavi. These guys are ferrents."

The image steadied as one of the clinic's front doors opened and two broad-shouldered bullet heads in civilian clothes, right hands inside their jackets, trotted down the front steps toward the Interior Police vehicles.

The staff car's door opened, and a man in a brown trenchcoat and slouch hat stepped out and toward the Yavi guards.

I whispered, "My guess is we just walked in on round two of the turf battle over the prisoner."

The man in the trenchcoat and the two Yavi met at the curb. He held out a paper, then pointed at it, then at the clinic.

One Yavi shook his head, while the ferrent waved his arms. Their voices echoed off the stone buildings.

Alia said, "They sound mad."

A second ferrent stepped out of the staff car. Then the tailgates of the two lorries banged down, and two squads of uniformed ferrent riflemen, like the checkpoint guard who had passed us through, clambered out.

A third Yavi appeared at the top of the entrance steps. A short-barreled Yavi needle gun with a drum magazine dangled by its sling from his right shoulder.

"Things are warming up."

"Are they going to fight?"

I shrugged and slid off the snoops to adjust the sensitivity. "Maybe. At the least they're gonna argue."

Alia whispered, "This is perfect!"

"Huh?"

"Pyt says the best time to attack is when the enemy is distracted."

"Well, in this case Pyt just may be wrong."

Alia sniffed. "What kind of hero *are* you?"

I slid the snoops over her eyes, thumbed the autofocus, then pushed her head out around the building's corner. "The kind who can count! How many do you see?"

Alia pointed her finger in the air. "One. Two. Three—"

I snatched the snoops back and stared down at her. "Twenty-nine! Counting the Yavi."

She rolled her eyes and pointed to the side of the building. "You don't *storm* the castle, of course! The doctor said there's a side door. I saw explosives in your bag. Blow it open."

I did have door bores with me, and the Tressens didn't have much in the way of remote alarm systems. But I shook my head. "Even if I circled behind those other buildings, I'd finally have to cross a hundred yards of open, floodlit ground. That's suicide."

In the shadows, Alia crossed her arms and snorted. "Some hero!"

"Stop that!" I drew my bush knife and waved it. "I can't just wave my magic sword and make—"

Bam!

It was more a crackle than an explosion. The clinic lights flickered, something else popped, then the building and grounds were plunged into total blackness.

Forty-seven

Polian shuffled forward, arms extended, in the suddenly pitch-black room. He stubbed his toe and fell. "What the hell did you do?"

The interrogator's disembodied voice echoed in the darkness. "I told you there could be glitches when we powered up! It's just a fuse or something!"

Polian heard the echoing footfalls of running feet on floor tile, and the voices of his men. "We're under attack!"

Pop-pop-pop.

A needler set for three-round burst.

Someone screamed.

"Cease fire! Cease fucking fire! Whoever that was, you almost hit me!"

"Lock the place down!"

Polian screamed into the darkness, loud enough that his men would hear him. He should have issued snoopers and just let the hospital staff be suspicious. "Stop it! Stop it, all of you! We're not under attack! It's a damn blown fuse! Stop locking things down! Go find a way to get the power back on!"

The interrogator's voice sounded in the dark. "Polian?"

"What?"

"Do your men have any idea how to restore power?"

"They're soldiers, not electricians. What about the hospital staff?"

"Who knows? This culture is new to electricity. They've got a rotten power grid. They don't even have backup power in a *hospital*."

"I don't choose our allies."

"Look, I think I can get the lights back. The electrical closet's just down the corridor. But I'll need an extra pair of hands."

"Hold on." Polian crawled on his hands and knees until he touched the metal leg of the chair into which the woman was taped. He pulled himself upright until he felt her head, limp and slumped forward. The first jolt hadn't knocked out only the lights. She was going nowhere.

This was, indeed, a minor glitch. It would remain minor as long as the lights were restored before some nervous idiot shot some other nervous idiot in a friendly fire incident.

Polian said to the interrogator, "Meet you at the door. Then we'll feel our way. Keep close to the wall or some fool will shoot us both."

One minute later, he and the interrogator stepped out into the pitch-black corridor. Polian barked his shin against the door guard's desk and swore. He felt across the empty desk and chair. The guard was gone.

Polian laid his hand on the interrogator's chest in

the blackness and stopped him. "Wait!" The woman was unattended in the interview room. Polian fished the room's key from his pocket, felt for the door handle, and locked her inside.

Forty-eight

I pressed my back against the stone wall of the building that hid us and listened to ferrent and Yavi shouts and footfalls provoked by the sudden darkness.

Alia crept alongside me and touched my arm. "Now, *that* was more like it!"

I shook my head and whispered as I peeped around the corner. "I didn't do anything." I turned the bush knife blade in my hand as I sheathed it. "At least, I don't think I did."

Through the snoops I saw the ferrents, all prone, rifles aimed and facing out in a ragged, circular perimeter that surrounded their vehicles. The Yavi, without snoopers, had also frozen in place, guns drawn but with nowhere to shoot in the dark.

I whispered, "Maybe a power outage. Maybe the Yavi cut the lights to slow down the ferrents." If so, why were people shouting and shooting inside the building?

Chaos and uncertainty ruled the moment.

Military history was littered with the regrets of soldiers who failed to seize the moment. It was also littered with the bodies of more of them who seized the wrong moment.

If the lights came up while we waited, hidden here, we could just go ahead and recon the place as I had planned. No problem. Except that we would then have to try to come back and start over.

Alternatively, I could run four hundred yards mostly behind cover, then the last hundred yards concealed in darkness that was like green daylight to me. If and when I got inside I had to navigate another hundred yards of corridors that I knew only from a non-military observer's secondhand reminiscence. Then, in some eleven-year-old's fantasy, I would somehow rescue the princess. Hell, in my fantasy, too. This was what I came for.

I bent, reached into my rucksack, and drew both machine pistols and chest holsters.

Alia held out her hand and wiggled her fingers.

I slipped the right holster over my shoulder as I stared at her hand. "What do you want?"

"My gun. I'm not going in unarmed."

"You're not going in at all."

Her jaw dropped. "Why not?"

I hesitated. "Because I said so" was likely to get me as far with an eleven-year-old girl as it always had with a thirty-three-year-old woman.

I said, "Uh, because this is a raid. Did Pyt teach you about raids?"

She raised her chin. "Naturally."

"Quick in, quick out. If the raiding party gets separated during the raid, they need a secure place to reassemble. A rally point. You're the rally point security element."

She rolled her eyes. "You made that up. You're just scared I'll get hurt."

No to the first, yes to the second. I shook my head. "No."

"Yes, you did! You can't get separated from *yourself*."

I exhaled. Why me? There wasn't time to argue. "There's only the one set of snoopers."

"Oh. I guess you're right."

Not that I was crazy about leaving her here alone. I dug in my rucksack again, stood, and held out an object. "This is—"

She squinted in the dark. "A six-shot double-action .38 with a three-inch barrel and iron sights. Inaccurate, compact, reliable. Good backup gun."

"Oh. Can you use it?"

"Pyt taught me more than raids."

I handed her the pistol. She flicked open the cylinder, checked it, then tucked it into her trousers' waistband while I hefted the rucksack onto my shoulders. My teeth were clenched, and I expected the power to flash back on every instant.

Alia stood in front of me, rearranging my holster straps and the knife scabbard. Finally, she patted her palms on my chest, then stood back and looked me up and down in the dim light. "There! Now you look ready to rescue a princess! You should've shaved, though."

I didn't feel ready. But I ran, crouching, into the dark, weighed down by my load and by anxiety that the lights would expose me in the open, that Alia wouldn't stay put, that after all this Kit wouldn't be there, or . . .

I circled behind another building and made the clinic's

side door in three minutes without incident. I set the ruck on the ground, tugged out a door bore, and grasped the doorknob to fit it in place. The door opened, and I swore at myself for time wasted by not trying the door first.

Then I was inside. The door led in to a level lower than the level on which Kit was, I hoped, being held. The stairwell up was empty, and I navigated the stairs easily with my snoops.

The public corridor at the top of the stairs bustled, if you can call nurses stumbling around searching for candles bustle. I padded down the corridor in total darkness, an unseen shadow breathing hoarsely. The T-junction where a Yavi guard was supposed to be posted was deserted. I peered left down the corridor that led to the front of the building and saw two Yavi peeking around the half-open entry doors with guns drawn. The ferrents had been kind enough to divert my opposition.

I crossed the corridor intersection behind the preoccupied guards' backs, then counted doors as I walked.

I stopped in my tracks when I heard two male voices behind one door on my left, realized that the door was closed, and bypassed them.

Finally, I saw ahead the fourth door on the right. I didn't really have to count. The physician had said that a desk and chair had been set up in the hallway as a station for the all-hours guard. The desk and chair were right where they were supposed to be. The all-hours guard wasn't. I suspected he was one of the two now guarding the front door. I smiled as I ran. Chaos could be a spook's best friend.

When I got to the door, I stood back and cased the job.

The door to the right of the desk was supposed to lead to the room where Kit was being held. The door to the left of the desk, according to the physician, led to a smaller room from which patients in the room next door, head cases, could be observed.

Both doors were steel, with massive, keyed locks set below their knobs. Each was hinged to open out to the hall, so the door couldn't be removed from its hinges from inside. Apparently Tressen head cases could get feisty.

I tried the knob on the door behind which I was supposed to find Kit. Unlike the outside door, this one didn't budge. I eyed the exposed door hinges. Unhinging a door to open it was noisy. So was a door bore. And both had the undesirable side effect that thereafter the door couldn't be closed if plans changed. And the one certainty in a planned operation was that plans changed.

As the mental clock ticked down in my head, I shrugged off my ruck, opened it on the vacant guard desk, and retrieved my lockpick set. Then I knelt in front of the door handle and reset the snoops for close work. I also cursed myself for dozing through Lockpicking and Safecracking 101.

That wasn't the real name of the class. The spooks euphemistically named it Defense Against Methods of Entry. Trueborn case officers would never, ever break in to somebody else's locked property, of course. We just needed to know how bad people might try to do it to us. Same thing for Defense Against Sound Equipment. I also had loaded a regular bughouse of listening devices into my ruck.

I glanced left and right. This corridor remained deserted.

The distant murmur of distracted nurses and doctors in the dark soothed my nerves.

Still, as I slid the first slim pick into the keyhole and wiggled it, my fingers trembled.

Then something clunked in the distance, and I jumped.

Overhead, the corridor lights flickered.

I whispered, "Crap."

Forty-nine

"It was just a circuit breaker." In suddenly restored light, the interrogator turned and smiled, blinking, at Polian. The two of them were wedged into a cramped room, barely an elongate closet, walled with vertical pipes and insulated conduits.

The man lifted his hand off of a copper knife switch bolted to the side of a gray steel box on the wall of the tiny room. Polian released the heavy top-hinged access panel that he had held open while the interrogator had worked. "Done?"

The interrogator wiped his hands on his trousers. "I think so."

Polian backed until he touched the door that led from the utility closet to the corridor, then turned and looked down the bright-lit, white corridor toward the interview room. He blinked.

The interrogator backed out and stood by Polian. "What's wrong?"

Polian shook his head as he peered down the corridor

at the vacant guard's desk. "Nothing. But the guard hasn't returned." Then he jerked a thumb back toward the T-junction of the corridors while he stared. "He must have gone to cover the main-entrance door when the power quit. Go back down there and fetch him, will you?"

The interrogator nodded, then walked away, his footsteps echoing on the floor tiles while Polian kept staring. Elsewhere, he heard the voices and footfalls of hospital staff as normalcy returned.

Then Polian walked slowly down the corridor toward the interview room where he had left the woman shocked senseless, bound, and gagged. Though the little recent excitement had passed without incident, he breathed faster now. It was as though an undercurrent was pulling him forward.

Fifty

Heart pounding, I pulled the heavy door shut behind me and heard it lock. Then I stepped into a suddenly bright, classroom-sized room, windowless on three white walls. A blacked-out window ten feet wide, with its lower sill waist high, was set in the fourth wall's center. In the room's far corner was a cot. Closer to me stood a table and two chairs. A man's jacket hung half-off one chair back, like someone had left in a hurry.

I tugged off my now-unnecessary snoops to widen my field of vision and saw a console on the table. Cables ran from the console to the floor, then crossed the floor to a metal-frame chair.

My heart skipped. In the chair sat a person, back to me, wearing a loose gray smock and trousers. Blonde, female, head bent forward, she slumped, motionless.

I sucked in a breath as I stepped toward her.

Her arms were taped tight to the chair's legs, her arms to the chair arms. Copper wires were taped to her palms and the soles of her bare feet, and were wrapped around the chair frame.

"Oh, God. Oh, God," I whispered as I came around in front of her, knelt, and looked into her face. "Kit!"

Her eyes were closed, and her tongue protruded, bloody and swollen, from her mouth.

I shook my head. "No! Oh, no!"

She breathed, barely. I peered at her. It wasn't her tongue, it was some sort of bloody rag.

At least I had paid attention in first aid, even during Legion Basic.

Step one. Clear the airway. I slipped trembling fingers into her mouth and freed the bloody rag. I felt around her tongue. Not swallowed. Airway clear.

She breathed deeper.

Step two. Stop the bleeding. I searched her torso and limbs but found no bleeding. Good. But if she was puking blood, she was bleeding internally. I couldn't put a tourniquet on that. All I could do was watch her die. "Goddamit! In the middle of a fucking hospital!" I tore off my rucksack and flung it on the floor.

Her eyes opened. She looked up at me and blinked.

My eyes burned as my throat swelled.

Her eyes widened, blue, enormous, and bloodshot. "Parker?"

She shook her head and asked again through lips dark with dried blood, "Parker? If it's you, am I dead?"

I took her face between my palms and held it until I got her to look into my eyes. "Kit. Look at me. Listen to me. Do you know where you're bleeding?"

"What?"

"Ribs? Gut-shot? Chest cavity?" I drew back, looking down at her torso. No bloodstains.

She looked sideways, at the bloody rag in my hand. "That's not my blood, Parker. You should see the other guy."

I turned my face up and closed my eyes. "Thank you!" Then I leaned forward and kissed her cheek, stranger's blood and all.

"Cut me loose, Parker."

I retrieved the rucksack, tugged out my knife, and sawed at the tape that bound her legs with the knife's serrated edge. "What the hell is all this?"

"Yavis."

"That I know."

"Electric-shock interrogation."

"Bad?"

"Do I look like it was good?"

I cut the last tape off her arms and smiled at her. "Better now?"

She threw her suddenly freed arms around me and hugged me. I slid my arms around her, too, gently, and nearly recoiled. Beneath the smock she felt tiny, wasted. Then she began to shake and sob.

She whispered, "God, I missed you."

I felt wetness on my ear, then the touch of her lips.

Alia had been right. The princess had kissed me.

I held her and cried, too.

After a few seconds, she drew back from me and wiped her eyes and nose with the back of her hand.

I stared at her hair, which was frizzed out like a scouring pad, then pointed. "Love what you've done with it."

She narrowed her eyes in a stare I hadn't seen for two years. "Bite me, Parker." Then she pointed at my rucksack. "You bring the usual suspects?"

I nodded.

"Good. I got a couple things to attend to."

Thirty seconds later we stood together in the center of the room.

Clack-clack.

Behind my back, the room's doorknob rattled.

Fifty-one

As Polian stood at the interview-room door, his relief that it remained locked turned to annoyance. He grunted as he tried again to force the mechanical metal key into the mechanism.

The interrogator trotted up, the missing door guard in tow, and asked Polian, "Jammed?"

"Hasn't been." Polian turned to the door guard. "You had any trouble with this lock?"

"None, Major." The man shook his head, then jerked it back up the corridor. "Sir, we got a problem. Just before the lights went out, two truckloads of ferrents pulled up to the front door. Two full rifle squads. They say they got a warrant to take the prisoner. The others have been holding 'em off 'til they could come and get you. Then the power went."

Polian nodded. "Alright." He had expected the ferrents sooner or later. Not in force, but in some fashion. He raised his palm. "I'll go argue with them in a moment."

"You might not want to, sir. The ferrents are real

jumpy. When the lights went out, it almost started a firefight. Our guys are jumpy, too." The broad-shouldered guard pointed at the door. "You want me to break it down, Major?"

Polian glanced up the corridor. Two nurses, arms full of linens, paused there, watching casually. They probably, and correctly, blamed the power outage on their visitors. Polian had no desire to advertise the Yavi presence further by breaking down doors.

He shook his head at the guard. "As long as the woman's still unconscious in here, we can take the time to work on the lock." He pointed at the observation closet's door. "I'll check."

Fifty-two

Kit and I stared at the wiggling door knob as we crouched alongside the metal chair that had held her. The conversation beyond the door stopped.

Kit whispered, "They can't get the door open."

I whispered back, "I think I broke the pick off in the keyhole."

She rolled her eyes at me. "Better lucky than competent."

"Thanks."

One set of footsteps sounded in the hall, and Kit gripped my arm.

"What's wrong? They can't see us in here," I said.

She pointed at the dark window in the side wall. "One-way glass. I always hear them going around to the room next door to watch me. They'll be able to see us in a minute."

She reached across me and drew one of my machine pistols from its holster. A shoot-out with the half-dozen Yavi commandos who would soon burst through the door to this sealed room was a terrible option. Especially because the shots would probably spook twenty-plus ferrents, who would rush the place. I closed my hand over hers and the pistol. “No.”

She stared at me. “Parker, I’ll go down blazing before I’ll go back in that chair.”

“Me, too. But we may not have to.”

“We can’t just disappear.”

Fifty-three

Polian opened the door to the observation closet, flicked on the dim light, then stepped to the window, turned, and peered into the interview room.

He gasped. Then he stepped forward and pressed his palms and nose against the glass. "What the hell?" He pounded the thick glass with a fist, and his voice rose to a shout. "What the hell?"

In the room's far corner stood the woman's cot. Off center was the table upon which the interrogator's control console and the hologen rested. Polian's jacket still hung half-off the chair back where he had left it. Wires snaked from the console on the table to the bolted-down chair. Nothing had changed. Except the chair was . . . empty. The tape that had bound the woman dangled in slashed strips from the chair's arms and legs.

Not only was the chair empty: the room was empty.

The interrogator and the guard rushed into the observation closet where Polian stood, eyes wide, pointing at the empty chair.

"Damn. She's disappeared," said the interrogator as he stared into the room, jaw slack.

Polian shook his head, slowly. "It's impossible."

The interrogator said, "Trueborn case officers really are freegging magicians."

The guard said, "Maybe the ferrents got in here and took her."

Polian paused. She was no magician. And this wasn't the ferrents' work.

Fifty-four

Kit and I stood, guns drawn and pointed up at the ceiling, backs pressed flat against the observation window wall, to its right. Two more pairs of feet had just run into the room that lay on the opposite side of the glass. From there, they couldn't see us and the room would appear to be empty.

My heart thumped. All that this child's trick would buy us was perhaps thirty seconds. Then common sense would overtake the Yavi's surprise at the apparently empty locked room.

But people who have never experienced close-quarters battle don't realize how often the difference between life and death turns on who plays peek-a-boo better.

I pointed the remote that I held at the door bore shaped-thermite breaching cone that I had stuck over the door lock, then turned to Kit one last time. She nodded. I thumbed the remote's trigger.

Pop.

The charge fired a pencil of four thousand degree Fahrenheit flame into the lock's guts, which dislodged the lock cylinder, then popped it out the opposite side of the door. The lock's seared guts clunked onto the corridor floor beyond, and the heavy steel door swung out on its hinges without a squeak. Say that for Trueborns. Nobody in the universe was better at breaking stuff.

Kit and I dashed for the door, side by side, before the smoke even cleared.

We popped out into the corridor and turned back to back, sighting down our gun barrels.

The place was empty.

I shoved the observation room's door shut until its latch clicked, put my shoulder to the guard's desk until it squealed, and jammed it against the observation-room door.

Kit looked up and down the corridor as I stood and turned. "Which way?"

I grabbed her hand and tugged her in the direction of the stairwell that led to the door through which I had entered.

Behind us, muffled shouts and banging leaked from the blocked observation-room door. Ahead loomed the corridor junction where, to our right, lurked maybe five Yavi and two ferrent rifle squads. Across the junction, nurses and hospital orderlies drifted out into the corridor, curious about the commotion.

A nurse saw us running toward her, guns drawn. She screamed, dropped the tray she was carrying, and disappeared into a side door.

I looked back. Already, the feeble desk that blocked the door shuddered. The Yavis my cheap trick had trapped wouldn't be trapped long.

I skidded Kit and me to a stop before we reached the corridor junction, then peeked around the corner. The front doors remained ajar, and through them I could see Yavi, weapons drawn and backs to us. But the corridor between us and the doors was deserted. Kit trembled, weak and coughing, in her bare feet, after running twenty yards. The two of us healthy might have simply made a run for it, but in her condition we couldn't win either a footrace or a shoot-out. I had to do something to change the game.

Fifty-five

Polian had been the first of the three of them in the observation closet to realize that the woman, or an accomplice, had somehow managed to shut them in.

He drew back from the observation closet's door, shoulder aching from the first ineffectual blow that he had struck against it. His rage at being fooled welled up, and he threw himself again at the door with a snarl. It budged an inch. They had blocked it.

The guard laid a hand on Polian's arm as the older man stood, panting. "Sir, let me."

Polian turned and eyed the big soldier, the man's needler still holstered. Polian couldn't order him to shoot off the lock. The Trueborns did it all the time in the entertainment holos they exported to glorify themselves.

Earth's armaments industry produced what armies used to bludgeon one another, including large-caliber firearms that could hole modern body armor. Yavet had been a monolithic society for a century. Its armaments industry produced what it needed to control unorganized, unarmored, barely armed citizens who lived and worked in stack cities. Civilian suppression required gunfire that penetrated clothing and people but lacked the mass and velocity to continue on and damage property.

Normally Polian took pride in the elegance of Yavet society and the weapons that secured it. But at the moment he wished for a Trueborn gunpowder blunderbuss that could blow the door into scrap iron.

Instead, he had to stand back and let the soldier take a run at the blocked door. The man backed up against the observation closet's far wall to build momentum. As the man pushed the interrogator aside, Polian looked down at his 'puter. The whole foolish business had only bought the woman momentary freedom. In her condition, she couldn't get far. In the end, her desperation would gain her nothing, except, perhaps, a less painful death.

Fifty-six

It took only seconds for me to drag Kit to the front doors. We stopped, and I motioned Kit to lay on the floor while I low-crawled to the half-opened door and peeked around.

Three feet from me, five Yavi stood shoulder to shoulder with their backs to me on the clinic's front steps. They blocked the clinic entrance. Two had sidearms drawn: three leveled drum-fed needle rifles at the ferrents beyond.

Since I had left them in the dark, the ferrent rifle squads had redeployed into a semicircle. Each ferrent held his rifle against his shoulder and sighted along its barrel at the Yavi.

One of the Yavi, eyes front on the ferrents who had a bead on the Yavi, was whispering to the others.

"Mark a target. Hold your fire."

Between the two groups, one Yavi and one ferrent stood, the ferrent waving a paper sheet, the Yavi shaking his head.

"What if they fire?" asked one Yavi.

"Then you return fire. But nobody's gonna shoot anybody. Take it easy."

I peered between the calves of the Yavi. The faces of the ferrent troops looked as jittery as the Yavi sounded.

The Trueborns called this kind of guns-drawn confrontation a Mexican standoff. I called it opportunity.

I raised my pistol and peered between the lower legs of two Yavi and toward the trench-coated ferrent out front who was waving his search warrant or whatever it was, selected semiautomatic, and thumbed off the safety. I made the range twenty yards.

Sight alignment. Sight picture. Relax. Breathe. Squeeze.

Bang.

My pistol kicked; the round caught the ferrent in the fat part of his calf. He yelped, clutched at his leg, and crumpled to the pavement in full view of his troops.

I was already skittering backward, like a crab on 'phets.

By then, the first itchy-fingered ferrent rifleman had returned first fire at the Yavi. Who had not, in fact, fired the shot that the ferrent was returning.

The five Yavi probably knew the shot had come from behind them but were too busy ducking and firing at the ferrents to turn and investigate.

Kit and I low-crawled back up the hallway as behind us needlers hummed like angry Barrens dragonflies and ferrent rifles crackled off rounds that exploded the translucent windows of the clinic's doors, as well as the transom above them, and sprayed glittering shrapnel that tinkled down on our backs and shoulders.

Glass rained down on floor tiles. Men screamed.

The exchange of fire petered out in seconds, and I pulled Kit to her feet. We ran, crouching, back to the corridor intersection and turned right, toward the stairwell that led to darkness and safety.

I glanced left and saw three Yavi dashing toward us. Behind them the guard desk sat at an angle in the corridor. One of the three was bullet-headed and broad-shouldered and carried a needler. The second, gangling and tall, trailed. The third man, florid and half a head shorter than the other two, grimaced as he ran.

Kit and I were halfway down the corridor to safety, dodging screaming, white-coated hospital staff, when the first needler shot whizzed past my ear.

I dropped back and interposed myself between the Yavis and Kit as I pushed her forward toward the end of the corridor.

Ziizz.

My left shoulder burned as a needle tore through my jacket sleeve.

I looked back and saw the florid-faced Yavi in the middle of the corridor intersection. He held a needler in two hands, apparently the gun that the other Yavi had been carrying, and had dropped to one knee to improve his aim at Kit and me.

He fired again. A needle burned my back, and I staggered. When I fell, I dropped the pistol I held in one hand and the rucksack I held in the other. Both skidded along the tile and came to rest beyond my reach.

Fifty-seven

When Polian, peering past the front sight of the needler in his hands, saw the woman's accomplice sprawl after the shot struck him, he pumped his fist.

The instant that Polian saw the man's face, he recognized him as the armored figure he had glimpsed in the boat in the Eastern Sea.

Polian had just brought down the son of a bitch who was responsible for Sandr's death.

Polian shifted his aiming point. The woman had nearly reached the door at the end of the corridor when Polian's shot had struck down her accomplice. Now she rushed back and knelt beside him.

Polian smiled. The woman had already given them enough. He slid the needler's selector to full automatic. The rounds would riddle her head to foot. She would die painfully and slowly, principally from blood loss.

Sight alignment. Sight picture. She looked up, and her eyes bored into his. Not fearful, not pained. Cool and murderous.

Relax. Polian savored the moment. He released a breath, held it, and began to squeeze the trigger.

Fifty-eight

"Jazen! Get up!"

"Can't."

Kit knelt and tried to drag me toward the door. Healthy, I had seen her fireman's-carry a partisan my size a hundred yards, no problem. But tonight? No chance. I shooed her away. "Go!"

She looked across me, back in the direction of the Yavi who had shot me, and drew her own pistol.

Fifty-nine

"Drop it!"

With the woman in his sights, Polian felt warm steel press against his right temple as he knelt on the clinic's tile floor.

"Drop it, you son of a bitch. Or don't. Blowing your brains out suits me fine."

From the corner of his right eye, Polian glimpsed a uniformed ferrent who had rushed up the corridor from the clinic's front doors and now held a service rifle pressed against his temple. The man's hands shook so badly that the rifle's muzzle vibrated against Polian's skin.

Polian also saw the interrogator and the door guard, each facedown on the floor, hands behind his head, each straddled by a ferrent rifleman.

Polian lowered his needler very slowly, then rested it on the floor and drew back. He continued to stare straight ahead as the woman dragged her accomplice, inch by inch, closer to the door at the corridor's end.

Very slowly, Polian pointed at them. "They're getting away!"

"Shut up!"

Polian said, "You don't understand!"

"I understand! I understand three of my friends are dead because you fuckers opened fire on them."

The woman and the man reached the door.

Polian hissed, teeth clenched. "No! They duped us all!"

Down the corridor, the two of them disappeared, and the door swung shut.

"Who did?"

Polian pointed down the suddenly empty corridor at the closed door.

The ferrent kept his rifle on Polian while he turned his head and stared at the empty space. "Right."

Polian looked over at the door guard, facedown on the ground.

The man turned his head to face Polian. "We have three dead, too, Major. Maybe the Trueborns really are magicians."

Sixty

I lay on my stomach on the landing just inside the cold, dimly lit stairwell where my floundering and Kit's dragging had landed me.

A needler burst will kill a person just as dead as a gunpowder assault-rifle round. But a single needle-gun round won't, unless it tags a vital. The wound does hurt like hell, bleeds like an open faucet, and the trauma can shock you into momentary immobility if the right spot is hit.

Kit dumped my rucksack and machine pistol alongside me. She shook two happys from a tube into her palm, then slipped them between my lips. I gulped them down dry. Then she sprayed my wound with a topical and dressed it. "I don't think the kidney's lacerated."

The stairwell was, at the moment, our dim and quiet little hideaway. But when the ferrents and Yavis who were fighting amongst themselves fifty yards from us reached a truce, my kidney would be the least of our worries. I rolled over and pushed up onto my knees. "We gotta move."

We emerged from the clinic into the darkness without incident. Kit limped stiffly on bare feet that had to be half-frozen. She leaned on me, and I was already bent by my wound and by my ruck. I was moving too slowly, but without Kit and the happys, I wouldn't be moving at all.

We circled back behind buildings, retracing the path I had taken to break in. As we crossed one open space, I had a straight-shot view back at the results of the diversion that I had started by winging one ferrent in command.

A dozen occupied litters lay within the hemispheric glow shaped by the clinic's grounds lighting. The litters lay in a row on the pavement between the shattered front doors and the little convoy of ferrent vehicles that remained parked at the curb. Hospital staff knelt alongside some of the wounded, but a half dozen of the litters held still, blanket-covered bodies.

Kit and I together had fired a grand total of one shot, which had only wounded one bad guy. Yet a half-dozen people had died, and the wounded were too many for me to count. Kit wheezed and pawed my arm for a rest stop.

As we stood in the darkness, panting, hands on knees, another long-hooded ferrent staff car pulled up behind the two canvas-topped lorries. The driver leapt out, circled the hood, and opened the rear door for the passenger.

A ferrent sat up on one of the litters, then stood and limped toward the car and its passenger. The limper was the ferrent that I had winged, touching off the melee.

The two senior ferrents met, talked there in the night, then walked together into the clinic. Broken glass crunched and tinkled as they reached the clinic's front steps, then passed inside. Another litter, bearing a dead body, lay near the doors. A Yavi KIA, no doubt.

I whispered to Kit, "Couple hundred yards more. Can you make it?"

"I dunno."

"Kit, we've gotta get out of Dodge before they regroup."

The best time to escape any situation, as present circumstances had just shown, was sooner, rather than later, when the enemy was confused and disorganized.

"I know. I taught you that, remember? You go on ahead. I'll be along. Just in second place."

I would have carried her in a minute, until I dropped. Her protests notwithstanding. But wounded, I physically couldn't. "I'm not leaving you."

In the distance, I saw healthy ferrents organizing. Too soon, they would be hunting us. "Kit, second place tonight isn't just first loser. It's dead."

She nodded, and we shuffled toward the shelter of another intermediate building. Five yards before we reached the protective shadows, I heard the metallic click of a pistol being cocked in the darkness to our front.

Crap. The ferrents had reorganized faster than I expected.

Kit swung her pistol up and aimed at the sound.

Sixty-one

Polian sat in the now-disconnected metal chair in the interview room. He stared at the dark window of one-way glass. Alongside him in an unwired chair sat the interrogator, who leaned forward, forearms on knees. The door to the corridor was open, but the ferrent who had held his rifle to Polian's head blocked the doorway, rifle trained on the two of them while he scowled.

The ferrent glanced away from them, down the corridor, and his eyes widened. Then he snapped to present arms and stood aside.

A different ferrent, this one in a trench coat, swept past the guard and into the room a heartbeat later. The new arrival walked straight to Polian, then stood, feet planted in front of him. "I warned you that woman was trouble!"

Polian looked up. The black-eyed chief inspector, who Polian had argued with on the clinic's steps weeks before, glared down at him.

Polian nodded. "But you were wrong about why she was trouble. She's a Trueborn spy."

The ferrent rolled his eyes.

Polian said, "You need to lock down the city. Mobilize every asset you have. The danger to Tressen—"

The ferrent's eyes widened. "Are you insane?" He pointed a brown-gloved hand toward the carnage he had just passed through. "The danger to Tressen, Polian, is you! And your trigger-happy skinheads. Three of my men are dead!"

"That was the Trueborns' doing."

The ferrent snorted. "You mishandled a low-level Iridian terrorist. Now you want to deflect the blame for it."

Polian shook his head. "The woman confessed!"

The ferrent narrowed his eyes at Polian. "Really? Pity the Interior Police missed it. Oh, that's right. We weren't invited."

"That's beside the point. She's escaped!"

"Or you've hidden her someplace else. I find it hard to believe that your skinheads couldn't handle a single woman."

"There's another Trueborn spy."

"Ah." The ferrent nodded. "A one hundred percent increase."

"I can prove what I say." Polian nodded toward the hologen on the table. "I can literally let you watch her confession. If I prove to you that she's a threat, will you concentrate on stopping her instead of on blame-fixing?"

The ferrent snorted, spun on his heel to leave. But when he reached the doorway, he bent and lifted the burnt and misshapen lock cylinder that lay there. He frowned. "I know these locks. They're unbreakable."

Polian raised his arms. "Every minute you waste—we waste—their trail gets colder."

The ferrent turned the twisted steel in his hands, then pointed at the hologen. "Show me."

Polian stood, hurried to the table, then lifted the hologen into play position and tapped the start button.

Sixty-two

At the sound of the pistol cocking, my heart rate spiked, and I gripped my own machine pistol tighter.

Kit raised her off hand to grip and aim her machine pistol. I reached for her arm. "Wait!"

"Jazen?" Alia's voice hissed from the darkness.

By the time my arm touched Kit's, she was dropping the pistol back to her side. Alia stepped out of the shadows, into the pale light that leaked from the clinic's grounds. The .38 she gripped two-handed and pointed skyward.

I flapped a hand at Kit and her pistol. "It's okay. She's with me."

Kit looked Alia up and down. "Well, well, Parker. Lost your appetite for older women?"

I held out two hands, palms spread, at Alia. "What the hell? You were supposed to stay back at the rally point and secure it."

"Pyt taught me to take initiative. You picked a dumb rally point. This one's just as secure, and it's closer. Now we can get away sooner. By the way, you missed an excellent gunfight." Alia tucked her pistol back into her trousers' waistband. Then she looked Kit up and down.

So did I. Kit stood, shaking in dirty smock and trousers, and hugged herself with her bare arms, one of which was sheathed in a cast. Her bare feet were blue with cold and bloody from our run across broken glass. Dried blood painted her chin, and her teeth chattered. She was so thin that, if she had been a chicken, a dozen of her would have been required to boil down to a cup of soup. Captivity and torture had sunk her eyes deep into her face, and electricity had exploded her hair into a dirty blond feather duster.

Alia waved me close and tugged my arm so my ear was alongside her lips. Then she whispered behind her hand. "Are you sure you got the right prisoner? For a princess, she looks a little shopworn."

Sixty-three

Polian stared down at the hologen, then depressed play again. He swore and stabbed the button. The machine just sat there. He looked up at the interrogator. "What did you do to it?"

The interrogator shrugged. "Never touched it."

Polian lifted the machine and shook it.

"What am I supposed to be seeing, Polian?" The chief inspector crossed his arms, then glanced down at his old wristwatch, sighed, and jerked his thumb in the direction of the clinic's front. "I have wounded to attend to." He turned on his heel and said to the rifleman in the doorway, "Come with me!"

The uniformed ferrent's jaw dropped. "What about these two, sir?"

"Released on their own recognizance for now. We can find them. Apparently the only aliens capable of disappearing are Trueborn spies."

After the chief inspector had left the two Yavi alone in the interview room, Polian dug his fingernail under the hologen's side-access panel, then flipped it open.

Soot dribbled out and formed a conical, black pile on the tabletop.

The interrogator stared, then slammed his hand on the table. "She fried it!"

Polian ground his teeth. The woman had been left alone with the hologen. A simple incendiary straw in the hologen's memory slot and the most unassailable and valuable evidence of Trueborn misconduct that had been developed over the entire course of the Cold War had been reduced to rubbish.

Polian sat, shoulders slumped, staring at the floor. Then he realized that he also had casualties it was his responsibility to see to. He pulled himself together, rubbed his face, and straightened his shirtsleeves, using his shadowy reflection in the observation window's featureless dark glass.

"Long day." The interrogator stood and walked toward the corridor.

Polian followed. As he reached the doorway, he turned back into the room, then looked around. His Tressen jacket hung off of a chair back. A bedraggled commander was the last thing that his men needed to see after this debacle. Polian slipped the jacket on and smoothed its collar where it lay across the back of his neck. The fabric was comforting. After this night, he needed all the comfort he could find.

Sixty-four

Normally, Tressen checkpoint soldiers care who enters the Government Quarter, not who leaves. If Tressen society communicated in real time, though, the abnormal events of that night would have had those soldiers on high alert in seconds.

But the Tressens didn't communicate in real time. So Alia and I, supporting Kit, bundled into my jacket, between us, slipped past a checkpoint and out into the narrow, twisting streets of the Old Quarter within minutes.

Since the Republican Socialists had taken over, Tressen's official religion was Republican Socialism. But on Tressel, like on most of the outworlds, old-time monotheism had acquired a certain momentum that even totalitarians hadn't been able to arrest. The Church of Tressel had managed to keep its doors open across Tressen. Literally.

We found a twisting side street that led up a hill. The Church of Tressel apparently believed in building as close as possible to its principal shareholder, and there was, in fact, a church on top of the hill. Its doors were unlocked, because you never knew when somebody might feel the need to be saved. But apparently we had picked a light-need night, because the place was deserted inside. We rummaged through the church poor box and built a wardrobe for Kit. It didn't make her look less shopworn, but it improved her morale.

The three of us sat in a rear pew while Kit tried on shoes that Alia passed to her. Alia pointed at the shoes. "We're taking those from the poor. Shouldn't we pay for them?"

I sighed. In the first place, we had spent the last of our Tressen currency on tea and brot at the bakery. In the second place, the only other suitable tokens of value we still had were a couple of Weichselan diamonds apiece, which were not only gross overpayment for secondhand shoes but a tipoff if they turned up in the poor box. But the wound in my back ached. Also, as I came down off the happys, fatigue wedged itself into a corner of my consciousness.

"Those?" I pointed at the shoes Alia wanted to pay for and shook my head. "I think the poor already gave those back."

As I was getting weaker, Kit, ratty shoes and all, was getting stronger. She pointed at the rucksack in my lap, and I passed it to her. She rummaged, handed me an object, then pointed at a steep, spiral staircase behind us that wound up and into an opening in the ceiling. "Bell tower?"

I stared at her. "I have to do the rescuing *and* the climbing?"

Alia stuck out her hand. "Give it to me. I'll do it."

I stared at her. "Do what?"

She eyed the unfamiliar thing. "Oh. I don't know."

I sighed, lifted myself onto my feet, and shuffled to the spiral staircase with the object in one hand.

Five minutes later I wound down the bell-tower staircase, rubbing a knot on my head where I had hit it on the bell that hung in the tower. Tired soldiers make mistakes. The sooner we got out of here the better.

I stepped back down onto the marble-tiled floor and found the pews empty. The clothing Kit hadn't appropriated had been returned to the poor box, and the two females in my life were dressed and waiting on me at the door, arms crossed.

Kit said, "We've got a train to catch."

Successful field espionage isn't just about being smarter. It's about being smarter, sooner.

Before sunrise, the three of us had snuck aboard a freight that had already begun to roll south but hadn't yet reached even walking pace. Once the Yavi and the ferrents resolved their mutual dysfunction, or at least reined it in, trains like the one we had hopped would be searched. Eventually, telegraph alerts would go out through the cables buried in the roadbed to the strongpoints down the line. The three of us would become an even more endangered species. But at that moment, we remained ahead of the game.

At midmorning, Kit, Alia, and I sat in a boxcar facing the open door and watching Tressel roll by as we headed south into Iridia. The cargo crates against which we leaned contained manufactured goods, not fish, so the car smelled better. The car rocked, and I rocked with it.

I drifted, half asleep, down off the stimulants that had driven me, sedated against the pain of my wound and bleary even without the drugs.

I watched through half-closed eyes as Alia peered into Kit's face.

"You have pretty eyes. Not pukey green like mine."

Kit stared out at the landscape. "Thanks. Where I come from, blue eyes are common. Green eyes are rare. With those eyes, boys would go nuts over you."

"Like Jazen is nuts over you?"

I closed my eyes before Kit could glance at me, and pretended to sleep, which didn't take much pretending.

Kit sighed. "Maybe once."

Alia said, "Are you nuts over him?"

If the hole in my back didn't kill me, the waiting to hear her answer might.

Kit said, "Things are different in situations like this."

"I don't mean like now, when you're both all sweaty and gross."

"That's not what I meant, either. Physically intimate case officer pairs are fairly common. The problem between us was mission orientation."

"What does that mean?"

The sedative tugged me toward unconsciousness.

Kit said, "I wanted to save the universe, which was our job. Jazen just wanted to save me."

"He got in *trouble* for that?"

"No. But because of Jazen's misplaced focus, I finally had to recommend that we be repartnered. Jazen quit rather than serve with anyone but me."

"Why was it so important?"

"In our business, misplaced focus gets people killed."

"I mean why was it so important to him?"

"Living without someone who you"—I heard her swallow—"someone who you work closely with is painful. Every day of your life that you wake up and realize that they're gone, it's like somebody reached into your chest and squeezed your heart."

"Oh. He saved you just now. Does that mean you will take him back, or you won't?"

I fought to stay awake. But before Kit answered, I lost the fight to the healing sedatives. That meant that when I woke up the next day I was still going to feel somebody squeezing my heart.

Sixty-five

Polian turned up his Tressen jacket tighter as chill wind tore at him and at the other mourners in the stone line at the Tressen cemetery. The wind scudded a low cloud ceiling across the morning sky and caused already-bowed heads to dip lower. The place itself was bland, treeless granite, punctuated by waist-high stone mounds. Polian stared down at the fist-sized granite cobble in his hand, then glanced at the similar stone carried by Gill, who shuffled in line alongside him and to his right.

Ten feet to Gill's right, in a parallel line, walked the ferrent chief inspector with whom Polian had locked horns, somber and carrying his own stone. Ten yards farther ahead, the two lines would pass three stone cairns, and he and Gill would confront the ferrent across the stone-covered bodies of the three ferrents who had been killed by Yavi needle rounds the previous night. Not, Polian reminded himself, by Yavi. At least, not in a causational sense. The three Tressens and the three dead Yavi were victims of an exchange of gunfire triggered, Polian was sure, by the Trueborns.

As he shuffled along, it occurred to Polian that one could tell a lot about a society by how it handled death. The three dead Yavi had already been cremated and their ashes sealed in envelopes. The ceremony had been appropriately brief. Yavet couldn't spare space for holes filled with decomposing flesh, nor waste emotional energy on afterlife fantasies.

This Republican Socialist funeral was mercifully atheistic, compared to Iridian or Trueborn rituals. But equally barbaric, except for detail variations imposed by differing physical environments.

Seventy percent of Tressen, Sandr had told him, was soilless, moss-covered granite. So bodies weren't buried, they were simply covered with loose stones.

The Tressens were, at least, better than the Trueborns, who buried their corpses, then left them to rot in the ground.

Gill was the first to reach the stone cairn. He bowed as he laid his stone atop the waist-high cairn, then backed away. Polian copied the old man's behavior, but glanced up, across the stones that covered the dead men. His eyes met the black eyes of the ferrent chief inspector, who glared as he placed his own stone.

Afterward, Polian and Gill left the cemetery together in the backseat of a Tressen staff car driven by a Yavi trooper.

Gill stared out the car window at the chief inspector, who huddled alongside the now-deserted cairn, smoking, with a knot of ferrents.

Gill said, "Polian, you ever wonder whether the other folks have it right?"

"General?"

"The three men we lost? Didn't give them much of a send-off, did we? Maybe we hold human life too cheap."

Polian stiffened his back against the car seat. "The Tressens have systematically exterminated a nation of eleven million people, sir."

Gill waved his hand at the ferrents. "Not those butchers. The Trueborns. They call our population-control policies mass murder."

"Sir?" If Gill had been an ordinary citizen, Polian would have been tempted to arrest him for treason.

Gill waved his hand again. "Don't worry, Captain. I'm not a subversive. Just an old man who's seen too much death."

And one who hadn't reprimanded Polian for this entire fiasco.

"Major, allying totalitarian societies is like stuffing two fire-ant colonies into one bottle. The Tassini on Bren do that."

"I don't follow you, sir."

"When the bottle gets shaken, the ants fight. But if you pour enough sugar into the bottle, they go their separate ways."

"Sir?" Polian stifled an eye roll. Gill didn't think like a Yavi. At least, not like a legal one.

"Major, you were right about these Trueborns. They're more real than the ferrents thought. Frankly, maybe more real than I thought. And they're pretty good at shaking up this bottle."

"Uh—thank you, General."

"What we need to do now is accelerate a positive result before it's too late."

Polian sat back in his seat as the car pulled up in front of Gill's hotel.

As Gill stepped to the curb, he leaned back in to the car and said, "Ruberd, you're a bright guy. Think me up some sugar, will you?"

Polian managed a smile. "How soon, sir?"

"Before the Trueborns figure out what's going on and shake the bottle again."

Sixty-six

The day after I had slept through the most interesting part of Kit and Alia's girl talk, the three of us managed a happily uninteresting disembarkation from our boxcar at the spot where we were expected. Pyt and a detachment escorted us to a different rebel encampment, to which Celline had displaced during our absence. The place was as old and understaffed as the first one.

We were supposed to return from Tressia with information and a plan. When we showed up with a warrior princess to boot, it was natural enough that she was invited to dine with the only other warrior princess at large on Tressel.

Alia and I were invited, too. The four of us dined in Celline's quarters, a cabin as spartan as her troops' billets. We ate the same menu as Celline's troops, too, and dinner wasn't served until after the troops had eaten.

Halfway into the fish course—who am I kidding? All Iridian courses are fish courses—Celline turned to Kit. "Colonel, why did you come here?"

I paused with a forkfull of crabmeat in front of my

mouth. It wasn't the kind of question a soldier answered for a just-met semi-ally who didn't need to know the answer, especially in front of an eleven-year-old. But a case officer in the field was no ordinary soldier, and Kit Born was no ordinary case officer.

Kit and I both knew that we needed Celline's cooperation, and we wouldn't get it if we treated her like an untrustworthy hick.

Kit looked up from her meal. She still looked thin and pale, but already the light had returned to her eyes, and she filled out her Iridian fatigues better with every meal. She dabbed her lips with her napkin. "Ma'am, your friends the Republican Socialists would love to have a technically advanced ally like the Yavi."

Celline stared at her, eyes suddenly cold. "As we say it, Colonel, every bully wants a bigger stick. Apparently the stick Earth gave the Tressens the first time wasn't big enough."

Kit inclined her head. "I'm sorry. I really am. Earth understands Iridian anger. We didn't even try to link with you when we were inserted."

Celline shifted her gaze to me. "Obviously that changed by the time Lieutenant Parker was inserted. Earth figured out that we were too angry to ask, but not too principled to bribe?"

Kit ignored the barbs. "Ma'am, what we need to figure out is what the Republican Socialists offered that bribed the Yavi. One of my interrogators was a major, and the way he was getting bossed around, his superior was a general officer. The Yavi don't send generals to command routine outworld brush fires."

Alia asked Kit, "How did you get caught?"

I watched Celline. If Alia hadn't asked, Celline would have.

"My partner and I didn't come down on a shuttle. But we knew all the Yavis had to come and go aboard one. So we staked out that vacant lot they call a spaceport in Tressia. When the next party of Yavi imposters arrived, we followed them."

Alia leaned forward, eyes wide. "Where did they go?"

Kit shrugged. "North to the Ice Line by commercial rail. That was an easy tail for us. We just bought tickets on phony ID papers. Then the Yavi went on, even farther north, by ice train."

Celline's eyes widened. "The RS doesn't sell tickets for the ice trains."

Kit wrinkled her forehead at Celline. "You know the ice trains?"

Celline frowned. "Too well. Please, Colonel. Continue."

"You're right. They don't sell tickets. It's a military-run train. We stowed away on the undercarriages." Kit glanced at me. "Eternads are a case officer's best friends. But once the Yavi arrived at the end of the ice-train line, they continued on farther northeast, out across the snow flats. Jazen, they've downsmuggled more than that one skimmer you saw. They must have been at this for years. It's just one more indication how big this is."

Alia asked, "They got away?"

"No. They would have, but I made the decision to follow them on foot." Kit stared down at the table and shook her head. "Hostile, unfamiliar environment. Weather went to hell. Risky." Kit's face darkened, and she swallowed. "My junior died in a crevasse fall during a storm. Took our uplink with him."

And another piece of her heart. More victims sacrificed to her Trueborn delusions of duty.

She took a deep breath. "My luck just got worse from there. I wound up in that damn clinic broken in a half-dozen places, with the ferrents and Yavi intelligence pulling on me like dogs with a chew toy. The rest, you know."

Actually, I didn't know. And I didn't want to know. It was obvious that the hologen that Kit had fried before we escaped contained a confession that the Yavi had wrung from her by drugs and torture. One thing I did know was that I owed the Yavi payback for that. Worse for them, Kit Born owed them, too.

Celline wrinkled her forehead. "Do you have any idea what they were doing up there?"

Kit shrugged. "I didn't see much before things went to hell. They had opened a small-scale excavation surrounded by disproportionate security. Buried treasure. Mining, maybe."

Celline nodded. "Ah. Both, actually, I think."

Kit and I both stared at her, jaws dropped.

I asked, "What?"

"They're after the stones."

Kit stared at her. "What stones?"

Celline said, "Your father's stones, Jazen."

Sixty-seven

Three days after Gill and Polian had parted, they met again in the makeshift office that Gill's predecessor had made out of an urban hotel room.

"At ease, Major. You look cold." Gill nodded at a teapot set on a warming plate on a sideboard. "Pour yourself a cup, then sit with me."

It was cold. Polian buttoned another button on his Tressen jacket.

Once the two of them were seated at a conference table set to the side of Gill's desk, Polian tugged a hologen from his bag, switched it on in the center of the table, then pointed at the graphic that hung in the air between them.

"This red pancake is a threedee schematic of the deposit. The vertical scale is exaggerated because the deposit is so thin that if it weren't exaggerated it would look like a circular sheet of paper."

Gill stared at the holo while he rubbed his chin and nodded. "You're saying that the stones aren't buried even as deep as you thought?"

Polian nodded. "The burial depths turn out to be about the same as they are for the weapons-grade cavorite at the west end of the fall. Weapons grade behaves like a less dense material than propulsion grade, so we expected that we'd have to dig for this stuff."

Gill sipped his tea. "Major, what's the soonest you could begin full-scale extraction operations?"

"Do you mean from now, or from the time we downsmuggle the mining equipment, General?"

"What equipment do we need?"

Polian cocked his head, then ran a finger along the perimeter of the image. "Actually, sir, the way this has shaped up, we wouldn't need equipment. We could literally put troops to work raking stones up from under the snow."

Gill cocked his head. "How much of this stuff could we get like that?"

Polian waved up another figure, this one a threedee numeric matrix. "You know, sir, given good weather and motivated workers, we could harvest enough stones to power a cruiser fleet for a decade in three weeks."

"How big a mountain would that be?"

Polian cocked his head as he stared at the ceiling. "You'd be surprised. I think you could load it all into ten skimmers."

Gill nodded. "If that's all it amounts to, we could pack the stones into the leftover containers we used to downsmuggle skimmer parts and upsmuggle the whole thing on a single shuttle. Nobody cares what leaves Tressel. Just what arrives. We'd be out of here before the Trueborns knew what they missed."

Polian didn't answer. He stood, walked to the room's window, and looked out across the city. In the distance, he saw the spaceport's silver hemisphere, the runways, and the broad, exposed plain across which the shuttle runway stretched.

Gill came and stood alongside him, then clapped him on the shoulder. The general's bony hand felt light through the soft fabric of Polian's jacket. "Something bothering you, Major?"

Polian pointed out at the spaceport. "It's pretty exposed. I'd like to do something about that."

Gill frowned. "The Iridians haven't mounted a meaningful operation inside the Tressen border in years."

"They haven't had Trueborn help in years."

"According to the spy, she didn't know what she was looking at up in the Arctic. She certainly doesn't know how fast this thing is going to move from here forward. We didn't know ourselves until five minutes ago."

"I'd still like to fortify the place."

Gill nodded. "I'd rather prepare for the worst and be pleasantly surprised when it fails to occur. Do it, Major. Do all of it."

Sixty-eight

After Celline had dropped the bomb about my father, she called for Pyt to take Alia off to bed. Then Kit and I walked with her out to the base of a low rock face at the edge of the camp. There, the racing moon's light reflected off two dozen stone grave markers that were tucked back beneath an overhang. There, presumably, godless Tressens would never find and desecrate them.

Celline bent and touched the nearest stone. "Jazen, each of these men and women survived the Long March with me. There are only a few of us left now."

"Ma'am?"

"After Earth handed the war to the Tressens, and before there was a rebellion, the Tressens began the wholesale extermination of the Iridian people. The ice trains carried unknowing Iridian families north by the trainload to freeze and starve. Colonel Born, that train you rode carried you through the grave of a nation."

Kit whispered, "I didn't know the specifics."

Celline sighed. "That was the Tressen's intention, of course."

I bent and squinted at a marker. "You said that my father—"

"Long before I knew him, your father was a soldier who was sent here to Tressel to help the Tressens win the war against us. A high-level military advisor."

My heart sank. No wonder nobody wanted to talk about General Jason Wander. He helped kill a whole nation. As I knelt there in the vanishing moonlight, I cradled my head in one hand. Howard had finally led me to an answer. He had never promised that I would like it.

Celline touched my shoulder. "Jazen, nations pick wars. Soldiers only fight them. It wasn't the loss of the war that destroyed Iridia, it was what the Tressens did afterward. I've never blamed your father for that."

A Legionnaire learns early that soldiers don't pick their wars.

I said, "But you said you knew him."

"That came years later. The Trueborns sent Jason Wander back to Tressel."

"To make things right?"

She shook her head. "Nations do the right thing for others when it's also the right thing for themselves. He was sent back because the Trueborns needed cavorite."

I shook my head. "The Trueborns have all the cavorite in the known universe. On Bren. I know. I got blown up there once helping them keep it flowing."

Kit touched my shoulder as she shook *her* head. "No. This makes sense. Not that Howard would ever admit it."

Howard Hibble wouldn't admit that the sun rose unless somebody electrocuted him first.

Kit said, "Jazen, the only reason the Slugs bothered to

impress human slaves in the first place was because cavorite was poison to them, but not to us. There have always been rumors about how the war ended. That we weaponized a grade of cavorite that couldn't be used for fuel."

It did make sense. The Trueborns were always belly-aching about everybody else's human rights violations. Everybody knew we won the war. The history chips said we won a massive battle, out at the edge of the universe, between gigantic fleets of colossal starships. But if we actually won by wholesale poisoning of the only other intelligent species known in the universe, we wouldn't advertise it. How could Earth argue that its brand of genocide was different than the Tressen brand?

Celline said, "Hibble sent your father back to get the stones. And your father did. But he also risked his life, shoulder to shoulder with me and other Iridians, to strike out against the Tressens."

"Why?"

"The stones were under the death camps. Then your father helped me and the core of what became the rebellion escape from the Tressens."

"My father was part of the Long March?"

Celline shook her head. "He had another war to fight. Not just for our survival, but for the survival of mankind. However, without him there would have been no Long March. And without the Long March from the Arctic, there would have been no rebellion."

Kit frowned and crossed her arms. "But why would the Yavi want weapons-grade cavorite? It's useless for starship fuel. All it's good for is killing a species that's been extinct for thirty years."

The moon began to set over Tressel, and the three of us walked back toward our billets.

Celline gazed up at the vanishing moon and smiled. "Only the Yavi know. And they aren't about to tell us."

I looked at Kit and raised my eyebrows.

She nodded, then said to Celline, "Actually, they might."

Sixty-nine

The Tressen sentry snapped to as Gill, Polian, and the Tressen Regular Army major approached him across the tarmac of the spaceport runway. Gill returned the rifle salute, looked the sentry up and down, smiled and nodded. He turned to the Tressen major, and said, within the sentry's earshot, "Your men look sharp, Major Vendl."

Gill still had the Chancellery fiat letter, so the compliment was no more necessary here than it had been to silence the ferrents yet again, after the funeral. Gill effectively commanded here, whether these Tressens liked it or not. But Gill was what the Trueborns called a GI's general. He knew how to make them like it, rather than not. He had now made a friend of one soldier, of every soldier that one told, and of the major who commanded this Tressen infantry battalion. That battalion was now erecting a defensive perimeter around the landing strip.

Vendl, the Tressen major, jowly and gruff, paused as the three of them walked along a double row of concertina wire strung between sandbag guard emplacements.

Major Vendl crossed his arms. "General, may I speak frankly?"

"It's the only way I want my soldiers to speak."

"Sir, the Iridian rebels haven't mounted an assault of any magnitude inside Tressen proper since I was a boy. All this"—he waved his hand at the ring of emplacements and wire that his battalion was building around the landing strip—"is probably for nothing."

Gill nodded. "Actually, I agree with you, Major. I'm preparing for the worst case. What I need to know from you and from Major Polian here is what the worst case may be."

Vendl, the Tressen major, pushed back his steel helmet and scratched his forehead. "The latest intelligence I've seen about rebel order of battle is that they can't field more than one company-sized light-infantry unit."

Polian stepped in before the other major stole his thunder entirely. "The Iridian rebellion's been reduced to irrelevance. For the last ten years they haven't attempted more than assassinations and occasional hit-and-runs on Tressen positions down in occupied Iridia. The best estimate is that once Celline dies—if she hasn't already—without an heir, the old guard will fold completely."

Gill pursed his lips. "Take it from an old guardsman—they may want to go down swinging. Tell me more about their capabilities."

The Tressen major shrugged. "Extrapolating from what they were, we should expect basic, leg infantry. Well-trained, minimally equipped. Highly motivated."

Polian said, "No body armor like contemporary infantry. Needlers will cut them to ribbons. Typical partisans. But typical partisans are more likely to try to hit us elsewhere, while the"—he glanced at Major Vendl—"the material is in transit. An ambush."

The Tressen major said, "They're pretty good at ambushes. The best defense against an ambush is to not walk into it in the first place."

Polian said, "We won't pick the route until the last minute. Use decoys. Ambush won't be a problem. For that matter, nothing the Iridians might throw at us should be a problem."

Seventy

About Kit's and my freight-hopping return trip to Tressia, the less said the better. We anticipated that the Tressens might be watching the trains more closely since the Great Big Clinic Shoot-out, so we stood watches back-to-back, one asleep, one awake. Therefore, we had minimal time to get reacquainted. We also anticipated that the rail yards would be watched more closely, so we bailed out of our boxcar on the outskirts of Tressia, split up so that we didn't fit the two-person profile the Tressens were looking for, then legged it in to town separately.

It was past moonset when I rounded the corner and reentered the street where we had raided the church poor box. I climbed the steep cobbles toward the church, the street deserted except for a single drunk passed out in a doorway. I was so jumpy that for a moment I thought it was Kit.

The church looked to be as cold and empty as it had been during our last visit, but I noticed a gray scuff on the left side of the entry door jamb, six inches above my eye level. That mark signaled me that Kit was already inside.

I took the stairs two at a time and smacked my head on the bell again at the top of the stairs.

I rubbed my head. "That's gonna leave a mark."

"That's what *he* said." Kit sat on the belfry floor with her head bent below the waist-high wall that enclosed the open space within which the bell hung. The single bell, which was both as tall and wide as I, was capped by a wood frame that suspended it between timber beams that supported the belfry's pyramidal roof.

"That's a stupid place to hang a bell. That's what *who* said?"

Kit peered down at the data panel of the remote-activated telemetry recorder that I had placed during our last visit. It now rested in her lap like a black plastic rodent with a wire tail.

"The bad-cop Yavi at the clinic. After I broke the good cop's nose."

"No wonder you don't get dates."

She looked up. "You're late to this one. Trouble?"

I shook my head. "You're early." I pointed at the recorder. "We got anything on the RAT?"

"Couple hours."

I raised my eyebrows. The bug that the recorder was set to listen for was voice activated. It was common to revisit a RAT and find nothing, if the bugged subject was quiet. A normal office day often yielded only a half hour of audibles, farts included.

She smiled. "The bad cop seemed attached to his jacket. He must wear it all day."

A micropowered flexibug, like the one Kit had slipped into the hem of the Tressen jacket that had hung in her interrogation room, transmitted a signal deliberately weak in order to be virtually undetectable. Therefore, we had to set the RAT high, such as in this tower on top of a hill, so the bug's transmissions would reach it no matter where the subject took the bug, as long as it stayed within a city-sized radius.

And RATs didn't retransmit, because the signal could reveal *their* location. They had to be serviced by a live asset who exchanged drained batteries and full chips for fresh ones. It was clumsy, dangerous, and all very last-century. But the outworlds were last-century places. They lacked contemporary infrastructures within which to eavesdrop. You can't hack a Net that hasn't been invented yet.

That wasn't the only reason I didn't like this situation. We were cornered up here. I slipped on my snoops and peered out over the waist-high wall of the open bell tower into darkness that the snoops turned bright, ghostly green. The street below remained deserted. I asked Kit, "Pull the chip and listen someplace safer?"

She shook her head. "We're already here. Once we leave, we won't be back for a while. We could miss something that gets said in real time."

We could also get trapped up here like rats, lower case. I sighed and plugged my phones into the RAT's second jack. But I remained standing, with eyes on the street below. Actually, the view wasn't bad. I could see all the way out to the spaceport.

After a half hour of breakfast orders and routine

chatter, another voice joined the subject, who turned out to be an intelligence major named Polian.

We couldn't see the holo the two of them were watching, but we got the gist. Kit paused the recording and said, "I know that guy. Nice for a baby-killer." A minute later Kit spoke again. "Propulsion-grade cavorite! No wonder the Yavi sent a general to take charge of this! Rat-bastard Howard could have told us both about this."

I shook my head. "I don't think he knows. He misfigured that Tressel cavorite was all weapons grade." Over the years, Howard Hibble, like most spooks, was more infamous for what he got wrong than he was famous for what he got right. Despite the periodic public outcries, it wasn't so much that intelligence services were dishonest, and it wasn't so much that they were stupid. They just absolutely, positively knew a lot of stuff that wasn't true.

Kit looked up at me. "Then the most important thing we can do right now is get the word back about this, Parker. The Yavi without starships are pains in the ass. The Yavi with them, and allied with the Tressens? That's an interplanetary war waiting to happen."

"Neither of us has an uplink. There's no commercial transmission off Tressel. We have to get out of here aboard the next shuttle."

"That may not be easy."

We resumed listening. Then we got to a three-way conversation among Polian, his boss, General Gill, and what appeared to be a Tressen infantry major. They were talking about the shuttle landing strip. I leaned out of the bell tower, maxed my snoops, and studied the spaceport. "Crap."

Kit looked up at me. "Why crap?"

I tugged off the snoops and handed them down to her. "Stand up here and take a look. It's really not going to be easy to get on to the next shuttle."

Kit studied the distant perimeter, then whistled. "That's a battalion-sized unit. And the strongpoints are manned by Yavi with crew-served needlers."

"We could send out a physical message with a clean courier."

"Pass a note in study hall?" Kit shook her head. "No Earth diplomats, no Earth diplomatic pouch. The only people who upshuttle from Tressel are Yavi, and Tressen diplomats."

"Maybe—"

"The shuttle crews?" She shook her head. "They're all Rand."

Rand was a major hub, like Mousetrap, but famous for tight-ass neutrality instead of sex, drugs, and vomit. The Trueborns called Rand the "Switzerland of Space," and we were as likely to bribe a Rand contract pilot as we were to hack a Rand numbered account.

Kit sighed. "Besides, we can't trust even an honest novice courier to deliver a message this important."

Kit wasn't just a nose breaker. She could fly a shuttle. I'd seen her do it. However. "We can't fight our way in and hijack the flight. Not through what we just saw out there. This is lousy."

Kit leaned forward as she stared into the darkness. Then she whispered, "No. It's worse."

I turned and peered out of the bell tower. Two Tressen canvas-backed troop trucks were now parked sideways, nose to nose, at the base of the hill, blocking the street that dead-ended in the square that fronted the church.

Kit said, "How the hell did they find us?"

I closed my eyes and swore. "When we were here last time, who put the clothes back in the poor box?"

"Alia. Why?"

"She left Weichselan diamonds in the poor box. To pay for the stuff we took."

"She told you that?"

"Do women ever tell me anything? But it's obvious now. If somebody told the ferrents, and here somebody tells the ferrents everything, diamonds would attract attention. Even if the Tressens didn't recognize the diamonds as a Trueborn calling card, their new friends the Yavi sure did. They might not have guessed why we came here. But they probably staked the place out for days, just in case we came back." The drunk asleep in the doorway. I swore.

Bam. Bam.

The two trucks' back gates slammed against the trucks' rear bumpers as they swung down. A helmeted Tressen infantry platoon piled out into the street at the base of the hill, then fell in alongside the trucks.

Seventy-one

Polian leaned forward and tapped the car's driver on the shoulder. "Faster!"

The staff car rounded a bend, then squealed to a halt in front of two Tressen troop trucks parked nose to nose across a narrow street walled on both sides by stone row houses.

Polian leapt from the car, ran around the trucks and up the street as it climbed uphill. He was panting by the time he caught up with the Tressen major, Vendl, who walked behind an advancing phalanx of troops, his sidearm drawn.

Polian drew alongside the other officer and touched his arm.

Vendl smiled at him, panting too. "Such a nice night for a walk, I came myself. Glad you asked us out, Major." His smile disappeared. "Major Polian, we staked this place out like you asked. And the stakeout saw two people enter the church, at different times, earlier tonight. But it's just as likely to have been a couple tramps as a pair of spies. It's gonna be a cold night."

Polian shook his head. "It's them." Why they would have left coated diamonds mystified him. A dead-drop payment to a local asset, perhaps. But the undercurrent he felt was strong. "There's no other way out of the building?"

The Tressen major shook his head. "Or in. We're dealing with two people inside, tops. In the Old Quarter the buildings were built with one stone back against another stone back. Especially on hilltops with views and a summer breeze. Space was at a premium."

Polian nodded. Yavi didn't understand views or breezes. But every Yavi understood the concept of too little space. Ruberd Polian was on the verge of changing that for Yavet. And he wasn't about to let two Trueborn spies stand in his way.

The advancing phalanx that had dismounted the trucks crested the hill and spread out as it moved into a small, open square in front of a church, which had to be the one where the diamonds had been found. It was a narrow, spartan stone building, and a short stone staircase rose from the street to the church's arched wooden double doors. They were closed.

As he and the major strode across the square's center, Polian frowned. "Major Vendl, don't leave these men in the open. Don't underestimate these people. They—"

Bam.

The formation began taking fire from a gunpowder weapon.

Polian dove for the curb, rolled up against a building, drew his needler, and looked around. A Tressen writhed on his back in the square's center. The man clutched his thigh with two hands, immobile and screaming. The rest of the troops had scattered into the shadows, as Polian had.

He peered up into the dimness. A bell tower rose from the church's facade, perhaps sixty feet above the square. The belfry, open on four sides, made a perfect sniper's perch. One round, one hit. The woman probably had night-vision equipment, and the Tressens didn't. As long as they all cowered out here, she would pick them off one by one. But inside, in close quarters, sheer numbers would work to their advantage and against her marksmanship.

The obvious course of action was to withdraw to defensible, covered positions, then await reinforcements. The Trueborns weren't going anywhere. But one of the people in that church was responsible for Sandr's death, and the other, the woman, had humiliated Polian. And both threatened his mission.

Ruberd Polian, the staff officer, the bookish boy, got to his knees in the shadows, gripped his pistol tighter, and prepared to lead the first, and perhaps last, charge of his military career.

Seventy-two

Kit leaned out of the bell tower as she tapped a fresh magazine into her machine pistol to seat it: then she pitched the removed magazine, which was down a round, to me to reload. I peered down into the dark stairwell while I pressed another round down against the magazine's spring-loading. Outside, the only sound was someone screaming.

I said, "Why do you get the snoopers?"

"Because I'm a better shot. The screamer's their C.O., I think."

"Where'd you hit him?"

"Left thigh. So he'd be conscious and vocal."

She meant so he'd be bait. Not only had Kit decapitated the organization below us with one stroke, she had left its commander bleeding his life out through a severed femoral artery in the middle of a pan-flat open space.

In a minute or two, the most courageous and daring among the wounded man's troops would crawl out and try to drag him to safety, and she would plink the poor hero.

One of the new casualty's braver buddies would crawl to *his* rescue, and she would plink him. And so on. It was a very effective tactic to winnow out an outfit's designated as well as latent leaders, and thus paralyze it as a fighting force.

It was cruel. But as the Trueborn general Sherman said, war is cruelty. The crueler you make it, the quicker you replace it with peace.

The trouble with this tactic in this situation wasn't its ruthlessness but its math. We would run out of bullets before the Tressen army ran out of replacements. We had to break out of this trap now, before the Tressens could reorganize and reinforce.

A force of two case officers was equipped to multiply itself and defeat a numerically superior force in a pinch like this. But the force-multiplying equipment of Kit's team lay entombed in an icy crevasse with her junior. My team's mines, grenades, and microdrones lay scattered across the land and sea of northern Iridia like sneezed-out snot.

We remained handsomely outfitted for eavesdropping and for burning holes in locked steel doors, which helped us here and now like pants helped pigs. What we needed, it seemed to an old tanker like me, was a dose of shock power and mobility. A tank didn't really have to kill infantry. It just had to come rolling toward them, and its appearance would clear them from a battlefield like an overhead light cleared roaches from a kitchen floor.

Pop-pop-pop.

A needle pistol. There was at least one Yavi down there.

Somebody was yelling down below, loud enough that he almost drowned out the wounded screamer.

Bam-bam-bam. Kit's machine pistol spit yellow flame in the darkness.

"Dammit!" Kit hissed.

Bam-bam-bam.

This time, somebody else below started screaming. Several somebodies.

Then the crackle of Tressen gunpowder rifles began, slow at first, like rain pattering on a roof. Then it grew into a deluge. Rounds splintered the beams above Kit and me, and ricochets bonged off the tower bell itself.

Kit and I ducked, covered, as a debris storm pelted us.

In seconds, the shooting stopped. But below us, now inside the church, running feet thundered.

Kit brushed plaster and wood off her sleeves. "Some hero got half of them up and moving. And the other half laying down a base of fire. I got a few, but—"

"I hear 'em down there." But I couldn't see them, and neither could Kit, snoops or not.

Outside, the screams of the wounded faded as shock and blood loss drained them.

Below, I heard a creak, barely louder than the thumping of my heart, then more of them, as the Tressens started climbing the stairs toward us.

Seventy-three

Polian knelt behind a pew, staring at the staircase that spiraled up through the church's arched ceiling and into the bell tower. His breath came in ragged gasps, not so much from exertion as from a combination of terror and exhilaration. He had led and men had followed.

He nodded at four of the Tressen riflemen among the thirty who knelt behind him in the church and waved his needler toward the staircase. In single file, the four crept forward, rifles at the ready and eyes upturned, and began to climb.

Seventy-four

I lay on the belfry's plank floor, extended my machine pistol over the floor's edge into the stairwell, and sprayed two unaimed, three-round bursts down into the dark. For my trouble, I got twenty rounds of returned Tressen rifle fire that splintered beams and spalled clanging splinters off the great bell, one of which laid my cheek open like a split pomegranate.

Kit, lying on the opposite side of the stairwell, looked across at me and shook her head. She didn't need to speak. Tight spot. Maybe, finally, too tight.

How many steps had I climbed from the church floor to the belfry floor? I guessed fifty. Forty-five feet? Fifty? How many riflemen could they pack onto the staircase at one time? Too many of them. Too few of us. And not a tank in sight.

I rolled over on my back to reload and stared at the bell. Then I rolled back, tugged my rucksack toward me, and dug out two door bores.

I pointed out bolts above us that secured the iron

supports for the axles upon which the great bell pivoted. Kit nodded.

A rifle barrel poked up in sight, and she sprayed a burst down the stairwell.

There was a scream, then a thud.

Then more creaks as more Tressens climbed toward us.

Kit sprayed another burst, and under its cover I scrambled to the bell, leaned out, and slapped the two door bores on the bell supports' bolts. Then I ducked back before the return fire gouted up into the belfry.

I nodded to Kit again. She pulled back from the bell and dialed down her snoops against the impending glare. Then I triggered the charges with the remote in my hand.

The smell and smoke of molten steel and charred timber filled the belfry. Kit coughed. The bell creaked.

But it just hung there.

A dozen shots whizzed up from below.

Our adversaries were getting more aggressive, if no more accurate.

I wedged myself between the belfry wall and the bell and shoved with my feet.

Nothing, except a burst from below.

I looked across at Kit.

Her sleeve was shredded, and a red stain spread across it. She waved her other hand and mouthed, "Scratch."

The next one might not be.

I stared at her again. Then I backed up two steps, jumped across the gap between the belfry floor and the bell, and my chest thudded against the curved iron. I hugged the bell like it was an overweight prom date, while my split cheek bled against the iron. But still nothing budged.

Bwee.

A round zipped past my ear. I shinnied up the bell and threw a leg across the inverted yoke of timber from which the bell's axles protruded into the charred pivot points. Seconds later I sat atop the bell like a Trueborn cowboy on a rodeo bull.

I threw myself forward, back, and side to side. The bell creaked, then swung so hard that the clapper thudded against the bell's wall, muffled by the human wart that clung to it.

The overbalanced bell swung back, wood splintered, and the bell tore free.

In a blink, it plummeted down into the stairwell. And so did I.

Seventy-five

Bong!

At the base of the spiral staircase, Polian squinted up into the deeper darkness when he heard the thunderous peal overhead, so loud that he reflexively covered his ears.

Next came a rumble, a human shriek, and then a rifle clattered down and struck one of the soldiers creeping up the staircase on the man's shoulder. The stricken soldier's rifle discharged, and a man above him screamed.

The repeated peals of the bell crescendoed and alternated with great crashes. A limp human body thudded to the floor at Polian's feet; then the great bell tumbled into view thirty feet above him. It crashed into the tower's stone wall, then caromed back as it rolled toward him like a runaway train.

Polian's exhilaration of moments before turned to terror as his eyes widened. He screamed, then turned and dashed toward the church doors.

As he slammed his shoulder against the thick doors he looked back and saw that the bell was gaining on him. The doors parted before him, and he sprinted for his life.

Seventy-six

Each time the bell struck and was redirected by the bell-tower walls, its gong deafened me. As I tumbled, I saw back up the bell tower's dim shaft. The bell had ripped out the belfry floor as it fell, and a hail of snapped floorboards followed behind me. So did Kit, arms and legs flailing as she fought for balance or a handhold.

The bell rebounded off one wall and caught a Tressen infantryman between itself and the opposite wall. His face was a foot from mine as his eyes bulged, and I smelled his last, sour breath as his chest collapsed with an audible crunch of rib bones.

Then the bell and I were past him. The iron mass, then my body, fell on in nose-to-tail formation, bouncing and deflecting off shattered stair treads and supports that protruded from the stone walls.

The bell spiraled down to the church floor, and the impact of iron lip against marble exploded tile fragments like shrapnel. The bell bounced, deflected off a pew as it crushed the bench, and, redirected, rolled toward the now-open front doors.

Shouting Tressen soldiers flattened themselves against walls to let the bell rumble past, or dashed ahead of it, then tripped and tumbled down the outer stairway and into the square.

I landed facedown on my machine pistol, which knocked the wind out of me. Stunned, I gulped for a breath.

Whump.

Something as soft and heavy as three flour sacks struck me between the shoulder blades and drove the breath back out of me before I could enjoy the oxygen.

Kit lay on top of me, wheezing into my ear. She got to her feet before me, scooped up her own gun, and dragged me to my feet.

The two of us dashed after the bell as it toppled over the church threshold, bong-bonged down the steps, and rumbled, rolling on its side, across the cobbled square.

By the time the rolling bell began to accelerate down the hill, we were sprinting, crouched and sheltered behind it as Tressen infantry fired. Maybe at the careening bell, maybe at us.

Kit panted, "That was sentimental crap!"

"Huh?" I stumbled over a cobble, then righted myself as a round spanged off the rolling bell.

"You jumped on this bell because you saw me get hit."

"What?"

"I saw it in your eyes!" Kit ripped off a full auto burst in the general direction of a Tressen who aimed at us while kneeling in a doorway. A halo of orange sparks flashed around the man as bullets caromed off the doorway surround, while our personal steamroller led us past him in the darkness.

We were three-fourths of the way down the hill now, and the bell rumbled straight toward the midsection of the right-hand Tressen truck. Three Tressens between the bell and the truck scattered.

Kit ejected her spent magazine. It clattered to the street; then she wiggled her fingers at me. "Magazine?"

I ripped a spare one out of the pouch in my chest strap and handed it across. As Kit took it, the bell struck the truck so hard that it rocked on its suspension, then toppled onto its side.

Whoom!

The truck's fuel tank exploded in an orange fireball so wide that it licked the house fronts on both sides of the street. The concussion knocked us flat on our backs, and the heat from the blast swept across us like someone had opened a furnace one yard in front of us.

I blinked away my daze as Kit rolled on her side and faced me. "You can't play hero whenever I bleed, Parker. I'm a big girl. And I care about something bigger. You *do* see that's the problem between us?"

Bang. Bang-bang.

Rounds buzzed over our heads, Tressens rushed us, and I returned fire.

As I reloaded, I sighed. In the vast cosmos of human experience was any situation so dire that it could divert a woman bent on discussing The Relationship?

I said, "Could we do this later?"

"Hmph."

"This is a *gun*fight, for God's sake!"

Whump.

A secondary explosion aboard the burning truck

brightened the street again. An instant later, the new fire must have reached ammunition in the truck. Rounds cooked off like popcorn, flashing green tracer streaks in all directions that ricocheted off the stone of the buildings and the street.

While the Tressens had their heads down, I tugged Kit up by the hand and we sprinted, dodging the cook-offs, toward the narrow gap between the nose of the flaming, toppled truck and the nose of the intact one opposite it.

We drew closer, and I saw the church bell. It had burrowed into the burning truck's twisted frame and lay, a cracked and crackling iron lump, glowing red hot and spent, like a meteorite newly delivered from heaven.

Religion and I were strangers, but it did seem that the godless had just been smitten by an engine of the righteous, pretty much like the Gideon Bible predicted they would be. It wasn't enough to convert me, even to the secular Trueborn idealism that Kit wanted from me. But it was enough to make me think about it.

We squeezed through the searing opening between the trucks. Then we ran, limping and leaning on one another, into the quiet darkness beyond.

Seventy-seven

Polian dragged himself, breathing hoarsely, over the square's cobbles toward the prone and motionless Tressen major. Polian's right foot dangled, swollen and useless, the ankle crushed by the great bell as it had leapt and bounded from the church. He paused to rest, chest heaving, and stared down at the base of the hill. A ruined truck burned, and its flames lit the dark bodies, and the limping wounded, rifles dragging behind them, as they gathered around the remaining truck.

He had seen the whole fiasco unfold, indeed he had made much of it unfold, yet it seemed unreal. He reached the fallen Tressen major and felt Vendl's neck for a pulse, but the cold flesh beneath Polian's fingertips told him not to bother. And that it was all real.

Polian stared at the dead man's shattered thigh. An adult human body, whether it originated on Yavet, on Tressel, or even on Earth, had only perhaps five quarts of blood to give up. It seemed that all of Major Vendl's quarts had pooled there among the cobbles.

Polian clenched his teeth, dragged himself into a sitting position, and stared out across the dying flames at the darkness into which the two Trueborns had escaped, again.

They would never stop him. But now he hoped they would try.

Though he would probably be hanged for this catastrophe before they could.

Seventy-eight

Kit and I hit the jackpot after we limped aboard our return freight before sunrise. Our boxcar was loaded with household goods. We drew straws for first watch, then decided we were both too exhausted to stay awake alone, anyway. So we each wrapped up in blankets, trusted the espionage gods to protect us against waking up in leg irons, and slept like corpses.

We got away with it not, I think, because the gods *did* care, but because it had been so many years since Iridian rebels had mattered that the Tressens *didn't* care.

I woke to sunshine filtering in through the rolling boxcar's slatted sides, and Kit's fingertips gentle on my cheek. Even better, her face was six inches from mine, her lips were puckered, and her eyes were closed.

I leaned toward her, and her eyes opened.

She said, "Oh. I tried not to wake you." Her fingers smoothed a plastitch strip over the slash in my cheek, while she blew on it. That would dry the solution which would pucker my wound's edges together so the nano 'bots could knit them.

She drew back and examined her work; then her mouth turned down at the corners as though she was about to cry. “Oh, Parker. I did my best, but it was open down to the bone. I really do think that one is gonna leave a mark.”

I smiled though it stung. “Bigger mark on the Yavi and the Tressens, though. How about you?”

She laid her left hand on her right shoulder, then rotated her right arm slowly, and winced. “Okay. You’re a good pillow to land on. But I’ve got bruises on bruises in places you can’t imagine.”

“I can imagine plenty. I could blow on them for you.”

She rolled her eyes. “It really is the first thing to come back, then?”

I paused, swallowed. “It never went away.”

She blinked. Then she turned her back and dug through my ruck for a couple of Meals Utility Desiccated. “Like I said. You haven’t changed.”

“Neither have you. It’s not good enough that I risk my life to save yours, is it? I have to risk it to save the universe. Doing the right thing’s never good enough for you! I have to do it for the right reason. That Trueborn crap about the happy few who shed blood with one another? I still wouldn’t hold my manhood cheap if I’d been lucky enough to avoid it.”

She squeezed my breakfast tube to start it warming, but so hard that her fingers whitened. “You still don’t get it, do you? It’s not about misplaced testosterone. It’s about giving yourself to something bigger and better than your own welfare. Or even your buddy’s welfare.”

“Idealism’s a luxury. Downlevels kids can’t afford it.”

“But rich Trueborn kids can?”

"If the tiara fits . . ."

She chucked the MUD into my lap, then squeezed her own.

I lifted the warmed tube, read the label, and raised my eyebrows. "Buttermilk waffles with maple syrup and bacon. My favorite."

Kit whispered, "You think I'd ever forget?"

The boxcar's door was open, and she turned her face toward it, and away from me, while she ate.

She always did that when she didn't want me to see her cry.

The rest of the trip, we were both very quiet.

Seventy-nine

Polian lay in a white-walled, plain private room at the clinic where his last bloody contest with the Trueborns had gone awry. He lay atop the linens, the bed's head cranked vertical, so he could see the clumsy plaster boot with which the Tressen surgeons had weighed down his throbbing right ankle.

He snorted at the irony. The interrogator was the only Yavet-trained medical professional attached to this task force, but he was forbidden to treat Polian, or any other member of the task force, by modern means for fear that would blow his or their covers. At the moment Polian thought it was an idiotic rule, even though he had made it.

Polian looked up as he heard a rap on the jamb of the room's open door.

Gill cocked his head at Polian, then pulled the door shut behind him and strode to the younger man's bedside. Gill looked down and smiled.

Polian frowned back. Gill looked different, and yet

more normal. Then it hit Polian, and he widened his eyes. "General, you're in uniform."

Gill grinned as he held out his arms and looked down at the Tressen battle dress uniform that hung from his thin frame. "Major, we haven't been fooling anybody on this planet except ourselves. We're in a shooting war of consequence now. We may as well act like it."

Polian shook his head. "We aren't authorized—"

"We are. I do the authorizing until my notification gets back to Yavet and the chain of command's response arrives. Which will be months from now."

"How do you intend to proceed, sir?"

"I leaned on Zeit himself. The battalion guarding the shuttle strip and convoying the cavorite down here's been seconded to us. And our own troops will operate openly and integrated within the force. Divided command is confused command."

Polian turned his face away. If he, Polian, had recognized that sooner last night, how many casualties could have been avoided?

Gill patted Polian's uninjured thigh. "Don't whip yourself, Major. That Tressen commander didn't know what he was up against. You tried to tell him. He paid for not listening. Now his battalion's grieving for its major and in need of a commander."

Polian nodded.

Gill laid his hand on Polian's shoulder. "Soon as we get you a walking cast, I want you to step into that command slot, Ruberd."

Polian stiffened his back. "Sir, I'm a staff officer."

Gill made a fist. "You got those riflemen off their

bellies! You're a leader! And you seem to be the only person on this planet who outguesses these Trueborns."

Polian felt his throat swell. He had expected a court-martial. Gill had instead given him far more than the benefit of the doubt. Finally, he said, "What schedule do you intend that we follow now, General?"

"The next cruiser's due in four weeks. We should deliver the cavorite inside the spaceport defensive perimeter in time to conceal it in other cargo before the down shuttle arrives. But no earlier. Then we load the stuff. Once it's aboard the cruiser, the parcels will get lost in the shuffle and offloaded at intermediate ports before the Trueborns even know they exist."

Polian said, "Their intel down here seems to be better than we expected. They may know our schedule."

Gill smiled at Polian. "The schedule I'm most interested in now, Ruberd, is yours. How soon will you be up and around?"

"Before the Trueborns know what hit them, if possible."

Eighty

When Kit and I met with Celline again, she had returned to the encampment sheltered against the cliffs where I had first been taken.

The three of us sat together in Celline's plain quarters around a conference table. Kit and I laid out what we had learned, and we asked Celline to help us derail the Yavi, who were our enemy, and the Tressens, who were hers, because together they would become a more dangerous threat to everybody. Celline wasn't dumb. She agreed.

We evaluated our options.

If we could simply have communicated what we knew to the Trueborns, the cavorite would become a useless, embargoed rockpile here on Tressel. But we couldn't get so much as a birthday card off Tressel in time.

That simplified our objective. We had to make sure that the Yavi couldn't get the cavorite off Tressel. But simple objectives rarely can be simply accomplished.

We couldn't shoot down the shuttle, because we lacked the means. Besides, nobody in Human Union history had ever shot down a neutral-flagged vessel. It wasn't ground any of us wanted to break.

We couldn't attack the cavorite mine. If a case-officer team in Eternads couldn't reach the mine in fighting trim, Iridians in overcoats certainly couldn't.

We couldn't intercept the shipment in transit from the Arctic to the shuttle landing strip, because we couldn't intercept what we couldn't find or catch. A skimmer convoy could take any route over any terrain, change it at any time, and could outrun any vehicles the Iridians had or could steal.

The only *time* the Yavi's cavorite would be vulnerable was shortly before the next cruiser arrived, in four weeks. The only *place* was at the so-called spaceport. Unfortunately, the Yavi and the Tressens had recognized that vulnerability and had converted a joke of a spaceport into an improvised fortress that was no laugher.

Irregular armies historically penetrated fortresses by infiltrating them. Belly-crawling in the dark was a staple of guerilla warfare. However, the Yavi military was an offshoot of a culture that sniffed out and killed people wholesale. The shuttle strip was now surrounded by a buffer of antipersonnel sensors that could detect a house cat at a thousand yards.

All of the above left us one very bad option.

In the table's center, where the hologen usually goes in meetings, I unrolled for Celline a flat paper map of the city of Tressia. It was an old map, and I had drawn in the shuttle strip north of the city with a wooden-shafted pencil. Kit and I had also drawn in the details of the perimeter surrounding it, from sandbag strongpoints to barbed wire, to antipersonnel sensor arrays, based on our observations.

Celline spread her hand so that the little finger and thumb spanned the distance between the first of two doubled rows of concertina wire and the nearest covered position from which infantry could mount an assault on the perimeter. That cover consisted of a single row of attached working-class houses that backed on the rail line from the south that led into the main rail yards.

Celline shook her head. "Infantry would have to cross at minimum a mile of open ground, exposed to an enemy firing from covered positions within their perimeter. Every army is made up of few teeth supported by a long tail. Our tail is longer than most, because a higher proportion of our troops are no longer able to perform combat service."

I frowned. "What could you put up, total, ma'am?"

Celline frowned back at me. "Lieutenant, my army can deploy perhaps two combat-ready platoons, totaling one hundred."

My jaw sagged. That wasn't an army. Trueborn college football teams dressed that many for home games.

Celline stared at the map. "The Tressen battalion you've observed numbers nearly one thousand. Plus these Yavi of yours. We would field one attacker against ten defenders. The textbook preferred ratio is three attackers against two defenders."

I sighed. The beautiful warrior princess could do command math. That didn't make her sums prettier.

Celline tapped a finger on one of the emplacements that had been erected behind the concertina. "These needle machine guns you say these people have. How much fire can they lay down?"

I cocked my head. "They run cool. They can sustain three thousand rounds a minute until the ammunition or the nitrogen runs out. They always have plenty of both."

She raised her eyebrows. "Three thousand rounds?"

Kit said, "Darts, really. Yavi weapons systems are designed more for population suppression than war fighting. If we had body armor—but we don't."

"My soldiers are valiant and competent. But I've wasted too many in impossible set-piece battles before. A frontal assault won't work. All of these ideas won't work." Celline's shoulders slumped. Even Kit's did.

Celline ran a hand through her hair as she looked at Kit, then back to me. "I believe in my cause and in my troops. But I do not believe that God will send another rolling church bell to smite our enemies."

I glanced out the window. Alia ran past, Pyt trailing behind slowly as she ducked behind a rock and hid from him.

I looked back at the group. "The Trueborns say that God helps those who help themselves, ma'am."

Celline cocked her head. "We say that, too. Lieutenant, do you have an idea that *will* work?"

I shrugged. "The next cruiser's due in four weeks. In three, you'll be able to tell me whether I do."

Eighty-one

Polian sat in a parked skimmer, warmed by his armor, and looked out across the brown, Arctic plain. Acres of ground now lay open to the sky. Tressen combat engineers had scraped snow away that had lain undisturbed for centuries.

More Tressens, great-coated infantry, shuffled across the frozen ground in skirmish lines, their rifles replaced by simple rakes. Moment by moment, a man would halt, stoop, and place a plucked red stone into his cross-slung cloth bag. It more resembled a harvest than a military maneuver.

Yet he was witnessing, indeed was in charge of, this most militarily significant operation in the history of his world. He shifted his weight, then lifted his armored thigh with both hands and moved it closer to the skimmer's floor heat vent. The Tressen cast on his ankle, that protruded below the sawed-off leg segment of his armor, was neither light nor warm.

But except for the cast, Yavi technology was now

employed openly. Polian turned and counted down the row of skimmers parked to his left on the snow. Five were loaded with harvested cavorite. Five more soon would be.

He glanced at the calendar in his visor display. Two weeks until the shuttle lifted off. Two weeks more to plan and to agonize over what might go wrong.

Gill, who had remained at the fortified shuttle strip, gave Polian wide latitude to plan, to agonize over, to command this operation. The old moustache had proven to be the best officer Polian had ever served under. And yet, Polian agonized more about Gill than about the Trueborns or the rebels or the downshuttle's schedule.

Polian was an army officer. But Yavet's domestic tranquility made the army, and army intelligence in particular, little more than a slightly better equipped police force at home, and little more than paramilitary mischief makers on the outworlds.

So Polian, like his father the cop, was as offended by crimes against Yavet as by military operations mounted against her. And uncertificated birth was a capital crime.

Polian's suspicions about Gill had begun with the simple bigotry of physical appearance. "If you're looking for an Illegal, look first beneath the table." A simpleton's joke, but true. Illegal births were a vice of the lower classes. The lower classes got less to eat, and less space in which to live. Over generations, only the small among the lower classes survived.

And Gill had begun his military career not through enlistment, but after time in the Legion. The Legion offered Illegals a way off Yavet alive. And, if they banked their pay and their luck, they survived their hitches with enough money to buy a new, phony identity when they got out. But while a scrub identity might make an Illegal look legal in the eyes of the world, he remained an Illegal in the eyes of the law. There were whispers that some returned and served Yavet, some who didn't tell. There were also whispers that if they served well, no one asked.

All that pricked at Polian, he reminded himself, was an undercurrent of suspicion that ran counter to everything Polian felt about Gill. But Gill himself had told Polian that it was an intelligence officer's duty to be suspicious.

"Major, Number Six is loaded out!" A combat engineer, bright and earnest, saluted as he approached Polian's skimmer.

Polian returned the salute, which was the only right thing for an officer to do. Polian watched as the engineer walked down the skimmer line, bent against the arctic wind, and checked loading manifests. Returning a salute was a right thing that was easy for an officer to do. But not all right things were easy. If a Yavi officer, police or military, believed beyond reasonable doubt that he had encountered an Illegal, it was the officer's sworn duty to summarily execute him.

Eighty-two

Three weeks to the day after Celline and Kit bought my plan, I sat outside my billet, in the chill moonlight, on a rock bench. I bent over a fire-warmed pot of soapy water, washing grease off my hands and forearms so that I could see what new blood blisters, tool gouges, and cuts decorated my skin.

Celline walked toward me holding two steaming mugs of tea. When she handed one to me, then sat down across from me, I saw that she was as stooped from fatigue, and as grimy, as I was. But tonight her green eyes glowed in a face that had begun to show the wear of years locked to a struggle spiraling downward.

I raised my cup to her, and the thin veil of steam softened her features for a blink. "Thank you, ma'am."

"No, Lieutenant. Thank you."

I shrugged as I wiped my hands with a rag. "I've never been afraid of a wrench."

"For that, certainly." She shook her head. "But more for rekindling hope. I see it in the faces of my soldiers. I've failed to inspire them, for far too long, to anything like this. If we fail, the rebellion will be done. But if we succeed visibly, we may inspire others to challenge the RS. By the thousands."

I threw down the rag. "I'd like to see a few thousand of 'em show up tomorrow."

Celline bent a tired smile and raised her eyebrows mockingly high. "I thought a Trueborn would say, 'The fewer men, the greater share of honour . . . I pray thee, wish not one man more.' "

I rolled my eyes. "I didn't know the Trueborns had pushed Shakespeare this far out along the jumplines."

"Actually, *Henry V* is no favorite of mine. Your father would say it's too gung-ho. That there is no glory in war." She set down her tea, rolled up her sleeve, and washed dust off an old and purple shrapnel gash that furrowed her forearm from elbow to wrist. "Though, as Shakespeare wrote in *Henry V*, I'll strip my sleeves and show my scars from this day to the ending of the world, alongside anyone who's ever shed his blood with me."

I nodded. "Ma'am, I'll shed my blood for a friend. I have. But not for somebody's idea of glory."

"Ah." She nodded back. "The disenchantment of the soldier, who by definition can't choose his war. The idealist, by definition, always chooses hers. That's a source of tension between you and your Colonel Born, isn't it?"

I shook my head. "Mine? Hardly."

"Alia seems to disagree."

I paused. "What happens to *her* tomorrow?"

"She will remain here, safe under the protection of Pyt. At first she will call it bad luck to miss the fight, as

Shakespeare's actor does. But someday she will understand how many dead soldiers would ache to share her luck."

I should have known that Celline would have thought not only about her troops but even about the simple war orphan who had fallen under her protection.

I raised my eyebrows. "Pyt's staying behind? He doesn't seem the type to miss the fight, either."

"Pyt knows where his greater duty lies. He will do that duty, from now until the ending of the world." She shifted herself on her stone bench, and shifted the subject, too. "Are they ready, then?"

I shrugged. "We're out of time and daylight to make them any readier. But they should be fine. Your idealists are surprisingly good scroungers. Is your side of things ready?"

"After so many years and so many battles, there are no surprises. Except for Colonel Born, whose strength is a welcome one." Celline yawned, then stood. "Until tomorrow, then, Lieutenant?"

I smiled in the moonlight and touched my forehead. "Or until the ending of the world, ma'am."

Eighty-three

Polian felt himself nodding off in the skimmer's right-hand seat as the convoy whispered south, changing direction at random intervals, the outriding skimmers alert for any sign of ambush. His driver slewed the hovercraft ninety degrees, and Polian rocked against the side curtain so hard that he half awakened.

The Trueborns, even with any help they could bluster or borrow from the Iridians, even with the great good luck they had thus far enjoyed, had to be off balance about this entire operation. No more, Polian thought, than he was about Ulys Gill.

The skimmer changed direction again, and leaned Polian inboard this time. Regarding Gill, Polian didn't know which way to lean. Fortunately, when it came to denying Yavet the treasure he and this convoy carried, neither did the Trueborns and their meager allies.

Eighty-four

"Here it comes! Right on time." The Iridian staff sergeant who stood at my side pointed to the south, out between the fern fronds that concealed us. He peered through brass binoculars, while I wore my snoops set for full daylight. We saw the writhing black smoke plume that hung above the Tressen Patrol Train's locomotive before we saw the train itself.

I shifted my focus eight hundred yards to our immediate front, to the railroad tracks. The ground looked completely normal. I smiled. If that was what I saw, the train's engineer and lookouts would see the same thing as they stared ahead at the flat, unthreatening monotony of the Bloody Corridor. The name had in recent years become merely historic, but we were about to change that.

Our force had left camp before the dawn that followed my discussion with Celline about soldiers and ideals. The trek that had brought us to this vantage overlooking the Corridor had taken us all of the following day and night.

I shifted the snoops back to the approaching train.

I could see it now: engine, tender, troop car with roof pillbox, and the usual flatcar pair behind, both empty.

"Perfect!" said my staff sergeant.

Two minutes later the patrol train was five hundred yards short of being directly in front of us. I heard its wheels as they clacked over the joints between rails, saw the helmeted guards swaying lazily atop the troop car, even smelled steam and burned engine oil as the wind drove the engine smoke toward our hiding place.

Someone, among the other six men I directly commanded, who were huddled around the sergeant and me, hissed, "Now!"

I nodded up my snoops for an instant and glanced at my staff sergeant. His fingertips were white where they gripped his binoculars.

I nodded my snoops back down and flicked my gaze from the locomotive to an apparently empty space alongside the tracks. Now just four hundred yards separated them. I swallowed, myself. *Now!*

The train rattled forward.

I muttered, "Do it!"

I felt my heart pound as I stared at the empty spot.

The flash blackened my snoops for a heartbeat. Then I saw a smoke-and-dust cloud hovering in a ball above the roadbed. One rail curled toward the sky, the coppery spider silk of our det wire dangling from it and glinting in the sun. The companion to the curled rail remained arrow straight, but it protruded at an angle from the ground fifty feet to the side of the roadbed, where the explosion of our charges had spun it. Then the explosion's thunder boomed across us there in the forest.

The locomotive's drive wheels froze as it braked. One hundred fifty tons of train screeched atop the rails, squeezing fountains of orange sparks up along the locomotive's flanks, that glowed even in the daylight. The engineer tried to halt the train short of the gap we had blown in the tracks, lest it derail, then accordion onto itself in a jumble of wreckage.

The engineer could have taken his time. The commander of our lead infantry platoon, concealed fifty yards off the tracks in a camouflaged hole, had detonated the charges so far in advance of the train's passage that the train would halt easily fifty yards short of the gap. We didn't want to derail the patrol train. We just wanted to borrow it.

Our loan was, however, subject to the approval of the Tressen infantry aboard the train, and we expected them to be tighter about it than bark on a tree.

Boom!

The commander of our second infantry platoon detonated our second charge as soon as the train's tail had passed forward of *her* concealed position. The first purpose of the second charge was to cut the tracks behind the train, to assure that its engineer couldn't reverse back in the direction it came, to safety.

The charge's other purpose was to signal our two infantry platoons to attack, even before the train had shrieked to a stop and its defenders began to realize the trouble they were in.

Two platoons of Iridian soldiers rose up from the flat soil of the Iridian Corridor like armed zombies on Trueborn Halloween. They stormed the troop car and the engine before the troops atop the car could think about traversing the crew-served machine gun and depressing its elevation to engage the attackers.

Inside the car, small-arms fire crackled for perhaps thirty seconds. One Tressen dove out through a window, rolled to his feet, and ran. An Iridian bullet cut him down within thirty yards.

Then there was silence, except for the periodic hiss of steam as the locomotive's brakes automatically released pressure, and the wind that blew in from the sea and across the Bloody Corridor.

I won't say it was a fair fight. But a fair fight is the last thing a soldier wants to give his enemy. The Tressens never knew what hit them, and that's the way we planned it.

The commander of the lead infantry platoon, whose timing had been critical to the success of the ambush, climbed an outside ladder at the end of the troop car, swung a leg up, and stood atop the troop car's roof. She waved a green scarf that she held in her left hand, which signaled us, hidden back in the treeline, that the train was secure.

I zoomed my snoops to look also at her upraised right fist, from which her index finger extended in our prearranged signal for number of Iridian casualties suffered. I also looked at her face. Kit wasn't smiling. One casualty suffered was a miraculous number, considering. But any number greater than zero isn't miraculous to the commander whose unit suffers it.

I peeled off my snoops and turned to my staff sergeant. I turned around and pointed at two lurking objects camouflaged beneath mounded fern boughs. "Sergeant, let's get the twins moving."

Fifteen minutes later, my crew of seven and I led the way as our two-vehicle column of smoke-belching, clattering, squealing crawler tanks rolled forward. Over the past three weeks, their crews and I had resurrected and rebuilt two operable tanks by cannibalizing the other two of the four in Celline's junk-heap arsenal. Meanwhile, engineers had cleared a path from camp to this spot, one that the old crawlers could navigate. Now the resurrected machines lurched across the uneven ground at the tree line and into the sunlight for the first time in four decades, like regrown dinosaurs.

The Iridian crawlers were the first tanks used in combat on Tressel, during the final Iridian-Tressen war. Like so many things in the parallel human cultures that had grown up within the parallel environments of the outworlds, the Iridian tanks resembled the first tanks used in combat on Earth. The Trueborns invented their versions during the war that the Trueborns had designated as their first, but hardly last, world war.

The tanks were probably alike because the wars that spawned them were alike. The British Mark V and Iridian Thunderer crawler tanks were both designed to shelter advancing infantry formations, which had been getting slaughtered and reslaughtered in back-and-forth assaults across open ground, swept by machine guns, that lay between trench lines.

Both tank designs rolled on continuous, flexible tread bands that rotated around their armored flanks. Both were riveted-together, rectangular steel boxes that looked like a giant had kicked them in the ass, causing the box top to slide forward relative to the box's base, creating a rhombohedral profile. The up-angled prow that the shape created enabled the tanks to crawl up and over obstacles that weren't crushed beneath their thirty-ton weight.

Both lacked the familiar top turret of later crawlers and contemporary hovertanks. The old crawlers' main cannons fired sideways, swiveling within enclosed sponsons that bulged from the vehicles' armored flanks like steel saddlebags. Four machine guns whiskered out below aiming slits, one from the nose, tail, and the side of each sponson.

Even an early 2000s Trueborn crawler could travel cross-country at nearly fifty miles per hour. But it took our crawler pair ten minutes just to rumble across the few hundred yards of open plain between the treeline and the railroad. That was because both the British Mark V and the Iridian Thunderer were designed to be too slow, and in fact were too slow, to outrun the walking infantry that sheltered behind them as they advanced toward enemy machine guns.

By the time our little convoy lumbered alongside the patrol train, our infantry had removed intact rails from the roadbed behind the train, carried them forward on their shoulders, and were spiking them into place in front of the train to replace the rails that Kit had blown.

We didn't care about leaving a gap in the tracks behind us. In fact, we wanted a gap, to slow down any trainload of Tressens that might pursue us from the south. We were taking our borrowed train not back south, but north, into the heart of Tressen.

Kit's soldiers had also cut the telegraph cables that ran in the roadbed, which was supposed to preserve for us the element of surprise as against our enemy in Tressen.

We also uprooted ties from the roadbed behind us. These we used to construct ramps, then drove the crawlers up onto the two flatcars. Then we chained our thirty-ton girls into place for the journey north. Finally we tied tarpaulins fashioned from sailcloth over the tanks, in hopes that they would attract less attention when the train rolled past strongpoints and, once we crossed the border into Tressen, villages and towns. Most of that travel would happen during the oncoming night, after moonset, but we needed all the surprise we could get.

The last thing we did was attend to the dead.

The lone Iridian casualty, who had been a widower corporal, we buried back within the wood line in an unmarked grave. Celline said a few words, and there were moist eyes, including hers and mine, though the moment was brief. We didn't really have the time to spare, but nobody wanted the Tressens to get hold of the body.

The Tressen dead, who numbered ninety-seven, we could have pitched into the shallow fighting holes along the roadbed in which our infantry had hidden. But the Tressens entombed their dead above ground, covered with stones.

It took us two hours that we couldn't spare, and we could barely scavenge enough rock to veneer each body. But Celline insisted.

When we had finished, Kit, Celline, and I stood on the open back platform of the troop car as the train inched forward. In the locomotive's cab, an Iridian private who had once worked on the railroad opened the engineer's throttle.

We looked back across the makeshift grave mounds.

Here and there a bit of uniform or even a limb was exposed.

Celline sighed. "It's unfortunate that we couldn't have done a more thorough job."

It seemed to me that a ninety-seven-to-one kill ratio was plenty thorough. But, of course, she was referring to the burial. As the train accelerated toward the Tressen border, I raised my eyebrows. "After what Tressen's done to Iridia, ma'am? I wouldn't have blamed you if you pissed on 'em."

Maybe that was why she was a duchess and I was a soldier.

But twenty-four hours from that moment, Celline, myself, and everybody now aboard that train would be soldiers. Or worm food.

Eighty-five

The first skimmer of the convoy from the Arctic, with Polian in its right front seat, a command pennant flapping from its windscreen, slid to a halt. The hovercraft drifted in front of the first gate that marked a passage through the rows of concertina wire that now surrounded the spaceport.

The gate guard came to attention and saluted. Then he raised the gate bar and waved the convoy through. Two minutes later, the cavorite that would change the balance of power in the human universe came to temporary rest inside the shuttle strip's hangar.

Gill was waiting for Polian, smiling alongside a small mountain of plasteel cargo containers waiting to be repacked, first with contraband cavorite and then with an assortment of unsuspicious goods.

Polian's skimmer settled onto the floor of the great dome, and the echoes died as its engine shut down.

After thirty-six hours of being vibrated into jelly, Polian could barely stand. He tried, clinging to the windscreen with his left hand while saluting with his right.

Gill motioned him to remain seated. The older man walked to Polian's side. "How was the trip?"

Polian shrugged. "Uneventful."

Gill nodded. "Those are the best kind." He leaned into the skimmer and looked down at Polian's ankle. "We'll see if this shuttle carries a flight surgeon. We need to get that looked at by somebody besides a local physician. And in the meantime, you should go and rest it. You must be shaken to pieces."

"I thought I'd stay here while the stones are unloaded and repackaged, sir."

Gill shook his head. "They're surrounded by a battalion now. And nobody inspects what leaves Tressel, just what arrives. Ruberd, your job is ninety percent done. Take it easy. Do I have to make it an order?"

Polian said, "No, sir, you don't. And thank you." But what he thought of was what the interrogator had said before the abortive attempt to torture Born, the killer. A job ninety percent finished was only half done.

It occurred to Polian that the interrogator had probably interrogated dozens of imposters who had been unmasked as Illegals, then executed. No warrant was required to subject any Yavi to interrogation, just like the interrogation that had been conducted on the woman, so long as the crime under investigation was serious. No crime was more serious than unauthorized birth. Technically speaking, Polian was duty-bound to follow up his suspicions about Gill. He had the authority. He had the means. He certainly had reasonable suspicion. It was the right thing to do. After all, Polian's father had spent his life tracking down suspect Illegals.

Yet the suspect had recently been more a father to Polian than his own had ever been.

As it had during Polian's long journey back from the Arctic, the profane notion that a man should be judged by what he made of himself, rather than how he had been made, abraded the edge of Polian's conscience.

Gill's hand lay on Polian's shoulder armor. "I'll take care of things. The downshuttle's on schedule to land tomorrow, take on cargo, and take off within an hour. I don't think we're going to have any trouble."

Eighty-six

We thundered north in our peculiar Trojan horse of a train all night. Nobody came out and waved at us. But then nobody came out and shot at us, either. Maybe that was because nobody on Tressel had ever seen a horse.

More likely it was because a half hour after dark it began to rain buckets big enough to drown Troy. In these, the good old days of warfare, before Doppler radar and satellites, weather wasn't a planning element, it was a blind date.

Kit and I stood, swaying, side by side on the troop car's back platform, clutching the railing in front of us, as rain rumbled off the platform's steel roof.

A lightning flash lit the rain-slicked sailcloth covering the two tanks on the flatcars behind us. The thunder rumble came two beats later, and another flash cracked down before the first rumble died.

It was eight a.m. Tressia time, though the storm made it look like midnight. The train was two hours away from our objective.

Kit snugged her oilskin jacket around her throat, leaned toward me, and shouted in my ear. "This is great, if it holds!"

I nodded.

Historians of warfare hold that awful weather favors the defender. They hold this even as they write about all the complacent defenders who got creamed when they were attacked under cover of awful weather.

Kit pounded my shoulder and pointed at the sky to our left. A wedge-shaped shadow tipped by winking red navigation lights slid down through the cloud ceiling and was immediately backlit by lightning. The shadow flashed across our path, showed two dots of orange engine exhaust for a blink, then vanished again, in the direction of the landing strip outside Tressia. It left behind a roar nearly as loud as the storm itself.

Kit said, "Shuttle."

I shouted back, "So when Lockheed says all-weather, they mean all-weather? Maybe they won't be able to take off with the stones and we can all go home."

She shook her head. "Landing in this crap is the hard part, not taking off. I've gotten one of those old heaps off the ground in worse than this, and the Rand can fly circles around me. 'Course what a pilot can do if she has to and what she will do if she's prudent are different. Like they say, old pilots, bold pilots. But no old, bold pilots."

"Game on, then."

One hour and fifty minutes later our engineer shut the train off. Ten minutes later the train coasted slowly, and as silently as two hundred tons of steel can roll, through the unabated storm and came to rest with just a pinch of brake squeal alongside a house row two hundred yards longer than the train, that blocked us from line of sight from the shuttle strip.

No curious faces appeared at the windows of the houses. No Tressen or Iridian outpost sentries marched the walks in front of the modest homes. The row was deserted.

The weather was good luck. The empty house row was good planning.

From the handle of every door on the row hung a drenched red quarantine ribbon. Our good friend the physician had, at the request of the rebellion and at great personal risk, quarantined and cleared the house row on the grounds that it was a deadly cesspool of influenza. It was even money that he wasn't lying.

We stripped the tarps off the tanks within three minutes. Then my crew and I clambered aboard tank one while tank two's crew did the same.

Compared to a modern tank, an old crawler interior's a regular concert hall. Even a Trueborn-tall type like me can almost stand up in most of it, and the biggest usurper of open space is the engine. It's bigger than an upright pipe organ and sits smack in the middle of the main compartment, as if the organist were about to take center stage and play a solo.

Starting a hovertank, or even a 2000s vintage crawler, is easier than starting a family four-place. Switch on, push a button, and the turbine sings.

Starting a Mark V or a Thunderer, however, was more like playing chamber music with sledgehammers. My staff sergeant began the process by priming each engine cylinder with local kerosene. Then he and three other crew members stood, grimacing like a row of galley slaves in a synchronized dead-lift contest, rotating a long crank like they were twisting the engine's tail. As tank commander, I switched the magneto on and off while they cranked, and exhorted them to greater efforts. This division of labor normally continued until the engine finally fired. Sometimes command isn't such a burden.

After two minutes of unrequited cranking, my staff sergeant shook his head and panted. " 'S no good in the wet, sir."

Plan B in case of high humidity involved wrapping a pinch of gun cotton, which was a low-grade explosive, in a kerosene-soaked rag, then lighting the rag with a match. The burning wad was then thrust inside one of the cylinders in the hope that the engine caught before the uniform and hair of the person who did the thrusting burst into flames.

This job fell to the tank commander. We were under way in no time, and I only lost an eyebrow.

I took up my position in an iron box top-center, while my staff sergeant drove from a position in another armored box that stuck up above the tank's nose. Four of the crew operated the two side cannon and four machine guns while two more worked the gears and engine.

Outward visibility was through slits left at various spots around the tank. On clear days visibility was abysmal. In that day's driving rain, it was worse.

Once we got both tanks started, off the flatcars, and idling nose to tail alongside the train, I waddled forward, then hand-signaled—they didn't call it the Thunderer for nothing; interior conversation was impossible when the tank was running—my sergeant that I was going outside for a final meeting with the leader of the infantry platoon that our tank would lead into battle.

Kit and her platoon had formed up behind my idling tank. Celline's platoon would follow behind tank two.

I pulled Kit by the elbow away from my tank's bellowing exhaust, then pulled her close and yelled, while rain sheeted down, "Remember, keep it closed up behind us."

She nodded. "No bad guys on your back, no machine-gun fire on our front."

"Okay. Let's do this." I nodded and turned.

But she caught my arm and spun me back to face her. "After this, don't look back for me, Parker."

"I know. I have a job to do."

"No. Because if you did look back, I might be afraid to do *my* job. Too afraid I'd lose you again." She grabbed me by the webbing straps that ran from my shoulders to my belt, pulled me close. Then she kissed me as though it was the first and last time, while rain cascaded over us and peals of thunder shook the ground. It sounds erotic, but between the ammunition pouches, first-aid packs, trench knives, and pistols we were each wearing, I couldn't even tell if she had boobs.

Then she was gone, back to her platoon.

Despite instructions, I watched her walk away. Then I ducked back through one of the tank's side hatches, in the rear of the left sponson, weaseled past the engine on my right and the six-pounder cannon's breechblock and its cannoneer on my left, and twisted myself into the commander's seat.

I peered out through my forward peephole and jerked

a cord that I had tied to my seat frame. It ran the ten feet forward that separated me from my driver and was tied around his bicep. He glanced back over his shoulder when he felt the tug. I signaled, and Thunderer One lurched forward into the storm.

Eighty-seven

Polian stood, wearing Tressen battle dress uniform and a belt-holstered needler, in the vast, rolled-back doorway of the shuttle hangar. He stood, one leg angled to accommodate his new walking cast, and stared out past the parked shuttle and into the rain beyond.

Water poured in pencil-thick cascades through a thousand leaks in the hangar's vast dome roof and wound in ankle-deep rivers across the stone floor. A puddle had formed at the base of the cargo-loading ramp that angled down beneath the great shuttle craft's upturned tail assembly. The storm was apparently so hard and so general along the continent's eastern seaboard that it had knocked out the telegraph lines that the Tressens used to communicate with the occupation forces in Iridia, even though those lines ran underground, in the railroad's roadbed.

A figure strode down the shuttle's ramp. The shuttle's pilot wore a characteristic Rand full beard and black coveralls that stretched across broad shoulders. The man reached the ramp's base, leapt the puddle, and walked to Polian. "We're loaded and fueled. 'Puter forecasts a weather break in an hour. And an orbital matching window from right now 'til noon."

"You'll take off in an hour, then?"

"We'll take off when it's safe. That may be in an hour. It may be at midnight. Is there a hurry, mister?"

"Major."

The pilot waved his arm at the open hangar door, at the distant revetment and barbed-wire perimeter barely visible through the rain. "We've never had this circus here before."

"The Iridian rebels have become more active recently. I think you'd be well advised to take off as soon as possible. Our cargo could be in jeopardy."

"Mister, I care about your cargo. It's my job to care, and I really do. But I care more about my ship. The Iridian rebels may be a myth. Wind shear out past the end of this runway is no myth."

"You're saying you can't take off?"

"I'm saying that my ship's safer here at the moment"—the pilot pointed at the clouds—"than up there. The moment that changes, I'll be off this rock before you can tap dance on that cast of yours."

Gill walked up to the two of them, hands clasped behind his back and smiling. "Captain Berger! Wet enough for you?"

The pilot shrugged, half smiled at Gill. "We'll see."

"Sir!" A Tressen private ran to Polian, stopped in front of him, and saluted. He held out a handtalk. "Something going on beyond the perimeter."

Polian frowned, snatched the receiver, and held it near his ear. Gill stood close and listened. Polian spoke. "This is Base One."

"Outpost Six reports. The machine shows something inbound."

Polian rolled his eyes. The "machine"? Outpost Six was manned by Tressens. There weren't half enough Yavi to go around. "Be more specific, man!"

"There's two of them. Tractors or trucks or something. They're barely moving."

"Range?"

"Twelve hundred yards."

"They're tanks!" Another voice, this one with a Yavi accent, broke in.

Polian recognized the voice. "Mazzen? Are you looking at a sensor display, or do you have visual?"

"Both, sir. They're old crawlers, but their turrets have been removed. We've got indicators of a platoon-sized infantry unit tucked in behind each of them."

"Infantry? Is anyone shooting?"

"Uh. No, sir."

Polian touched his chin. A Tressen farm tractor resembled a tank without a turret. "It could be locals demonstrating for influenza vaccine. There's a quarantine site out beyond OP Six."

Polian rather hoped it was a demonstration. Skimmers and needlers were designed to control unruly civilians. Though neither Yavet nor Tressen had spawned much in the way of civil disobedience over the last few decades.

Gill whispered, "Ruberd, I gave you this show, and it's yours to run. But do you think you should send a pair of skimmers out past the wire to probe them? Just in case?"

Polian realized that the normal skimmer patrols out beyond the wire had been suspended after one crashed into a sensor array in the rain. He called over the soldier who had fetched him the handtalk. Polian pointed to the hangar's far wall, where twenty skimmers were parked, two in ready-reserve status with crews strapped in place and side-mount needlers loaded. "Corporal, tell the two ready-reserve skimmers to slide out to OP Six and challenge some inbounds the post has identified."

Ping.

The Rand pilot thumbed his 'puter. "What'cha got, Mr. Sciefel?"

The pilot's 'puter squawked back at him. "Hole in the weather, sir. For the next twenty minutes. After that, we're socked for four hours, guaranteed."

The pilot scratched his beard, then turned to Polian. "Is there any chance these things your people are seeing may endanger my ship?"

Polian shook his head. "None. We're a thousand strong. This demonstration, or whatever it is, involves a hundred people. You're one hundred percent safe in here."

The Rand pilot spoke into his 'puter. "Heat 'em up, Mr. Sciefel. No time to wait on a tug. We'll power out."

He spun on his heel, but Polian caught his arm. "Captain, if . . . if these so-called tanks with no turrets do turn out to be a threat, that runway is in the line of fire. You're safer in here for a few minutes."

"I'm sure you know your job, Major. But I know mine, too. I intend to have my ship gone, out of harm's way, long before your 'if' turns to 'when.' " He strode away from Polian, up the ramp, and disappeared.

Whuummm.

Polian turned toward the sound that echoed in the hangar so loudly it was audible above the rain's rumble. It was the two ready skinks. They had just popped off the stone floor, and now wobbled while their drivers trimmed them. He caught the eye of the lead driver and waved him to slide the skink over. The second followed *en echelon.*

Polian motioned the trooper in the right-hand seat of the lead ready skimmer to dismount, and took his place. Polian had to lift his cast leg up and over the flank armor, but then he was in.

"Ruberd?"

Polian turned and realized that Gill still stood there and had reached out and touched the younger man's sleeve.

"Yes, General?"

"You know, if this is enemy armor, it could present a meaningful threat."

"Sir, with respect, I doubt it. But that's why I'm going out there to see for myself." Polian nodded to his driver, and the skink slid out toward the rain.

Booom. Booom.

Polian jumped a fraction of an inch in his seat. Ahead of the skimmer the great bells of the shuttle's engines glowed orange and shuddered as the big ship came to life. The engines' thunder half drowned the hydraulic whine as the shuttle's loading ramp rose and sealed the shuttle's belly.

Polian smiled, a witness to history. The magical stones,

now hidden throughout the cargo in the space plane's hold, were about to embark on the next leg of their journey to free Yavet from Trueborn domination.

The second skink slid alongside them, and Polian's eyes widened when he saw a flash of silver gray in the right-hand seat. The old moustache was coming, too. Was it because he didn't trust Polian? Polian frowned when he realized that the mistrust in the relationship now ran precisely the other way. Polian had concluded that the slight old man who had befriended him would have to be killed, on suspicion of the crime of having been born.

Polian reached up and snapped his goggles down over his eyes, just in time, as the open skink slid out from beneath the great protective umbrella of the hangar's dome roof and a torrent of rain blinded him.

Eighty-eight

For the first three-fourths of a mile after Thunderer One and Thunderer Two clanked out from behind the cover provided by the quarantined row houses, I kept waiting to be slammed by a cannon round, or at least to run across a patrol, either on foot or in a Yavi skimmer. But it didn't happen. I supposed it was possible that we did run across a patrol but passed in the downpour without seeing or hearing or smelling one another. Most likely, though, the Tressens and the Yavi had suspended patrols due to the weather.

For us inside Thunderer One, it seemed that no one else could miss us. We couldn't see much through our slits, but we were wider than a mag-lev and nearly as long. The engine roar and vibration that left us deaf and battered surely outshouted the unabated thunder. Also, the mixture of one-hundred-twenty-degree internal temperature, unvented carbon monoxide, kerosene exhaust fumes, and the vomit that the combination of the above had already provoked from the right-side cannoneer, would alert anyone who got within sniffing distance to our presence.

As unpleasant and dangerous as it was to be route-marching behind us in a chill maelstrom, I would have preferred to be out there in the downpour with Kit.

Ping-ping-ping-ping.

At two hundred yards out from the perimeter wire, even though we couldn't see the perimeter emplacements that were four hundred yards from us, we began taking fire.

At first the needler rounds just sounded like tinnier rain against the hull. But even after we recognized them for what they were, and as we came close enough that they became an incessant hail against our forward plating, they were as ineffectual as pelting us with handfuls of jelly beans.

One improvement we had made on the tanks as originally designed was to rig polished steel mirrors that we could swing into place angled behind a couple of the slits. That allowed us to close most of the slits against the few, but deadly, needler rounds among thousands that would have found their way in through the slits. We were kidding ourselves, because really the mirrors were scarcely better than blindness. But it was better than a needler round in the eye.

If Kit's infantry behind us had charged without the cover we provided, they would all be dead or wounded already, without even reaching the concertina wire.

Spang.

My head snapped back as something seared my eye.

"Oh, God!" My hand flew to my eye. Somehow a

needler round had found its way inside our armor and rendered me half blind.

I opened my eye, closed the uninjured one, and could still see.

Running my fingers beneath my eye, I felt a bloody gash, but hardly a needler wound.

We had just taken our first round of conventional Tressen gunpowder machine-gun fire. It had struck the armor plate in front of my face. The steel plate on a Mark V or a Thunderer stopped such rounds, but the impact spalled steel slivers off the plate's backside, like struck billiard balls. British Mark V crews had actually worn chain-mail masks to protect against secondary internal shrapnel. If the mix of machine guns we faced that day had been more conventional Tressen and less Yavi needler, the inside of our tank would have been a steel hailstorm.

I peeped out the slit again, grimacing.

Ten yards to our front loomed the concertina barbed wire that blocked our way forward. Multiple tubular razor-cut coils that would slash a man's flesh like knives gleamed slick with rain in the dim light.

We crossed the wire without a hiccup. Frankly, anybody who owns a family electric has run over a Styrofoam cup and been more jostled. Thirty tons will squash a lot of wire.

Ahead of us loomed the perimeter fortifications. The Tressens had built up, rather than dug in, because they wanted to be able to see their attackers coming. Every hundred yards, strongpoints of chest-high sandbags shielded crew-served needlers and were connected by a three-foot-high earth berm behind which Tressen riflemen sheltered.

If the Tressens and the Yavi had paid any attention whatsoever to the possibility that they faced armored attack, they would have dug into the Tressen arsenal and emplaced a few direct-fire cannon in those strongpoints. If they had done so, they would have blown us all to hell before we reached the concertina.

That was where intelligence, so often maligned, had saved our butts before the first shot was fired. Kit and I had bugged the Yavi-Tressen defense-planning sessions. That had nearly gotten us killed in the bell tower, but we knew with absolute confidence that our enemy was preparing to defend only against light infantry. So that was exactly what we hadn't attacked with.

Thunderer One and Thunderer Two rumbled forward, side by side, at a stately but unstoppable four miles per hour and plowed into the berms defended by Tressen infantry. By the time our tanks crested the berms, they were long-since deserted. The infantry had fled, helpless and terrified. The driver and sponson gunners hosed the fleeing men with machine-gun fire as they ran away. Some fell, wounded, in our path. We couldn't have steered the beasts around them if we had tried. They disappeared, screaming, beneath the treads, their bones offering the resistance of Styrofoam cups.

We struck the Tressen line midway between two sandbagged strongpoints. These we reduced, meaning blew the crap out of, with our side-firing sponson cannons. The cannons were massively inaccurate given the lurching of the tank and the tiny slits through which the cannoneers peered to aim them.

But the strongpoints were placed just a hundred yards

apart, so that the Yavi needlers could overlap their fields of fire.

That meant that the range to target for our cannoneers was less than fifty yards, virtually point-blank.

I actually saw a blown-up Yavi needler spin through the air with its tripod legs still attached. Also attached was a hand, that still grasped the gun's pistol grip.

Any unfortunates who escaped us were dealt with by our following infantry.

I learned later that one brave Yavi soul, a corporal, was actually openly wearing Yavi armor. That breach of Cold War etiquette told us how desperately they wanted to keep their cavorite. It also must have persuaded the Yavi that he was bulletproof. He climbed aboard our slow-rolling tank and tried to stick his needle pistol through the commander's view port, which would have ruined what was left of my day.

Kit had clambered up on the tank from the rear and shot him through his armor's neck-ring latch gap with one pistol shot from thirty-five feet. The neck-ring latch gap is the chink in Yavi armor, but it's only a quarter-inch wide and a third of an inch tall. Considering conditions, it was a shot that the Trueborn markswoman Annie Oakley would have been proud of. Except that the only pride a sane soldier takes in a shooting is surviving it.

After we breached the perimeter, I wasn't sure precisely where we ought to head next.

Then two shapes loomed up ahead, dim through the rain.

They were open Yavi skimmers, inbound for us at sixty miles per hour, rooster-tailing spray from beneath their skirts as they came. Both were equipped with crewed dual-sidemount needlers, spraying rounds at us as voluminously as the rooster tails sprayed rain.

In that moment, the wind and rain abated for a few heartbeats.

Behind the skimmers and to our left, an enormous, blunt black shape slid into view. The shuttle. They surely hadn't fired up the space plane and rolled it out of the hangar in a rainstorm because the pilot wanted to spin doughnuts on the tarmac.

We had come so far to get to this point, but if the shuttle lifted off with the cavorite aboard, we would have failed completely.

Kit had told me that the shuttle, fully fueled and loaded, needed all twelve thousand feet of runway to get airborne, and then spaceborne, in the atmosphere and gravity of Tressel.

If we could get one of the thirty-ton Thunderers out onto the runway, then, as long as it remained there, the shuttle and the cavorite would remain here on Tressel, too.

I peered out a side peephole. Thunderer Two had apparently reached the same conclusion I had. The tank adjusted course, then leapt—who am I kidding, crawled—at all of five miles per hour toward the long runway.

The distance to the runway was only about four hundred yards. But between our two tanks and the runway the two skimmers buzzed like frenzied hornets. Their drivers hovered them, and juked them left and right, while their gunners hosed out an ineffectual curtain of needler rounds at us. They could literally run circles around us, but they couldn't get under our skins. We, on the other hand, could penetrate each skimmer's skin with our machine guns like it was foil. To say nothing of our cannons.

We rolled forward toward the runway.

In the distance, the pitch of the shuttles engines rose until it overmatched the thunder.

Eighty-nine

Polian peered through his rain-drenched goggles at the two drab-painted vehicles that lumbered toward the skimmer in which he rode. He vaguely recalled seeing something similar to them on a history chip. They *were* crawler tanks, and not tractors. They had already breached his meticulously designed and executed perimeter.

Tressen riflemen by the dozen dashed by the skimmer, away from the relentless, bellowing behemoths. As the tanks lurched and rumbled, they spit yellow flame from machine guns that protruded, seemingly in all directions at once, from gimbaled mountings set in their sides.

A retreating Tressen ran straight at Polian, looked up with wide eyes and dodged only a blink before he was run down. As the man dashed past, he threw away his rifle, and it clattered off the skimmer's flank.

Polian reached out and grabbed the man's arm. "Stop! Pull yourself to—"

Bam-bam-bam-bam.

The man stiffened, and his head snapped back as a

burst from a tank machine gun struck him in the back. He fell away as the skimmer's driver sideslipped the craft to dodge the burst.

Polian felt heat in his right thigh, looked down, and saw that a bullet had torn his trouser and grazed his leg.

A neat row of holes stitched the skimmer's armor, which was effective against the needler rounds a criminal might fire at it back home, but useless against a gunpowder weapon's heavy bullet.

Another man ran toward him, zigzagging through the rain. This one was an armored Yavi private. He, too, carried no weapon. The private's face shield was raised, and he panted, wide-eyed, as he threw a leg over the side and rolled into the skimmer's rear compartment.

Polian turned back to the man, who lay gasping on the floor. "Get up, man! And fight back! You're wearing armor!"

The man shook his head. "No. Mazzen. They killed Mazzen right through his armor!" The man pointed his index finger against the back of his own neck, like a pistol.

Polian balled his fists, then stared at the oncoming tank. In his mind, he saw Mazzen, good, solid, promising Mazzen. Kneeling while these ghouls executed him with a pistol shot to the back of the head. He muttered, "Bastards!"

Another machine-gun burst, from the tank directly in front of Polian's skimmer, ripped through the skimmer's flank on the driver's side.

The driver screamed, then collapsed forward onto the wheel.

Polian twisted in his seat. One of the crew was gone.

Out over the side? Deserted? In this chaos, who knew? The others slumped grotesquely, dead or unconscious.

He slumped himself, dazed, while the unguided skimmer spun slowly in a perpetual left turn, as aimless as his thoughts.

He had failed as a commander. He had failed dead young men of promise like Sandr and Mazzen. He had failed his father, who had admonished him to beware the undercurrents. The only failure that remained to him lay in the future, to betray Gill, the man who had been a better father to him in weeks than his biological father had been in a lifetime.

Polian straightened himself, then dragged the unconscious driver into the rear compartment and slipped behind the skimmer's wheel himself. He peered out through the skimmer's spiderweb-cracked windscreen at the tank clanking toward him. Now a figure knelt atop the tank, alongside the slitted, topside forward box. Polian realized that the box housed the driver. The exposed figure was a woman, in Iridian uniform, and she leaned down to shout directions to the blindered box as she pointed ahead with her free hand.

She looked up, and Polian recognized her rain-slicked face from the hospital wanted-poster sketches. Celline. The mythic heart of the rebellion that had now spoiled so much.

Ruberd Polian's hands gripped the wheel so tightly that it quivered. Then the heat in him receded and a cold rage replaced it. He drew a breath, held it.

Pointing the skimmer's nose at the tank's oncoming prow, he rammed the throttles to their forward stops.

Acceleration slammed him back against the driver's seat as the skimmer roared head-on toward the tank and the woman at over sixty miles per hour.

Ninety

As Thunderer One rolled on, I peeked out a side peephole. Thunderer Two was fifty yards closer to the airstrip than we were, hare to our tortoise in the glacial dash to block the shuttle.

The shuttle's engines, which had crescendoed moments earlier, settled back and purred like a three-hundred-foot-long cat. I had upped ship the old-fashioned way often enough that I knew the pilot had just run his engines up, against the brakes, to test them. Given a shuttle's checklist—and the Rand followed their checklists as surely as cats purred—that meant we had three minutes before the big ship rolled out for real.

The Yavi had either given up on wasting needler rounds on our armor, or had run out of them. Celline had clambered up onto Thunderer Two's turtle back and was leading the charge with one arm thrust forward like an animated war memorial.

Maybe you have to be nuts to be a hero. Maybe when people think you're a hero it drives you nuts. I'm too sane to join the club, so I'll never know.

Suddenly, Thunderer Two's bow machine gun, which had been quiet, flashed, firing straight ahead. Celline dropped into a crouch like the tank had become a Trueborn surfboard.

I switched peepholes to see what Celline saw.

A skimmer dead ahead of Thunderer Two streaked straight toward the tank's prow. It hit a bad air patch inbound, wobbled, and one of the limp Yavis in armor in the rear compartment, who seemed to be reclining in back, bounced up and was catapulted out of the skimmer like a stuffed doll.

Behind Thunderer Two, Celline's troops scattered and ran.

The skimmer driver hunched over the wheel, his face obscured by the cracks that veined the windscreen. I don't know whether he was a member of the hero's club. I do know he was nuts. A skimmer's listed best military speed is sixty-one miles per hour, but if this one wasn't making seventy when it hit Thunderer Two, dogs don't bark.

Four tons traveling at seventy meets thirty tons traveling at five. Kit the college girl was fond of saying that physics were a bitch. So you do the math.

Skimmers are really pretty flimsy, like most things that fly. But their fuel is highly flammable, and the pressurized nitrogen vessels that power the needlers are such bombs in their own right that they're located inboard, protected by the vehicle frame, and armor plated.

Therefore, when the skimmer hit the tank, pointed prow against pointed prow, the skimmer just seemed to disappear into itself, the way an empty beer can did back at the bar when I stomped it.

Then the compressed lump that remained of the skimmer exploded in a ball of yellow flame that engulfed the front half of Thunderer Two and reached up into the rain higher than a three-story Tressen row house. I saw Celline fly through the air like the stuffed-doll Yavi had; then I lost track of her. The explosion's heat puffed through my peephole hot enough that I blinked. Then my eye teared.

Seconds later, Thunderer Two sat within a semicircle of flaming metal bits that sizzled as rain washed them. The tank looked exactly as it had before the collision. Except that it was stationary, and silent.

That meant that my tank was the last chance to block the shuttle from taking off and changing the balance of power in the known universe. I dunno. It's a living.

I shifted in my seat, looked ahead, and dropped my jaw.

The other skimmer sat, hunkered down on its deflated skirt, presenting its left flank to us broadside. It was thirty feet in front of our prow. The half-dozen Yavi in its open cab blazed away with the skimmer's sidemount needlers, with short-barreled carbines, and one, in the right-hand front seat, with a needler pistol. As the range between the tank and the skimmer closed, the Yavi fired away like it was their last stand.

Which, fifteen seconds later, it was.

Our left track bit the skimmer's flank first, and we tilted up on the left for a moment; then the skimmer collapsed. I counted five screams. The tank continued on across the pancaked skimmer, rocking front to back and side to side as it crushed one element of the machine after another. Metal groaned and snapped.

I don't know whether the Yavi had powered down to block us, thinking that four tons squatting would be harder to bulldoze than four hovering tons. Or they had a mechanical. Or they were just nuts. There's always a lot of nuts-ness going around during a firefight. An unfortunate truth about combat is that your enemy rarely tells you why he did what he did. Especially if he's dead.

I grabbed a peek and saw the shuttle still stationary, but time had to be short.

We continued to lurch forward toward the runway, but something had hung up on our underside. It howled like a cat from hell as we dragged it, which was merely annoying. But it also slowed us down too much.

Maneuvering a Thunderer was a team sport. Two gearmen behind me had charge of one track each. I signaled the gearmen to reverse the left track, then the right, then repeat. The pattern would twist the tank the way you might twist your foot to scrape something unpleasant off your shoe sole.

On the second twist, whatever was caught on our sole exploded so violently that it lifted the tank, dropped it, and knocked us all senseless.

"Jazen?"

Kit peered down at me, blue eyes wide.

I lay on my back on my tank's floor. Behind Kit, light and rain entered the tank's interior through the open rear left sponson hatch.

I blinked. "What happened?"

"Whatever you were dragging blew. Skimmer nitrogen bottle, I think."

I looked around. "Crew?"

"Okay, I think. Bells rung. Like you. Most of my platoon, too."

It suddenly occurred to me that we were inside my tank, but we were talking.

I sat up. "We're stalled!" There was no time to restart. Besides, I only had one eyebrow left. But I still heard the shuttle's engines purring steadily in the distance. I couldn't have been unconscious for more than a few seconds.

I pulled myself up by the six-pounder's mount. "We'll never get this thing onto the runway in time."

"You're right."

I squinted down the cannon's coaxial telescopic sight. The shuttle still sat, but as I spoke its engine pitch changed.

Kit said, "Crap. He's running them up." She turned and stared down at the six-pounder's square breechblock. "This thing work?"

I widened my eyes. "We can't blow up a neutral shuttle! We already talked about this."

"That was then. This is now. Besides, we won't blow it up."

I pointed my index finger from the breechblock along the six-pounder's barrel to the point where it poked out through the sponson as I raised my eyebrows. "You do see that this is a *cannon*?"

"We just put one armor-piercing round through one of the landing-gear struts and collapse it. No explosion. The worst case would be maybe a fuel-cell rupture."

I stood back and crossed my arms. "Seriously?"

She bent and peered through the cannon's 'scope at the distant shuttle. "It's only, what? Twenty-two hundred fifty yards?"

I had forgotten that I was in the presence of Annie Oakley.

Kit turned back to me, hands on hips, and stared. "It takes two to operate the gun, Parker. Move your ass!"

I had seen that look before. I had also forgotten that I was in the presence of a woman bent on saving the universe.

In the distance, the shuttle engines climbed the scale.

I turned to the ammunition rack, slid out an armor-piercing round, and loaded it while she cranked the traversing wheel.

Kit panted as she bore down on the wheel. "Jeez, Parker. Didn't you grease this thing?"

"That shouldn't make—" I wrinkled my forehead, peeked out past the cannon slit, then recoiled.

Glaring back at me through the slit was the face of a thin, gray-moustached old man. His face was smoke smudged, and the left sleeve of his Tressen battle-dress uniform had been torn away. But the leaves of a Yavi lieutenant general were pinned above his right sleeve. He straddled the six-pounder's barrel as though he were bareback-riding an anaconda.

I glanced at Kit. She had given up on the wheel, and bent, hands on knees, while she peeked out through the gap between the cannon's barrel and the sponson. "Parker! We can't aim this thing with that fucker on there! Shoot him."

If we couldn't aim the cannon with his weight aboard, we certainly couldn't wiggle it around and shake him off. Running outside and wrestling with him would take too long.

I drew my machine pistol and sighted down the barrel through the slit at the old man. Behind him, I could still see the shuttle. Its engines were now so near max that they shook the ground, and the space plane's vertical stabilizers vibrated.

I looked into his eyes, and in that instant I knew. I knew that he was the sixth man in the skimmer we had crushed, and the only survivor. I knew that with those leaves, he was also Gill, the general in charge here on whom we had eavesdropped. He knew the shuttle's importance, knew that the six-pounder was our last chance to stop it. And he was risking his life the only way he had left to stop us.

"Parker! I can still hit it on the roll. For God's sake, take the shot!"

I aligned my sights. As I did, I saw the old soldier's forearm, bare as he clung to the cannon barrel. Burned into his skin was a Legion graves-registration tattoo.

Just like the one I had. And that told me everything about him.

He was small, a downlevels birth. He had joined the Legion. The only Yavis who joined the Legion were Illegals who had nothing left to lose, like I had, once. The old man was living the lie that I would have lived. He was an Illegal with a new identity who went to sleep every night wondering whether it was the night that a bounty hunter would make sure he never woke up.

I stared into his eyes, then lifted my pistol barrel vertical and slid the safety on. I could no more shoot him than I could shoot myself.

The floor plates beneath my boots shook as the shuttle

rumbled in the distance. Then the sound Dopplered away until it mingled with the roar of the rain.

Kit touched my shoulder. "Parker, what the hell have you done?"

I glanced at her, then back out through the aiming slit. Gill was gone. So was the shuttle, and with it the stones that let men fly to the stars. I said, "Long story."

"Better be a good one."

Outside the tank, the rain diminished to a drizzle, and we heard the buzz of skimmers in the distance. We leaned together so we could peer out the slit. A half-dozen more Yavi skimmers had formed up, just inside the open door of the Yavi's grand memorial shuttle-hangar dome, a mile away. Soon we would have company.

Kit said, "We should run." Then she pointed at the six-pounder's locked and loaded breech. "Be a shame to re-rack that round."

I nodded, then traversed the gun while she set elevation. When she was satisfied, she poked her head out the sponson hatch and held a finger up into the wind.

Then she ducked back, tweaked the elevation wheel, and yanked the six-pounder's pistol-grip trigger.

Whoom!

The gun recoiled on its carriage, cordite smell and smoke swirled, Thunderer One rocked, and my unconscious crew stirred.

Kit and I rushed out through the sponson hatch and stood in the drizzle, hands visored above our eyes. We watched as the six-pounder's round Annie Oakleyed invisibly downrange, while my crew and Kit's platoon wandered up alongside us staring where we were staring.

The nonexplosive armor-piercing round barely seemed to jostle the third skimmer from the right when it struck. But it doesn't take explosives to blow a nitrogen bottle. A moment later, the skimmer exploded. Then it set off the other skimmers alongside it like a string of giant firecrackers. There must have been more skimmers and flammables inside the hangar, because secondary explosions erupted. They inflated the dome like a balloon, then the structure sagged back, collapsed on itself, and steam, debris, and flame erupted from all sides of the wreckage.

One minute later, the great silver symbol of Yavi–Republican Socialist brotherhood and cooperation had been reduced to still and smoking rubble, steaming in the rain.

Someone in the little crowd of Iridian partisans standing behind Kit and me whistled, then said, "They really aren't going to like this."

I shrugged as I stared at the rubble. "Not the prize we needed. But a solid second place."

Kit shook her head, arms crossed, as she stared at the smoking wreckage in the distance. "Second place? You mean first loser."

That was what she always used to say to me when she outsprinted me on a burn lap. I raised my remaining eyebrow. "Does that mean that *now* we run?"

She nodded. "Yep. Direction?"

"Your turn to pick."

She shrugged, shouldered a ruck, and limped east. I pulled on my own ruck and followed.

We didn't run fast. We didn't run in step.

But at least we ran together.

Ninety-one

On the night that I had broken Kit out of the Tressen Clinic, I had told Alia that a by-the-book raid had a rally point, where the raiders reassembled after action. The spaceport battle was a raid, alright, but not by the book.

We had always known that the tanks would be abandoned. The surviving raiders would, like successful guerillas always did, scatter, then melt away like fish in a sea of fishes, and live to bite another day.

Kit and I knew that south toward Iridia along the railroad was the most obvious, and so worst, escape route for us. So we headed east to the coast.

There we stole a boat and sailed—well, Kit sailed; I barfed—south. We scuttled the boat south of the Barrens, humped back through the canyons of the Inside Passage, then crossed the Iridian Corridor.

Two weeks after the raid, we reached the camp from which we had started.

Celline was already there, concussed and limping after being blown off of Thunderer Two. Sixty-six more raiders had also returned safely to that camp. Sixteen more had returned to other camps. Three wounded were being hidden by the physician who had helped us before, inside Tressia. One soldier had fallen when we took the patrol train. Four fell during the raid, all inside Thunderer Two.

Seven remained missing in action. We hoped they would be found. But we knew they wouldn't be forgotten. None of those who were already being called "The One Hundred" ever would.

The Yavi got creamed, but still pulled off the greatest heist in the history of Cold War II, though they couldn't advertise it.

Nobody had to advertise what Republican Socialism lost. The burst silver bubble whispered volumes about its vulnerability.

Recruits, not a gray hair on them, were already trickling into the rebel camps. Three meetings of something called the Free Tressen Resistance had been busted up in Tressia. Each meeting was being held in a church. In each case the conspirators escaped the ferrents because a lookout rang the church's bell.

As soon as Kit and I returned, we laid out our pickup-panel display in the cleared area behind Celline's quarters, then settled in to await a pickup that might never come.

A week after we returned, Celline held a private ceremony behind her place.

When Kit and I arrived, we found Her Grace standing, with her back to us, hands clasped behind her, wearing an unsoldierly Iridian-cut business suit. A delicate tiara was visible in her pulled-back hair. She stood alongside a nearly empty table draped in the Iridian flag, that rustled in the breeze of a cloudless day.

The rest of the crowd comprised Alia, who sat on a bench in the clearing, reading aloud from an Iridian grammar primer, to Pyt, who sat beside her.

Celline, who was watching Alia, turned, saw us, and smiled. The duchess said, "Please forgive the lack of grandeur. Not so much has changed."

Kit said, "That's not what I hear, Your Grace."

Celline nodded. "Yes, it's promising. But the Republican Socialists have scarcely toppled. This isn't, to paraphrase Shakespeare's countryman, Churchill, the end, or even the beginning of the end. But for us it is a new beginning. I won't see the end." She turned her head, and her eyes rested on Alia again. "But the fifty-eighth duchess will."

My jaw dropped. "Alia?"

"My daughter is hardly something to advertise, Jazen. I've had a target over my own heart so long that I sometimes pretend I'm dead. Churchill also said that in war truth is so valuable that it must always be accompanied by a bodyguard of lies." She smiled. "And by Pyt. His uncle served my family all his life, and now Pyt has taken his place. Families are tangled things, you know. That's why you deserve to know about her. About your heritage."

I squinted. "I don't understand."

"Part of the reason I allowed Alia to accompany you, though it placed her in danger, is that her destiny demands an education in danger. Pyt can train her up for her role, but he can't do it all. I also wanted her to know you, Jazen. She's half Trueborn, you know. The strawberry-blonde half. And, after a fashion, your niece."

I stepped backward. Then I said, "Tell me—"

The duchess cut me off with an upraised palm. "In time. Jazen, first I would like to present these."

She laid her palm on three flat, blue velvet boxes stacked on the flag alongside her and said, "The Star of Iridia."

Her Grace stood, motioned me to step forward and kneel, then slipped the medal over my bowed head and let it dangle at the end of a red velvet ribbon.

I stepped back and hefted the medal in my hand. I've always thought that medals were just ways to divert attention from mistakes that got somebody killed. And these were no different.

But when I watched Kit kneel, saw the ribbon slip over her hair and around her neck, and saw the way the medal lay over her heart when she stood, I cried. For the dead, for the missing, for our failure, certainly. But those tragedies and mistakes didn't diminish her valor.

Then Celline handed the third box to me.

I took it and wrinkled my forehead. "Ma'am?"

"Your father's. I've never been able to present it in person. It's my way of saying to you, Jazen, that I hope, I believe, that someday you will present it for me."

Now she had me crying again. This time I had to wipe my eyes. "What should I tell him?"

"That it's the greatest honor my people can bestow."

As I watched Celline, a shadow crossed her face, then darkened the clearing. I turned and looked up.

A matte-black ceramic watermelon seed fifty feet long hung motionless fifty feet above us. It radiated heat down on us as though the sun had reappeared twenty million miles closer to us. Juking through the atmosphere at four thousand miles per hour will do that to a spacecraft's skin temperature. The big watermelon seed was as silent as a C-drive ship always was, emitting just a crackle as its skin cooled.

I widened my eyes. "For once, they're early?"

The Scorpion sideslipped to the clearing's center as Pyt and Alia ran and stood alongside us.

Once they were clear, the Scorpion descended until it hovered just far enough above the signal panels laid out in the clearing that they didn't catch fire. The opaque canopy clamshelled open, and we glimpsed the pilot in the left front seat. The figure in the right front seat grinned down at us.

I groaned. "Howard?"

Howard's eyes darted around the sylvan, unthreatening clearing, then rested on Kit's and my well-scrubbed faces. He said, "Emergency extraction is for emergencies. Do you know what it costs to operate this thing?"

Kit rolled her eyes. "Seriously, Howard?"

Howard looked wounded. "It was a joke."

I raised my palm. "We got that, Howard. But there *is* an emergency."

"You mean the cavorite?"

Kit's eyes widened. "You know?"

"We pieced it together after we interviewed the shuttle crew."

I pumped my fist. "Then the Yavi didn't get away with it?"

Howard shook his head. "Oh, heavens, yes, they did! The cavorite is long gone."

My heart sank.

Kit ground her teeth. "Now the baby-killers have starships?"

Howard shook his head. "Oh, no. Without C-drive, they're like hitchhikers with a can of gasoline, but no car."

Gasoline? Was Howard *that* old?

I said, "Oh."

"But that's about to change, if we don't get busy. You think I came to sign your expense reports? I need a team. Actually, I don't need *a* team. I need you two. Now!"

The insulated ladder whined down across the Scorpion's flank.

I looked at Kit and raised my eyebrows. "The man needs a team. Does he have a team?"

I waited for her answer, every heartbeat like a hammer.

Finally, she grasped the ladder's bottom rung. "Maybe, Parker. Maybe."

Afterword

"Plus ça change, plus c'est la même chose" idiomatically translates from the original French as "The more things change, the more they stay the same." The Vietnamese (who used to be the French Indo-Chinese, but were pretty much *la même chose* when they were) say it a bit differently: "Old wine in new bottles."

The only nation that insists that things really do change at the drop of a bottle is the Republic of Speculative Fiction. Of which you must be a citizen, because you are reading this. These days you can't browse the Kindle store's aisles without tripping over a story that Defines a Totally New and Wildly Original Subgenre!!!

Once there was science fiction. Now there is hard science fiction, military science fiction, space opera, new space opera, fantasy, urban fantasy, paranormal romance, bit lit, alternate history, time travel, steampunk, splatter punk—I could go on, but already *Undercurrents* is hopelessly past deadline.

Undercurrents is also hopelessly searching for a subgenre. Or is it?

In January, 2010, *Pevnost*, the Czech Republic's glossy, premier print magazine of speculative fiction, devoted an entire issue to "military science fiction," in particular James Cameron's *Avatar* (surely you've heard of it) and the Jason Wander/*Orphanage* series (surely . . . okay, not so much). The Jason Wander/*Orphanage* books are the five-volume prequel to *Undercurrents* and *Overkill*. Their translations are popular with the Czechs (who used to be the Czechoslovakians, but their beer's the same. *Plus ça change* . . .).

Pevnost differentiated *Avatar* as a Totally New and Wildly Original Subgenre, roughly translated as "Military Science Romantic Fantasy." Ex-military/paramilitary protagonist, preferably a smartass; military hardware and panache; strong, independent female characters; a prominent love story, and alien worlds and creatures; all unstifled by NASA-level rigor. And that's probably a good Kindle store aisle within which to shelve *Undercurrents*, too.

But what *Pevnost* didn't say was that *Avatar*, and I hope *Undercurrents* and its precursors, were good because they were about what characters you care about would do next, and why. Or, as SFWA Grand Master, multi-Hugo/Nebula winner, and writer's writer Joe Haldeman once told me about *Orphanage*, they were the rare sort of story that keeps him turning the pages.

George R.R. Martin, who writes both science fiction and fantasy, says that "He engaged the hyperdrive, then . . ." and "She cast the spell, then . . ." are doorways into the same house, but with different furniture.

There are really only two speculative fiction subgenres:

good and bad. The difference isn't the furniture, it's characters you care about, what they will do next, and why.

I tried to make *Undercurrents*, and the six books that precede it, the good kind. Hope you enjoy them.

—Robert Buettner

Acknowledgements

Thanks, first, to my publisher, Toni Weisskopf, for the opportunity and encouragement to create *Overkill*, as well as for insights and ideas that helped make it better. Thanks also to editors Jim Minz and Danielle Turner, for wisdom, to my copy editor, Paul Witcover, for perfection, and to Kurt Miller for dazzling cover art. Thanks also to Laura Haywood-Cory and to everyone at Baen Books for remarkable support and enthusiasm.

Thanks, as ever, to my superb agent, Winifred Golden.

Finally and forever, thanks to Mary Beth for everything that matters.

About the Author

Robert Buettner's first novel, *Orphanage*, nominated for the Quill Award as best Science Fiction, Fantasy and Horror novel of 2004, was compared favorably to Robert Heinlein's *Starship Troopers* by the *Washington Post*, *Denver Post*, Sci-Fi Channel's *Science Fiction Weekly*, and others. Now in its ninth English-language printing, *Orphanage*, and other books in his Jason Wander series, have been republished by Science Fiction Book Club and released by various publishers in Chinese, Czech, French, Russian, and Spanish. *Orphan's Triumph*, the fifth and final book in the Jason Wander series, was named one of Fandomania's best fifteen science fiction, fantasy, and horror books of 2009—one of only two science fiction books to make the list.

In March, 2011, Baen Books released *Overkill*, Robert's sixth novel, and first in his Orphan's Legacy series, to which the Jason Wander books are prequels. *Undercurrents* is the second Orphan's Legacy book.

Born in 1947 on Manhattan Island, Robert graduated

with Honors in Geology from the College of Wooster in 1969, and received his J.D. from the University of Cincinnati in 1973. He served as a U.S. Army intelligence officer, a director of the Southwestern Legal Foundation, and was a National Science Foundation Fellow in Paleontology. He is a member of the Heinlein Society and the Science Fiction and Fantasy Writers Association.

As attorney of record in more than three thousand cases, he practiced in the U.S. federal courts, before courts and administrative tribunals in no fewer than thirteen states, and in five foreign countries. Six, if you count Louisiana.

Robert lives in the Blue Ridge foothills north of Atlanta, with his family and more bicycles than a grownup needs.

Visit him on the Web at www.RobertBuettner.com and follow his tweets @orphanscribe.

The Following is an excerpt from:

SUNSET OF THE GODS

STEVE WHITE

Available from Baen Books
July 2012
Trade Paperback

CHAPTER ONE

EVEN ON OLD EARTH, nothing was forever unchanging, as Jason Thanou had better reason than most to know—not even on the island of Corfu, however much it might seem to drift down the centuries in a bubble of suspended time, lost in its own placid beauty.

For example, the Paliokastritsa Monastery had long ago ceased to be a monastery, and the golden and silver vessels were no longer brought there every August from the village Strinillas for the festival of the Transfiguration of Jesus Christ, by a road which had led laboriously up the monastery's hill between tall oak trees and through the smell of sage and rosemary. Now aircars swooped up to the summit, and the monastery had been converted into a resort, bringing visitors from all around Earth and far beyond it, who stared at the ancient chambers, a few of those visitors at least trying to comprehend what must have been felt by the cenobites who had lived out their lives of total commitment under the mosaic gaze of Christ Pantocrator.

They came, of course, for the incomparable location. From the monastery balcony, one could look out on the endlessness of Homer's wine-dark sea. Northward and southward stretched the coast, its beaches broken into a succession of coves by ridges clothed in olive and cypress trees and culminating in gigantic steep rocks like the one that the local people would still tell you was the petrified ship the Phaecians, once rulers of this island, had sent to bear Odysseus home to Ithaca and his faithful Penelope.

Now Jason stood on that balcony and wondered, not for the first time, what he was doing here.

He could have taken his richly deserved R&R in Australia, where the Temporal Regulatory Authority's great displacer stage was located . . . or, for that matter, anywhere on Earth. Or he could have gone directly back to his homeworld of Hesperia—his fondest desire, as he had been telling everyone who would listen. Instead he had come back to Greece . . . but only to this northwesternmost fringe of it, as though hesitating at the threshold of sights he had seen mere weeks ago. Weeks, that is, in terms of his own stream of consciousness, but four thousand years ago as the rest of the universe measured the passage of time.

There were places in Greece to which he was not yet prepared to go, and things on which he was not yet prepared to look. Not Crete, for example, and the ruins of Knossos, whose original grandeur he had seen before the frescoes had been painted. Not Athens, with its archaeological museum which held the golden death-mask Heinrich Schliemann had called the Mask of Agamemnon, although Jason knew whose face it *really* was, for he had known that face when it was young and beardless. Certainly not Santorini, whose cataclysmic volcanic death he had witnessed in 1628 B.C. And most assuredly not Mycenae with its grave circles, for he knew to whom some of those bones belonged—and one female skeleton in particular. . . .

Unconsciously, his hand strayed as it so often did to his pocket and withdrew a small plastic case. As always, his guts clenched with apprehension as he opened it. Yes, the tiny metallic sphere, no larger than a small pea, was still there. He closed the case with an annoyed snap. He had seen the curious glances the compulsive habit had drawn from his fellow resort guests. The general curiosity had intensified when word had spread that he was a time traveler, around whose latest expedition into the past clustered some very odd rumors.

"Is it still there?" asked a familiar voice from behind him, speaking with the precise, consciously archaic diction Earth's intelligentsia liked to affect.

A sigh escaped Jason. "Yes, as you already know," he said before turning around to confront a gaunt, elderly man, darkly clad in a style of expensive fustiness—the uniform of Earth's academic establishment. "And what brings the Grand High Muckety-Muck of the Temporal Regulatory Authority here?"

Kyle Rutherford smiled and stroked his gray Vandyke. "What kind of attitude is that? I'd hoped to catch you before your departure for. . . . Oh, you know: that home planet of yours."

"Hesperia," Jason said through clenched teeth. "Psi 5 Aurigae III. As you are perfectly well aware," he added, although he knew better than to expect anyone of Rutherford's ilk to admit to being able to tell one colonial system from another. Knowledge of that sort was just so inexpressibly, crashingly vulgar in their rarefied world of arcane erudition. "And now that you've gotten all the irritating affectations out of your system, answer the question. *Why* were you so eager to catch me?"

"Well," said Rutherford, all innocence, "I naturally wanted to know if your convalescence is complete. I gather it is."

Jason gave a grudgingly civil nod. In earlier eras, what he had been through—breaking a foot, then being forced to walk on it for miles over Crete's mountainous terrain, and then having it traumatized anew—would have left him with a permanent limp at least. Nowadays, it was a matter of removing the affected portions and regenerating them. It had taken a certain amount of practice to break in the new segments, but no one seeing Jason now would have guessed he had ever been injured, much less that he had received that injury struggling ashore on the ruined shores of Crete after riding a tsunami.

The scars to his soul were something else.

"So," he heard Rutherford saying, "I imagine you plan to be returning to, ah, Hesperia without too much more ado, and resume your commission with the Colonial Rangers there."

"That's right. Those 'special circumstances' you invoked don't exactly apply any longer, do they?" Rutherford's expression told Jason that he was correct. He was free of the reactivation clause that had brought him unwillingly out of his early retirement from the Temporal Service, the Authority's enforcement arm. He excelled himself (so he thought) by not rubbing it in. Feeling indulgent, he even made an effort to be conciliatory. "Anyway, you're not going to need me—or anybody else—again for any expeditions into the remote past in this part of the world, are you?"

"Well . . . that's not altogether true."

"What?" Jason took a deep breath. "Look, Kyle, I'm only too well aware that the governing council of the Authority consists of snobbish, pompous, fatheaded old pedants." (*Like you*, he sternly commanded himself not to add.) "But surely not even they can be so stupid! Our expedition revealed that the Teloi aliens were active—dominant, in fact—on Earth in proto-historical times, when they had established themselves as 'gods' with the help of their advanced technology. The sights and sounds on my recorder implant corroborate my testimony beyond any possibility of a doubt. And even without that. . . ." Jason's hand strayed involuntarily toward his pocket before he could halt it.

"Rest assured that no one questions your findings, and that there are no plans to send any expeditions back to periods earlier than the Santorini explosion." Rutherford pursed his mouth. "The expense of such remote temporal displacements is ruinous anyway, given the energy expenditure required. You have no idea—"

"Actually, I do," Jason cut in rudely.

"Ahem! Yes, of course I realize you are not entirely unacquainted with these matters. Well, at any rate the council, despite your lack of respect for its members—which you've never made any attempt to conceal—is quite capable of seeing the potential hazards of any extratemporal intervention that might come in conflict with the Teloi. The consequences are incalculable, in fact."

"Then what *are* you talking about?"

"We are intensely interested in the role played in subsequent history by those Teloi who were *not* trapped in their artificial pocket universe when its dimensional interface device was destroyed—or 'imprisoned in Tartarus' as the later Greeks had it. The 'New Gods,' as I believe they were called."

"Also known as the Olympians," Jason nodded, remembering the face of Zeus.

"And by various other names elsewhere, all across the Indo-European zone," added Rutherford with a nod of his own. "They were worshiped, under their various names, for a very long time, well into recorded history, although naturally their actual manifestations grew less frequent. And as you learned, the Teloi had very long lifespans, although they could of course die from violence."

"So you want to look in on times when those 'manifestations' were believed to have taken place? Like the gods fighting for the two sides in the Trojan War?"

"The Trojan War. . . ." For a moment, Rutherford's face glowed with a fervor little less ecstatic than that which had once raised the stones of the monastery. Then the glow died and he shook his head sadly. "No. We cannot send an expedition back to observe an historic event unless we can pinpoint exactly when it took place. Dendrochronology and the distribution of wind-blown volcanic ash enabled us to narrow the Santorini explosion to autumn of 1628 B.C. But after all these centuries there is still no consensus as to the date of the Trojan War. It is pretty generally agreed that Eratosthenes' dating of 1184 B.C. is worthless, based as it was on an arbitrary length assigned to the generations in the genealogies of the Dorian royal families of Sparta. On the other hand—"

"Kyle. . . ."

"—the Parian Marble gave a precise date of June 5, 1209 B.C. for the sack, but it was based on astronomical computations which were even more questionable. Other calculations—"

"*Kyle.*"

"—were as early as 1334 B.C. in Doulis of Samos, or as late as 1135 B.C. in Ephorus, whereas—"

"*KYLE!*"

"Oh . . . yes, where was I? Well, suffice it to say that even the Classical Greeks couldn't agree on the date, and modern scholarship has done no better. Estimates range from 1250 to 1180 B.C., and are therefore effectively useless for our purposes. The same problem applies to the voyage of the Argonauts, the war of the Seven against Thebes and other events remembered in the Greek myths. And, to repeat, the gods tended not to put in appearances in the full light of history. There is one exception, however." Rutherford paused portentously. "The Battle of Marathon."

"Huh?" All at once, Jason's interest awoke. It momentarily took his mind off the irritation he felt, as usual, around Rutherford. "You mean the one where the Athenians defeated the Persians? But that was much later—490 B.C., wasn't it?"

"August or September of 490 B.C., most probably the

former," Rutherford nodded approvingly. The faint note of surprise underlying the approval made it less than altogether flattering. "By that period, it is difficult to know just how widespread *literal* belief in the Olympian gods was. And yet contemporary Greeks seem to have been firmly convinced that Pan—a minor god whose name is the root of the English 'panic'—intervened actively on behalf of the Athenians."

"I never encountered, or heard of, a Teloi who went by that name," said Jason dubiously.

"I know. Another difficulty is that Pan—unlike most Greek gods, who were visualized as idealized humans—was a hybrid figure with the legs and horns of a goat and exceptionally large . . . er, male sexual equipment."

"That doesn't sound like the Teloi," said Jason, recalling seven-to-eight-foot-tall humanoids with hair like a shimmering alloy of gold and silver, their pale-skinned faces long, narrow and sharp-featured, with huge oblique eyes under brows which, like their high cheekbones, tilted upward. Those eyes' strangely opaque blue irises seemed to leak their color into the pale-blue "whites." The overall impression hovered uneasily between exotic beauty and disturbing alienness.

"Nevertheless," said Rutherford, "the matter is unquestionably worth looking into. And, aside from the definite timeframe involved, there are numerous other benefits. For one thing, the more recent date will result in a lesser energy requirement for the displacement."

"Well, yes. 490 B.C. is only—" (Jason did the mental arithmetic without the help of his computer implant) "—twenty-eight hundred and seventy years ago. Still, that's one hell of an 'only!' Compared to any expedition you'd ever sent out before ours—"

"Too true. But the importance of investigating Teloi involvement in historical times is such that we have been able to obtain authorization. It also helped that the Battle of Marathon is so inherently interesting. It was, after all, crucial to the survival of Western civilization. And there are a number of unanswered questions about it, quite aside from the Teloi. So we can kill two birds with one stone, as people say."

"Still, I don't imagine you'll be able to send a very large party." The titanic energy expenditure required for displacement was tied to two factors: the mass to be displaced, and the temporal "distance" it was to be sent into the past. This was why Jason had taken only two companions with him to the Bronze Age, by far the longest displacement ever attempted. Since the trade-off was inescapable, the Authority was constantly looking into ways to reduce the total energy requirement, and the researchers were ceaselessly holding out hope of eventual success, but to date the problem remained intractable. This, aside from sheer caution, was why no large items of equipment were ever sent back in time. Sending human bodies—with their clothing, and any items they could wear or carry on their persons, for reasons related to the esoteric physics of time travel—was expensive enough.

"True, the party will have to be a small one. But the appropriation is comparable to that for your last expedition. So we can send four people." Rutherford took on the aspect of one bestowing a great gift. "We want you—"

"—To be the mission leader," Jason finished for him.

"Even though this time you have to *ask* me to do it," he couldn't resist adding, for all his growing interest.

Rutherford spoke with what was clearly a great, if not supreme, effort. "I am aware that we have had our differences. And I own that I may have been a trifle high-handed on the last occasion. But surely you of all people, as discoverer of the Teloi element in the human past, can see the importance of investigating it further."

"Maybe. But why do you need me, specifically, to investigate it?"

"I should think it would be obvious. You are the nearest thing we have to a surviving Teloi expert." Jason was silent, as this was undeniable. Rutherford pressed his advantage. "Also, there is the perennial problem of inconspicuousness." Rutherford gazed at Jason, who knew he was gazing at wavy brown black hair, dark brown eyes, light-olive skin and straight features.

Jason, despite his name, was no more "ethnically pure" than any other inhabitant of Hesperia or any other colony world. But by some fluke, the Hellenic contribution to his genes had reemerged to such an extent that he could pass as a Greek in any era of history. It also helped that he stood less than six feet, and therefore was not freakishly tall by most historical standards. It had always made him valuable to the Temporal Regulatory Authority, which was legally interdicted from using genetic nanoviruses to tailor its agents' appearance to fit various milieus in Earth's less-cosmopolitan past. The nightmare rule of the Transhuman movement had placed that sort of thing as far beyond the pale of acceptability as the Nazis had once placed anti-Semitism.

"If we were sending an expedition to northern Europe," Rutherford persisted, "I'd use Lundberg. Or to pre-Columbian America, Cardones. But for this part of Earth, you are the only suitable choice currently available, or at least the only one with your—" (another risibly obvious effort at being ingratiating) "—undeniable talents."

Jason turned around, leaned on the parapet, and looked out over the breathtaking panorama once again. "Are you sure you really want me? After my latest display of those 'talents.'"

Rutherford's face took on a compassionate expression he would never have permitted himself if Jason had been looking. "I understand. Up till now, you have taken understandable pride in never having lost a single member of any expedition you have led. And this time you returned from the past alone. But that was due to extraordinary and utterly unforeseeable circumstances. No one dreamed you would encounter what you did in the remote past. And no one blames you."

"But aside from that, aren't you afraid I might be just a little too . . . close to this?" Once again, Jason clenched his fist to prevent his hand from straying to his pocket.

Rutherford smiled, noticing the gesture. "If anything, I should think that what you know of Dr. Sadaka-Ramirez's fate would make you even *more* interested."

Deirdre, thought Jason, recalling his last glimpse of those green eyes as she had faded into the past. *Deirdre, from whom it is practically a statistical certainty that I myself am descended.*

He turned back to face Rutherford. "Well, I don't suppose it can do any harm to meet the other people you have lined up."

— end excerpt —
from *Sunset of the Gods*
available in trade paperback,
July 2012, from Baen Books

PRAISE FOR LOIS McMASTER BUJOLD

What the critics say:

The Warrior's Apprentice: "Now here's a fun romp through the spaceways—not so much a space opera as space ballet… It has all the 'right stuff.' A lot of thought and thoughtfulness stand behind the all-too-human characters. Enjoy this one, and look forward to the next." —Dean Lambe, *SF Reviews*

"The pace is breathless, the characterization thoughtful and emotionally powerful, and the author's narrative technique and command of language compelling. Highly recommended." —*Booklist*

Brothers in Arms: "…she gives it a genuine depth of character, while reveling in the wild turnings of her tale… Bujold is as audacious as her favorite hero, and as brilliantly (if sneakily) successful." —*Locus*

"Miles Vorkosigan is such a great character that I'll read anything Lois wants to write about him… a book to re-read on cold rainy days." —Robert Coulson, *Comics Buyers Guide*

Borders of Infinity: "Bujold's series hero Miles Vokosigan may be a lord by birth and an admiral by rank, but a bone disease that has left him hobbled and in frequent pain has sensitized him to the suffering of outcasts in her very hierarchical era…. Playing off of Miles's reserve and cleverness, Bujold draws outrageous and outlandish foils to color her high-minded adventures." —*Publishers Weekly*

Falling Free: "In *Falling Free* Lois McMaster Bujold has written her fourth straight superb novel…. How to break down a talent like Bujold's into analyzable components? Best not to try. Best to say: 'Read, or you will be missing something extraordinary.'" —Roland Green, *Chicago Sun-Times*

The Vor Game: "The chronicles of Miles Vokosigan are far too witty to be literary junk food, but they rouse the kind of craving that makes popcorn magically vanish during a double feature." —Faren Miller, *Locus*

MORE PRAISE FOR LOIS McMASTER BUJOLD

What the readers say:

"My copy of *Shards of Honor* is falling apart I've reread it so often.... I'll read whatever you write. You've certainly proved yourself a grand storyteller.

—Lisa Kolbe, Colorado Springs, CO

"I experience the stories of Miles Vorkosigan as almost viscerally uplifting... But certainly, even the weightiest theme would have less impact than a cinder on snow were it not for a rousing good story, and good story-telling with it. This is the second thing I want to thank you for... I suppose if you boiled down all I've said to its simplest expression, it would be that I immensely enjoy and admire your work. I submit that, as literature, your work raises the overall level of the science fiction genre, and spiritually, you work cannot avoid positively influencing all who read it."

—Glen Stonebreaker, Gaithersburg, MD

"'The Mountains of Mourning' [in *Borders of Infinity*] was one of the best-crafted, and simply best, works I'd ever read. When I finished it, I immediately turned back to the beginning and read it again, and I can't remember the last time I did that."

—Betsy Bizot, Lisle, IL

"I can only hope that you will continue to write, so that I can continue to read (and of course buy) your books, for they make me laugh and cry and think ... rare indeed."

—Steven Knott, Major, USAF

What do you say?

Cordelia's Honor
pb • 0-671-57828-6 • $7.99
Contains *Shards of Honor* and Hugo-award winner *Barrayar* in one volume.

Young Miles
trade pb • 0-671-87782-8 • $17.00
pb • 0-7434-3616-4 • $7.99
Contains *The Warrior's Apprentice*, Hugo-award winner *The Vor Game*, and Hugo-award winner "The Mountains of Mourning" in one volume.

Cetaganda
0-671-87744-5 • $7.99

Miles, Mystery and Mayhem
pb • 0-7434-3618-0 • $7.99
Contains *Cetaganda, Ethan of Athos* and "Labyrinth" in one volume.

Brothers in Arms
pb • 1-4165-5544-7 • $7.99

Miles Errant
trade pb • 0-7434-3558-3 • $15.00
Contains "The Borders of Infinity," *Brothers in Arms* and *Mirror Dance* in one volume.

Mirror Dance
pb • 0-671-87646-5 • $7.99

Memory
pb • 0-671-87845-X • $7.99

Miles in Love

hc • 1-4165-5522-6 • $19.00

trade pb • 1-4165-5547-1 • $14.00

Contains *Komarr, A Civil Campaign* and “A Winterfair Gift” in one volume.

Komarr

hc • 0-671-87877-8 • $22.00

pb • 0-671-57808-1 • $7.99

A Civil Campaign

hc • 0-671-57827-8 • $24.00

pb • 0-671-57885-5 • $7.99

Miles, Mutants & Microbes

hc • 1-4165-2141-0 • $18.00

pb • 1-4165-5600-1 • $7.99

Contains *Falling Free* “Labyrinth”, and *Diplomatic Immunity* in one volume.

Diplomatic Immunity

hc • 0-7434-3533-8 • $25.00

pb • 0-7434-3612-1 • $7.99

Cryoburn

hc • 978-1-4391-3394-1 • $25.00

Falling Free

pb • 1-4165-5546-3 • $7.99

Available in bookstores everywhere.
Or order online at our secure, easy to use website:
www.baen.com